ironvine

unraveled destiny series
book two

CAT PORTER

Wildflower Ink, LLC

Ironvine
Cat Porter ©2022
Wildflower Ink, LLC

Editor
Jennifer Roberts-Hall

Developmental Editor
Christina Trevaskis
BookMatchmaker

Cover Designer
Najla Qamber
Qamber Designs & Media

Special thanks to Alison, Jan, Larri, Natalie, & Jo

Visit my website at www.catporter.eu

ISBN: 978-1-954633-06-3

Notes from the Author

For all the readers who loved Wolfsgate and demanded justice
for Brandon & Justine
and the return of their necklace…

This is for you.

xx Cat

* <u>*Please note*</u>*: In the text, the name "Ryvves" is pronounced as "Reeves"*

England,1794

Chapter One

Charles

WHO IS THAT WOMAN?

"You sure you're not coming?" His brother's hand squeezed his shoulder, pulling his attention away from the flare of feminine glory he'd spotted in the distance.

"Coming where?"

"This one's mouth is not to be missed, I tell you. She's a damned good piece. I'm going to hire her to come to the house tonight for us both." On a laugh, Hugh left his side and headed down one of the many intricate dark walks of Vauxhall Pleasure Gardens, winding shadowy paths which were a favourite haunt of lovers, prostitutes, pick pockets, and all sorts of colourful villains.

"I'll come with you." Matthew, a friend of theirs from the country, darted after Hugh.

Charles didn't want to be serviced by a whore. He wanted to find out who this girl was.

He and Hugh had been coming to Vauxhall, London's leading venue for public entertainment outdoors, almost every night this week like everyone else, and Charles hadn't seen any such sample of feminine splendour. Splendour, in fact, had been hard to come by, but he was a picky bastard.

This one was sheathed in a glowing blue gown, just a rise of bosom exposed, elegant jewels dripping from her earlobes, jewels in her hair, not gaudy, simple. Lovely ringlets of hair, a long neck. An elegant profile withal.

She'd do nicely, wouldn't she?

He pushed up against the wall. Something was familiar about this one. The torches lighting the many pathways of the Vauxhall gardens cast a peculiar magical glow everywhere. Perhaps he was seeing a vision. But no…something else, it was something else, he was sure of it. He'd have to point her out to Hugh once he finished with the prostitute.

Hugh had joined Charles in London over a month ago to attend every damned social event the ton had to offer. His brother, the newly named Earl since their father's recent death, was on the prowl for a wife.

But not because he wanted to marry. He had to in order to inherit the rest of his money. Their father had left that particular point in his will a surprise. If Hugh had gained the title and still wasn't married by the age of thirty, he would lose half his income and would not regain the other half for another ten years.

Hugh had been livid, and although Charles had been shocked, he also had been secretly amused. Their father had been quite a scoundrel himself, yet he always upheld the responsibilities to the family title above all else.

And everyone else.

Hugh had two weeks left. Still, no girl had caught his eye for a bride. *"If I'm going to be stuck with some woman for the rest of my days, she'd better be pleasing to my eye and pleasant to be with,"* he'd remarked.

Hugh had been out of the swirl of the ton in London the past two plus years, and his return was heralded by all, especially the ladies, and most especially their ambitious mothers. He'd swiftly made up for lost time on the social carousel: a bored Marchioness, a couple of young widows, a married

Portuguese noblewoman whose husband had come to England to speak at Parliament this week, and of course, plenty of whores at his favourite clubs and at private parties with their friends.

It had become a tedious task to scout for candidates at every single social occasion, at every morning walk in St. James Park, but he did it. It was his duty to his brother, to their family.

Father had been pushing Hugh to marry for years to prepare to take on his role as the Earl of Ryvves, but Hugh had refused. He was much too busy enjoying his longtime mistress, the very married Duchess of Oakley.

However, upon discovering their father's deadline for marriage, Hugh promptly broke things off with Her Grace and set on a course for hunting down a bride and marrying immediately. Great wealth was a mighty motivator.

The crowd was thick here tonight. So many making merry, as if the pleasure gardens offered something so incredibly fresh and novel. He liked being out of doors rather than inside a crowded ballroom or someone's home, but he'd grown accustomed to Vauxhall's offerings and weary of the endless procession of well-dressed people he knew and knew of.

"Montclare." William Treharne, an old friend from the country, dipped his head at him as he and his wife, Amanda, walked past. She caught his eye, lifting her chin as she shot him a sharp look dripping with disdain. He averted his gaze.

Since their dalliance had ended badly almost two years ago, Charles had shown Amanda only indifference, and she had shown him that cold disdain. He'd known her and William forever; they'd all grown up together in the country. Amanda had been the prettiest girl, the most accomplished, the wittiest, and the vainest and arrogant. She had been almost engaged to his best friend, Brandon. But when Brandon's father had suddenly sent him on a trip to the West Indies, she'd gotten impatient and bored and married his cousin William.

Charles had found her to be exquisitely challenging at the beginning of their brief affair. She'd made it quite a game between them. He enjoyed games, and together they played a number of them. But then one of those games hurt Brandon and his new wife, Justine, which led to Brandon and his cousin William having a terrible falling out that had never been repaired.

Charles had not been proud of the consequences of his selfish actions and that was when he'd broken off with Amanda. He'd kept his distance from her and her husband ever since.

But Amanda enjoyed casting him a dismissive look or a sardonic comment in society. He knew it gave her a sense of power to do those things for she was attempting to maintain a connection between them, a bitter one. He knew she could not fathom a man no longer being consumed with her, especially one who'd ridden her.

He brushed all those thoughts away and kept his focus on the delightful girl in the distance. Fireworks burst and crackled in the sky over them. Laughter and shouts rang out, and she turned her face upward, laughing at the artificial starlight over her.

Beautiful.

He'd like a bite of her himself.

Charles groaned inwardly. He recognised the young lady she was with—Alice, Alice Dunsmore, who he knew all too well. She was the stepdaughter of his Aunt Vivian. His aunt had wanted Hugh to marry Alice, but Hugh had refused and rudely so. *"Are you joking? I cannot marry that!"*

Alice was not pretty, yet she was not too plain a creature. A somewhat giddy and very innocent girl, she had a chirping laugh that both Hugh and Charles found irksome. She smiled shyly, blushed often, and could barely hold a conversation worth having. Alice and her friend were greeted by a male. He knew that male, another childhood friend from Gloucestershire, Thomas Hackelton. Thomas took Alice's arm in his and entreated the perfect girl to do the same. He knew her? She turned at last.

A red hot poker pierced Charles's chest. "Well, I'll be damned."

The perfect girl, the exquisite young lady, the splendid woman was none other than Thomas's sister, Georgina, who he knew. "Damn me," he muttered to himself.

He hadn't laid eyes on Georgie—as she was fondly called by their mutual friends, Brandon and Justine—in months and months. She hadn't been here in town this season, that was certain, although her brother had been at almost every party he and Hugh had attended.

Where had she been? He knew she'd never missed a season since she'd come out, and she dazzled at every dinner and dance she attended. His back straightened as he took her in from head to toe. How she'd grown.

She was only two and twenty at most, but since he'd seen her last, she'd altered. Perhaps it was the more revealing gown she wore so well tonight, or the stylish turban wrapped around her gleaming dark hair instead of the more delicate hairstyle favoured by most of the girls? She'd always been graceful and elegant, even as a girl, but tonight her demeanor seemed even more sophisticated if that were possible.

They had sparred much in the past. She was close with Justine, his best friend's wife. And he and Georgina had run into each other many times over the past two years. Her cleverness, her sharpness of tongue, her directness he'd found refreshing. He always knew she'd become a fine lady, and she had indeed.

He smiled to himself. Had she reined in that tongue, he wondered?

Matthew approached, and Thomas greeted him, bowing his head. Was Matthew done with the prostitute already?

Matthew bowed at Georgina in an exaggerated fashion,

and she dipped her head and smiled gently, which he was sure masked her great delight. His jaw tightened. If he remembered correctly, she'd always been sweet on that fool.

Matthew said something to her, she laughed, and he immediately gestured for her to accompany him on a walk. Charles's jaw tightened as Georgina joined him, the two of them strolling together behind her brother and Alice.

Matthew had dark good looks that he used to his advantage. On one occasion he'd told Charles he'd perfected a particular glance that was "full of mystery" in order to lure ladies into his sphere, and that Charles should practice one as well.

For fuck's sake.

Matthew worked hard to lure Georgie. He talked incessantly, pausing frequently to shoot her this odd smirk, and she only continued to smile at him and attempt to reply. Charles followed them in the crowd. They rounded a corner where they stopped to admire a group of jugglers. Thomas and Alice hadn't noticed they'd stopped and kept walking, and Matthew now had Georgina to himself.

Charles rubbed at his eyes. He'd had a lot to drink this evening and had welcomed the warmth and looseness to his limbs, but now he desired full clarity. Charles moved in their direction, his every instinct demanding they be followed.

"Ah, there you are–" A familiar voice stopped him in his tracks.

"Aunt? Good evening." He bowed at his mother's sister, a tall, slender woman elegantly dressed in black and silver. She'd recently lost her husband.

"I was hoping I'd see you here tonight."

His eyes darted to where Matthew and Georgina walked. "We're here every night."

"I was most insulted by Hugh's reaction to my proposal that he marry Alice."

"He has a rather indelicate temper, as you know."

"Indelicate temper? He's a spoilt, selfish brat. Much like your father was."

"May he rest in peace."

"May he not." She sniffed in air, fluttering her fan. Aunt Vivian detested his father, always had done. "Alice would make you a fine wife, Charles."

"She is indeed a lovely girl, Aunt, but I have no intention of marrying. In truth, I have never considered it."

"Of course, you haven't." She narrowed her eyes at him, letting out a bitter sigh. "Mark me, soon enough, all your usual entertainments shall become tiresome to you."

On a grin, Charles took her arm in his, and they walked in the direction Matthew and Georgina had taken. "You were most fortunate, Aunt, to have married someone you had fallen in love with."

Her face beamed at him. "Very true, very true. Quite a shame 'tis so rare a phenomenon."

"Indeed." His thoughts went to his close friends, Brandon and Justine. Although their marriage had been arranged, they had fallen deeply in love and shared a very close, trusting bond.

"Perhaps one day you shall meet a girl you find you cannot do without."

"What a shocking idea."

"It is, isn't it?" she said. "And when that happens, I shall have the last laugh."

"You certainly shall," he murmured. The women he preferred were the married kind who were bored with their husbands, eager to be bedded, and could make no claims upon him. Brief affairs where he could walk away whenever he liked without censure or responsibility.

"Once your brother marries, you will be living at Penrose Park, will you not? Hugh did promise the house to you?"

His lips pressed into a firm line. No, Hugh hadn't.

Penrose Park was his mother's family estate where her

elder brother lived. His mother had been born there, she'd grown up there, and when she'd left his father, she had gone to live there. Met her end there. It was at Penrose Park that she was buried.

That estate was the one thing of his mother that remained, and he'd always wanted that piece of her. It was important to him. Significant. And now upon the death of his uncle, it was Hugh's, the eldest remaining male relative.

Charles cleared his throat. "Certainly, Hugh has no use for the estate."

"Are you quite sure of that?"

He shifted his weight. It hadn't occurred to him that Hugh would not give him Penrose Park, for it was the logical, practical thing to do. But when was Hugh ever logical and practical?

Aunt Vivian squeezed his arm. "I very much appreciate Hugh's allowing me and Alice to stay there when we are in the country."

"Come now, of course. It is your family home. You will go there after London?"

"We will, yes, in about a week's time." Aunt Vivian brought a hand to his cheek, her expression softening. "Charles, your owning Penrose one day was your mother's wish, and it is mine too."

Revelers bustled past them, laughter and shouts resounded, but they all faded, as Charles held his aunt's clear gaze. That sentiment meant more to him than anything. Taking her hand in his, he cleared his throat. "Perhaps I can be of use to you, Aunt. May I help you find a suitable husband for Alice?"

"Oh, my darling, would you? It was her father's dearest wish for her to be secured with a good and kind gentleman, and on his deathbed, I promised him I would see to it. She is almost two and twenty." She let out a sigh, her lips twisting.

"Alice is a gentle, sweet girl with an extremely healthy

dowry. Leave it to me. Shall I join you both tomorrow morning at St. James?"

"Yes, wonderful. I look forward to it. Thank you, Charles.

"Has your brother found himself a suitable bride yet?"

"No."

She let out a sharp laugh. "He'd best get on with it. That pendulum blade your father left behind is swinging."

A grin swept his lips. "It most certainly is, and I assure you, Hugh feels its sharp edge." They laughed together. He and his aunt shared the same biting humour.

Behind his aunt, the jugglers finished their performance to great applause, and he spotted Matthew leading Georgina around the performers. His jaw tightened. Charles knew there was another dark walk in that direction which was reserved for private pleasures. Was Matthew hoping to take advantage of the girl? Insanity. No, he wouldn't let him try.

"Forgive me, Aunt. I must take my leave."

"Yes, yes, off with you."

Charles pushed through the thick crowd, torches lighting their faces like unnatural beasts. The smells of bodies, heavy perfumes, grease-laden food cooking, and spilt liquor became unbearable.

Bloody hell.

He'd lost them.

Chapter Two

Georgina

"Matthew, where are you taking me?" *As if I didn't know.*

"Darling, Georgina, I've missed you so much. When you managed to write me, which was most illicit of you, and said you would be coming to London at long last, I could not sleep for craving your company."

"You did not send a letter back. I waited."

"I did not wish to put you in any danger, my sweet. What if your sister or brother were to intercept my passionate missive?"

"It would have been passionate, your letter?"

"But of course."

"Well, I've always taken the risk of being found out, but you've never once written back to me."

They were in a shadowy aspect now, rows of hedges and tall trees secluding them from the crowds milling about the gardens. She knew of these areas of Vauxhall used for intimate privacy.

Guttural moans and manic cries rose in the distance. Mutterings filled the space.

"Yes, sir, yes. Oh, yes."

"That's it, wench."

"Where have you brought me, Matthew?" She knew very well where they were, but she wasn't about to betray that she knew.

"I am rendered powerless before you and act with great recklessness. You must forgive me with a kiss of those most beautiful lips."

"A kiss?"

Yes, yes, yes, she'd wanted a kiss from him for so long. She'd been infatuated with Matthew, her brother's closest friend, for as long as she could remember. And now, at last, he was seeking her favours. *Yes.*

She'd been looking forward to returning to town, not only for its usual entertainments but for the chance to see Matthew again. He and Thomas had been in London since the very beginning of the season.

His fingers pressed into her sides, and she let out a small gasp. Eager, she leaned in closer to him. The warm skin of his lips touched her cheek, brushing her skin toward her lips. *Yes. Finally.* She'd been dreaming of this moment for so lo —

"Get your hands off her," came a deep, sharp voice, separating her and Matthew like the slicing *swoosh* of a sabre.

"Who's there?" Matthew pushed Georgina to his side.

Georgina recognised the voice immediately. "Charles Montclare, is that you?

"What?" Matthew moved toward the tall figure in the dark.

Charles moved forward, his sculpted features visible in the muted light. "Penry, how dare you risk Miss Georgina's reputation and well-being by bringing her here? Are you daft or only supremely selfish?"

"How dare you speak to me this way, Montclare. We were watching the jugglers, and Miss Georgina became overwhelmed with the heat and the wild doings, and I took her away."

"And I'm taking her right back." He held out his hand. "Come, Miss Georgina."

"But, Charles…"

"Now."

She knew he was right. Her skin heated as she brushed past Matthew and went to Charles.

"Montclare, damn you, you'll answer for this." Matthew stomped out of the pathway leaving them alone.

Charles turned to her. "You know better. I know you do."

Her face heated, but she did not avert her gaze.

"Where have you been, dear girl? Did the earth swallow you up? I have not laid eyes on you for nigh upon a year, I think. Could that be right?"

"You missed me?"

"Terribly. Had no one to tease, no one to share a good laugh with."

"I have been at my sister's in Devonshire. She was with child, and I stayed with her until the birth of her son."

"Ah, wonderful."

"Yes. But having missed most of the season was trying."

"I, on the other hand, did not miss a single event this year. Hugh surprised me with a visit. Wanted to attend everything, so we have."

"I haven't seen your brother in years, I don't think."

"Lucky you."

They both laughed.

"Did Matthew kiss you?"

"You ruined it."

"Good. I'd bet twenty pounds sterling that he wouldn't kiss you the way you should be kissed."

"That's quite a lot of money. You're either very sure of yourself or you're an utter spendthrift."

Charles let out a laugh. "You wanted a kiss from that arrogant boy?"

"I did."

"You've always been infatuated with him."

"Not always."

His thumb stroked her chin, lifting her face to meet his, and her pulse ticked up. "You're all grown up now, Miss Georgina."

There was a gleam in his eye that had her shifting her weight. Charles was her brother's friend, a few years older than the rest. Both Thomas and Matthew had always looked up to Charles because he was the experienced, sophisticated, polished gentleman they both wished to be, even if they didn't have the lavish income nor the titled family Charles did.

"Is that a rakish compliment, Mr. Montclare?"

"Whatever do you mean, young lady?"

"If it was a typical gentleman's compliment, you would say what mesmerising velvety eyes I had. How my cheeks are the very bloom of spring, my lips the promises of sweet delights. That sort of thing."

His lips twisted into a smirk. "Is that the sort of florid rubbish Matthew said to you?"

"Yes."

"Did you like it?" He grinned at her, that sardonic grin of his, and she took in a slight breath at the sight. Had she missed it all these months? "I am not florid, Georgie. Never have been, never will be."

"I know." She'd always liked that about him.

He moved closer to her, closing her in around the tall hedges. "Was that your first kiss?"

"It would have been, but you interrupted us."

His eyes flashed at her, stinging her flesh. "And I'm glad I did."

"Such impudence."

"I saved you from mediocrity just now with Matthew."

"And such arrogance."

"A kiss is not merely a meeting of lips, Miss Georgina. A first kiss, most especially, should leave you with a wild, mad impression on your senses."

She raised her chin. "I am aware."

"Are you? A good kiss is a taste of the illicit that you didn't know you needed, a rush of feeling." He stalked her with his wild words, his tone fierce. "Not those sweet delights you just spoke of.

Her breath stalled. "Illicit?"

"Yes. And a shared promise."

"A promise of what exactly?"

"A hint of the bliss that awaits. A prelude to many more sensual pleasures."

"Ah, I see…"

"No, you don't." His gaze had landed on her mouth as he shook his head, and in one swift movement, his cool hands slid around her jaw, cradled her face. Pulling her to him against his hard body, his lips pressed against hers. Warm and firm. His tongue, wet and sleek, demanded entry and sought hers. She gave herself freely. A groan rose in his throat, and it vibrated through her as her tongue danced with his. Every inch of her flesh blazed. She tasted him. Tasted his wild fervour.

Tasted Charles Montclare.

Music blared around them, the rousing chorus surging in her veins. He released his tight grip on her, his lips leaving hers, and their gazes met. His was positively troubled. Both of them breathed hard as if they'd been running across a field.

Her hand reached out and touched his heaving chest. "Charles?"

"I—"

"What the devil is going on here?"

Both of them turned, and a chill raced up her spine. Her brother, Thomas, stood at the end of the pathway. "Montclare, how dare you take my sister and bring her here?"

"No, Thomas, Charles was helping me. I'd wandered off to see the fountain and lost my way."

"Matthew told me you left him and took up with Montclare. That was quite ill-mannered and presumptuous of you."

That double dealing…

Her brother moved forward, the dim light exposing his tight features. "And look where he's taken you. Have you no sense, girl? You know very well what he's about."

Georgina took in a breath. "Matthew had stopped to speak with friends, and I wandered off to see the fountain. Luckily our friend, Mr. Montclare, found me and was about to lead me back into the gardens."

Scoffing, Thomas grabbed at her, pulling her next to him. "You will not leave my side for the rest of the evening. And you, sir—to divert yourself with my young, innocent sister? I know you have no bounds, but this goes beyond the…"

Charles said nothing in his defense as Thomas rattled on. He only glared at him, a muscle along his jaw ticking.

Georgina met his gaze. "Thank you for your assistance, Mr. Montclare. For your kind words. It is lovely to see you again after so long."

Giving her an appreciative smile, Charles bowed his head as Thomas pulled her out of the dark pathway. Away from him.

Away from the dangerous beast and back into polite society's roaring carnival.

Chapter Three

Charles

THE FRENCH BRANDY Hugh kept in their coach had done nothing to quell the fiery nerves pounding in his head this evening. Nothing.

They hadn't stopped pounding since he'd kissed Georgina the night before.

He'd kissed her. Their lips had met, their tongues. And it was no chaste kiss. It was laced with desire, and that desire had exploded in his veins quite unlike anything he'd ever experienced before.

From just one kiss.

A kiss that wasn't supposed to happen. For God's sake, he was saving her from being compromised by Matthew, and instead, he ended up compromising her himself. He let out a groan.

"You need more, Charles?" his brother asked.

"No." Charles's gaze remained outside on the dark streets of London.

"Do you think everyone's going to this damned ball?"

"Last ball of the season at Lord Eccleston's? Everyone will be here."

Hugh's rumbling dark laugh filled the coach. "You sound as

enthusiastic as I. I'm sure Aunt Vivian will be there with young Alice in tow. You were so very kind this morning at St. James walking with her, introducing her to gentlemen."

"I'm trying to be helpful."

"Why don't you just marry her?"

"Whatever for?"

"I would be thoroughly amused to see you married to such a creature."

"I do not exist for your amusement."

"Come now, brother. Ah, I have the perfect inducement for this match, one you cannot deny."

"Nothing would induce me to—"

"Nothing?" Hugh's eyes lit up, and a chuckle rolled from his throat. "Not even Penrose Park?"

Charle's pulse jammed in his neck. "What are you saying? Otherwise, it won't be mine? Do you intend on keeping Penrose? You've just inherited the title, our entire estate, and the income that goes with it. Why would—"

"That house is a lovely property, and I have plenty of friends who are looking to rent a house in the country. It could generate a tidy little income to have at my disposal. If I remember correctly, there was very good fishing to be had in that lake, and deer roam the park freely. Uncle Henry did love to hunt and shoot, and he always…"

Hugh went on, but Charles could no longer listen through the pounding in his veins. He only stroked a hand across his tight jaw in an effort to keep his tongue prisoner within its walls. He remembered how Hugh had barely commented on the acquisition of Penrose Park when Charles had taken care of the paperwork with the lawyers upon their uncle's death. Owning it was nothing to Hugh, but it was important to Charles.

What a fool he'd been for not having secured that house in his name. Fool for having assumed it would be plain to his brother that it should go to him, that something should go to him. He knew that if he showed any sliver of anger or emotion, his brother would only find it amusing and use it against him. He averted his gaze out the window.

Unlike his brother, he'd been close with their mother. Their father had forbidden Charles and Hugh to visit her at Penrose. Hugh obeyed, but Charles had not. He'd gone to the house in secret on at least three occasions to see his mother.

As the years had passed, Charles and Hugh rarely spoke of her. Their father had raised them not to need her, not to care about her; it was a weakness. Only Charles had needed her and cared about her, and he still did. But she was lost to him.

Since her death, Hugh had behaved as if she hadn't even existed. Either he didn't care one jot, or he cared too much and hid it away. Charles had never been sure which.

Beside him, Hugh stretched out his long legs. "I say, I very much like this new frock coat. Tailor did a damn fine job, eh?" He smoothed his hands down his wide lapels. "I'll have to go back for more before I quit town." He'd spent a small fortune on new clothes since he'd joined Charles in London for the season, along with the small fortunes on cards, women, private parties, and the like.

Tidy little income to have at my disposal. Hugh's words seared through him afresh.

Hugh let out a small groan. "For weeks, we've been plowing through dinners and assemblies, concerts, and balls, and not one female has tempted me thus far for a wife."

Charles threw his brother a sidelong glance. "All females tempt you by virtue of their cunt. But for a wife, you seem to have criteria."

"I have standards for a wife. Why shouldn't I? A wife is … a wife." Hugh let out a breath.

"How then would you classify your former mistress?"

"The Duchess is a singular woman." Hugh's gaze remained on the crowded streets outside the carriage window, but his voice had gone lower, serious.

That woman's cunny had bewitched his brother, Charles was certain. Their illicit relationship had lasted for almost three years and was known only amongst the Duke's very small and very tight-lipped inner circle. And, of course, the Duke himself.

To be together freely, the pair would mostly stay at the Duke's remote estate in the north as well as travel abroad as often as possible. Last year they'd lived in Naples for several months at a house she'd rented for them. But now, it had come to an end. Hugh hadn't wanted to speak of it, and frankly, Charles did not want to hear his tale of woe.

"For both of you, the only future in that relationship was scandal eventually." Charles let out a sigh. "I must say, I find it quite remarkable of His Grace to allow his wife her own lover."

"The Oakleys are enlightened minds, Charles. I'll have you know, he very much enjoyed watching me swive his wife. It would excite him exceedingly."

"Did Her Grace know?"

"Of course she knew."

"And how did she find it?"

"Made her even more feral."

"Enlightened indeed."

"What a time it was…" Hugh's voice took on a huskier tone as he absently rubbed a hand down his chest. "You can't begin to imagine what we'd get up to at that house. The Duke enjoys a diverse assortment of pleasures, and I learned much from him."

Charles said nothing in reply. He leaned his head back against the cushions. *Well done. Father would have been so proud of you,* he thought to himself.

This was the first time Hugh had ever told him anything about his life with the Duke and Duchess. Charles had heard vague rumors of exclusive gatherings at the Duke's northern estate for his inner circle of which Hugh had been a member.

Debauchery and revelry on a grand scale for a select few were on an elaborate menu of sordid delights to indulge in. Delights that his brother obviously very much enjoyed and probably missed.

But Charles was not an enthusiast of covens or of despotic veneration, and he much preferred to hunt and indulge on his own.

"Is Frederica Ashton still Oakley's mistress?" Charles asked.

"Not sure." Hugh kept his gaze trained on the road.

"You don't know?"

"So many women would come and go, and I minded my business. Some lasted for months, others only a matter of weeks."

"The Duke has refined criteria too, eh?"

"He most certainly does. And if he loses interest for whatever reason, they're cast out."

"Perhaps he should consider keeping a variety of females to suit each particular interest. Like a Sultan. That would certainly make his life easier."

"Oh, do shut up," Hugh snapped at him through gritted teeth.

"Zounds, I thought you'd enjoy the jest. I only asked because this morning at St. James, Aunt Vivian had asked me if I'd seen Mrs. Ashton. It seems they'd been friends and lost contact in the past months. I told her last year I'd seen Mrs. Ashton with Oakley quite often here in London and then in Bath. But this season I hadn't seen her at all. I thought to ask if you'd seen her at the estate up north?"

"As I said, I minded my business."

"Of course you had to mind your manners with the Duke. You were fucking his wife, after all."

Hugh ignored his comment and poured himself more brandy. "Mutual consent makes the Oakleys' marriage work brilliantly. Something for us all to learn from and aspire to."

"Do you endeavor to be that sort of enlightened husband, then?"

Charles's slightly caustic tone was not lost on Hugh, and he shot him a cool look. "Do you forget so many of our forbearers kept high-born mistresses as well as a wife?"

"No, I have not forgotten. Our own father did, but he was certainly no enlightened husband."

"He was a traditionalist, as am I." Hugh's laughter rumbled through the coach. "All of the men in our family were pleasure hounds, rakes, scoundrels, eh?"

"Except for the very first Montclare."

"I do enjoy the irony that we have sprung from the loins of a monk who married. I do indeed."

Charles's laughter joined his brother's. "These many weeks, you've diligently shown all the ton that you are a free man and very much a Montclare as you ever were." When Hugh wanted to put effort into a project, he certainly did.

Hugh slapped Charles on the thigh. "You enjoyed our festivities last night, did you not, brother?"

"I did."

Hugh had brought that prostitute from Vauxhall back to their house. She'd swallowed his cock down her throat as she took Hugh's from behind, and then they'd switched off. With each new coin Hugh offered her, she performed more dazzling feats for them.

Yet, this morning he'd woken up with the feel of Georgina's lips on his, Georgina's taste on his tongue. His lungs had constricted in his chest, so startling had been the feeling of her actually lingering over him. No ordinary memory, no. He could *feel* her flesh on his, her warmth, smell her scent. What madness was this?

Their coach turned down a road. "I fully expect the young ladies tonight will gather about you like flies to honey as they have every night," said Charles. "One is sure to strike your fancy, in particular, for a wife."

"Christ, I've come to bloody hate that word—wife."

"I wholeheartedly agree, brother. But the Earl of Ryvves cannot be the plaything of a Duchess all his life."

"I am no woman's plaything," Hugh spit out, his eyes daggers. "That's not how it was."

"My apologies." Charles cleared his throat. "By the way, my lord," said Charles in a lighter tone of voice. "You didn't come to our appointment at our solicitor's today. You should have been there. It's you they want to talk to, after all. You need to take an interest in your estate. I've been taking care of everything since Father—"

"You've always done. Isn't it easier that way?"

"No. No, not anymore." Charles hadn't expected him to reply any differently. Hugh had barely ever shown an interest in the family's holdings, only the rewards. The estate is now yours and thus, your responsibility."

"Oh, for fuck's sake. I'm very well aware of my responsibilities." Hugh drained his glass of liquor. A spindly silence fell between them. "I'll have you know, I've been considering marriage for some time. Even the Duchess and I had discussed the necessity."

"Had you?"

"She's a practical sort."

She'd have to be, married to that man, thought Charles. "And did she provide you with a list of appropriate contenders?"

"She did. A long list of noble virgins."

"Amuse me, brother. Who did she name? Perhaps I can offer you insight into the ladies."

"I'm sure you could." Chuckling, Hugh leaned in closer, his brandy-scented breath fuming the air between them. "But I took no heed of the particulars. No one tells a Montclare where to plant his cock."

"Too right." Charles raised his chin, his lips twitching into a slight grin matching his brother's.

Hugh settled back against the cushioned seat and held his glass aloft. "Here's to the future Lady Ryvves. She will be unlike our mother, who was a selfish wife —"

"Selfish?" Charles bit out. "Perhaps our father should have tried to be a better husband."

Hugh only made a face as if he'd had a sour drink. He had no patience for the topic of their mother. "I shall ensure that my wife stays firmly planted at our home always and between my legs for however long I fancy her."

"*If* you fancy her." Charles laughed.

"It could happen. It very well could." Hugh wiped at his lips through his laughter. "Nonetheless, my wife's prime obligations shall be to her husband, and she shall see to those many obligations with grace, gratitude, and humility like a proper wife should."

Charles winced at his brother's remarks. "You sound more and more like Father every day."

Hugh chuckled. "We'll wed, bed, and beget an heir." He drained his glass. "And so on and so forth."

"That's what marriage comes down to in the end, doesn't it?" Charles's gaze remained on the coach window to the crowded streets. "A bargain. A contract both parties agree to with a purpose. Everyone gets something out of it so life can push on."

Their father and mother's marriage had distilled into nothing but a contract of requirements. Appearances were all, and they both knew how to present as the perfect couple when necessary. Distance and congenial coolness became the hallmarks of his parents' relationship. And it became perfectly normal to all of them.

He'd learned early on that marriage was a cold, selfish place, where there was no such thing as affection or love only obligation and tribulation. To survive it, you had to bargain for what you wanted, and you always had to play by the Earl's rules. Or else.

That was marriage.

That was his family.

Charles smoothed his hair back. He wanted none of that for himself. Nothing of what Hugh was imagining for himself. None of it.

The coach slowed its pace, finally coming to a stop behind a long line of other carriages in front of Lord Eccleston's home. The blazing lights of the torches set off an eerie glow in their coach. Finely dressed young ladies and gentlemen, their faces full of excitement and expectation, crowded the entrance to the house.

Would Georgina be here tonight?

Hugh let out a rolling laugh. "Look at them all."

"Enjoy it." Charles's hand smoothed over his necktie. "You're sure to cause a stir, as you do everywhere you go."

The coach door was flung open, and Hugh's lips curled. "I should hope so."

Chapter Four

Georgina

"I'D QUITE FORGOTTEN how grand Lord Eccleston's house here in town is. Unmatched," remarked Georgina to her sister and mother.

"Quite." Her sister, Philippa, slid her arm through hers. "I realise I kept you away from all that glitters all this time in Devonshire. But, my dearest, were you terribly bored with my company?"

"Philippa, you know I was glad to be with you during your confinement. To be with my nephew. There were dances and assemblies in Devonshire, to be sure. But this...I've missed this."

"London is grand and exciting, isn't it?" said Philippa.

"Today being on Oxford Street and seeing all the shops... Behind all those great glass windows absolutely everything one can think of is neatly, attractively displayed."

Philippa sighed. "And in such abundance of choice as almost to make one greedy."

"Almost? I confess I became quite greedy, sister."

"I'm so glad we were able to be here this last week. For you to have missed an entire season–"

"There are times when being in London is important," said Mother sipping her wine.

"*And wonderful,*" thought Georgina. Meeting friends for tea and sweets, walking in St. James Park to see and be seen, shopping for new hats and scarves and turbans that she'd fallen in love with. She and Philippa and their mother had visited friends and had accepted visitors at theirs.

They'd gone to the theatre, to concerts, to coffee houses. She'd even gone to an exhibition of landscape paintings one morning. Philippa hated leaving their rooms until midday, but not Georgina. She'd gone with their brother, Thomas, who had to be dragged there, but no matter, it had been splendid.

The ball tonight was the grandest event of the season, and she was so gratified that they'd been invited. Already the day after next they'd be leaving town. Philippa and John would return to their baby in Devonshire, and she and her mother and Thomas would finally go home to her beloved Gloucester-shire. How she'd missed home, her friends.

"This is actually quite a special evening." Philippa sipped at her wine.

"How so?" Georgina could not tear her eyes away from all the finely dressed young gentlemen. She recognised quite a number of them and knew not an even greater number. She caught many an appreciative glance and carefully chose at whom she returned a smile and who she ignored. Yet, none of these many gentlemen were Charles. Surely he would be here tonight?

Charles Montclare. A man she'd known all her life. She'd always enjoyed his witty company and clever, lively conversation at social events. He was of the finest of dancing partners. Of course, he had a reputation as a scoundrel, as did most of the very handsome and extremely wealthy young gentlemen of her acquaintance. She'd never considered him any kind of…

No.

She'd had feelings for Matthew Penry for years now. Yet one kiss, one wholly unexpected, wildly passionate kiss from Charles Montclare, and she could think of little else since it had happened there, in the shadows of Vauxhall of all places. Her first true kiss, not simply a pressing or brushing of lips, no indeed, had been everything she had hoped it would be…and more.

Her sister moved closer to her, bringing her back to the commotion of the ball. "Sir Reginald will be here tonight."

"John's friend from Devonshire?"

"Yes. He's been in town attending Parliament. As you know, he is quite dedicated to his work."

"He and John would speak of little else but politics at every dinner since I landed in Devonshire." It had been quite a relief once he'd left for London many weeks prior, but she wouldn't tell her sister that. She and John doted on the man and held him in the highest regard.

"Tonight, you shall dance with him," said Philippa.

"And you shall be bright and charming." Her mother eyed her in *that* way of hers which meant, *this is of the utmost importance, and you must behave perfectly.*

A flick of cold raced over her flesh at her mother's firm tone. "To what end?"

"An engagement, of course," replied her mother.

Her head flew back. "Engagement?"

"Isn't it exciting?" Philippa sipped on her drink.

Georgina had no words. Her lips parted, but none came for perhaps the first time in a very, very long time.

"Sir Reginald is a fine gentleman," said Mother. "His manners are impeccable."

"Hmm. He is respectable, above reproach." Philippa dabbed at the corner of her mouth. "Unlike some of our acquaintance." Thomas must have told Philippa about having caught Georgina with Charles Montclare at Vauxhall the night before.

Georgina let out a huff of air. "Yes, yes, his manners, but he is so much older than I am. He is like an uncle to me."

"He wishes to marry again, and he's taken quite a liking to you these past months. It is a perfect match."

"How is it perfect? He has grown children —"

"Yes, his eldest daughter has just been engaged to a naval officer."

"She is younger than I!"

"Indeed she is, and that is precisely the point." Mother's sharp tone pinched at her insides. "You should be married already. You've turned down two proposals, and I cannot allow you to dally any longer. Your bloom is passing."

"I am but two and twenty, Mother."

"I was seventeen when I first married. And your sister nineteen," said Mother. "And judging from your recent behaviour, you need a firm hand to guide you, and Sir Reginald is certainly such a one."

It seemed they'd told Mother about her little adventure with Charles Montclare. Her heart sank. A night that she'd been so looking forward to had now suddenly become tainted. "I always thought I would be able to choose a husband. You'd always said I would."

"Having already rejected two perfectly good offers —"

"They most certainly were not perfectly good in any way. I did not even like either gentleman."

"Knowing that you have done so, men will be loathe to pursue you. You've become quite willful and reckless much like your late father, unfortunately," Mother said. "I will not have it. Your marrying well is not the game you seem to think it is. It is essential to all of us."

"I know it's not a game. I never said it was."

"My darling." Philippa squeezed her arm. "Tonight, the two of you shall dance, and tomorrow…"

Her breath caught in her chest. "Tomorrow?"

"Tomorrow, all the arrangements shall be made," her

mother said. "He shall come to the house and ask for your hand, and you shall accept him."

Georgina's pulse pounded, and her throat burned. Her mother, Philippa, and John wanted her and Sir Reginald to be seen together this evening. Seen dancing, seen talking. A pair expected to …

Philippa slid her arm through Georgina's. "Sir Reginald has always looked after us. Done right by John and his investments in Devonshire. He has been most kind, quite generous."

"Am I to be repayment? Am I to be the gesture of goodwill between you?"

Mother pressed her lips together, and an eyebrow arched. She was frustrated. "We are uniting our families, forging a lasting bond."

Forging a bond. Making a gesture.

A business transaction.

Georgina's blood went cold, the music blaring around her.

Philippa's fingers puffed up the fabric on the shoulder of Georgina's pale blue silk dress. "He's a good man, an intelligent man. Would we ever direct you falsely?"

"No, I don't believe you would, but…"

"Of course not, my love."

"I know you had hopes for a certain young gentleman," said Mother. "But you have been hoping and waiting on him for almost two years now." She directed her gaze at Matthew, who was dancing with a striking young woman not far from where they stood. "Gentlemen his age are never interested in marrying. Furthermore, he has not ever shown a serious interest in you, and I warrant he never will."

Her mother was right about Matthew, wasn't she? Cold hard truths she could no longer deny.

"Recently, you have shown very poor judgment when you put yourself in a terrible position with that Charles Mont-clare." Mother's voice practically seethed upon uttering his name. Obviously, Thomas had told Mother as well. "You must inspire goodness in a man, Georgina, not tartness."

"Perhaps I shall find a man who enjoys my tartness."

"Georgina!" Her sister bit her lip.

"So like your father." The lines of their mother's thin face tightened. "You could have been ruined. A disaster for all of us. You have a responsibility to your family."

"It's time for you to be sensible, sister."

"Sensible?"

"Yes, sensible. You need a firm hand to guide you, and Sir Reginald is such a one." Mother lifted her chin, daring her to object.

Georgina's lips parted. *A firm hand?*

Her sister squeezed her arm. "You haven't had a single suitor call on you in a long while."

"I have been at your home, tending to you in your confinement. Not here in London enjoying the season, meeting new people."

Her mother's eyes narrowed. "Come now, you attended quite a number of social events in Devonshire and met many new people."

Her sister slid an arm around her waist. "Darling, think of it. We would be neighbors. Sir Reginald's stature in the county is most high. And you would be coming to London regularly as the wife of a respected politician. Uniting our families would be a huge boon for all of us. His income alone..." Her voice, although barely above a whisper, now flared with delight.

"Sir Reginald is not a peer of the realm and he comes from new money," said Georgina, her tone crisp. "I would have thought you would find that highly objectionable, Mother."

"He is a fine gentleman who has been honoured by the Crown with a knighthood. He owns his own estate which is one of the finest homes in the county. He is a success and is well-liked and admired both in Devonshire and London. And having been married before, he knows very well how to be a husband."

"Only his wife could tell us that," quipped Georgina.

Her mother's eyes flared. "That tongue of yours…"

Her sister pulled her in close. "Mother makes a very good point. Having been bereft of companionship for so long, Sir Reginald is certain to cherish you."

Georgina shuddered. She knew what her sister meant. They spoke of sexual congress often enough between them. Georgie always had a healthy curiosity about the intimacies, and Philippa was always eager to educate and inform from her experience.

How could her sister possibly think such a man would please her? Philippa knew better. Over the years, the two of them had often amused themselves by analyzing the positive and negative attributes of the available young gentlemen as possible husbands for Georgina as they'd once done for Philippa. They'd made it an entertaining game between them.

This, now, was no game.

"Georgie, he has an elegant air about him, does he not?" murmured Philippa. "He is a most attractive man."

"He is not."

"How silly you are," her mother's voice lashed at her. "What matters is what kind of man he is."

"You have been discussing this, planning this for some time? Without telling me?"

"We want the best for you, my darling." Her sister turned slightly to greet a passing friend. "Oh, hello, how lovely to see you…"

Georgina averted her gaze to the elegant couples lining up for a dance in the centre of the grand room. Was all of this to be now taken away from her? She thought she had time still. Plenty of time. Plenty of opportunities.

There was no more plenty.

Her own family had chosen for her, had made plans for her future, and Georgina had no choice. No voice.

When had sharing all things changed in their family? How could she not have noticed?

Her mother moved closer to her. "The time has come for you to be settled with a husband and not to be taken up with frivolous pursuits which waste your time."

"Frivolous pursuits? Like father's you mean? I am glad to be like him. Father was more a free thinker than most. He—"

"Stop this instant. Sir Reginald is a most suitable husband for you, and you shall settle very well with him."

Settle? Suitable? Sensible?

Despicable sentiments, hateful words.

"I do not agree."

"It's already been agreed upon," her mother's voice snapped at her. "'Tis done."

"Done?"

"And you cannot undo it. Your time has come to do your duty as a daughter, like all of us have." Her mother's words pierced her like a flaming arrow.

Philippa joined them. "Shh, there he is now with John."

Her sister's husband, John, approached them along with Sir Reginald. Georgina's heart thudded in her chest, her lips pressed together.

Now she looked at the man with new eyes. Eyes that noticed every detail of him in a different way. Slightly stooped upper back, a paunch to his middle. His face mottled with red, his eyes small, a shiny new wig. His clothes were very fine, perhaps too fine. His shoe buckles polished. He had an air of confidence, or was it pomposity?

Georgina's back straightened as the two men reached them. An unusually charged smile pushed up John's lips as his arm gestured out to her.

Georgina's flesh prickled as if she were bare naked to the world at this very moment.

"Good evening, Miss Georgina." Sir Reginald bent his head at her, and she did the same.

"Good evening, sir."

"Mrs. Townsend. Mrs. Holyfloke." Sir Reginald bowed his head at Mother and Philippa. "Such a pleasure to meet here in London, is it not?" He cast another appreciative gaze at Georgina. "A great pleasure, indeed."

Mother and Philippa agreed with him, and they all laughed together. Georgina said nothing. Her mind feverishly clacked away, imagining she and Sir Reginald living together, him touching her, those lips kissing her, him undressing her, rutting over her, demanding of her, delivering his babies one after the other…

"I do hope you will be free to dance with Georgina this evening?" Philippa's suddenly arch voice extended. "That is, if you are not otherwise engaged, of course?"

John cast his wife a sharp look. Philippa couldn't contain herself, but realising she had said a mite too much, her fingers tightened over her fan.

"I most certainly hope to dance with Miss Georgina if she is free?" With a small smile, he slanted his head in her direction.

Their heavy expectant gazes trampled her.

"Are you not free, sister?" Philippa's voice was tense, so impatient.

"I am." Her voice came out small.

"Excellent," he replied, a grin curving his lips.

Everyone smiled at each other, their shoulders' eased. Everyone except for Georgina. Smiles full of anticipations, hopes, plans, prospects. Calculations and carefully laid designs were being formed. Triumphs were ahead.

Music flared, and her body tensed.

"Shall we?" Sir Reginald offered his hand to her.

Georgina's spine stiffened as she placed her hand in his thick, cold one. He led her to the dance floor, and they lined up for the dance.

They took the first steps. As she turned in the line, Georgina took in all the other dancers. She spotted Matthew with a new partner, Miss Alice Dunsmore, who they'd met earlier this week.

Matthew was her brother's closest friend, and they'd known each other for ages and ages. She'd always had a soft spot for him. He was handsome and witty and enjoyed flirting with her and she with him. He had shown an interest in her, a true warmth on many occasions since she'd come out.

But she'd been in Devonshire this year and had missed all the parties in London and in Gloucestershire that Thomas had attended. She'd always gone along with him. Always danced with each of his friends and especially enjoyed dancing with Matthew.

She knew she was luckier than most girls. Having an older brother, she was introduced to his friends from an early age and had grown accustomed to the male sex. She was not frightened to speak her mind to them, to laugh. To dance.

But Matthew Penry was always different.

And now she was here, at the final event of the ton for the season, and instead of feeling that giddiness and glorious anticipation that she'd felt all day, it was as if a lead weight were in her bowels instead of the butterflies that had been there when they'd first arrived. She could barely move, let alone dance and keep the steps gracefully.

Sir Reginald circled her and she kept her gaze downward. She didn't feel proud and pleased like she did when she danced with Matthew or any other fine young gentleman whose gaze she would hold. A sting erupted in her belly. How could her whole world change so completely in a matter of moments?

Couples laughed and smiled at one another, whirling around each other. Gaiety reigned, the very air thick with it like a perfume. It stifled her.

If only her dearest friend, Justine, were here, but she and

her husband, Brandon, had left London after a very brief visit over a fortnight ago to return to their children at their estate in Gloucestershire.

Georgina and Sir Reginald swirled past Philippa and John, whose pleased gazes were fixed on them. She was drowning. If her family meant to affiance her so very quickly—as on the morrow—would she be returning to Devonshire with them instead of going back home to Gloucestershire with Thomas and Mother?

Of course.

Matthew bowed to his partner. A year ago, at another ball in London, he had brought her a glass of wine, his twinkling gaze holding hers so steadily. Dancing with her, laughing, squeezing her hand, sharing *bon mots*. She'd been so sure that he'd come to the house to call on her in the following days. And yet, he had not. There had never been any such visits from Matthew Penry.

He'd been the only man with whom she'd ever felt a flutter of feeling. Always, always, she'd hoped that as time had gone on, he'd see her as his choice for a wife, not simply as his good friend's younger sibling to dance with, flirt with, tease.

That's all she'd been to him, hadn't she? He had no intention of pursuing her. All this time, wasted time, all her hopes had been in vain. A disappointment. Dashed hopes and disappointments were her familiar friends, weren't they?

She turned to face her partner in time with the music, and Sir Reginald took both her hands in his, and they proceeded down the line. She raised her chin as they approached where Matthew stood. He caught her gaze, a soft grin sweeping his lips as she passed once more. She did not return his smile.

Alice delicately spun into Matthew's loose embrace, and his lips brushed her hand. Tenderness laced with a sly promise. A hot sting seared Georgina's chest at the sight. Alice's cheeks flushed as they proceeded down the line.

And yet, he had tried to kiss her last evening. Said pretty

words full of desires. He'd probably do the same with Alice tonight, wouldn't he?

"Miss Georgina?" Sir Reginald's husky voice interrupted her chaotic thoughts, and she met his gaze. No sparkle. Only obligation. Servitude. Her heart thudded in her chest. The dance had finished. They applauded the orchestra.

Her life as she knew it, as she'd always seen it, was over.

Smiling, he guided her back to her mother, sister, and brother-in-law. "Miss Georgina, I look forward to dancing with you again this evening." He bowed his head, and she bowed hers to him without reply.

"So lovely." Philippa beamed.

Liar. Sour rose in her throat at her sister's theatrics.

Casting her a hard glance, Mother lifted her chin and elegantly bowed to Sir Reginald.

Sour filled her throat at her mother's brittle formal cordiality.

John introduced Sir Reginald to one of his friends, and they turned away from the ladies, and Georgina let out a breath. Philippa offered her a fresh drink. "You seemed to enjoy the dance."

She gulped at the wine, a flame down her throat. "I did not."

Chapter Five

Georgina

GEORGINA FOUND her brother at the entrance to the gaming room. She had to know his role in all this.

"Thomas, did you know of their plans for me?"

He shifted his weight. "They only told me last night."

"Sir Reginald is not my choice, nor could he ever be."

"Our mother and sister are of the mind that no man will want you if you wait any longer, especially having rejected two suitors already. And that would most certainly be a waste—a girl of your accomplishments and worth."

"My worth indeed."

"Isn't it nice that he is not a stranger to you? And Mother is most pleased that you'll all be living in Devonshire together."

"Mother is planning on moving to Devonshire? She will leave Fairthorn?"

"She wishes to be close to her new grandchild and welcome yours soon enough. I have been considering marrying for some time now, and perhaps it will be best to have Fairthorn to myself when I do."

Her heart twisted. Fairthorn had been the only home she'd ever known. It was the estate of Philippa and Thomas's father, who had died young. Their mother had married a second time to Georgina's father, who had owned a very fine house in town, which her mother had promptly sold after his death.

"Oh. I see," she said. "But you've never approved of Matthew for me, have you? Even though he's your friend."

Thomas let out a huff of air. "I know you've always had a soft spot for him, Georgie, but you know he's a terrible flirt. But there is more to it than that. Matthew's family's circumstances have changed drastically. He now needs to marry for money, and all he has to offer is his handsome face and talent at cards."

"And he does not offer opportunity like Sir Reginald?"

"You have a sizable fortune, Georgina. Although Matthew is my friend, in his current state, I would not trust him with my beloved younger sister. He is only interested in saving himself, and I doubt he has been humbled by this experience."

That was why Matthew had suddenly wanted to kiss her the other night.

"And frankly, Montclare is another kind of pirate," continued Thomas. "Charles is only ever interested in one thing from a female. One thing only. He is cunning, and most importantly Charles has nothing to lose, which makes him all the more dangerous. He would ruin you on a whim, ruin all of us. You need protection from such vultures. Sir Reginald is a mature gentleman, a father, a successful investor, and a respected politician. He does not see you as a passing entertainment nor as a full purse to pluck bare."

"He does not appeal to me as a husband should. I cannot—"

"Appeal?" Thomas crossed his arms.

"Brother, I am quite sure that if you were to be pressed to marry the female version of Sir Reginald, you would balk."

"Oh, Georgie, what do you know of the world other than gaiety? Think of it—your marriage will secure the happiness of all your family. Is that not wonderful? Is that not gratifying? We have this one chance, and we must make it count."

She blinked. "Do you stand to gain from this union to Sir Reginald, just as our sister and her husband would?"

"I cannot deny it would be most favourable to my new investments with John, and naturally, there is the considerable political influence Sir Reginald yields. He's quite a figure in Parliament, don't you know? Such a lasting alliance with him would be highly favourable."

"Dear God," she murmured, her fingers curling into the silk of her dress.

Her brother let out a sigh. "I am considering my future."

Investments. Influence.

"This is the real reason we came to London this week? To make a show to the ton? So we would all be seen together, so I would not be able to reject him?"

"And you almost ruined it all last night with Montclare, which only made me realize that this is a sound decision. Tomorrow it will be officially settled, and then you shall return to Philippa and John's with Mother to make arrangements for the wedding. Won't that be lovely?"

Her heart thudded in her chest. "I shall not return to Fairthorn?"

"One day soon, you shall visit with your husband. When I return to Fairthorn in a few days, I shall send all your and mother's belongings on to Devonshire."

"Fairthorn is the only home I've ever known."

"You will soon have your own home with your husband, Georgina, and you will make of it what you wish. There are some improvements I would like to make to my house before I marry, and now will certainly be a perfect time to do it."

They'd never separated *yours* and *mine* before. Not really. Her chest squeezed. "Why is suddenly everything changing so completely?"

"Because it must, my love. You must. It is time."

Georgina had never heard her brother speak this way. She

was stranded in a foreign land where she understood not the language nor the currency. She was alone, deserted.

"I must dash, Georgie. I have to find my partner for the next dance. It's Miss Alice who we met the day before. Such a sweet girl. I'm rather taken with her."

"Are you? You'd better hurry, for I believe you'll find her with your dear friend Mr. Penry. She may have forgotten all about you by now."

Thomas only scowled at her and took off into the crowd to find his Miss Alice.

Cheering rose up in the dark and smoky gaming room. Well-dressed gentlemen and finely gilded ladies sat at tables playing card games, hoping and strategising for luck to go their way, for triumphs large and small.

Games and triumphs of all kinds were to be had here tonight.

An opportunity had arisen, and all her family desired to partake. Her future, simply a coin tossed on the table to make the winnings fatter. A card turned over and met with lustful glee. Her life a game played by others for their entertainment, for their particular gains.

No. Her life was not a game.

Chapter Six

Georgina

GEORGINA HAD TAKEN leave of her brother and sister on the excuse that she saw friends she wished to greet. Amanda, an acquaintance from Gloucestershire, and several of her friends spoke excitedly by the punch bowl.

"So handsome, it's almost sinful," Amanda remarked.

"Yes, sinful," purred Henrietta.

"Sinfully divine," giggled Charlotte.

Georgina took a glass of punch. "Who are you discussing so that I too may adore this awe-inspiring divinity?"

"Oh! Have you not heard?" they said.

"Obviously, I have not."

"The Earl of Ryvves is here in high form as he has been at every event this season."

"The Earl of Ryvves?" Georgina sipped on her punch, its sweet pleasantness spreading through her veins. "You mean Hugh Montclare?"

"The one and only," said Charlotte.

"Do you know him, Georgina?" asked Henrietta.

"I do. Their home is not far from ours in Gloucestershire. The Montclares and my brother have been friends since childhood. I have not seen him in quite some time. Years, in fact. He's been abroad mostly, I think."

Charlotte's cheeks flushed. "Look at him."

Georgina followed Charlotte's gaze and took in Hugh's figure. Long, sturdy legs. A full head of golden hair, sharp eyes, deep laughter, generous mouth. In his bearing and the tilt of his head, there was confidence and that trademark Montclare *hauteur*, just like Charles.

Charles stood with him and seemed bored whilst at attention. She grinned to herself.

"The Earl of Ryvves is the most dashing gentleman here tonight," whispered Henrietta.

"He is, isn't he?" Georgina hadn't laid eyes on Hugh Montclare — now the Earl of Ryvves — in a very long time.

"He's recently taken the title," remarked Amanda. "Their father passed away."

The other girls tittered and murmured their appreciation of Hugh.

"What do we think of his brother, Charles, in comparison?" Amanda asked on a short laugh.

Georgina cast her a glance. She knew that Amanda and Charles had once had an affair not too long ago, which had ended badly and quickly, after which Amanda and her husband had left Gloucestershire for good.

"That one has an edge of unkindness to him, I think," murmured Charlotte.

"There is something callous about him." Henrietta tilted her head. "So unlike his far superior brother."

"Hmm. Indeed." Amanda's lips curled.

Spreading malevolence wherever she goes, thought Georgina. *She can't help herself.* Amanda enjoyed casting shadows on Charles, even now.

"I find Mr. Montclare most handsome as well." Georgina cast a heavy glance at Amanda.

"The Earl is the clear winner here this evening," said Charlotte. "What a warm smile he has, such a charming and elegant disposition."

Hugh did seem the warmer sort of the two. Relaxed, easily amused, a generous conversationalist. Charles seemed more removed, which was rather unlike him. Had he changed over the past year? Grown wearier of society?

"The Earl must be looking to wed, don't you think?" Henrietta raised an eyebrow.

"A title, a vast estate, and a most prodigious fortune by all accounts." Charlotte sipped her drink. "And he's a wonderful dancer."

"Did you dance with him tonight?" Henrietta's eyes widened.

"Not tonight. Last week." Charlotte pursed her lips.

"Oh, to capture his attention. To be the object of his affections," said Henrietta, and they all laughed softly.

Georgina's heart thumped in her chest. *To capture his attention...*

Suddenly, the room seemed brighter.

Hugh Montclare blotted out all the Sir Reginald Talbots with one magnificent, blinding stroke. She took in a quick breath, her pulse beating loudly, her fingers tightening around her glass.

Insanity.

Reckless.

Outrageous.

Georgina placed her empty glass on the crowded silver tray, pulled back her shoulders, and moved toward Charles.

"Where is she going? Georgina!" rose up behind her, which only gave a more pronounced sway to her hips as she moved across the room.

They were all waiting to be introduced. To be noticed.

She would not wait on anyone to do this for her. She would take the chance. After all, she had an in.

Charles spotted her, his body straightening, his eyes gleaming, his bow graceful. "Miss Georgina? Delightful to see you as always."

She bowed in return. "Thank you, Mr. Montclare."

"Would you care for refreshment? I believe they've opened a new Madeira just now."

"I would indeed."

His head flew up at the flare in her voice. There was a sparkle in his golden brown eyes, and Georgie's pulse quickened under the shimmer of their inspection. His attentions in the past were always probing and sweeping. He missed nothing.

He handed her a glass of wine, their fingers brushing. "Very good to see you here tonight, Georgie." His voice always grew warmer when he used her nickname, that ease of familiarity flaring between them.

"No lady has caught your fancy this evening? What a terrible state of affairs, you standing here alone."

"Have you come here to save my reputation, then?"

"I don't think anything can be done to save your reputation, Mr. Montclare."

"Such a brazen tongue…"

Was he remembering her brazen tongue against his the other night? She certainly hadn't forgotten it. She could feel it even now. Sparks flew up her spine, over her flesh as they held each other's gaze, the muscle along his sharp jaw flexing. How is it she felt as if she were bare to him?

Georgina cleared her throat. "I've always enjoyed our conversations, Mr. Montclare. I know with you I can speak freely without censure."

"Indeed." His features eased, his lips curving into a grin. "I do remember you once called me a helpless, insatiable rogue."

"Did I?"

"You're blushing."

"'Tis the wine."

"You've emptied your glass."

"More, please."

"Your wish is my command." He signaled a servant, who promptly offered him a fresh glass. Charles handed it to her.

"Thank you." She sipped. "I was quite sorry to hear of your father's passing."

"Although he had been ill for some time, it was most unexpected."

"The loss of a parent is always unexpected."

"Yes. Unfortunately, you are familiar with this as well."

"I am." Her father had perished in a horrible carriage accident years ago, and it had left a hole in her heart that still remained deep, wide, and dark. "And now your brother is the Earl of Ryvves?"

"He is, yes." Charles shifted his gaze to the crowded ballroom. "How do you find this evening's ball? Is it to your liking after being away from town for so long?"

"I find it quite sparkling." She laughed softly.

"As are you." He raised his glass to her. "You are resplendent this evening. You are…quite changed."

If she were changed, it had happened in the last hour, to be sure.

"I thank you, Mr. Montclare." She sipped the wine, and its warmth blossomed through her. "I do miss our dear friends, Brandon and Justine. I am most impatient to see them again."

"When do you return to Gloucestershire?"

"Of that, I am not sure. I expect your godson has grown this past year?"

"Indeed he has. He is speaking now. An advanced child for his age."

She laughed. "Have you taught him how to play a good hand at whist?"

"Oh no, not yet. But soon, I warrant. Quite soon." They laughed. "You will save me a dance, I hope? If you are not fully claimed for the evening?"

"Are you not claimed for the evening?"

"I can't say I've made an effort."

"If you're not in the mood then…" She turned to leave.

He clasped her hand in his. "But I am." His grip on her hand tightened, his eyes piercing hers as he leaned in closer, taking her breath away. That danger that Thomas spoke of pushed through her like a thick wave in the sea. "Shall we dance this one?" he asked.

"We shall."

He quickly dispensed with their glasses and led her to the floor.

"I noticed you dancing earlier with the gentleman." He slanted his head to the left, where Philippa and Sir Reginald were dancing toward the end of the line next to Amanda and her surly husband, William. "Do you know him well?"

"He is a friend of my brother-in-law, Mr. Holyfloke."

"He is eyeing us quite decidedly." He'd lowered his voice and laced it with a teasing tone.

"Most probably, he is admiring your ease and facility in the dance, Mr. Montclare."

His lips curled into a sly grin. "I am a fine dancer, am I not?"

"You are, sir."

They turned and took each other's hands and stepped down the line.

She and Charles nimbly kept up with the now faster steps of the dance, neither losing sight of their direction or time with the music.

"I had quite forgotten what a fine dancer you are, sir."

"Are you saying you'd forgotten me, dear Georgie?" He raised an eyebrow at her.

"No, that's not what I meant."

"I'm glad to hear it. How is it that you are not yet married? No young buck has caught your eye?"

"None."

"What? Matthew Penry already forgotten about?"

"Don't tease me."

"Why ever not?"

She stopped. "I'm not a child."

"Oh, I know." He took her hand once again as she moved alongside him. "I can see that quite plainly."

Her blood quickened at his suddenly low, gruff tone, at the firmer grip of his hand on hers, at his hard form brushing against her. Why was she reacting to him this way? This was Charles, who always spoke glibly with his slightly outrageous and very clever wit. In fact, she had missed their repartee, hadn't she? She had, but right now, she must not be distracted from her course of action.

"And you, Mr. Montclare? No fiancée?"

"No."

Amanda and her husband, William, danced between them. William cast a dark glower at both she and Charles. Amanda ignored them.

The music ended. *Was it over already?* They bowed to each other, but Charles kept her hand in his. A warmth glowed through her and she wasn't sure if it was only from the dancing.

He squeezed her fingers. "Shall I return you to your sister and the gentleman?"

"No, please. No."

He chuckled. "Your wish is my command, Miss Georgina. But there will be a fee."

"Of course there will be."

"You must tell me the reason. I feel there is a reason." His voice had gotten deeper, darker, and it sent a flicker of heat over her flesh in a strange, delicious way.

She moved closer to him. "My family wishes for me to marry the gentleman."

"Ah. And your answer?"

"I do not wish to. He's…not my sort."

"I would agree."

"I'm glad to hear you do."

"He seems a fine man, to be sure." He cleared his throat. "Although…"

"Although?"

"He does seem dour."

"Dour, yes. That is a fine, fine word." A smile curved her lips.

"And you, Georgie, are such a lively sort. But, perhaps you would make him less dour, eh?"

"I do not wish to have anything to do with him, Charles." Her voice trembled there at the end, and she instantly regretted it. His brow furrowed, and he turned them around so as to have more privacy from the passersby.

She bit her lip. She always said too much. When would she ever learn? But with Charles, she'd always felt that she could be forthright as was her wont. And he always appreciated her candour in a way that was quite satisfying.

"Is there anything I could do to help?"

Yes, actually there is! She grinned. "You always do enjoy schemes and stratagems, don't you?"

"I do, but, in faith, I would like to help you if there is any way I can, scheme or no." His voice had become lower, serious.

She went to speak but just then, eyes much like Charles's peeked over his shoulder taking in Georgina. Her breath caught in her chest. *Hugh. Hugh at last.*

Hugh's gaze swallowed her whole, pinning her to the spot as he came up alongside Charles, an arm hooked on his brother's shoulder. "Brother, who is this beauty you've uncovered?"

Chapter Seven

Georgina

CHARLES'S FACE STIFFENED, and he released her hand. Hugh had found them.

Just as she'd hoped he would.

Georgina's back straightened, her lips deepening into a brilliant smile. Up close she saw the facial features that the Earl shared with his brother, but on Hugh, they were thicker, bolder strokes, not as refined. And while Charles had a certain cool disdain to his demeanor, Hugh had a positively devilish, warm, and unabashed way about him. He grinned at her, his head tilting. Quite devilish.

"Hugh, this is Miss Georgina. You might remember her from our childhood in Gloucestershire. Philippa and Thomas's younger sister."

"Ah, yes. Georgina. Of course." He took her hand in his and kissed it. "My, how the years have passed, and gloriously so."

Her lips parted at his lingering touch and at his appreciative zesty gaze in order to convey her being overwhelmed by him. That's what this occasion called for, and she knew that's what men like Hugh wanted to see.

Charles cleared his throat. "Miss Georgina, my brother—the Earl of Ryvves."

Hugh released her hand, and she bowed her head slowly. "A pleasure, my lord."

"The pleasure is all mine." His low, rich voice sent a tingle through her middle. Hugh spread out an arm. "Look who I found, Charles, and I've brought her to you to claim a dance—our cousin, Alice."

Charles's face went stony. "Alice." He bowed his head.

Alice let out a sharp giggle. "Charles."

"Miss Georgina, this is our cousin, Alice Dunsmore."

"We've met before." Georgina bowed her head.

"How wonderful to see you again, Miss Georgina," said Alice in her thin voice.

Hugh loomed over Georgina. "And I have found a new dance partner. Miss Georgina, shall we?"

"My lord."

Charles moved out of their way, and they proceeded to the dance floor with Alice and Charles behind them. A wide swathe was cut for their approach, and Georgina's heart beat faster under the weight of hundreds of eyes feasting upon them. She noticed Charlotte and Harriet whispering as they watched them.

Dancing with Hugh Montclare was a whirlwind. He was a most excellent partner. His eyes shone as they held hers. Indeed, they never strayed. She felt as if she were under a bright heavy light in his presence, but his touch was firm yet delicate, guiding. He knew every step, never faltered.

They conversed. They laughed. "I daresay, Lady Appleton's feathered hat may fall off her head at any moment. Shall we take bets on when and who will be the unlucky one to step on it in the line? Perhaps she is also wearing a wig this evening?"

"Then that too shall go flying along with the hat."

He laughed.

The dance over, she turned to thank him and take her

leave, but he only brought his body closer to hers. "Oh, don't leave me now. You cannot abandon me thus, sweet girl."

"Ah, but I must, my lord. We would be making a spectacle of ourselves."

"I would love to make a spectacle with you."

"Would you?"

A noise escaped his throat. "You are a delightful creature, and I would brave a dark forest of odious tongues and lascivious lies for you."

A shiver raced up her spine at his intriguing, dramatic turn of phrase in her favour. "I thank you, but I must find my brother. I'd promised him this dance." She smiled cooly as she delivered her lie.

He bowed his head most gracefully. "Very well. But I shall find you again, I promise you that. I require more from you." He lifted her hand to his lips, his gaze remaining on hers with a look that spoke of something secret only they shared. "Much more. You must come back to me soon. You've spoilt me for any other partner. I want no other."

"My lord. I would not want you to go unsatisfied."

His eyes flared. "Ah. I shall hold you to that, Miss Georgina."

She had made just the impression she'd hoped to make on the Earl of Ryvves. He enjoyed her company, and she'd left him intrigued.

And better yet, she quite enjoyed his. *Perfection.*

Her lips turned up into a slight smile. She made sure it was no more than that as she bowed and took her leave of him. They were being watched. She was sure of it. Her face hot, she turned. Lifting her chin, she glided through the crowd to find her brother. She wanted to shout and laugh out loud, but of course, that was impossible. Her blood rioted through her veins as she calmly made her way to Thomas in the gaming room.

The heavy smoke and humid air cloaked her as she entered

the room. This was the greatest game of chance she had ever or would ever play.

After all, her life depended on it.

Chapter Eight

Charles

CHARLES HAD to have a word with Georgina. Saying a quick thank you and farewell to Alice, he moved through the blur of the crowd, searching for Georgie.

His gut tied into thick blistering knots watching her dance with Hugh. Flirt with Hugh. She'd transformed into a woman before his eyes. A woman who very much enjoyed a man's attentions without fawning over him or giving into him. His cock had stirred at the sight of her graceful movements whilst dancing, her coyness as Hugh spoke with her. The little scoundrel knew what she was doing.

And he knew what she was doing. She was getting Hugh interested. And he was. If she were any other girl…

He must try to talk her out of this course of action.

His last resort was the gaming room. He spotted their friends, her brother…*There she is.* "You are enjoying yourself this evening, Miss Georgina?"

She gave him a quick glance. "I am, sir. And you?"

"Quite. How did you find the dancing? Has the music been to your liking so far?"

She let out a satisfied sigh as she gave him a knowing grin. "The dancing tonight has been wonderful."

She was pleased with herself and her plan thus far.

The relish with which she'd enunciated the word 'wonderful' stirred him. But she was describing her time with his brother. "You and my brother danced quite well together."

"He is an excellent partner."

She was all in. Charles's fingers fiddled with his necktie. "I would caution you, Georgie."

Her head raised at his serious tone, coupled with her nickname coming off his lips. "Whatever do you mean?"

"Although my brother is a fine figure of a man and looking for a bride, I do not think he would be a wise choice for you."

"As a dance partner?" Her lips had curved into an ironic tilt.

"My brother, madame, lives a most independent life uniquely his own." Did she catch his meaning?

"I admire that in a man."

She was being stubborn. She was determined.

"Georgie, I know what you are doing."

"I am enjoying myself at a ball, Mr. Montclare. That is what I am doing."

"My brother is extremely enthusiastic. One finds oneself easily carried away with that enthusiasm, like waves in the sea. But mark, those waves always crash on the shore and are no more."

Her brow furrowed. "I find Lord Ryvves's enthusiasm most appealing and quite compelling. He is not dour in the least." She raised her chin. She was pleased with herself.

"Years ago, I warned you that being in my company would tarnish your reputation, and you'd replied that you as yet had no reputation. After this evening—"

"Yes?"

"Make no mistake, Georgina, Hugh is a man of the world."

"Such as yourself."

"Yes, but you…you…"

"Charles." Her voice was raw, and his lungs constricted at

the desperation in the way she said his name. She pleaded with him to listen. "I do not wish to be mired in dour. I shall not survive it."

"Charles, are you going to play with us?" Thomas's loud voice sliced the air between them, and they pulled away from one another just as he had probably intended for them to do. "Matthew must dance, and we need you." Thomas glanced at his sister, and he went back to reviewing his cards with great intent.

"No. No, thank you." Charles cleared his throat and moved closer to Georgina once more. "I understand your predicament, but you are an innocent," he whispered. "And I would not wish that to alter." His insides tightened. Damn, why was this so hard for him to articulate his concerns to her for her well-being?

"Surely, a wife does not remain innocent, does she, sir? Is that what you would have for me? I would then truly be an unlucky woman."

The image of Hugh taking her maidenhood made his vision black. "Oh, Georgina—"

"Charles, I realise you've always thought of me as a young girl."

"Yes, but I do not now. I think of you as a pure spirit, untarnished. A vibrant young lady…" Damn, he'd said too much. Gone overboard. A ragged sigh dragged from his lips.

"I thank you for such fine compliments. But I assure you, I am quite capable of making my own decisions, especially now. If there is the slightest chance I can save myself, I will take it. That is unless you do not approve of me for the Earl." She bit her lip.

"You are the finest young lady of my acquaintance, Georgina. Be assured of that."

"I thank you." She swallowed hard. "I must find an agreeable prospect tonight, and not just any man, a spectacular man that my family could not possibly deny. If I do not, I will be taken back to my sister's, where I do not want to be, and married off to the dour gentleman, whom I do not want for a husband. Do you understand?" The urgency in her voice bore straight through his chest.

"I do, yes." *For fuck's sake, this is a disaster.*

"Tonight I have an opportunity. I have but one chance to make this right for myself. Should I not try? This is the only avenue available to me."

Hugh was surely the more impressive candidate for a husband than the dour older man, but if she married Hugh, it would change her intolerably. He was sure of it. She would be trapped, miserable, bitter. She would be forced to accept her husband's illicit behaviour because he was certain Hugh would not suddenly tame himself once he married, as he'd readily admitted.

And if he took up with a new mistress, which he was sure to do, that would be the ultimate betrayal for this girl and perhaps lead her to risky behaviour of her own.

But Georgie was right in her thinking. She needed a stellar candidate for her fiancé. To see her married and with child from that man made a cold sour sensation slither through his belly. The thought of a man such as he feasting on Georgie whenever he liked…

He tamped down the swell of bile at the images that thought conjured. He gave Georgina a softer, easy smile. "Be assured, you have danced with Ryvves once, spent much time in conversation. And it has been noticed."

She let out a small sigh. "How wonderful." She was pleased, relieved.

"Tread carefully. My brother pays his enthusiastic attentions to many young ladies at every party we attend. Do not think that simply because you have charmed him with one dance that—"

"I realise that. I understand. If you could—"

"There you are, Miss Georgina." Hugh's voice rose behind

them, and they parted at his appearance. "Has my brother been entertaining you or boring you?" Hugh stood before them.

"My lord," Georgina smiled up at him. "We were catching up on our mutual friends, the Gravens, in Gloucestershire, whom I greatly miss."

"I greatly missed you. In fact, I need you." His lips curved. "Stay and bring me good fortune as I play a hand or two here."

"Of course I shall." Georgina smiled brightly at Hugh.

Matthew stood up from the table, his gaze dragging over them. Hugh took his seat between Amanda and Thomas.

"Miss Georgina." Matthew bowed his head slightly. Georgina only tilted her head and kept her gaze firmly on Hugh.

Charles's throat burned. She was a woman with purpose. She had a strategy. She was on a mission that was life or death.

Hugh was dealt cards as he chatted with Amanda. Thomas told a ridiculous anecdote, and everyone at the table laughed. Georgina laughed. Georgina ordinarily wouldn't have found that tale amusing. She would have been the first to roll her eyes and share the irony with him.

Charles retreated from the table and made his way out of the clogged room, grabbing a fresh glass of wine from a servant's tray and swallowing the liquor down.

"SHE'S MAGNIFICENT, ISN'T SHE?" Hugh came up alongside him where he stood watching the dancing.

Charles rubbed his temple. The ache in his head would not cease. "Which female are we discussing?"

"My chosen bride."

"At last. Who is she?"

"The adorable Georgina, of course. She's far from the little scamp she used to be, raising her nose at us, always talking back, fiddling with her bow and arrow."

"Ah, you remember her then?"

"I remember. And I very much like what I see now. She has a fine profile, an elegant nose, and good teeth. She's not short, certainly not plain, an inquisitive mind, witty, gracious, lively. Lovely dancer. Money and not a bad pedigree. Exquisite bosom. She's tailor-made for me."

"You think so?"

"Out of all the females here tonight—nay, out of all the females I've met in London this season—I've enjoyed her company and dancing most of all. And I very much want her for my bed and for my wife."

"Find someone else."

His head jerked back. "Do you want her for yourself, old boy?"

"Miss Georgina and I are friends."

Hugh laughed. "You can still be friends when she's your sister-in-law."

"I would not wish to see her wounded in any way."

"Wound my wife? Why would I ever do such a thing?"

So like father. Arrogant, selfish…

"She deserves a real husband, Hugh. Not simply a title and a house and the obligatory heirs to bear. Georgina is a good girl."

Hugh held his brother's gaze, his jaw suddenly harder. "Have you tried to talk her out of accepting me?"

Georgina's desperate countenance flashed before his eyes. He had to help her, even if…

"No, I've done no such thing." He brushed a hand down his lapel. "In fact, she told me that her sister and brother are favouring another gentleman for her hand. And he is here tonight."

"Does she favour this man?"

"No," he pushed the word out his lips.

"Excellent."

Music swelled around them. Another dance had begun. Hugh suddenly stiffened, muttering a curse under his breath.

Charles followed his brother's attention to the dance floor.

Georgina danced, and her partner was the Duke of Oakley. Next to them danced the Duchess with Georgina's brother-in-law, John. Oakley and Georgina spoke, her countenance demure but pleased. Rather, the Duke did most of the talking, and Georgie was the perfect lady. Listening, nodding, smiling, replying briefly, to which His Grace smiled upon. And on and on it went.

Charles's black heart thudded in his chest. Was this simply a coincidence that Oakley had asked Georgina to dance?

The squall in the sea inside him churned and grew into a veritable gale. A fierce thunderstorm of thick black clouds fulminated directly overhead, rumbled, threatened.

Imminent doom.

A handsome, striking man, the Duke of Oakley was over a decade older than his wife, although you would never guess by looking at him. Unlike many of his peers, His Grace was fit, hardy, and robust. And like many of his peers, he was a commanding, imperious sort.

The Duchess, who was but a few years older than Hugh, was an elegant specimen of womanhood. Tastefully dressed and adorned with diamonds at her ears and a double strand of long pearls and diamonds flecked with rubies at her neck, she was every inch the grand noblewoman amongst them. She could have been wearing the plainest of muslins and a straw hat, and yet you would know that she was of noble birth.

The music came to a rousing finish. The dancers applauded loudly, their enthusiasm filling the room. His head ached with the noise. Georgina, her eyes shining, her cheeks flushed, hands clasped before her, spoke with the Duchess. Hugh gulped at his wine.

Oakley turned and caught Hugh's eye. He lifted his chin, a

slight smile on those chiseled lips of his. The hairs on the back of Charles's neck stood at attention. Hugh acknowledged the greeting with a discreet bow of his head, and a cold potion seeped through Charles's veins.

Oakley guided Georgina from the dance floor as they spoke. Behind them, his wife conversed with Georgina's brother-in-law.

Charles's instincts never let him down. They twisted and churned inside him now, blaring. "You haven't truly broken with her, have you? You got his approval for Georgina, is that it?"

Hugh did not reply. He only drained his glass.

"Why? Have you already planned the virgin sacrifice?"

"No sacrifice." He swiped at his lip. "A feast."

"You must find another," he said through gritted teeth.

His brother met his gaze. "I don't want another. She's perfect."

"You must." Charles leaned in closer to his brother, a hand at his broad chest. "Do this for me."

Hugh shoved his hand away. "I will not."

"Please, Hugh. You've put her in a risky position this evening with all the lavish attention you've bestowed on her."

"Miss Georgina has deeply enjoyed my brand of lavish, or haven't you noticed?"

"We've all noticed. But her family has arranged to formally engage her tomorrow."

He stilled. "Tomorrow?"

"That's what she told me."

"I shall act quickly then. Nothing shall get in the way of my plans for her."

Chapter Nine

Georgina

She and Hugh danced a third, then a fourth. It was most reckless of them, and with each step they took on the floor, she could feel her pulse beat in time with the music, with the stunned gawking of everyone. Destiny herself gawked.

With each step and turn, she and the Earl of Ryvves declared themselves to the world and they both knew it.

She declared her independence from her family and their plans for her.

Her feet flew over the polished floor. Somewhere down the line, she noticed Matthew who, when she caught his gaze, only glared at her coldly. Next to him, her brother's face was drawn as he danced with their sister. And Philippa's small mouth was now unusually pursed ever so tightly, giving her the look of a perpetually irritated fishwife. Discontent and reproach in one.

John and Sir Reginald, although engaged in conversation with a number of other gentlemen as they enjoyed their wine, seemed stony-faced.

She was making her point.

Her chest puffed up as she took the turn to her left. She reconnected with Hugh in the center, where he met her with a smile, her hand slipping easily into his. All eyes were on them.

The music came to an end, and her heart pounded in her chest as they applauded. Hugh took her hand and bowed his head. "Dancing with you this evening has been the most singular and exciting experience of the past few weeks here in London, Miss Georgina."

"Thank you, my lord. I, too, greatly enjoyed our dancing this evening."

"There are certainly more people in this ballroom now than there were before. It is quite hot in here, and we are both in need of fresh air. Perhaps you would like to join me on the terrace?"

Georgina took in a breath. Here, now, was the moment. The moment that would resolve or destroy all her hopes. She had to show him she was keen on him, but she also could not play the easily won naive girl. Although Georgina felt carried away by the power of this idea that had certainly blossomed in her favour, Ryvves must respect her if she wanted him to see her as a wife, not a dalliance.

She wasn't afraid to be alone with him, to be kissed by him under the stars. But she couldn't take the chance that what he wanted for them was but a passing fancy, a moment's desire, and not marriage.

She needed a marriage proposal posthaste. And to get it, she mustn't appear eager.

"My sister is waiting on me. I should go to her."

"Surely she would understand."

"What is it she would understand, sir?"

"That you and I have an undeniable connection." The rough timbre of his voice pawed over her flesh.

She lowered her eyes. "We do, yes."

"Such passions as you inspire, Miss Georgina, cannot be contained by boundaries or rules created by those who could not possibly understand what it is that you and I are feeling at this very moment. Blood runs hot, not cold, just like your hand in mine right now, our flesh touching…"

She withdrew her hand from his. "Sir, I beg leave of you for the moment. I must go to my sister. Otherwise, I fear…"

Suddenly, her arm was taken in a firm hold, and she was pulled deeper into the throng, out the veranda doors, quickly down the steps away from the other guests and into the gardens. Hugh's warm breath fanned the bare flesh of her chest. "You are a divine creature, and I must have you to myself."

She only laughed. Divine. Yes, that was the word.

"My darling, I must have you."

"I beg your pardon, my lord?"

"Yes, beg for it, the word I long to hear," he muttered against her hand, and her fingers curled. His wet tongue laid a trail up the inside of her bare arm, and she shivered. "Lord Ryvves, what are you doing? You mustn't—"

"Tasting you, of course."

Her insides tightened at his words, his darker tone. The meaning unmistakable. How she had longed to hear such things whispered under the moonlight to her by a handsome man one day.

One day had arrived, but was Hugh Montclare that man?

"I remember you as a child, Miss Georgina." His thumb stroked the edge of her jaw. He chuckled, a rich sound filling her ears that made her heart beat faster. Was this the same heady feeling Philippa had experienced when she'd danced with Hugh Montclare at a ball years ago?

They'd danced only once, but he'd remained a god among men for her sister, the one by whom she'd measure all other males thereafter. She spoke of him endlessly, dreamed of him. Even scribbled out her name "Lady Ryvves" on a sheet of paper. But Hugh had never expressed any interest in her, never called on her. Philippa had been deeply disappointed for weeks after. A month later, she'd agreed to marry John.

"You feel it too, don't you? This deliciousness between us."

Hugh's warm nose nudged along the sensitive skin of her throat.

The fragrance of his lavender-scented water filled her nostrils. The warmth of his skin flared against hers.

Positively outrageous.

Oh, her plan had succeeded.

She'd never allowed a man to touch her like this before. *"What would Philippa think if she could see us like this?"* roared through Georgie's wicked mind as she relaxed in Hugh's hold.

He murmured against her skin. "All night long, mothers and fathers and girls have paraded by me…"

"A great compliment."

"To be sure. But you appeared like a vision releasing me from a fog of mediocrity." His lips were only inches from her own. "Are you afraid, my beautiful creature?"

"Should I be?"

Two fingers trailed down her bosom, delving past the filmy fabric of her dress to brush the top of her breasts. "Ah…" His voice was an ache. She was sure he wanted to get a response from her. Was he testing her?

She was in this until the end. She would not show fear or panic or allow him to take more liberties than he already had.

The tip of his tongue traced a hot, wet brand over her bare chest, and Georgina's fingers dug into his taut arms as she pulled away from his grip. "Lord Ryvves, you mustn't. Someone will see."

He chuckled. "Yes, they certainly will."

"I would not wish them to."

He swiveled her around, pressing her back against the cold hard garden wall. Trapped. His eyes were just as cold and hard, and her body tightened. His lips touched hers. "I wish them to."

"Why ever for?"

"Dear girl, you are the most sparkling creature I have laid eyes on, and I must have you for a wife. You seem agreeable, but I cannot take a chance that you would deny me. I will brook no denial."

Victory.

"I heard talk that you may be promised to another."

"I'm not engaged, sir."

"But there is a man here tonight who has hopes and designs on you. Engagement may be imminent."

"My lord is well informed."

"I want you for myself, Miss Georgina. No one shall stand in my way." His hands cupped her buttocks, firmly pressing her against his firmness, and an icy shiver raced up her spine. The devil himself was clutching her, offering her the very thing she wanted most, and yet…

His knuckles brushed the line of her jaw. "Dear Georgina…."

She gulped in a breath. His rumbly voice made her flesh prickle and hum in a way that certainly Matthew had never. She had no idea that a different man could bring a different response. She'd assumed that the feeling of desire would be the same.

But Hugh? Hugh made her feel like she was standing over a black abyss. Exciting, yet…

"What in the devil is going on here?" Charles's sharp voice filled her ears, and her body snapped to attention. "Hugh— what in the bloody hell are you doing?"

"Only what you wanted of me, brother. What is required— securing a wife."

Chapter Ten

Charles

A HOT KNIFE slashed at his chest at the sight of Georgina in his brother's clutches, her face marred with red. Was it excitement? Desire?

"Is she not glorious, Charles?"

"Unhand her this instant."

A slow smile spread across Hugh's face as he held onto Georgie.

Fire blazed in his veins. "Let her go before someone sees. She's an innocent."

"Oh, not for long." He let Georgie go, and she visibly shuddered. "That flush on her skin, that hitch in her breath, those lips…Heaven awaits me."

"Enough!" Charles gritted out.

"How does Heaven await you, sir? I have yet to agree to anything." Georgina smoothed her hair and adjusted her dress.

"I've taken care of that for you, dear girl," replied Hugh.

"What do you mean?" she asked.

"Just over there is our dear friend, Matthew Penry. I had him follow us here to witness our little rendezvous."

Her eyes widened at the sight of Matthew in the distance. "Witness?"

"You bastard." Charles's voice seethed.

"I needed insurance that you would agree to marry me as you are within hours of being spoken for, or you might change your mind, as you pretty young things are wont to do. I will be coming to call on you tomorrow, and I expect a positive answer from you and your family."

"And if I do not agree?" Georgina lifted her chin. She met his gaze. "Then Mr. Penry would share what he'd seen between us, perhaps enriching the tale with his colourful imagination, and I would then be ruined?"

"She catches on quickly. I like that. Yes, my darling. What would your aforementioned would-be fiancé think of you then?"

Georgie pushed Hugh off her with a grunt. "You've thought of everything, haven't you? My oh my. Who knew that the Earl of Ryvves would have to trap himself a wife?"

A scowl flashed over Hugh's face. He obviously did not appreciate her remark. Had he expected tears and pleading?

Georgina's dark gaze shot to Matthew, who stood not far from them against the garden wall, his arms crossed, gaping at her, his cold expression tinted with disgust.

The bastard. Since they were children, he'd always done Hugh's bidding to gain his favour. Beneath his thin veneer of moral outrage, Charles was certain Matthew was jealous that Hugh had gotten his fangs into Georgina and not him.

Hurried footsteps thudded over the stone walkway. Thomas came to a halt before them, "Georgina? What have you—Montclare? Ryvves? What are you both doing with my sister? Are you taking advantage? Again? This is not to be borne!"

"Again? Hmm. Well, well, well, Charles." On a dark chuckle, Hugh took Georgina's hand in his and kissed it.

Thomas's eyes blazed, his gaze shooting from one Montclare to the other, his sister in between them. "She is promised to another! Spoken for..." he sputtered.

"Now I have spoken, and she is mine."

"You Montclares, libertines all of you. Always have been, always will be," exploded Thomas.

"He's insulting us, Charles. Insupportable —"

"For the love of God, Hugh!" Charles's voice simmered.

"You little fool!" Thomas grabbed his sister's arm, pulling her away from Hugh, and wincing, she gasped.

"Thomas!" Charles darted forward.

Thomas thrust a finger in his face, his voice seething. "Don't you dare attempt to make excuses for your brother's behaviour, Montclare. All night long, he knew exactly what he was doing. Now, everyone here tonight is talking about them both. By tomorrow noon, if there is no official engagement announced, my sister's good name will be tainted forever."

"I assure you, we shall settle this like gentlemen."

Hugh crossed his arms, a derisive twist to his lips. "Quite right. Like gentlemen."

"Ah yes, always gentlemen bargaining. Gentlemen deciding," Georgina spit out.

They all turned to her, surprised, aghast as if they'd forgotten she was there. Forgotten she could speak, think, had a mind of her own. Everyone except Charles who let out a short laugh at her outburst.

Bravo, Georgie.

Georgina yanked her arm from her brother's tight grip. "Then do so, Lord Ryvves. Decide. Bargain. Settle. Tomorrow we look forward to hearing your terms."

Chapter Eleven

Georgina

SHE'D WON.

This evening Georgina had set her sights on a goal, and she'd seen it through. What she wanted had come to fruition.

She'd saved herself from marriage to Sir Reginald.

Thomas had dragged her through the garden and ordered her to stay at his side for the rest of the evening. If they were to leave the ball now, it would be obvious that something was amiss. Everyone would attempt to guess what had happened, rumours would spawn, and it would be a nightmare.

He brought her to a table where her sister and her mother pretended to eat the supper that had been served. Her mother let out a breath as she carefully placed her fork on her dish. "Where have you been?"

Thomas explained.

Philippa gasped. Their mother's eyes narrowed, and her signature withering gaze descended attempting to shrivel Georgina.

This time, it did not work.

"Did you not think how making a show of yourself with that man in front of everyone would have consequences? This is the very thing we were trying to avoid."

"I danced with that man, as I danced with a number of other fine gentlemen. I even danced with His Grace, the Duke of Oakley."

"You did more than dance, sister," remarked Philippa.

"Do you know what kind of man the Earl of Ryvves is?" Mother's voice was pinched and made her stomach twist.

"Like all men."

"And what do you know of men?" her Mother hissed at her, her lips pursed, her face stony. Disgust.

Later, in their carriage, they were all silent. Once home, their mother immediately retired to her chamber, and Philippa, Georgina, and John went into the drawing room. Thomas was out with his friends.

Philippa sipped on her sherry. "Lord Ryvves may be a peer of the realm with a historic lineage and an outrageous income, but he—"

"He is a gentleman in want of a wife," Georgina interrupted.

"Tonight, he may have taken a fancy to you for all to see. But tomorrow he may attend a luncheon, a dinner, a tea, the theatre and take a fancy to another young lady, hmm? Perhaps all he wants—"

"He wants the same as you—an impressive congress of prestigious connections and bloodlines. An heir or two to secure his family's future."

"You must watch your tongue, sister." Philippa glanced at her husband.

John sniffed in air, placing his empty glass on the mantel. "The Montclares are a family of decadents going back generations."

"Indeed." Philippa's eyebrows flared. "He's probably forgotten all about you already. I am quite sure he will not come tomorrow."

"He will come," replied Georgina.

Philippa let out a stifled grunt. "John, if he does come and asks for her hand, will you refuse him?"

"How can I?" John's lips drew into a thin line. "It would be spectacularly foolish and utterly ridiculous to refuse such a man, such a connection. This is a bloody fine mess." He slapped his hand on the mantle.

Philippa straightened her back as the servant filled her glass once more. "He may not come. He may be all wind."

Another servant entered the room with a letter for John. Tearing it open, John read before the fireplace, the firelight making his taut features dramatic. His lips a snarl, he lifted his gaze to her, his eyes boring into Georgina, their glint obvious even in the dimly lit room, making her flesh prickle with ice. "I warrant you will rue the moment you invited his attentions."

"I did no such—"

He lifted his hand for her to stop, a grimace on his face. "Foolish, foolish girl. I am most displeased." He raised the letter in his hand. "Sir Reginald has quit London." He tossed the letter into the fire, and it crackled and flared in the flames.

Philippa let out a gasp. "Oh no! No!"

Georgina's heart thudded in her chest. She had saved herself indeed.

"This is a terrible wound to bear," her sister exclaimed. "John and I have always taken care of you, Georgina, always done our very best for you. And how do you behave when it matters the most? The one time we required your obedience and gratitude? Willfully. Recklessly. How shall I ever forgive you? How shall we recover?"

"If he does not come tomorrow," John bit out, his low voice a beacon of doom.

Georgina's mouth dried, and she cast her eyes downward.

Hugh will come, she thought. He will.

Her hands clenched tightly in her lap. *He must.*

Chapter Twelve

Georgina

THE NEXT MORNING, Georgina woke early, dressed, and readied herself. One had to be prepared. And she would be. Prepared for the road of her choosing. The road of her own making. Success or failure.

She had breakfast alone. Georgina could barely swallow the bread she'd buttered and slathered with jam as she did every morning. Thankfully, her mother took her breakfast in her room as was her wont, as did Philippa. No sign of John or Thomas.

She went to the drawing room, read her book, but barely understood the words. She sketched, but hardly knew what she drew. Thomas and John entered the drawing room as her gaze went to the clock for the hundredth time. It was nearly eleven.

The servant entered, and she held her breath. "The Earl of Ryvves and Mr. Charles Montclare for Miss Georgina."

John's brow furrowed. "Bring them through."

The servant left, and her pulse beat like a heavy drum. Her brother eyed her as she stood, her fingertips smoothing down her dress. *Now it all begins.*

The door opened, and the servant ushered in Charles, his

demeanor cool and crisp, holding a thick leather folder, and Hugh, unruffled and at ease, followed. They greeted her brother and John, and both their gazes finally settled on her. She bowed her head, her face heating.

"Miss Georgina, it is wonderful to see you in the light of day." Hugh took her hand and brushed it with a delicate kiss. "You are radiant."

"Miss Georgina." Charles bowed, his face remaining shuttered. Her heart shrank.

She gave her intended a brilliant smile as he handed her a small bouquet of blossoms. "I thank you, my lord. They are beautiful."

The Montclare brothers settled in the armchairs opposite her and John, and Thomas stood behind her. Charles glanced at her, a sober, heavy look, and swiftly averted his gaze.

"We trust you have recovered from last evening's many entertainments?" John crossed his legs.

Hugh let out a warm chuckle. "I shan't ever recover, Mr. Holyfloke. Seeing Miss Georgina there last night, a brilliant gem amongst pebbles, I remain in awe."

"Did the two of you not know each other in the country?"

"We did, but the last time I saw Miss Georgina, she was but a child. Now she is in the full bloom of womanhood."

"My brother traveled the Continent quite a bit once he came of age," said Charles. "He was rarely at home."

Thomas sniffed in air. "Indeed, rarely."

A silence filled the room, but Hugh didn't seem to care. He boldly held Georgina's gaze, grinning at her. "I have come today to ask for Miss Georgina's hand in marriage. Undoubtedly I am but one suitor among very many worthy candidates, but I entreat you to consider my proposal above all others."

Charles sat stoically, his jaw sharp, his features tight. They were all playing this game now, they had to utter and exchange all the proper niceties to fulfill society's demands. They had to impress John, that was a hard fact, but even John knew this was all bluster and dissembling.

They played on.

"Your high regard, my lord, is an honour I dared not dream of," said Georgina. "With all humility and great joy, I most gladly accept this great honour."

Hugh's grin deepened, and they both tilted their heads at each other. At her side, John let out a scoff and Thomas laid a hand on her shoulder.

Charles cleared his throat. "Mr. Holyfloke, Thomas, shall we proceed to specifics and complete the settlement of engagement of the Earl and Miss Townsend?" He cast his golden eyes on Georgina, and she felt a chill scrape over her flesh. Charles was most businesslike in his role on his brother's behalf. "I assure you, you will be quite pleased with our terms to unite our families."

"I shall tell you exactly how I feel, Mr. Montclare. Have no doubt." John stood up. "We shall go to my study."

Without a glance, Charles followed John and Thomas out of the room toward his commission being completed. She knew he did not wholly approve of this scheme, but he was acting on his brother's behalf to settle the particulars of their engagement.

"Darling, Georgina," Hugh took her hand and kissed it once again. His warm lips lingered over her flesh as his other hand stroked her arm. "How I look forward to our wedding day. I am most impatient for you to be mine."

Her insides tightened. Was it nerves at his eagle-like glare? "I, too, am impatient, Hugh."

He bowed to her once more and left her to join Thomas, John, and Charles, his even, steady steps sounding down the hallway as her pulse pounded in her ears. Hopefully, all the Montclares' terms would be agreeable to her brother and John, and any of their terms on her behalf would be agreeable to the Montclares. Over the years her brother-in-law had taken on the role of advisor in their family on a range of issues. John was certainly much more discriminating and shrewd than the younger Thomas.

She was alone while the four men dissected and reconstructed the anatomy of her future. Decided how much would go here from there for this and that. She would now be under Hugh's protection, be his responsibility.

Her stomach curled, and she went to the window, opened it wider, and sucked in fresh air. This day had finally come, but it had not come the way she'd always hoped, the way she was sure it would.

The day of her engagement she had piled high with dreams and designs, but it didn't feel like she'd always imagined it would like a sugary bonbon's sweetness bursting then melting in her mouth. No, it was not a match born of esteem and affection. Her hand had been forced, and by some confluence of the stars, her mission had crossed with Hugh's.

Her spine straightened. She was pleased and proud that, ultimately, it had been her choice. There would be no Sir Reginald. And although she and Hugh barely knew one another, he was closer to her age, charming and witty, amiable and good-natured, and very handsome. He was Charles's brother, and she liked Charles very much, didn't she? Which was good since she imagined they'd probably all be living together at the same house.

Living together?

The memory of Charles's searing kiss stung through her, and she bit her lip hard to stop it. She had to wipe that memory from her brain, from her lips, her tongue, her body…*oh damn, damn, damn.*

Georgina let out a heavy breath. It was up to her now to make of this marriage to Hugh what she would. She was an adult, no longer a girl. A woman engaged to be married, and to an earl. She would be the lady of a great house.

"He is here?" Philippa swept into the room.

"He is," Georgina replied. "They are discussing terms."

"Are they? Well, I—"

The door flung open, and John entered with Thomas, Charles, and a grinning Hugh behind him.

Philippa bowed her head. "My lord. Mr. Montclare."

"Madame."

"Mrs. Holyfloke," said Charles.

"It is all arranged," John announced, his arms crossed, his features sullen. He'd been bested, and he resented it, no matter the advantageous gain. "The wedding shall be in a week's time."

"A week?" said Philippa.

"We've obtained a special license," said Charles, adjusting the leather folder in his hands.

"You see, my father wanted me to be married by my thirtieth birthday," said Hugh. "And my birthday is in a week's time. Fantastic, eh, my love? What a celebration we shall have." He took Georgina's hand in his and squeezed her fingers. Philippa's gaze shot to the motion.

"Yes, very good news," said Georgina.

"Shall we celebrate with a drink?" said Philippa gesturing at the servant.

Georgina went to Charles. "I thank you, Mr. Montclare, for all your efforts on my behalf," she said. "You have done much to see this through."

"And now it is completed." Something like a frown settled on his face.

"And suddenly, you and I shall be family in a week's time."

"Georgina…"

"Yes?"

He leaned in closer to her. "I have done whatever was in my hand for your comfort."

"I am most grateful. I am sure the arrangements are most generous."

"I've seen to it." A muscle at his jawline flexed. "Every detail."

She held his troubled gaze. "I thank you."

"Do not thank me. Anything but that." His strained voice set off an ache inside her.

"This was the only way, Charles. And I am grateful for it."

From across the room, her sister and brother stared at them.

Georgina smiled at Charles as if they were having an idle conversation about the weather. "They were convinced you would not come today," she kept her voice low. "If you had not come, they were prepared to pack me off before midday, and then I would be at their mercies, of which there are none to speak of as they are all quite angry with me. My mother refuses to speak to me."

"I am most sorry to hear that."

"I know this is the best of all possible solutions. And how wonderful that I will be in Gloucestershire again close to our friends." Her throat burned. "Close to you."

His eyes shot to her. Burning eyes. Her breath cut.

Why had she said that? In that way?

"I realise a man such as yourself has not given much thought to what a lady suffers in the marriage process—"

"On the contrary, I assure you I have." The lines of his face tightened.

"I am quite sure Hugh and I will make a comfortable go of it as husband and wife. And then when you marry, we shall all be good friends, shan't we?"

A noise rumbled in his chest. He did not reply.

A servant entered the room and bent to speak to Philippa, a silver tray in his hand. She waved him on. He crossed the room and came to a halt before Hugh. "My lord, an urgent message for you." He lifted the tray. A small folded paper lay on it with a T melted into the wax seal. Hugh picked it up and opened it.

So urgent that the messenger found him here?

His brow creased, and his lips drew in a firm line, as he read. Folding the note, he tracked toward them.

"Charles, we must leave. Urgent business."

Charles's shoulders stiffened. "Very well."

Hugh handed the note to Charles as he took Georgina's hand, squeezing it for a moment. The master of distraction. "Forgive me, my love. So many responsibilities. We shall be taking our leave, but I trust you shall be busy preparing for our wedding."

"Yes, yes."

"You will make a resplendent bride."

"Come, brother," Charles bit out, sliding the note into his pocket as Hugh bid farewell to her sister and brother-in-law.

"Miss Georgina—" Charles bowed his head. "Always remember, if you ever need any assistance, anything at all, I will always be there for you."

Her heart thudded in her chest. Somehow she knew deep in her soul that this was no ordinary pledge. "I shall remember." She swallowed hard. "Charles, has something happened?"

"I must be off."

She clamped her hand on his arm, and his eyes snapped to hers. Eyes full of a dark storm. "Who sent the message?"

"Goodbye, Miss Georgina." He turned to Philippa and John. "Mr. Holyfloke, Mrs. Holyfloke, I thank you." He bowed his head and quit the room.

From the window where she sat, she spotted Charles adjusting his hat as he strode down the crowded street, tall, with purpose. Hugh waited for him. A footman bowed to him and held open the door to the Ryvves coach, emblazoned with the family crest. Charles and Hugh spoke heatedly, nay, argued. Hugh spoke to the footman with some urgency. The brothers entered their coach, and within moments, they were gone.

Something was wrong. She was sure of it.

She would find out.

Chapter Thirteen

Charles

"How could you? You idiot."

"Shut up!" Hugh hissed.

Charles glanced up from the carriage, and there was Georgina at the window, her face riddled with concern. With questions.

How could he tell her the truth? The dirty, foul truth.

"Quickly, man!" Hugh shouted at the driver, and the coach took off.

Last night, after they'd left the ball, Hugh and Charles had gone on to continue their revelries elsewhere with their friends.

"We must celebrate my engagement!" Hugh had clapped him on the back as they headed out for their favourite private club. But for Charles, the brothel had struck a false note. Hideous. The sight of so many female rumps and breasts bared and pitched for his strokes, his strikes, did not stir him. Right there standing at the head of a row of females writhing for their attention, a horrible thought had seized him. He had become a procurer of flesh for his brother.

And that "flesh" he'd peddled was Georgina Townsend.

Would he ever be able to look upon himself in a glass again?

As Hugh and their friends enjoyed their carnal entertainments, he swallowed back a drink in one quick shot and went home. But it was of no use. Georgie's bright gaze blazed before him and would not let him go. The squeeze of her hand on his arm as she implored him to secure his brother to save herself was seared on his flesh.

He brushed a hand across his mouth, the sour lingering.

Once home, he went straight to his desk and wrote up the terms of settlement of engagement for Hugh and Georgina. He altered the original draft that his father's solicitor had drawn up years ago to be ready the instant Hugh had decided on a wife. How many times had Hugh declared he'd found a bride and then at the last moment he'd pleaded how the girl was all wrong and he'd never survive it.

Soon.

Later.

Wait.

I shall.

I promise.

Too many to count.

Charles made it so that once she married Hugh, Georgina would not only have access to the usual pin money outlined for a wife but have control over her own money. It would be some kind of measure of security for her if she found her new life as Lady Ryvves was not to her liking. That it was only a prison of gilded disappointments that she needed to escape.

Like Mother.

"At least we've secured the bride," Hugh's voice broke his reverie. "Georgina and I are engaged. Nothing can break that now."

"Is that what you told yourself when you were thrusting your cock in Amanda last night?"

"Jealous, are you? She told me about the two of you."

"I'm sure she did. That's been over for two years now. Why, Hugh? Why her? And for fuck's sake, why last night?"

"When we were young lads she was always the prettiest girl. Always flirtatious in that difficult way I enjoy. But she liked Brandon then. When I first got to London, her husband and I rekindled our friendship, and Amanda and I caught each other's scent."

"Tell me it was only this one time."

Hugh didn't answer.

"How long has this been going on?"

"A fortnight, maybe more?"

"Why didn't you tell me?"

"She begged me not to. Said you'd be put off."

He scoffed. "William was with us at the club last night, was he not?"

"Yes, he was. I'd invited him along."

"As you have many times. Of course."

"Once everyone got settled, I left to be with her."

"Obviously you stayed with her too long because William saw you leaving his own house."

"That was her fault. She got upset when I told her that this was the last time, that I was to marry. She wanted to know who my bride is."

"Did you tell her?"

"No, of course not. She begged me not to leave her, not to marry. Even sucked my cock to impress upon me her deep adoration—which wasn't half bad. I left right after."

Charles let out a sharp laugh. "Yes, right after…"

"Oh stop it."

"If this news gets out, if Georgina and her family hear about this, they will have every right to break the engagement. They should because it will be—"

"They will not find out, and that engagement cannot be broken! I am marrying that girl, and no one will stand in my way. I have no more time."

"You should have thought of that last night." Charles rubbed at his eyes. "This indulgence of yours may make marrying Miss Georgina impossible. William has borne much with his wife and has done much in the past to blot out her offenses, and her offenses have been many—debts, lovers. And these past weeks, you were his friend, his friend of old whom he trusted, which must make this wound deep and sharp."

"You were his friend when you rutted his wife, were you not?"

"Yes, I was, and after, he swallowed it down because he was forced to by circumstances."

"I suppose getting cuckolded by two Montclares may be too much for any man."

"This is no time to joke, Hugh. He always loved her terribly, and he was always faithful to her."

"He certainly hasn't been this season."

"My point exactly. Things have changed between them, but she is still his precious wife. And now to see you leave his house…her very bed in his house." He let out a heavy breath. "Her note sounds quite desperate."

"It's a ploy, I'm sure of it. She's desperate to hang onto me. We have no business at that house. Does she expect me to intervene between them? To take her away? Ridiculous. What a man does with his own wife is his business."

And you bear no responsibility, do you? Charles rubbed a hand across his aching temple. "I, for one, await the worst."

Chapter Fourteen

Georgina

GEORGINA FOUND the servant who'd brought the note to Hugh. "Landon?"

"Ma'am."

"Do we know from where that message for Lord Ryvves was brought?"

"No, Miss. Although, young Sally was outside at the time of his arrival and offered the young man refreshment as he'd ridden hard to get here."

"Ah, of course she did."

Sally was the new scullery maid and had proven to be quite a chatterbox. She'd been told more than once by Cook to hold her tongue from what Georgina's lady's maid had told her. Georgina murmured a prayer of thanks that Sally had not yet taken to mending her ways.

Landon tilted his head. "Shall I inquire, Miss Georgina? I'm sure the girl learnt something."

"I shall ask her myself. If you could follow the Ryvves coach discreetly. They are just leaving now. I must know where they are going. If you are asked for, I shall tell them I've sent you on an errand."

"Very well, ma'am." Landon bowed his head and left.

Georgina went downstairs to the kitchen. The butler immediately appeared before her. She asked to speak to Sally.

"Is anything amiss, ma'am?"

"Not at all, Harding. I only wish to make an inquiry. A silly thing really."

Sally appeared, face flushed, curtsying deeply. "Sally, did you happen to speak with the messenger who brought the note just now for our guests?"

"Oh. Uhm, I…"

"I hope you did. Because I need to know from where that note came, and it would be wonderful if you could assist me."

The girl's face brightened. "Well, Miss Georgina, I did, in fact, happen to offer the young man a cup of ale as he seemed to have ridden quite urgently to bring his correspondence."

"How thoughtful of you, Sally. Did he happen to say from what house he'd come from?"

"He did say that he had been sent to his lordship's house from his mistress, a Mrs. Treharne."

Amanda. Her heart fell. Was Charles caught between that woman's legs again? In her web?

"—And I remembered the name, as I know the scullery maid there, for they are not far from here, and I've sometimes walked with her to market."

"Ah how nice."

"He told me that once he got to his lordship's house, he were told that the gentlemen were not at home but here, which irked him, for he'd just ridden across town for naught as the Treharnes are close by, and he could have delivered the important message much, much sooner."

"Poor man, to have ridden back and forth."

"That's just what I said, Miss. You poor man, I says. Have some ale for yer troubles. And he was quite pleased, I must say."

"I'm sure he was. Your kindness to strangers in need commends you."

The girl blushed. "Oh. I thank you, ma'am."

"And I thank you."

Sally curtsied and tracked back to the kitchen. "Did you hear that Mr. Harding?" her voice resounded from the kitchen. "Miss Georgina said I were —"

Georgina raced back upstairs and went to the library. Landon returned forthwith, and she nodded for him to approach, dropping the leather-bound volume of poems she was pretending to read on the cushions. "Tell me."

"I followed them as you asked, and I saw them enter a fine house. I inquired from a delivery man I saw at the next house, and he said it was the Ryvves home. 'Twas their own house they went to."

"Thank you, Landon. Please fetch me my cape."

SHE HAD TO DO IT.

Georgina took in a deep breath and knocked on the front door of William and Amanda's home. She announced herself to the servant and said she wished to see the lady of the house.

The servant returned. "Mrs. Treharne regrets she is unable to welcome visitors at this time."

"Tell your mistress I absolutely must see her, but briefly. I insist. We are old friends from the country, she and I. I will not leave until I've spoken with her. It is of grave importance and concerns Mr. Montclare and Lord Ryvves."

A figure appeared behind the servant, her long blond hair loose and mussed about her. It was Amanda, eyes glassy, a bruise on her cheek, her lips swollen, and in her hand a glass of dark wine. "What are you doing here?" The servant bowed her head and disappeared down the hallway.

Georgina passed through. "Your message for Lord Ryvves arrived at my doorstep and he and Charles seemed upset, and so —"

"They were at your house? They sent you here instead of coming themselves?"

Amanda was waiting for them, but they hadn't come here at all. They'd gone home. Georgina sucked in a tiny breath and exhaled the lie. "Yes."

Amanda glared at her, her lips pursing. Turning away, she swooshed into her drawing room.

Georgina followed her. "I was concerned as Charles is my friend and—"

"Your friend?" her voice sneered through a sharp laugh that she drank down with her wine. "This is a private matter, not for elegant young ladies."

"I shall be part of the family soon."

Amanda wiped at the edge of her lips. "What are you talking about?"

"I am engaged to the Earl of Ryvves."

She stilled, her face paler than before. "You …"

"Engaged to Ryvves. As of just an hour ago. Charles and Hugh were at my house settling terms with my brother-in-law."

Amanda let out a long heavy breath as if a sudden weight had been heaved on her person. "Engaged to Hugh?" Her voice was a husky whisper.

"Yes."

"You? You are his fiancée?"

"I am." Georgina pressed her lips together. "You're quite pale, Amanda. Shall I ring for tea?"

"Oh no, no. Your news calls for wine. We must celebrate your success, my dear. Come." She pivoted and sailed to a sideboard where the liquor decanters stood. She poured a glass of wine and topped up her own, adding a dark tincture from a small bottle.

"Amanda, are you unwell? Did you fall? Is that a bruise on your—"

"William and I had an argument. A rather fierce one. He

tried to intimidate me, but I was not intimidated only angry. It's always good to turn the tables on men, Georgina. Indeed, now that you will be a wife, you must learn these things." She handed the glass of wine to Georgina, who took it, glancing at the purplish red liquid. An elixir of the bedeviled, of the knowledge of a married woman. Was this her initiation?

Amanda sat on her settee and motioned for Georgina to join her, and she did. "For instance, your first night with your husband, let him have his way. Let him think you are his precious concubine and he the glorious conqueror. But you must look to finding your own pleasure in it, and then you shall use that knowledge to your greatest advantage with him in all things—if you dare." Licking her lips, Amanda swirled the contents of her glass and raised it. "So much to celebrate. To your engagement. To William's duel."

"A duel? With whom? Why?"

"Why do men challenge each other, Georgina?"

"To defend their honour." She held Amanda's gleaming gaze and she understood. *For you.*

Amanda sported a brittle smile as she raised her glass and clinked hers.

"Because of you and Charles? That was long ago." Her breath burned in her throat as the words unrolled from her lips. "Have you taken up with him again?"

Amanda let out a small laugh. "Are you in shock? Should I ring for tea after all?"

"No. Don't." Georgie gulped at the wine.

"You know nothing of what it is to be bound to a man you do not want or even like. You know nothing. I imagine you like Hugh very much."

"I do, yes."

"I imagine you've had a great many suitors call on you since you've come out."

"I have, yes."

Amanda reached out and touched a curled lock of

Georgina's hair. "You remind me very much of myself at your age. The world at your feet. All eyes bedazzled at the sight of you. Everyone wanting to breathe your air, to dance with you as an excuse to touch you, speak with you, be seen with you. Desirous of a moment to impress you with their wit, their charm. How I enjoyed it."

"Of course you did. You still do...bedazzle." Georgina shifted her weight, suddenly uncomfortable. Philippa had told her all about Amanda's great victories in their younger days. All the men of their circle had been in love with her at one point or another. Georgina remembered it herself, she may have been younger, but she had noted it.

"When I was younger than you are, I had fallen in love with a very handsome and very wealthy man. He had just returned from a tour of the Continent, but he was sent away once more, and we were to wait to be affianced. He left me and was all the way across the sea from me, on the other side of the world. Letters were rare and few...and..."

"And?" Georgina knew she spoke of Charles's good friend Brandon, who was now married to her close friend, Justine. When they'd been younger, there had been an affection between Brandon and Amanda, but then Brandon's father had sent him to the West Indies, where he stayed for almost two years to manage a new investment of his father's.

Amanda took a long sip of wine. "Suddenly, waiting, and pining were no longer terribly romantic. In fact, they had become quite dull. There was no end to it. I realised then that I no longer felt gripped by this love I thought I had in me. So I allowed myself the entertainments of men once again. Men who promised me all the wonderful things a man promises a woman when he is besotted. A man will say anything to claim a smile, a touch, a kiss." She eyed Georgina. "Isn't that so, Miss Georgina?" Her eyebrow was cocked, and her lips parted. She was teasing her, making fun of her, the innocent maid. Or she knew what had happened with Hugh at the ball.

"Yes, men make a great many pretty promises to get what they want from you," said Georgina.

"I very much enjoyed William's words, his ardour, his fierce intent. And I accepted his offer of marriage."

William was Brandon's cousin.

"And you were happy?" It seemed an insipid remark, but Georgina wanted to know.

"I do not think I could ever be what some people term happy. Is it like the satisfaction one experiences after a very fine meal and good wine? After a good ride on your favourite horse?" She raised her glass at Georgie and drank. "After triumphing at a game of cards?" Her gaze shot to Georgie. "After a passionate few hours spent with one's lover?"

Georgina's insides twisted painfully at Amanda's boasting veiled with a taunt, the smug smile sneaking over her mouth. She was implying that Charles was her lover. "Surely, Amanda, that is fleeting happiness, not —"

"It was very real to me. That was what I wanted more of."

"Is not your child a source of happiness?"

"Yes, of course, he is. But what about me, Georgina? What about me?"

Georgina had no answer.

Amanda moved about the room, drinking from her glass in a greedy fashion, at odds with the world. "Mark me, you will remember that question one day when you are married for at least five years. *What about me?* A haunting question every married woman asks herself.

"You see, Georgina, once your enthusiasm wanes with your husband and his with you, once you've achieved the necessary delivery of a healthy heir or two, you will find you need to establish a new set of rules. You mustn't take it personally. You mustn't be upset if your husband delights in another woman's body, looking for that very same searing yet fleeting satisfaction you long for. Why shouldn't we, too, claim it for ourselves?"

"Amanda, I—"

She raised her hand in Georgina's face. "I'm tutoring you on what to expect in a marriage. I am sure no one has spoken to you with such frankness on the topic."

"No." It was best to agree with her.

Amanda cupped Georgina's chin. "You need to know, Georgina. Be prepared. It's much better when you are prepared. No one tells you these things. I had to learn them myself. My mother was of the you-must-do-as-your-husband-your-master-tells-you generation. I find that ridiculous.

"I liked William well enough all along. Enjoyed his company. Found him attractive and most attentive. But as time crawled on, I became a bit reckless." She drank more. "After we quit the country and settled here in town, things changed. Suddenly, there wasn't the money we'd once been accustomed to. Suddenly, William was peevishly jealous of everyone and questioned every little thing I did or said. We argued frequently. One upped the other more frequently. And that, my dear, is a cold and slippery place to be."

"I know that last year you lost a babe. I was quite sorry to hear of it."

She nodded her head slightly. "Hmm." She drank again. Refilled her glass again. "I was unable to carry the child to term. I had so hoped for a girl." Amanda sucked in a breath, her eyes glistening. "And it was."

"I'm so very sorry."

She brushed her fingers across her chin. "I ask you, Georgina, are we put upon this earth to fester? To be miserable? It cannot be."

"No, it cannot be," Georgina said.

"So I take hold of any sort of happiness—as it so sweetly called—whenever I find it. And my husband has learned this lesson. He now keeps a whore or two."

"And in all this, what of love?"

"Love makes for delicious urgent whispers in the night,

nothing more." She let out a short laugh. "Oh, dear, do you fancy yourself in love with Hugh? Feel things for him you have felt for no other?"

"I…"

"Enjoy it now, for it's only a fleeting illusion that truly has no place in a marriage. I applaud you—securing the Earl of Ryvves is a great success." She drank more. "It's that sort of success that you and I were bred for, is it not? A match with a titled and handsome man of means."

"Yes, quite right," Georgie murmured.

"My advice to you is this: make sure you know what kind of field you are stepping into with a man. Is it muddy in the center? A swamp to the south? Where is it dry and bristly or fallow? You must know in order to lift your skirts in just the right way and best navigate it. Otherwise…"

"Yes?" Georgie swallowed hard.

Amanda's eyes flared dramatically. "Be aware, Georgina, the male of our species is a fragile beast. He is all sounds and spectacle and needs to be applauded regularly. Even if you are not pleased in your marriage bed, you must, must pretend to be so. And not only pleased but grateful. Yes, men require gratitude as well. They are the great providers, after all. And a man like Hugh Montclare? Well…"

Georgina's gaze took her in from head to toe as Amanda paced about the room, drinking. Red marks were scratched on her chest and her neck. The bruise on her cheek had swollen even more since she'd first arrived. Her dress bore a rip and tears were visible at the trim. Georgina's mouth dried. Had her husband done this to her?

"William is not a practiced shot, but he is a man of tempers. Perhaps that rage will embolden him to shoot well for the glory of his precious honour." Amanda came to a stop before her, so close, only inches away. Georgina could smell the wine on her breath, the warm sweat on her skin.

"Ah, to be your age again," she said. "I saw you dancing

with Hugh last night. Everyone saw the two of you enjoying such a simple delight, enjoying each other. You have much to learn of the world in which you dance so carefree, Miss Georgina." Her lips curled as her voice sharpened brutally, and a scratch ripped up Georgina's spine at the sound of it. "That dance floor you love so much is a deceptive and treacherous place."

The front door burst open, and Amanda's eyes widened, her back straightened. Heavy footsteps grew closer, their pounding matching the beat of her pulse. The drawing room door was flung open, and there stood William. His dark eyes were sunk in his face, his skin sallow, his lips a sneer. Ripping off his gloves, he went to his wife, took the glass from her hand, and drained it. "It's done."

Amanda glanced at the empty glass and then at him. "He accepted?"

"I did not offer him a choice." He wiped at his mouth, his dark gaze snagging on Georgina. "What are you doing here?"

"You know Miss Georgina, darling."

"Why is she here?"

"Georgina has the most delightful news she came to share with me—she is engaged. And the lucky gentleman is the Earl of Ryvves. Is that not splendid?"

William burst into loud, hard laughter, and something cold and slithery knotted in Georgina's belly. He put down the glass, his eyes narrowing at Georgina, his jaw flexing as if something hot and volatile were exploding inside him. "I suggest you go to Hyde Park tomorrow morning and give your fiancé a final kiss before I kill him."

Georgina's heart stopped. *He was fighting Hugh? Hugh was the one who....*

"As you see, Georgina, my husband is defending my honour."

"I'm defending mine!" His fierce voice slashed through the

room as he flung his glass against the wall and it exploded into shards.

The air in the room grew thick and hot. The walls seemed to move, to close in on Georgina. These two were locked in a perverse dark dance of their own. She must leave, but she must know.

Georgina rose, planting her feet firmly on the floor. "Mr. Treharne, do tell me, please—when tomorrow? Where exactly?"

"Are you going to save him?" He poured himself another and brought it to his lips, his eyes narrowing over her. "He's not worthy of it, or of a girl like you."

"Please tell me."

He drained his glass. "Tomorrow morning at six. Hyde Park." William described the specific spot for her as he tore off his dress coat and threw it on a chair. "Now leave us." His hands tugged sharply at his neck tie, loosening it as his harsh gaze fell on his wife.

Georgina bowed her head as her stomach twisted tighter. "Mr. Treharne. Amanda, I wish you well."

Amanda raised her glass. "And I wish you to hell."

Chapter Fifteen

Charles

WHEN HUGH and Charles returned to their house, William was waiting for them in their drawing room, slouched in Father's favourite mahogany armchair, a pistol in his hand. "Shall I shoot you now, and we can be done with this? Both of you at once, now that I would enjoy immensely."

Hugh began to growl and threaten, but Charles pulled him back and spoke calmly with William, the revolver sagging in his hand between his legs. They'd agreed on a duel, as gentlemen would.

Once again, he was cleaning his brother's messes. Making them passable with language, with his own ease, with insinuation, double-dealing. Finally, a weary William left.

"Do this for me," Hugh said.

"Do what?"

"The duel. In my place."

"Are you mad?"

"Can you not see how delicate my position is? I am the Earl and I've just gotten engaged, and that wedding must happen. This can be no great sacrifice for you. What do you have—"

"You astound me, brother. This is your responsibility, your mess, not mine. And I will not pay for it with my life."

Charles's heart raced in his chest. He had never said no to Hugh before.

"Oh, come now. You're an excellent shot, always have been. Better than me and Father."

Charles eyed him. Hugh only ever flattered him when he wanted something from him. "You're damn good yourself, and you've been doing a lot of hunting up north with your friends, or so you told me. William has not left town for over two years now. I'll bet his skills are not as fine as yours. Not to worry."

"How can you be so selfish at a time like this?" Hugh exploded, his face streaked with red.

"Selfish?" His voice shook. "This is my very life you are playing with. The better question is, why are you so desperate?"

"Do this for me, and I will give you Penrose Park, or I swear I shall burn it myself, raze it to the ground."

"Why, Hugh? Why can you not allow me this small happiness? I've always done whatever you and father have asked of me. Always. All I want is that house, and as the second-born son, it should be mine. What is Penrose Park to you? Nothing. Nothing!"

"But to you, it is everything," he said on a snarl. "You must do this."

Charles's breath tightened in his chest as if he were on a mountaintop and couldn't breathe.

Just like Father. Hugh had that same streak of ice-cold cruelty to make you bend to his will.

But Father was gone, and Charles would never bend again.

"I will not." His low, deep voice resounded darkly in the parlour. "I will not sacrifice my life for your follies. How dare you ask it of me?"

Hugh let out an agonised roar, grabbed a porcelain vase, and flung it at him. It shattered at his feet.

～

THE NEXT MORNING they rode to Hyde Park in silence. Charles kept his gaze fixed out the window.

While Hugh's only consideration was his inconvenience, Charles's greater consideration was Georgie. No, she was not some innocent doe who had been tickled by Hugh's attentions. She said she was fully aware of the kind of man he was and had made her own choice to escape a worse marriage offer. He had to cling to that for now.

They arrived, and William and his man were already there. He took in his brother smirking at William as they talked curtly before they picked up their revolvers to shoot at each other over Amanda. Or their honour.

Georgina deserved better than this lesser of two evils.

Was Hugh truly the lesser? How would she react to the news of her fiancée being involved with Amanda, a married woman who she held in disdain?

Charles ground his teeth as he nodded at William's second, who held the pistols for his perusal. He could hardly believe he was here at Hyde Park at dawn. He'd never been involved in a duel before, never been anyone's second either, like he was right now for his brother.

His selfish, arrogant, bloody reckless brother.

"Sir, we are ready."

Charles blinked. The servant bowed his head. "Sir?"

"Yes. Yes." Charles followed him to the starting point.

William's eyes gleamed as he stepped back. Ridding himself of his frock coat, he stalked off to his starting point. His servant faced Hugh, tilted his head and turned, and slowly followed his master.

"Perhaps if you'd trusted me sooner we wouldn't be here readying pistols."

"Stop worrying. It's done now." He gave him a small smile. "Stand off."

Charles stepped back. Away.

William readied himself, the sleeves of his chemise fluttering in the breeze. He placed a hand on his brow, closing his eyes, taking a breath, steadying himself. Was he feeling ill too? Hugh took up his weapon, stilling at his mark position. William went to his.

"Gentlemen, we begin!" the servant announced. "Twenty - nineteen - eighteen…"

Charles clenched his teeth, his insides dropping as the numbers seemed to hang in the air. The damp cold lay across his flesh. This was bloody stupid.

"…five - four - three - two - one."

Both men pivoted swiftly, raised their arms, extending them in their reach for honour, for vengeance, for Amanda and…

Charles's fingers curled into fists. Explosions ripped the air, one popping off, a second closely after.

Still standing, Hugh remained intent on his opponent. Charles let out a breath at the sight of his brother untouched, not bleeding. Yet.

A loud grunt filled the air, and Charles's body jerked toward the sound. William staggered, his eyes flaring, his body stiffening. Shock. His hand clutched at his chest, his white chemise seeped in red.

"Sir!"

"Holy fu —"

William collapsed. His servant fell to the ground beside him, cradling his head. He whistled sharply, and their footman ran toward them.

"Damn me." Charles let out a breath and ran toward William, Hugh behind him.

The servant raised his head. "Gentlemen, we are concluded."

"William…" unfurled roughly from Charles's throat.

The servant and the footman hoisted William's bleeding, sagging body away. His head fell to the side, his lifeless eyes open still. His hollow gaze seemed to hang on Charles. Sour bile rose in his throat, his chest caved in.

A whip cracked in the air, and their horses started on an uproar, jerking the carriage off the green, into the trees, away. Away.

Charles leaned over on his thighs, fighting the sick in his gullet, gulping in air. He blinked, his head dazed. William, his childhood friend, his best friend's cousin. Dead. Dead. He struggled to take in a deep breath of the cold morning air, air that was meant to be the freshest yet now seemed polluted and foul. "Hugh? You're all right? Hugh?"

"Not a scratch."

Charles raised up and turned to face his brother. His heart froze. Hugh held a pistol aimed at him.

"What are you…Hugh!"

Crack exploded in his ears. Smoke and gunpowder filled his senses. A stinging pain blazed in his arm.

His brother had shot him.

Chapter Sixteen

Charles

THE GROUND ROSE UP and slammed into Charles. A strangled grunt rose above him. It was his. "What have you done? What have you done?"

Hugh loomed over him, a giant, a terror. Charles scrambled away, but his limbs wouldn't cooperate, and a burning pain flared over him with every movement. He gripped his wounded arm that hung useless at his side, his hand filling with warm goo.

Blood, my damn blood. "Why?" he raged.

"It must be this way, Charles. I cannot be embroiled in a scandal right now, especially one such as this. I did well finding a girl to marry, now this within the very same twenty-four hours? Impossible. The engagement cannot be broken."

Suddenly his brother's tone of voice was cool and even. Logical. He'd planned on this.

"Now the worst part is over. William's gone and cannot speak. With your history with Amanda, you are the perfect foil. You're my answer. This is the answer."

"No!"

"I cannot take the chance that all this will be made public.

Georgina's family would use it to break our engagement. I asked you to take my place, but you refused. You left me no choice."

"Bastard!" Charles spit out as a tremor took over his body. His flesh chilled, a cold sweat slithering over his skin.

"I know how much you care for my fiancée and would not want her distressed on the eve of her wedding. This is the only way to leave no question unanswered for her, her family, and the ton. This works, Charles, it's perfect, can you not see that? In everyone's eyes, I shall be the reformed rake, and you simply remain the rake you are. It's perfect."

"No…" Charles heaved for air.

"You can go up north to the Duke's. You'll be well hidden there, and well entertained, I daresay. Months from now, you shall reappear and all will be forgiven and forgotten."

"No." His vision blurred. He grabbed at Hugh's coat. Hugh shoved him off.

"You have nothing to be mindful of. I have my title, my bride, and dammit, so much more. That's what's important here."

Treetops, clouds all swirled above Charles. All the lies Hugh told him swirled and swam around him, squeezing him, strangling him. A groan escaped his lips as the very sky spun over him.

"The loaded revolver, where, how?" Charles struggled for breath, the fiery sting shooting down his arm, over his shoulder, his hand filling with his own blood.

"I paid William's man a tidy sum to leave me another revolver to use."

"You bastard…you fucking bastard!"

"Enough. We must leave here. Let's get you in the carriage. Get you home." He grabbed onto Charles, and every fibre of his being revolted at his brother's touch. Grunting, he smacked him, pushed at him. Twisted away. Kicked.

"Charles!"

That voice. Her voice.

Two hands clutched at his chest, held his face.

"Georgina?" Charles blinked, struggling to regain clarity.

"Charles!"

"What are you doing here?" Hugh spit out.

"You shot him!"

"He dueled with William."

"I saw you. I saw it all."

"What you saw is not the truth of it."

"Are you mad?" she cried out.

The Ryvves footman appeared at Hugh's side. "Sir?"

"Take him up, Smythe. We must quit this park immediately. We've tarried long enough."

"Stay away from him!" Georgina hissed, and Smythe jerked backward at her sharp command.

"My darling, I understand this must be a shock for you," said Hugh. "But you cannot begin to understand what lies between brothers. You cannot interfere.

"Indeed, I can."

"I forbid it."

"You forbid it?"

"I do."

"That, sir, makes no difference to me in the least. I will not leave him with you, for you will likely kill him. I shall take Charles away—away from you."

"Georgie—" Charles's voice ached.

A servant appeared. "Landon, take Mr. Montclare to the carriage," directed Georgina. Landon scooped him up and Charles grunted as pain shuddered through his side.

"You impudent girl!" Hugh's exclaimed. "Do not do this!"

Georgina stood firmly. "Will you shoot me as well?"

"Georgina!" Charles groaned.

Hugh's eyes blazed. "I will ruin you, do you hear? I shall

say I shot him because I found you with my brother in his bed. That you are nothing but a trollop and a schemer who seduced both of us. Do not tempt me, for I shall crush you and him."

"Oh, my lord, I have no doubt you shall try." Georgina went to Landon and Charles, wrapping an arm around Charles's middle. "Do your worst."

Chapter Seventeen

Georgina

LANDON HAD BOUND Charles's wound with his own necktie, and Georgina held it tight as he'd shown her.

The carriage lurched forward as the horses picked up their pace.

"Where…where are we going, Georgina?"

"To my cousin Malcolm. He is a doctor. He will take good care of you. He is not far from here."

He clasped her hand, his blood marking her fingers. "Don't do this, Georgie. You will stain yourself."

"Why did he shoot you?"

"So that everyone will think that I fought the duel and killed William and not he. So your engagement will be saved. But if we are seen now, if your name is joined with mine in this dirty misadventure, you will not survive it. Your family —"

"The only thing that matters is your being tended to. You, safe."

He cupped her chin, lifting it, his fingers burning her skin. "Why would you do this for me?" he whispered roughly.

She held his glimmering gaze. "You're my friend, Charles."

"Yes, true. I am."

"Now, please, lay back until we reach our destination."

"So I won't be seen?" He slid down in the seat, his head in her lap. "My lying down in your lap is a trifle more scandalous, don't you think?" His lips tilted into the beginnings of a smile.

That flirtatious, knowing smile of his.

She grinned back at him. "Now I know you'll be fine. You haven't lost mastery of your tart, seductive tongue."

A low noise escaped his pale lips. "I'm sure I never shall. Certainly not with you." Even now, vulnerable, bleeding, he was making jokes with her.

The carriage charged through the streets to the north of London. Although the morning air was bracing, she was quite warm with this man laying in her lap, her hand on his chest.

Charles reached up and touched a lock of her hair. "One day, madame, may I prove worthy of your saving me."

"You are worthy of much, Charles Montclare."

His chest vibrated with an aching laugh. "I believe you once told me that a long time ago. If only it were true."

SHE AND CHARLES waited in the back of her cousin Malcolm's small house as Landon announced her arrival to him. Within moments, Malcolm and Landon were helping Charles out of the carriage and bringing him inside the house.

"Cousin, you are well?" Malcolm glanced up at her.

"I am fine, Malcolm. My friend here, Mr. Montclare, was in an altercation this morning and needs your medical attention. I would be forever grateful for your time and discretion, cousin."

"You can depend on it." He cut open Charles's sleeve to reveal the bloody wound, and Georgina bit her lip at the raw sight. He inspected it as Charles ground his jaw, his entire face tensing. "You are quite fortunate, Mr. Montclare. There seems to be no damage to any bones or vital tissue. Most fortunate, indeed."

"Thank God." Georgina's heart thumped in her chest. She was not fond of blood and cuts and gashes. "Is there anything I can do to help?"

"Bring the brandy from the drawing room. He's going to need it while I attend to the wound."

She nodded and dashed from the room. In the hallway stood Landon holding a bottle of spirit.

"Perfect." She took the bottle. "Ah, Landon, you must return to the house. I would not wish you any disfavour with my sister and Mr. Holyfloke. You must go home as if nothing untoward has happened. Do not tell anyone of all that you have seen and heard today. You simply accompanied me to my cousin Doctor Langham's home."

His brow furrowed. "Very good, ma'am."

"Mr. Montclare and I are old family friends. He is now recovering after having been seen to, but no one can know we brought him here or that we have seen him today. Do you understand, Landon?"

"I do, Ma'am."

"I am safe here with my cousin, and I shall return home shortly."

"As you wish, Miss." He bowed his head and turned to leave.

"And Landon —"

"Ma'am?"

"I thank you."

Landon's chin lifted for a moment. He bowed his head once more and left the back way from whence they had come.

She returned to Malcolm and Charles, placing the brandy bottle on a table where bottles of herbs, tinctures, and powders stood. Malcolm wiped at his hands and helped Charles sit up. Charles seemed even paler, and something twisted in Georgie's insides at the sight of him so weak.

Malcolm held the bottle to Charles's pale lips. "Drink, man. To your health."

"Dash my health," he breathed, grabbing the bottle. "To the courageous and caring Miss Georgina for bringing me to your capable hands." He gulped deeply, and Georgina took the bottle from him as his body shifted on the table. He let out a guttural gasp and a slew of curses.

Malcolm got to work inspecting, cleaning, dabbing. Georgina's mouth dried, her lips pressed firmly together.

"Go, Georgie, you positively hate this. I know you do," Malcolm murmured as he worked.

"I'm not going anywhere," she bit out, her body pressing back against the wall.

Malcolm glanced over at her. "You'd better have a swig of liquor yourself."

She took hold of the bottle and raised it to her lips. "To your health, gentlemen. And to mine." She put the bottle back down with a plonk on the table, and Charles's cold fingers grasped hers. She took his hand in both of hers, gripping it tightly, offering him the most relaxed smile she could muster.

"All right then. I'm going to sew the flesh."

"What?" Georgina exclaimed.

"Otherwise, it won't heal."

"Of course. Yes."

"Georgie…" Charles's voice was husky, and he squeezed her hand as she lifted her gaze to his. "Take a breath. Look at me."

Swallowing hard, she did as he asked, holding onto his molten golden brown gaze and letting it calm her. She let out a deep, long breath, and the walls of the room gave away around her.

At that moment, she didn't think of her sister and brother and John and what they were doing, what they were thinking. If they had yet noticed her absence. If they were worried or if they were angry.

If news of the duel and William's death had reached their ears and that of all the ton.

What Hugh thought of her, where he was, what he was planning.

None of it.

Her chest lifted in time with Charles's, and her heartbeat eased. His lips parted as he took in a deeper breath. His hand had grown much warmer in hers, his eyes brighter, and his blond hair, now loose of its tie, was splashed across Malcolm's table. How many different tones of blond it was, some light, some dark…it was beautiful.

"There. You're smiling," he whispered.

"Am I?" She bit her lip.

His hold was steady, and her pulse ceased its dreadful pounding. Charles closed his eyes as his jaw tightened with the pain of Malcolm's work on his arm. The desire to help him, to comfort him, overwhelmed her.

She stroked his large hand. Charles Montclare was human, vulnerable.

Imagine that.

Chapter Eighteen

Charles

MALCOLM HAD CLEANED up his bandages and instruments, prepared and packaged tinctures and powders for the wound, and left them alone.

"I must go home. I must talk to Hugh. I need to assure him that all is as he wishes," Charles said, his voice low and tight. He was determined.

"You must rest. You—"

"I can rest later. Now I must speak with him. It is urgent."

"But—"

"Georgie, you and I took off together. You did so against his wishes. He threatened to tell a terrible lie about you—"

"About us."

"And I will not allow it."

"How could he be so cruel to you?"

"What matters is that your engagement is made public immediately before your family can break the agreement. Otherwise…"

Her shoulders sank. "Yes, you're right. News of the duel will only feed their righteous indignation against your family. They suffered your quick and unrelenting offer, and the very next day, my fiancé kills a gentleman who he had cuckolded."

"Knowing Amanda, I feel she may enjoy that the duel was over her and not some debt or insult, and she will not deny that she was the reason."

"How can everything twist and pervert in a matter of moments—"

"Listen to me. I won't let them break the engagement or take you away. I won't. Unless, of course, you no longer wish to marry Hugh?"

"I had no illusions about Hugh. I still need to marry, and I imagine so does he."

"Now, more so than ever before." The words were bitter on his tongue. "We must go find him and assure him that you are not his enemy. And I shall agree to take the blame for the duel."

"Oh, Charles, why must you?"

"It's nothing."

"It's not! It's not right."

"I've been doing this all my life with Hugh and my father, Georgina. But this time, it's not for them. I'm doing this for you." His vow vibrated in the air between them as he brushed her temple with his lips. Heat flared over her skin at his kiss, at the press of his body against hers. The citrusy scent of him filled her senses.

"I can't let you do this, Charles. This is all my fault. I—"

"It's not your fault. This truly has nothing to do with you, my sweet girl."

Indeed it did not. It was ages old.

Every time he was close to her, something inside him spiralled out of his control, something molten and hot. Clearing his throat, Charles stepped away from her. "Indeed, how did you find out about the duel? Where we were?"

"After you and Hugh left my house, I went to see Amanda."

"To find out about the note?"

Her face reddened. "Yes."

"Zounds, woman, you went to Amanda's yesterday?"

She bit her lip. "I did. I found out that she had sent that message which arrived at my home for Hugh. You both seemed so surprised and angry. I wasn't sure if it had to do with you or with Hugh, but I had to find out. I'm glad I did. She was waiting for you. She assumed that you'd sent me."

"And you let her assume so."

"Yes. She and I had a rather odd conversation, and then William came home and told us Hugh had accepted his challenge. I asked him for the particulars, and he told me."

"Your curiosity and insistence were spot on, Miss Georgina." His shoulders eased as his fingers brushed the side of her face leaving a trail of warmth on her flesh. He owed her his life.

"I do remember your finding my insistence rather irritating once upon a time."

"I did. But that was because your relentless pursuit of the truth would shed a merciless light on my lies and my vanity."

"I never meant to be merciless," she said softly.

"I'm glad you were." His thumb stroked her soft skin, his gaze landing on those generous lips of hers. Fetching lips. Sensual lips. He let her go.

"Now that William is dead, I wonder how Amanda will react. Of course, she and William must have argued terribly, but she was not her usual poised self when I saw her."

"How do you mean?"

"She'd had quite a lot to drink, and her face was not only flushed for it but bruised."

"Bruised?"

"Yes. She was still in her dressing gown, her hair wild. She spoke quite frankly with me about men and marriage. To school me."

"Bloody hell."

"When I told her that Hugh and I were engaged and that I was concerned for his and your safety, she became sharp with me. Taunting me in her way. Of course, I quickly realised the reason for the duel was that William had caught her out with one of you, and at first I wasn't sure which one of you it was."

"It seems Amanda and Hugh have been carrying on these past weeks."

"Did you know?"

"No idea. Felt like an utter fool."

"A jealous fool?"

"God, no, not that. Because I knew nothing about it."

"She seemed quite taken with him. Will Hugh continue on with her, I wonder?"

"Georgina—"

"It's all right. I am not shocked. I have no illusions about Hugh. At the ball, I didn't see him as my dream prince or a great love. He was only my perfect solution in a very handsome package."

"Not afraid of the sordid truth, Miss Townsend?"

"I prefer the truth, even if it is sordid," Georgina replied. "Do you think he might want to marry her now? Could he—"

"That is impossible. Before you arrived at Hyde Park, he was quite adamant about preserving your engagement. He didn't seem attached to her in any way. If even I was unaware of their dalliance, I should hope it was not known."

"William found out," she said.

"Now he's gone."

"Now Hugh is angry with me."

"You challenged him with the truth, and he was taken by surprise. You see? Merciless."

She only laughed softly.

"At that very moment, he had no control over you, and he reacted in a panic."

"He does like to have full mastery of a situation, does he not?"

"I am certain that once he calms down and you assure him that nothing has changed for you—"

"But everything has changed, Charles. You shall falsely bear the blame for cuckolding William, for killing him, and I shall be the well-behaved wife who knows her place in her husband's life."

Their heavy gazes met, and an ache spiraled in his chest. She was right. They would both be living a lie.

He swallowed hard and cleared his throat. "We should go to my brother. Assure him all is as he wants it to be. And then you shall return home and prepare for your wedding."

"When they ask where I've been, I shall tell them I came here to inform my cousin of my engagement." Her teeth clawed at her lower lip.

His lips turned up. "Yes. You took a walk together."

"Of course. It was a fine morning, after all."

He let out a stiff chuckle. "Very fine."

She moved, but his fingers gripped her upper arm, stopping her. Suddenly his face was close to hers, his breath warm on her skin, his grip tighter, demanding. "I wish everything were different, Georgie. This is no way for you to begin a marriage, with adultery and death and so many damned lies. This is not what I would have wanted for you. You deserve—"

"I do not know what it is I deserve, Charles, but this is what I have forged. And, still, it is better than the alternative."

"I thank you for bringing me to Malcolm." Releasing her, he let out a dry laugh.

She shifted her weight, smoothing down her dress. "Pray, what do you find so amusing, Mr. Montclare?"

"Only that you were always the young chit, my friend's young sister. The girl we all felt we should protect and shield. And now...now you are a bold woman of great determination and fire who risked much to protect me." A swell of emotion rose inside him. "And I admire you," he breathed.

He never wanted to forget this moment. A moment of utter truth between him and Georgina. The second they left her cousin's house, everything would be different between them. It would have to be. Forever.

By the end of the day, her engagement with his brother would be made public. Charles would be known as the rake who killed his paramour's husband. Georgina would begin shopping for her trousseau, and Charles would soon be calling her "sister."

Sister. His insides hardened like a lead weight at the thought. They might even be living in the same house once she and Hugh married.

His lungs constricted in his chest. No, that he would not be able to bear.

Chapter Nineteen

Georgina

MALCOLM GAVE Charles a cloaked cape to wear to hide the blood and ripped fabric of his frock coat, and also to keep him warm as he had the chills. "I shall never forget your assistance, Malcolm. I thank you."

"I am very glad I could help." They shook hands, and Charles and the servant went out the back to find a carriage whilst Georgina waited with Malcolm in the vestibule of the house.

"You are not scandalised by my behaviour, cousin?" she asked.

Malcolm tilted his head. "That you brought a wounded man in need of care to my attention? Absolutely not."

"Oh, dear Malcolm, if only life were as straightforward as you are."

"Georgina, you weren't scandalised by my behaviour when I did the outlandish thing and attended medical college."

"I admired your commitment."

"It's always meant so much to me that you believed in me, in my work. That you'd defended my choice to the family."

"Your work is a true calling, Malcolm. Not many people

are blessed with such a calling or such a talent. Tell me, Charles will be well?"

"As long as the wound is tended to properly. Kept clean, bandages changed."

"That is a great relief."

"I must say, Mr. Montclare seems familiar to me."

"Our families have known each other for many years in Gloucestershire. You've probably met there on many occasions."

"Quite right."

She slid her arm through Malcolm's. "I am engaged to his brother, the Earl of Ryvves."

"Are you? Congratulations, dear one."

"Thank you. I would ask you another favour, cousin. I would not want my family to know that I brought Charles here for your care. I would rather we said that I came here alone to tell you of my engagement, and we enjoyed an early morning walk and breakfast together."

"I have thoroughly enjoyed our morning stroll, cousin."

She smiled, touching his arm. "As did I."

A carriage came to an abrupt rumbling stop in front of them, the horses snorting, their hooves clomping on the stones.

It was no empty carriage for hire.

The door burst open, and a gentleman darted forth.

It was Thomas.

With Georgina's arm through his, Malcolm greeted Thomas on his front steps. "Cousin, how good it is to see you. Georgina came and surprised me today. She's told me her news and—"

"Did she now?" He cast a cold glance over them, and Malcolm's brow furrowed at Thomas's sharpness.

Georgina's fingertips dug into her cousin's arm. "Yes, I did. It's been too long since I've seen Malcolm, and I wanted to tell him about my engagement in person. I'm sorry I did not leave a note. I was so excited and in my haste—"

"Come inside, cousin," said Malcolm.

Thomas ignored Malcolm's invitation. "I had to find you, Georgina, once I heard of a duel and the death of William Treharne. It is said that a Montclare is responsible."

"Are you certain?"

"I'm sure I'll find out all the details at my club later today."

"Of course you will."

"You must come home with me now. You will be returning to Devonshire posthaste with our sister and John. They are preparing for the trip as we speak."

"Whatever do you mean?"

"You must leave London right away."

"I must prepare for my wedding."

"There will be no wedding."

Chapter Twenty

Georgina

"No wedding?" said Malcolm glancing at Georgina.

The wind had been knocked out of her. She could not speak. Could not move.

"Under these vile circumstances? Absolutely not," replied Thomas. "We must separate ourselves from the Montclares immediately."

"Hugh and I are engaged."

"Your engagement is only hours old, and luckily, has not yet been made public, so all is not lost." His intent gaze searched her face for tears, for emotions, but she betrayed none. She had none left to give.

Again, in a matter of seconds, everything around her spun like a whirligig in a gale of wind. She cleared her throat. "Perhaps we should go see Amanda, brother. Pay our respects. Inquire as to her well-being. After all, she and William are our friends from home."

His eyes narrowed. "I'll do that later. You need to leave." Thomas shook his cousin's hand. "Malcolm, good to see you again, old man."

"You too, Thomas. Georgina." He took her hand and pressed it between his, his lips in a firm line.

"Do stay in touch, Malcolm. Please."

"I shall." He leaned in close to her and whispered in her ear: "Whatever you may need, call on me. I shall help you."

Thomas gripped Georgina's arm and led her to his carriage. Her breath cut, her legs numbed, her feet barely remembered how to walk. Was this to be the end? Treated like an insolent child? Packed up and sent away? Punished for her sins? Blurry darkness squeezed around her. She stopped. It couldn't be the end. No.

The footman held the door of the carriage open. The horses whinnied and stomped on the ground.

Her brother held out his hand to her. "Come."

If she took that hand, if she took that hand—

"Georgina!"

His voice pierced through her haze, fisting in her chest. She swerved.

Charles. Charles in Malcolm's black cape, which was bulky for his slimmer frame, making him look like some sort of Medieval villain. His face had gone pale again, his eyes shadowed, his jaw a sharp, stony line. His long blond hair was loose and ruffled, feet planted wide, eyes cold and fierce. Her pulse charged in her veins. This man would brook no denial.

"What are *you* doing here?" Thomas thundered. His gaze darted to his sister, Malcolm, and back to Charles. "What is going on?"

Charles came to her. "You don't have to go with him, Georgie."

"The devil you say!" Thomas exclaimed.

"You cannot take her away. You cannot marry her to someone else. Your sister, sir, is engaged to the Earl of Ryvves. An agreement for Miss Georgina Townsend for marriage has been signed. A legal, binding agreement."

The air was sucked out of her lungs. Her heart pounded.

Thomas's gaze darted between them. He was on alien ground. "I don't know which one of you killed William today, but that agreement is now broken." Thomas pointed at her. "Georgina, get into the carriage this instant." He turned back to Charles. "You, sir, are an arrogant licentious lout, just like your brother, and your father before you." Thomas held his hand out to his sister. "Georgina, come!"

One decision.

One action.

One life.

She grabbed Charles's hand, and on a grunt, he pulled her into a carriage that stood behind Thomas's. Slamming the door behind them, he thumped on the roof. "Now! Go! Quickly!"

A whip cracked, the horses bolted, and her heart flew out of her chest. The carriage pitched as the horses charged down the road, and their bodies jolted back, the two of them colliding against the cushioned seating.

Their lips a breath apart, Charles grinned. "Well then, Miss Townsend, your sordid downfall at the hands of a Montclare has now begun."

Chapter Twenty-One

Charles

"Don't worry. Hugh won't bite you."

"Are you certain?" Georgina's shoulders tightened as they entered the Ryvves townhouse. She was worried.

"My brother has inherited our father's temper, but I'm sure that by now, he's cooled off and is grateful that he escaped the duel unhurt. It's good we're here together to speak with him."

"Yes, I think so."

They were greeted by a manservant, who took their cloaks.

"Is his Lordship at home?" Charles asked.

"Yes, sir. He's been in the drawing room. Said he did not wish to be disturbed for any reason."

"Very good."

"Sir, I did hear glass crashing and such, but I did not dare enter."

"You did well. Thank you."

Letting out a heavy breath, Charles directed Georgina to the drawing room. "Hugh often throws objects, breaking anything in sight when he's angry and frustrated. Something he inherited from our father."

"I see," murmured Georgina.

Charles opened the double doors of the drawing room.

Shards of broken glass littered the floor, as well as pieces of a shattered vase. The sweet dank smell of spilt brandy wafted around them.

His spine prickled as they entered the drawing room. "Hugh?"

Georgina cried out.

His brother lay on the floor before the fireplace. Motionless.

Charles rushed to his brother's side, his wounded arm flaring with pain. Georgina crouched next to him. Blood and bone matted Hugh's blond hair on one side of his head. Blood on the floor. Blood everywhere. A small bronze figurine of a monkey on the floor at his side.

"No, Hugh…no," he whispered roughly.

"This cannot be…it cannot be." Georgina's tiny voice faded around him. "We just saw him. We…"

Charles's hand reached out and slid the lifeless eyelids closed. His stomach turned. *Still warm.* "Georgina, send for your cousin to come immediately. Compose yourself—do not tell the servants anything."

"No. I won't." She darted from the room.

Charles locked the door behind Georgie and scoured the room with fresh eyes. The bottom of the broken brandy glass was on the floor. Hugh's favourite brandy stood open on the writing desk, and he went to it. A French brandy for which he paid dearly to smugglers.

On the desk, the bottle of ink was open, the quill lay on the blotter, and ink pooled underneath it. Had he been writing a letter? Charles brushed his fingers over the textured surface of the blotter. Only Hugh's signature was still evident.

He grabbed Hugh's half-empty bottle of brandy and gulped, the liquor streaming from his mouth. He wiped at his face as a knock came on the door. "Charles?"

He opened the door for Georgina. "I sent word to Malcolm to come immediately."

"Good."

She clutched his arm. "Are you unwell? You're quite pale and—" She brought him to a large armchair and wiped at the cool perspiration beading his forehead. She sat with him, the two of them quiet, staring across the room at Hugh's lifeless body.

The crazy thought of William faking his death and coming here after the duel to finish off Hugh raced through his addled brain. William was always a crafty bugger. Always had to have the last word. But he'd seen the blood spewing from William's chest this morning, heard those awful final moans of his, witnessed that slackness in his limbs.

No.

He dragged his hands through his hair. There was another jealous man, wasn't there? The Duke of Oakley.

Although Hugh had expressed confidence that the Duke was not jealous of his affair with the Duchess, even approved of it, the three of them being friends who often lived together, it seemed unlikely to Charles and much too convenient.

And if the Duke's wife was very much attached to Hugh and he to her, not simply enjoying a dalliance, would that not be a threat to any husband? A threat to his ultimate possession of her, his possession. Oakley was a man of great privilege and power, and the Duchess was his wife, his lawful property.

Once Hugh and the Duchess had separated, perhaps Oakley had taken the opportunity to punish Hugh.

Charles blew out a breath. *Punishing husbands.*

Even though their father had a mistress living at their house whilst their mother was there, he was still very possessive of his wife. And even though he'd allowed her to live elsewhere, he had strictly forbidden her from taking lovers.

Charles knew this because he'd heard his father threatening his mother every time she visited them. Threatening her in unforgettable punishing ways that sickened him to this day.

Charles's arm and head pounded with pain. Dizziness

swirled in his head, and he fought to breathe enough air. After all, the Duke made lovers he no longer favoured disappear, did he not?

A knock at the door shook him from his riotous thoughts. Georgina opened the door.

"Malcolm, at last. This way."

Malcolm inspected the body. "He's been bludgeoned."

"Yes," said Charles. "Whoever it was grabbed this small statue from the table and–"

"That would do it."

Georgina handed Malcolm a glass of brandy and he drank.

"Imagine, a ridiculous dancing monkey brought down my brother," muttered Charles.

"We only just saw Hugh," murmured Georgina. "He was alive, he was… What is happening, Charles? What is happening?"

"I don't know. Hugh had no debts, no outstanding insults, no enemies, only William at the end. Then again, I did not know about Amanda, did I? What did I know of my brother? The past few years, he spent most of his time with the Duchess and Oakley's inner circle of friends."

"It's true then? Hugh and the Duchess of Oakley were lovers?"

"It's true. Being in town together these past months was the first time Hugh and I had lived together in several years." A heavy sigh dragged from his lungs. "Perhaps he did have enemies and debts."

"Or perhaps those debts were not financial," said Georgina.

"Indeed. Excellent point." He rubbed his injured arm. "I do not wish his manner of death to be made public. We will say that William got a shot in as well. That Hugh came home straight away and died from his bleeding wound."

Georgina squeezed her hands together. "Malcolm?"

Malcolm wiped the blood from his hands. "Is that what you wish, Charles? Because whoever did this is out there."

"That is what I wish. This way, the duel takes care of the mess cleanly." *Hugh's mess.* "There will be no questions, no inquiry. It will be accepted as these things are: two gentlemen having claimed their fucking honour."

Malcolm rose. "Very well. We shall say he was shot in the belly, lasted an hour, and died."

Charles glanced down at his brother's lifeless corpse. "Is that a painful way to die?" He twisted the Ryvves signet ring from his brother's stiffening hand, his cold fingers splattered with ink.

"It is, in fact. Quite painful."

"Good."

BLACK RIBBONS WERE PINNED to the front door. The wool shroud for the corpse had been sent for. The drawing room had been cleaned.

Charles had dressed his brother's body. He didn't want anyone to see the actual wound. He encased the corpse in the horrid shroud, and now Hugh lay on the dining room table, lit candles on either side of him.

Charles and Georgina stood together, taking in the still unbelievable sight. "I have no fiancé any longer," she breathed.

"You now have a choice to make, Georgie. Once the news of Hugh's death reaches your family tonight, or on the morrow, your brother will arrive here to take you back. Is that what you want?"

"That is not what I want, but now I have no other choice."

"Yes, you do. Marry me."

"Marry you?" Her eyes widened. "You have done so much for me already, and I cannot burden you further. My little scheme crossed perfectly with Hugh's need to marry. But it was obviously not meant to be, and I must finally accept my fate."

"Not meant to be? Fate can go fuck itself. You are no burden to me. Georgie. Marry me. Unless you want to go to Devonshire, be punished somehow for your willfulness, and marry whomever they force you to."

"You know I don't want that."

"We'll go to Gloucestershire tomorrow, bury my brother, and marry. You would like that, wouldn't you? To marry there?"

"Tomorrow?"

"Tomorrow, first thing."

She bit her lip. Her chest heaved with rapid breaths as she moved closer to him, her gaze never leaving his. She kissed Charles, and his body stilled. His body hummed with the gentle touch of her most perfect lips on his. A simple yet dazzling stroke of innocence. Of sensation.

Invitation.

"What are you doing, Miss Georgina?" he whispered against her lips.

"Fate can go fuck itself. If we are to do this, then we need to make our engagement utterly binding so that it cannot be denied or pushed asunder by anyone. Even Fate herself."

"Careful what you say…"

Her hand pressed into his chest. "Thomas and John will surely come tonight, and when they do, there can be no question of our purpose, and there shall be no other choice than for you and I to marry. If you take me to bed now, my value to them will be ruined."

His pulse charged like a steed entering a battlefield under siege. "You wish me to ruin you?" His fingers stroked the side of her face, the soft silkiness making his blood simmer. "You wish me to make my mark on you? Take your innocence forever?"

She blinked, her tongue shot out and licked at her lip, her face flushed. "Dear Lord, you have a way of making it sound positively sordid yet infinitely delicious."

A growl escaped his grin. "I'm gratified to hear you think so."

She shifted her weight. "It must be plain that our intent has been completely and utterly resolved, save for a vicar's blessing."

The breath burned in the back of his throat as his thumb stroked her lips. "You did not answer my question."

"What am I doing? I am seducing you."

"Not that question."

"You didn't ask me a question. You made a statement."

"True. I shall ask you now. Miss Georgina, will you marry me?"

"I thank you, sir, and yes, I will. Now, Lord Ryvves, will you take me?" She pulled on her corset strings, loosening their grip on her body. "There is no time to spare. We must be quick."

His breathing deepened. He swallowed hard, utterly focused on her movements, on every inch of bare flesh she revealed to him in the warm candlelight. His hands cuffed her neck, bringing her close to him and his lips brushed hers. His tongue lashed hers. "Your first time should not be quick nor with the corpse of your former fiancé nearby."

"That is of no matter to me. Hugh made his choices, as are we. You and I are alive, Charles. We are living."

Her steady gaze met his and rooted him to the ground. To her. "Yes, we bloody well are."

"And we must be quick."

"You are sure?"

"Quite sure."

"Well, then, Miss Georgina." Charles tugged at the fastening of his breeches as her dress fell to the floor. "Let us complete your sordid downfall at the hands of the last remaining Montclare."

Chapter Twenty-Two

Charles

Swift plunder was what he excelled at, was it not?

She stood before him in her chemise, her beautiful breasts, the curve of her waist clearly visible.

"Dammit, Georgie. On the chaise, now." She quickly did as he directed, scrambling atop the wide and long chaise. His balls pounded with her quick and eager obedience. His hand went under her chemise, sliding against silken skin. She drew in a breath as he pushed past her bloomers…

"Of course, you're wearing these French garments."

"I am a fashionable young lady."

He loosened them and slid his hand over her mound. "You are most certainly a lady."

"Oh…" Her nails dug into his arms, her hips tilting.

"Have you ever touched yourself here?"

"In fact, yes, I have—"

"Hmm." His fingers sank into her luscious, untouched by any man quim. Wetness slicked through his fingers as they churned and stroked. Her breathing grew ragged. Her hips twisted. She was excited. He was delirious.

She let out a low moan. "It's quite different when you do it. Oh…oh…."

He grinned against her skin. He would be her first. Not Hugh. Not anyone else. Him.

He'd never before been any woman's first. Ever.

She was not a servant, not a prostitute, not someone else's wife. This was *Georgie*. Georgie was giving herself to him to claim, and he was claiming her for his very own.

His heart thudded in his chest. Georgie was now his to protect, his to marry, to pleasure, to reap his pleasure from. His blood roared in his veins. His cock was painfully hard, his pulse beating jagged and wild.

"Charles…what should I do?"

His mouth brushed hers, and she didn't close her eyes. She held his gaze. His thumb stroked her beautiful lips. His cock demanded freedom. Freedom to plunder, to claim.

Plunder or no, he would be good to her.

"Georgie, are you aware of how this is done?"

"I am. My sister told me —"

"Don't talk to me about her or anyone else at this very moment."

"I am aware of how this works." Her jaw was firm. She was resolute.

His fingertips stroked along that hard line of jaw. "I am going to do something to make this first time easier for you."

"Oh? Yes, thank you."

"So polite." He let out a short laugh. "I want it to be as enjoyable as possible for you in this short amount of time." His fingers dipped into her wet cunny as he held her burning gaze. She was on the edge of a new world with him. "Hold onto me."

"What are you —OH!" She gripped his shoulders.

His face sank between her legs, and she cried out, her body twisting in his hold. His tongue lashed over her, swirling through her centre, teasing her sweet nub.

Georgina whimpered, her body tensing, jerking in his hold. "I did not know that one could…ooh!"

He glanced up at her. "Are you disgusted?"

"No, no…" she cried out, her body shuddering. "Oh….oh…" Her release was coming.

Immediately, he disengaged his hard shaft and, cupping her buttocks, found her entry. Her eyes widened at the sight of his stiff length entering her. "Georgie…" dragged from him. He eased himself inside her inch by wet inch, sinking himself in her tightness. "This is our wedding ceremony. This right here…" Her fingernails dug into his flesh as he rocked in deeper. He met resistance, and her brow furrowed.

Something inside him ached at the sight of her tense, in pain. He held himself in check as she grew accustomed to him inside her. She took in a breath and rocked her pelvis against his, and he let out a long groan. That determination of hers would be his undoing. Her chin stiffened. She braced herself.

Charles pulled himself out slightly and on a breath, thrust inside her once more, filling her. He groaned at the sleek tightness, at her moans, her hands clutching him, the scent of her skin. He kept still as she throbbed around him.

This.

This was a moment they would never live again.

His lips searched for hers. Found them. He swallowed her defenseless cry.

"We are alive. Alive," she'd said earlier. Yes. They were alive and claiming their lives together. Claiming their pleasure together.

Damn Hugh, damn her family, damn them all.

He cradled her face. "Look at me, Georgie." Her eyes blinked open. "You are now mine. My wife. My Countess."

Her fingers tightened around his neck. "And you are mine," she breathed.

His pulse charged at her own declaration of possession. "Yes, I am yours." He thrust inside her quicker, her words thrilling him. "I am yours."

These were their vows, this lovemaking their pledge—their oath as one as they were one. He reveled in the feel of her sweat against his skin, the musk rising between their bodies, her perfume, a faded floral, mingling with the raw scent of their possession.

Crushed innocence.

A new life.

Her grip on him tightened as he filled her over and over. Her tiny moans and cries exploded inside him, and a groan escaped his throat as the pleasure built, overwhelmed. A groan of a different order. His eyes blinked open. He wanted to see her, as they were one, one body. One beast.

It wasn't only about his own pleasure, or some game, or a distraction to blind him for a few sweet moments. There were no lies, no bending of truths. Everything around them had contorted and changed, but there was an anchor for them both, body and soul.

Her chest heaved, and her eyes glistened as she took him in. Yes, his brave, remarkable Lady Ryvves. Pleasure tore through him. That compulsion to pull out and pull away as was his wont with a woman flew past him. He only surged deeper into Georgina, needing more of her for his satisfaction. Completion of a different kind.

A moan unleashed from her lips. "Charles…Charles…"

Banging thundered on the front door, loud voices yelling. The servants knocked, calling out to him.

He stopped, her body stiffening in his grip. "Dammit. Our guests have arrived."

Thomas shouting.

She sat up. "Are we finished?"

"No."

"Oh."

"But 'twill serve." He winced as he tucked himself in and fastened his breeches. His cock throbbed for not having finished after such a ride. Blood was smeared down her thigh and he ran his fingers through it.

Would she regret what they'd done? Would she cry and be

upset with herself, with him, and thus turn on him to her brother? He knew not what to expect.

"Yes, 'twill serve. It is done," she murmured softly against his cheek, planting a kiss there as her fingertips skimmed the curve of his jaw. Her hand slid around his blood-stained fingers, and she grinned. "I am ruined."

Chapter Twenty-Three

Charles

GEORGINA ADJUSTED HER DRESS. Her hair had fallen, and Charles smoothed an errant lock from her face. Her rosy cheeks reddened even more at his delicate gesture.

"Stay here, collect yourself," he said.

"The point is to not appear collected but pillaged."

"Be assured, Miss Georgina, you shall have your moment, but first allow me to greet them." He left her and entered the foyer where a servant stood with Thomas and John.

"Sir—"

Charles lifted his chin. "Thank you, you may go."

Thomas tracked toward him. "He's dead, eh?" his loud voice hurled at Charles. "They killed each other. We were just at Amanda's. She's beside herself."

"I'm sure she is."

"Where is my sister?"

"This is a house of mourning. If you are here to pay your respects to my brother, the body is this way—"

"We are here to bring Georgina home," said John.

Thomas crossed his arms. "Are you keeping her prisoner, Montclare?"

"I am not."

"Her being here alone with you is highly inappropriate," said Thomas, his lips pressing together tightly.

"Her fiancé is dead," said John. "Thus, there is no more engagement to the Earl of Ryvves. There is no more—"

"Miss Georgina Townsend is engaged to marry the Earl of Ryvves," Charles asserted. "And I am the Earl of Ryvves."

In the thick, loud silence, Georgina moved forward from the shadows and stood at his side.

"No. No. Come away, Georgina," said Thomas. "All is forgiven. You cannot possibly trust this man. You can't. He does nothing but lie and dissemble to suit himself, just as he is doing now."

"Be careful, Thomas, for you are insulting me in my own home," said Charles.

Thomas ignored him. "Whatever he has told you, he is only taking advantage of you, using you for his own nefarious purposes. But there is still time to save you."

"I don't need saving, Thomas," said Georgina. "And if anyone has used me or lied to me, it is my own family."

"Listen to me—" Thomas took in a breath, his jaw shuddering. "With Hugh dead, we can start afresh."

"We? You mean you. I shall be forced to go to Devonshire and marry whomever else you all choose for me. I do not want that."

"Only your family has your best interests at heart," said John.

"They are your interests alone. Mine are not being considered. I am not going with you."

"You will do as you are told!" erupted John. "Ungrateful child."

"I am to marry the Earl of Ryvves," was her only reply.

"Mr. Holyfloke, you must respect the generous marriage settlement that we signed," said Charles. "Miss Townsend is marrying a peer of the realm with an enormous income and a very healthy estate, surely the finest of connections for your family. And let us not forget, I've paid handsomely for the dissolution of the banns. The wedding shall take place as soon as possible."

"Your brother signed that document as well as you," said John.

"In all things, I was his second, and he was mine." Such a bitter truth now had a fresh new meaning. "She shall be my countess."

"You bastard!" Thomas exploded. "I will not allow—"

Charles threw him a dark look. "I might add that Georgina has been with me all day."

John and Thomas shared a quick glance.

"There are witnesses," continued Charles. "She has been in my carriage riding through London, and she has been in my house alone with me for hours. You understand my meaning?"

Thomas's chest expanded as his piercing gaze went from his sister to Charles. "No. No. It cannot be."

Georgina pushed that loose lock of hair from her flushed face. "It is true." She slid her hand in Charles's, and he raised it to his lips and kissed it slowly, tenderly, his gaze shooting to Thomas as his tongue peeked out and stroked her flesh.

"Oh Lord, no," Thomas muttered.

"What have you done?" John raised his hand in the air.

Darting forward, Charles grabbed it. "You dare to strike my fiancée?"

"She is not yours."

"She is. In every way—save for a vicar's blessing."

Georgina met John's gaze. "In every way."

John shoved off from Charles. "You are a fool, Georgina. And you, an evil seducer. Did your brother have her first, and now that he's dead, you're cleaning up the mess he's left behind?"

"How dare you say such a thing about her." Charles gritted his teeth against the burning tide of anger fomenting in his throat.

"Your brother dies in a duel and within the hour you are claiming his fiancée for yourself? I find it all quite suspicious, my Lord Ryvves. Do your ambitions and carnal passions have no bounds? What of respect, honour, morality?" John turned his blazing eyes on his sister-in-law. "And you—"

"You have spewed quite enough sewage, sir. Leave my house."

"You shall pay for this."

"I expect to—" Charles put his hand on Georgie's belly, her body seizing under his possessive grip. "—in nine months' time when my heir is born."

A grunt left John's mouth. He was outraged. Disgusted. "Come away, Thomas. We are done, here." His eyes narrowed. His lips a snarl.

"I never expected this of you, Georgina," said Thomas. "I am utterly shocked. How shall I ever tell our sister and mother? This is folly. You shall only find unhappiness and despair on this course you have chosen because he—"

"Get out. Now," said Charles.

John cast her a final spiteful glance as he and Thomas stalked out the door and it was shut behind them.

It was over.

He and Georgina had accomplished their objective.

Marriage.

"Georgina? Are you all right?" his voice the roughest whisper.

"I am," her voice the softest whisper.

"I am certain you've never gone against your family's wishes before and in such a way."

"No. Never."

"How did it feel?"

"Awful. Exciting. Horrible." Her glassy eyes met his. "Liberating." She was emotional, yet not distraught. She stood on the edge of a cliff, breathing in the crisp fresh blustering air. "I am now utterly free."

"Yes. Free." His heated blood tore through his veins at the sight of her. He was right there on the cliff's edge with her. "We need a drink." They went into the drawing room, and he poured her a glass of brandy and handed it to her.

She swallowed greedily. "Tell me, am I being an insolent child?"

"You are brave. Holyfloke did not get his way and he is angry. That is all." He took a swallow from the bottle. "You need rest, Georgina. Choose any bedchamber you like. There are many. We have a long journey ahead of us tomorrow." He threw himself on an easy chair by his brother's corpse.

A small weary smile flickered over her lips. "I shall finally see my beloved Gloucestershire again. Will we wear black to marry?"

He let out a sharp laugh. "I rather like the idea of that. Our wedding was founded on a death, after all." He drained the bottle.

She took it from his hands and knelt before him. Blood rushed through his veins at the sight of her kneeling between his legs. "You must be exhausted," she murmured, her hands on his boots, searing through the leather to his very flesh.

"What are you doing?" He licked at his lips, his pulse charging.

"Helping you." She pulled on a boot, and he let her. He had no energy left. Only aches of all kinds. She helped him remove the other as his gaze landed on the curve of her bosom, the bosom he hadn't had much of a chance to savour. "Will you not go to bed?" she asked him.

He averted his gaze from her ravishing body, those gleaming eyes of hers. He could drown in those eyes. "I have a responsibility, as is the custom, to stay up all night with my brother's corpse to verify that he is well and truly dead."

"What a good, responsible brother you are."

He let out a weary scoff. "Oh, I always have been."

Her hand stroked his thigh, and a molten heat surged over

his flesh. "I imagine you've always been good and responsible, haven't you?"

He took her hand in his and brushed it with his lips. "Go before I change my mind."

"Good night then." She left him and went upstairs.

His head fell back against the chair as he stared at his lifeless brother. Hugh dead. What a waste it was. Who had killed him in his own house? He scrubbed a hand down his face in an effort to scrub the images of his brother's lifeless bloody corpse from his memory.

"I wonder," he said aloud. "Are you with our father in hell or our mother in Providence? Perhaps you stalking the underworld trying to seduce Persephone herself?" He let out a dark laugh. "Idiot, idiot…" He closed his eyes, but images of Hugh did not dance before him.

No, it was Georgie.

Her body quivering all around him as he licked her. Her melted gaze as he filled her, her surprise as their bodies surged together. Oh, that surprise of hers, that was…priceless. Her cries of sensation and feeling, sensation and feeling she had never known before.

He indulged himself in those infinitely satisfying and fresh memories, and his muscles finally eased.

The pink light of morning glowed through the windows, reflected on his brother's waxy lifeless flesh. He stood over him, taking in his scent. "You are well and truly dead, brother. *Adieu.*"

Tracking up the staircase, he yanked off his chemise as he went. He wanted a bath, a good scrubbing. What he really wanted was to rub himself off. That taste of Georgina last night had set him off in a way he had never been set off before.

Maybe it was the intense contrast of death and pleasure, the eruption of violence, and the spoiling of innocence.

Maybe it was simply Georgina.

Charles entered his chamber, and there, on his bed, lay Georgie. Her long, thick hair cascaded over his pillows. Her lips were parted, her breathing deep and soft.

His chest filled with heat, and his pulse quickened. "I promise you, I shall always keep you safe," he whispered. "No matter what I have to do. I shall do it."

He reached out and touched her cheek, traced a line down her neck, across her exposed clavicle. He was getting married. He would have to get used to living with a woman. In his house. In his bed. Sighing softly, Georgina turned over, a bare shoulder peeking out from the large chemise.

It might not be too difficult a task.

Chapter Twenty-Four

Charles

As he was dressing, a servant informed him that his Aunt Vivian had arrived to pay her respects to her deceased nephew and the new Earl of Ryvves.

Charles went into his bedchamber where Georgina stood before the wash basin in his chemise, dabbing her wet face with a cloth. His breath cut at the sight of her. Her hair was loose, falling below her shoulders, the full curves of her breasts visible beneath his thin cotton shirt.

"Good morning, Charles." Her pale cheeks reddened under his gaze. She was beautiful in this raw state. More beautiful than he'd ever seen her at balls or parties, gilded and bedecked with fine clothes and jewels. This Georgina was…oh, she was his now, wasn't she?

Yes, she bloody well is.

When was the last time he'd seen her like this? When she was a young girl practicing archery or riding her horse much too quickly along a wooded path in their neighborhood.

How would she look in the morning after a night of rough lovemaking in his bed? His veins surged with heat, and something twisted deep in his gut at the thought.

"Charles?"

"Good morning." He took in a breath to steady himself. "My aunt has arrived to pay her respects, and I would not wish her to know you are here or that we are to go to Gloucestershire together and marry. I would ask you to stay here in this room and do not come out until she is gone and I send for you. Although it pains me to lie to her and not have her at our wedding, I will not take any chances of our plans being thwarted before we are even able to leave London."

"Yes, I agree."

He left her and, once downstairs, found Aunt Vivian standing before Hugh. "How tragic, this waste of a young life over…"

"A woman, most likely."

"Yes, I thought as much. I wonder what your father is saying to him now?"

"Do you think they've ended up in the same place, Aunt?"

She let out a laugh and shot him a derisive look. "Most likely. What do you say?"

"Most likely. I shall see you in Gloucestershire soon, I hope?"

"Yes, you shall. Alice and I should be at Penrose Park by the end of the week." She put a hand on his arm. "There, you see? Now Penrose Park will be all yours as it should be. Who could have possibly foreseen all this when we'd had that conversation?"

He walked her to the front door. "Aunt, my wish is that you live on at Penrose for as long as you like and whenever you like."

"Thank you, Charles." She planted a kiss on his cheek. "Farewell, my boy." She cast a final glance at Hugh. "Get him home."

～

At last, Charles and Georgina left London. Their carriage pulled a cart with Hugh's body in a wood box.

They'd spent the night at a coaching inn, and Charles had insisted she stay in his room with him. "I'm not taking any chances some evil will befall you. As it is, we have a dead body with us, and we are as yet unmarried. What if your brother's hired some louts to take you away? Although that may be rather a dramatic action for Thomas, I do not know what your brother-in-law is capable of, and so I will not tempt fate."

"Quite right. We've come this far." She tended to his wound with the powders and tinctures Malcolm had left with them. His body released its tension at the initial stinging. She was focused on her work, her teeth biting on her lower lip. The sight still made her uncomfortable, and yet, there she was tending to it. To him. Not complaining, not upset, not anxious about all the choices she had made. None of that. Only helping him.

"You've become quite good at this."

She glanced up at him, a smile on those gorgeous lips of hers. "You're a good patient."

They'd eaten in their room so as to not attract attention. After, she pulled down the covers on the lone bed in the chamber.

"I'll take the armchair," he murmured.

"You will not. Charles, we are well past chivalry and the virtues. We are to be married, and we've already shared congress. Now we shall take sleep side by side in the same bed. We've done it all backward, but there you have it. It would be preposterous to not share a bed in these circumstances as we are both extremely tired and have another long day of traveling ahead of us."

"Merciless and sensible."

She pulled her hair from its pins. "What did you expect of me?"

"Any other girl of your age and station would be mortified if not terrified."

"With all that has happened, I am well past any such mortification or terror. Even before the duel." She let out a sigh. "And I am no longer a girl."

"No, you're not. We've seen to that, haven't we?"

She glanced up at him for but a moment and the long, dark waves of her thick hair fell about her shoulders. His heart stopped in his chest. The desire to dig his hands into that silken mass, to tug and pull as he took her mouth. Took her…

Once they both dealt with their clothing and got into the bed, Charles blew out the lone candle at his side. "Do you feel safe, Georgie? I want you to feel safe."

"I do, Charles. I also feel great relief that we are this much closer to home. I thank you for asking," she whispered. "Good night." Her hand touched his arm in the darkness.

"Good night." The gentle brushing of her fingers sent a warm thrum over his flesh.

IN THE MORNING he woke to find her curled up at his side, snuggled to his body as if she were rooted there. As if it were the most natural, organic thing in the world.

It certainly felt so.

He let go of the breath he was holding and gave in to the temptation to touch her. His fingers trailed down her bare arm, and she let out a sigh in her sleep. Her skin was soft, smooth, and warm under his touch. The silky mass of her hair had fallen over his arms, tickling his chest. That delicate floral scent of hers rose from her skin, and his cock stiffened between his legs.

Bloody hell. Stop it, not now.

He had to get out of bed and get dressed. He moved, and

she immediately stretched out. That glorious body with peaks and curves twisted and turned. "Is it morning already?"

"Yes." He planted his feet on the floor. "We really should prepare to leave." He rubbed at his sore wounded arm

She sat up, her chemise falling off a shoulder, and a groan rose in his chest. "Quite right." She scrambled off the bed. "Let me help you."

He stepped back. "No, no, you don't need to bother with me. Malcolm said I should move the arm as much as I can bear to keep things circulating."

"Very well."

He finished dressing, quickly so that she could get on with her own preparations in privacy. He wanted her to be comfortable. Or was he the one who felt uncomfortable? He shoved his boots on. "I shall go find my man and make sure all is ready. I shall return for you."

"Very well. I won't be long."

After a quick breakfast in their room, Georgina covered her head and face with the hood of her cape, and Charles led her to their coach.

Hours later, they finally arrived in the village, their carriage swaying as it made its way up the high street, through the crowd. Georgina peered out the glass as they passed the old tavern, The Fang & Feather. "There she is," she murmured.

"Happy to be back?" he asked.

"You have no idea."

He leaned his head back against the cushioned upholstery. "Oh, I think I do."

Chapter Twenty-Five

Charles

THE CURATE'S WORDS WERE BUT a dull repetition, and Charles did not pay them any heed. His eyes were glued onto the wooden coffin in the ground at the family grave on the estate.

Only days before, his brother had cavorted over the earth, entertaining himself. Laughing loudly, making pronouncements, making plans. No longer. Not ever again.

All that was left of all that was Hugh lay deep in the earth. And Charles would walk away. He would bloody well prosper, spend their money, make more money, and create his own family.

Ah yes, he had to confirm the wedding with the vicar. The vicar had stopped his recitations and with a twist of his lips, muttered, "Sir?"

"Ah. Thank you. I have a question. I need you to perform a wedding. My wedding. Tomorrow night."

"Tomorrow night, sir?" He took off his spectacles. "There are banns—"

"I have the dispensations from the Archbishop himself."

The vicar's face folded in a scowl. "I'm sure you do."

"Is there a problem?"

"No, my lord. What time would be best for your lordship?" They settled on the hour for the service.

A tall dark figure appeared. "Charles?"

Brandon.

"My lords." The vicar left them, Charles's servant escorting him off.

"My condolences, my friend." Brandon hugged Charles and pain thundered in his upper arm, a grunt escaping his lips.

He released him. "What is the matter?"

Charles told him about Hugh shooting him, the duel, and how his cousin William died. All of it.

"Amanda wrote to me. I cannot say I am sorry about the loss of my cousin. Killing William was something I'd always wanted to do, but I held myself in check because I did not want his foul blood on my hands. My family was far, far more important."

"They most certainly are. You were right not to pursue that line of vengeance," said Charles. "Now William got what he deserved."

"Indeed. But for Hugh to have shot you?"

"My brother and I, as you know, were never very close, but this action of his was most unexpected."

"And most foul," muttered Brandon.

"And now he too is gone." Charles's gaze remained fixed on the coffin below. "I know he would have wished an evening burial complete with the pomp of a procession as befits his station, but I find I cannot give him more than this."

"He is in the earth with his family. The rest is meaningless."

"And William?"

"Amanda arrived last night, and I brought William's body to the church cemetery and had it buried alongside his father. Surprisingly, she did not insist on any pomp or ceremony. 'Tis done." He rubbed his hands together. "Now you will live your life with much freedom, Lord Ryvves."

"Not knowing who killed Hugh and why is not affording me great ease."

"It was most likely another jealous man. Hugh always had quite a reputation, and it had only renewed itself during your time in town this season."

"It certainly did."

"Let us focus on thoughts much more deserving than these two soulless bastards who lost their lives by their own doings. Whatever is left of them, cold and dank, is now deep in the ground below us. Earth to earth, dust to dust, and all that."

"That, my friend, is a far better eulogy than the one I just heard."

Brandon chuckled as he led Charles away from the grave. "Georgina arrived safely at ours this morning."

"I'm glad. She was so looking forward to seeing the two of you again. Thank you for taking her in until we marry tomorrow."

"Of course. Is everything set then? The ladies will ask me the moment I return home."

"It is. Tomorrow at eleven. We shall have a wedding breakfast directly after at home."

"No, no. I insist you let Justine and I do the breakfast, a small token for our dearest friends. Never did I think I'd see the day that you would actually marry—and to Georgie."

"Not more surprised than I."

"Let me assure you, my friend, there is something to be said for a surprise marriage," said Brandon. "I wasn't even aware I was married when I came back to Wolfsgate after the shipwreck, thanks to my uncle and William's machinations. But like me and Justine, you and Georgina have known each other and been friends for years. That, Charles, is something to build on. And yes, there were difficulties and mistakes, but we achieved much together, and we are very, very happy."

"You certainly are. Ah, Brandon, I want Georgina to be

happy. I don't want to disappoint her. For the first time in a very long time, I feel …" He let out a groan. "I don't know…"

"Go on, say it."

"I feel helpless. Incapable."

"That is good."

"How is that good?"

"You have a conscience. You feel the weight of your many responsibilities. Perhaps it's something new for you, Ryvves. And your estate now lays on your shoulders alone. You will be deciding everything. But you're experienced. I really did not have much of that experience before it landed in my lap, and Wolfsgate was in an awful mess. Your estate is in good health, is it not?"

"It is. Luckily, my brother didn't get a chance to enjoy himself as Earl for more than two months, and so it remained under my guidance and intact."

They reached Brandon's horse. "Leave the dead behind you, Charles, and live your new life. Enjoy it. Embrace it. And know, I am here for you."

"I thank you, my friend."

Brandon mounted his horse. "We shall bring the bride on time. See that you are there waiting."

"Oh, I shall be."

Chapter Twenty-Six

Georgina

"You're sure you like it?"

"It's gorgeous. Absolutely perfect." Georgina's fingers delicately fluffed at the cream silk dress detailed with gold that she wore. "Mademoiselle Therese is one of the finest dressmakers in all of London. To wear such a gown for my wedding…"

"I'm thrilled to have you wear it. I never got the chance as I grew quickly when I was with child. To have you wear it for your wedding makes me so very happy. Are you sure you're not disappointed that you won't be wearing a new frock you've chosen on your own?"

"Everything about this wedding is unordinary. Wearing this dress will make it truly special to me." She hugged her friend. "I'm most pleased. Indeed, I feel blessed."

"I never had a proper wedding, never mind a pretty dress, so I am very gratified that in this small way I am able to help you with yours."

Arm in arm, they both turned and faced the looking glass. "You know that your and Brandon's marriage has always been an inspiration to me. Perhaps by wearing this dress, a little of that good fortune shall rub off on me."

THE VILLAGE DRESSMAKER arrived and made a few small adjustments to the fit of the dress. Georgina also ordered an entire new wardrobe befitting the Countess of Ryvves. They did not, however, tell Mrs. Thompson that Georgina and the Earl of Ryvves were to marry. Otherwise, it would spread like wildfire across the village in an hour's time.

Mrs. Thompson took quick notes in her small notebook. "Underthings, chemises, night dress, dressing gown, muslins for day, and elegant dinner dresses."

"And, Mrs. Thompson, do not send the bill to Fairthorn." Georgina kept her voice light. "I shall come by your shop and make arrangements myself."

"Of course, Miss. As you wish."

After Mrs. Thompson departed, the two friends enjoyed their tea on the wide stone terrace in the shade.

"Now you will be the lady of a grand estate," said Justine. "I have not been to Charles's home for quite some time. With his father having been ill for so long, they, of course, did not entertain. Now, you who have such exquisite taste will remake that house however you like. You will let me help you, won't you?"

"I shall take great pleasure in having you assist." Her smile faded as she sipped at her tea. "Although, perhaps Charles will not want any changes made."

"You'll soon find out. You'll soon find out a great many things." Justine laughed softly. "Are you anxious about the wedding night?"

Earlier, Georgina had explained how the engagement had come about to Justine over cups of hot chocolate and biscuits. But, not entirely everything. One day she would tell her, but now she wanted to only focus on the present.

Georgina only smiled in reply.

Justine bit into a small sugar biscuit. "I realise you are very well aware of how things…work."

"Yes, I am. I was always eager to learn, and my sister was quite willing to inform."

"If I may add one thing."

Georgina set her tea cup on the table. "Please do."

"This is your time. Your experience. You must wipe all those stories from your head and embrace what you and Charles have to share. It's a unique bond that the two of you shall create. Its result is a closeness that grows and grows between you, a closeness that you build together. That will make you strong."

"I've never thought of it like that. I always thought of it simply as…a temporal pleasure."

"It is that, of course, yes." Justine put her empty tea cup on the table. "Frankly, it can be many things. I have found it to be a unique form of expression and feeling and trust between a man and a woman. I know you've always been eager to experience it."

Georgina only let out a laugh.

"I am sure your husband will be generous and good to you and that you will be delightfully surprised withal."

Oh, he is, and I already am.

"I'm sure I will be," said Georgina.

"That was a lovely break, but we haven't a moment longer to waste. Shall we go to my dressing room and try on shoes? Luckily we are the same size, you and I."

As they climbed the great staircase, Georgina took in the magnificent paintings of Brandon's ancestors along the coffered wood walls. "Oh my…"

"What is it?"

"This is Brandon's mother, Lady Caroline? They have the same sea green eyes, don't they? As does your daughter."

"They do, yes. She is beautiful, isn't she? And so very happy."

Georgina's gaze was riveted on the pearl, diamond, and ruby necklace Lady Caroline wore. She'd seen that piece somewhere before. She was sure of it. And recently too. But where? On whom?

"You are quite sure your mother and brother will not attend the wedding?" Justine's voice interrupted her haze. "I did hear that they have returned from London."

"Oh, have they?" Her insides sank. "I shall certainly write and invite them. I do hope they've brought my things on from town. I shall have to go to Fairthorn and gather my belongings from there shortly. I especially look forward to having all my painting tools at my disposal once again. I've been without them all this time whilst I was in Devonshire."

They continued up the staircase. "Tell me you're still sketching, still painting. You did not mention it in your letters to me," said Justine.

"I did sketch and draw at my sister's, but painting, no. My sister and her husband disapproved, and they didn't allow me any patch of space in their grand home to work. Philippa frowned upon the mess. Just like our mother."

"You've missed it."

"Beyond anything."

"Oh, I'd quite forgotten—we must decide on the menu for your wedding breakfast. Cook gave me a list of ideas earlier for us to review." Justine took out a folded paper from a pocket.

"Speaking of a menu, as I'm going to be the lady of Ryvves now, you must educate me on all things in running a house."

"My love, you know all this."

"But everything has happened so quickly, and I haven't had a chance to give it a thought. I want to make sure I do well. And you, having been married to the Lord of Wolfsgate for the past two years have much experience to share."

"Once you are settled, I shall help you with anything you wish."

"Thank you." Georgina let out a breath. "Charles deserves

a good wife after all that he has done for me. He did not expect to marry nor to be Earl. I would not want him to be riddled with regrets or disappointments on any score."

Justine opened the door to her chamber. "I firmly believe you have nothing to fear."

Chapter Twenty-Seven

Georgina

CHARLES HAD SENT a message to Georgina assuring her that all the arrangements at the church had been made, which she already knew as Brandon had told her of his conversation with her fiancé earlier.

But it pleased her to see that he had taken the time to tell her himself. She wrote back, thanking him for the note and letting him know that she looked forward to seeing him at the church.

She did. She did miss him, in fact.

They had spent three heady, intense days together, and had depended on each other for truth, for trust. And so to be without him felt odd. An ache spiraled inside her at that admission to herself.

His kiss, his touch, had also been heady and intense. She was now no longer a virgin maid, and she had been the one to instigate it. Charles could have refused her bold request, and if he had done, she'd be in Devonshire. Or he could have laughed at her, and she would have felt utterly humiliated. Or he could have taken full advantage and abused her, but he had done none of these things. He had been understanding and kind, and attentive.

A grin swept her lips. Most attentive.

That feeling he had invoked in her body had been unlike any other she had ever experienced. His hands on her, his mouth, his tongue. Her legs pressed together.

How would it be once they were married and they would have all the time they wanted to themselves? All the privacy?

Another thought seized her. Did Charles have a mistress? She hadn't considered that. Perhaps he did, and now she'd ruined it for them. She hadn't even thought to ask him. Perhaps he had a prostitute he favoured regularly? Would he continue to indulge?

She would have to navigate all that just as she had planned on doing with Hugh. But why was her heart thudding in her chest at the thought of finding out the truth of Charles's private life?

Justine's lady's maid brushed out her hair, and Georgina stared at her reflection in the glass. It was her wedding day. To prepare for her wedding without her mother and sister had seemed unthinkable. And yet here she was, but she was glad of it for instead, she could be at her sister's house being doted on by her mother and Philippa whilst Sir Reginald, the eager groom waited for her at the church.

Justine blasted into the room. "Darling, a letter and gifts have arrived for you from your fiancé." She placed a jeweler's box on the vanity and a bouquet of white roses and a letter with a large R wax seal on it.

Georgina's face heated as she lowered her face to the roses, taking in their perfume. Her pulse was suddenly giddy as if the rich fragrance had blasted away all her uneasiness and replaced it with delight. "They're beautiful."

"They are indeed, Miss," said the maid.

She broke the seal on the letter and quickly unfolded it.

My dearest Georgina,

Please accept these gifts as a token of my esteem for my wife-to-be.

Both are from my great, great grandmother's collection and are now yours, my dazzling Countess of Ryvves.
There is also a ring, and I shall place it on your finger myself.

I hope you will come to the church bearing these roses, as they are from our gardens that I have picked for you this morning, our wedding day.

Yours,

Charles

Her eyes filled with water as she brushed her fingertips over his elegant signature. Georgina opened the large box where inside were two very old jewellery boxes. Her pulse beat wildly as she opened the larger one. A tiara with tiny diamonds in a leaf motif glittered from within the velvet. "Lord."

"It's magnificent." Justine took the tiara from her as Georgina opened the next box.

Matching diamond drop earrings lay in the smaller box. "Beautiful," breathed Georgina.

The maid placed the tiara on Georgina's head, nestling it perfectly in her hair, and securing it. Next came the earrings. Georgina trembled at her reflection in the looking glass.

In the rush to prepare, she hadn't allowed herself to think or linger on the hows and wherefores. Now this moment was here. It was real. And this incredible tiara marked her as his chosen bride in a spectacular and intimate fashion.

If she were marrying Hugh today, she would feel proud and satisfied wearing this tiara. But the gift from Charles, antique diamonds and handpicked roses, had her heart racing and her blood humming. She felt capable of anything. Dauntless. Sure of herself in a way she had never felt before. And deeply stirred by her groom's thoughtfulness and care.

"Oh, Georgie…" sighed Justine. "You are a vision."

She took her bouquet in her hands. "We must go."

"Yes, the Earl awaits." Justine took her hand.

At the appointed hour, Georgina and Brandon and Justine arrived at the church in the Graven coach. The front steps and porch of the village church were strewn with flowers, rushes, and herbs. The vicar's wife greeted them, and Brandon took Georgina's hand on his arm and led her inside. The same church where she had been baptised, where she and her family attended services every Sunday.

Now it was empty.

"Thank you, Brandon," she whispered.

"I thank you for such a privilege, Georgie. I've known you since you were a child, and you've become a fine young woman and the dearest friend of my beloved Justine. To support you now, as you marry one of our closest friends, is indeed an honour." His fingers squeezed her arm gently as he led her down the aisle.

Yes, Brandon and Justine and Charles were her family now.

She blinked back the tears gathering suddenly in her eyes and, taking in a small breath, focused on the man who stood waiting for them at the head of the aisle.

The man who would become her husband. Who already was hers from that first night alone together in London. Now they would receive the formal blessing of the rite they had claimed so expeditiously.

Charles's heavy gaze remained on her, and her skin flared with heat. His blond hair was swept back in a tie, and he wore a formal frock coat in black with gold buttons which gave him a crisp, and very dashing appearance which suited him.

The cream silk rustled about her body, and the earrings

brushed her skin as she moved with Brandon toward Charles and the vicar. Towards her new life.

Like any female, all her life had been a slow procession toward a husband, hadn't it? And now here she was, in the ultimate procession toward her fate. But a fate that she had created for herself. No, she and Charles had done it together.

Brandon stopped, and she blinked, the breath burning in her throat. They had arrived.

Dipping his head, Brandon held out her hand to Charles, who took it in his warm one. Brandon receded, and Charles took his place next to her. "You are absolutely breathtaking, Georgina." Charles's raw whisper had her insides tightening.

"Thank you."

The vicar cleared his throat and recited from his service book. Within moments Charles produced a ring. Taking her hand in his, he fit it in on her finger, sliding it all the way on. It fit perfectly. A sparkling diamond ring with other smaller diamonds surrounding the brilliant rectangular centre stone. A Ryvves ring.

My wedding ring.

The rich fragrance of his roses filled her senses as her husband, his eyes gleaming, whispered, "We are married, my Countess of Ryvves."

Chapter Twenty-Eight

Georgina

THEIR WEDDING BREAKFAST at Wolfsgate was thoroughly enjoyable. Georgina drank perhaps too much sherry, but it was a day of celebration with their dearest friends.

Hours later, the time came that they were to leave. "Come, my Countess, we must go to our home now." Justine and Brandon and little Jeremy had applauded, and they all laughed. A thrill had raced through her at his words, but the teasing tone of his voice did not match the heavy gaze of his eyes on her.

She was off to her new home with her new husband, the Earl of Ryvves. She was no longer the younger sister, the resplendent Miss Townsend, the delightful Miss Georgina. No. She was the Countess of Ryvves. *His countess.*

All was different. All was new.

Their carriage shuddered and rocked as the horses took them from Wolfsgate. Took her in a different direction than Fairthorn, her brother's house, the house where she was born and raised. Where she was no longer welcome.

"Did you enjoy the wedding?" he asked.

"I did." She fingered her rose bouquet in her lap. "Very much."

"I hope it was not too difficult for you as your family was not present."

"Charles, this entire day has been so lovely. The morning at Justine's, the service, the breakfast. It was truly perfect. I loved it. I hope you—"

"It was perfect."

"Your gifts were magnificent."

"You like them?"

"Very much. It was the most extraordinary surprise. I shall always treasure them."

His lips blazed with a wide smile. "The jewels are indeed magnificent on you as I knew they would be."

The carriage descended into a valley, the road winding through an endless field of green. She had not been to Charles's home for many years. Truly, she barely remembered it. "Charles, you must tell me the moment we cross into your property."

"You want to know what you own, madame?"

"My lord, you know very well that as a woman, I own nothing. What I want is to know everything about your home."

He put a hand over hers. "Our home. It's our home now."

His warm, firm touch and carefree affirmation sent a ripple through her. Yes, she had a home. Her very own home now. There were no more worries of where to go, where she was welcome, would she have to leave. No more. She belonged somewhere.

"We are crossing over onto the estate now." An enormous valley of green sloping hills burst forth around them. The horses found a swift rhythm as they entered an avenue of tall beech trees. They knew they were home and were eager to reach their beloved destination. At last, in the distance, the old stone wall of the property appeared.

Charles rubbed a hand down his thigh as they passed through a tall medieval gate. "This gate used to distress me as a child. It always seemed forbidding and sinister."

"I can understand why."

He only pressed his lips together and kept his attention on the road. Was he looking at his home with new eyes? Charles was the great estate's lord, its foundation, its pillar. Hugh was gone and all was his.

And there, on a hill in the distance, rose the great house. Imposing, striking, towering. Stone magnificence in the Elizabethan style. Stone weathered yet taken care of, clean. A long stretch of formal gardens stood on either side with a fountain at its centre.

The horses made their way around the immense circular front drive. Their hooves clopped heavier, louder. Georgina's back straightened as the carriage finally came to a stop. On the stairs stood all the staff to greet them.

The door of the coach swung open. "Sir," his manservant greeted him with a bow. "Welcome home."

"Holt. Good to see you." Charles grinned at the man as he got out of the carriage. Turning, he held out his hand to Georgina, and she placed her hand in his.

He grinned at her, that knowing teasing grin of his she knew so well. "Lady Georgina, Countess of Ryvves, I welcome you home to Ironvine."

CHARLES INTRODUCED Georgina to the servants, and they entered through the imposing doorway into a large marble hall with a vaulted ceiling, which offered a procession of rooms and a grand staircase leading to the upper story.

Although the exterior of the house was in an old style, the interior had obviously been renovated in the Baroque. Gilded accents were everywhere, rich colours and lavish fabrics emboldened tapestries and curtains and upholstery. The furniture was elegant and of the highest quality.

"Would you like a tour now, Georgie, or some refreshment?"

"I'm quite eager to see the house."

"Holt, I'm going to show Lady Georgina her new home now. We'll take tea in the Blue Silk drawing room in an hour's time."

"Very good, sir."

Charles gestured for Georgina to follow him. "Over the years, with each Earl's increase in income and arrogance, the house was built upon, redecorated. My grandfather was the one who modernised and refreshed the structure. The one thing he was most proud of was the orangerie."

"Ah yes, the glass-walled conservatory. That I remember."

"Do you?"

"It's so unique. Walls of glass, light everywhere. As a young girl I'd never seen anything like it before, then or since. Our house—I mean, Thomas's house is rather dark. My father had once remarked how it had been built facing wrongly, and I daresay he was correct."

"I hope you never shared that remark with your brother."

"No, he and my father were never on very good terms. It would have made things even more wrong than they already were."

They made their way through the largest dining room Georgina had ever seen, several drawing rooms and studies, and finally, the library. Bookshelves filled each wall along with several armchairs, a dark blue duo of settees, and a massive mahogany desk.

"Ironvine's library is rather famous, is it not?" She touched the bindings of the volumes lining the shelves.

"Once upon a time, certainly. My grandfather was a great reader, and I'm quite sure that the last time a book was purchased and added to the collection was during his lifetime. My father was not a reader, nor was my brother."

"Are you?"

"I used to be. My mother enjoyed poetry. You like to read?"

"I do, very much. I look forward to going through the collection."

"If there are any books you would like, I shall order them for you from London, anything at all."

"Wonderful."

Her gaze landed on a framed illuminated manuscript sitting on the desk. The piece was painted in golds and bright reds, and deep blues, the calligraphy slightly imbalanced. "Is this a page from a medieval bible?"

"It is. That is the work of the first Montclare."

"Oh, the monk? 'Tis true then, that story of your ancestor, the first Earl of Ryvves?"

"What have you heard?" He crossed his arms as he leaned back against the desk.

"The first Montclare was a French monk who'd come to England to serve and was turned out of the monastery for his sins."

"His sins, eh?"

"They say he then became great friends with the local nobility and was eventually granted a title and this estate."

"As a reward for those many sins?" Charles raked a hand through his hair. "That's what everyone thinks. They find it amusing that my ancestor was a fallen man of the cloth, considering all his progeny acquired the reputation of rake."

"Something like that."

"They are wrong."

"Do tell me, Charles."

"The first Earl of Ryvves was indeed a French monk, Brother Laurent de Mont Clare."

"Did not William the Conqueror bring French monks with him to England, who then settled into the monasteries here?"

"He did, and they kept coming and brought their talents with them. Try as he may, Laurent was not a great proficient in

the fine arts of the Church." He picked up the framed illumination. "You see, here...and here." He pointed to several
sentences in Latin on the parchment. "They're crooked, and
this letter, he redid but not very tidily."

"Oh, yes...I see." She greedily took in the beautiful
coloured parchment poring over every detail. The exquisite
patient labour required to achieve just this small piece
astounded her.

"When he failed so miserably at illumination and greatly
disappointed his elders," Charles continued. "He begged to be
put to work out of doors."

"As a gardener? A farmer?"

"A vintner. He was well versed in the art of winemaking in
his native France, and so he grew his own vineyard, and eventually, he was able to provide the monastery with its very own
wine for the Eucharist."

"How wonderful."

"Here in England, it was the wine-loving Romans who
came and grew grapes and made wine. But when they left, that
died out. If you wanted wine, you imported it from Bordeaux."

"Only the war has put a stop to that, hasn't it?"

"Yes, for years now, England has had to look to other
sources for its wine, like Portugal and Spain. My ancestor
Laurent de Mont Clare had ambitions to make English wine
on English soil. Soon enough, his efforts caught the attention—
or rather fulfilled the appetites—of the local nobility, most
especially a duke who then shared his wine with the king."

"And the king was most impressed?" She took the framed
illumination from Charles.

"Very. Mont Clare's talents were much praised in all the
right circles. Around that time, Henry VIII dissolved the all-
powerful and very wealthy monasteries, and it was then that
Brother Montclare was given a title and this estate as a reward
for his unique talents."

"Extraordinary." Georgina's attention went back to the illuminated parchment. "Imagine, if Brother Laurent had been good at illuminating Bible verses, he would not have gone on to create such a wine that brought satisfaction to so many. Nor be granted his title and these lands by the king himself."

"Quite right. Who and where would I be without his wine?" He let out a short laugh, gesturing at the framed piece. "I've often wondered why he took this with him when he left the monastery."

Georgina put the framed piece back on its stand on the desk. "Perhaps as a reminder that his past failures and stumblings led him to his most rewarding present." She met his gaze. "I daresay, there's a lesson in that for us both."

Chapter Twenty-Nine

Charles

"COULD WE SEE THE CONSERVATORY NOW?" Georgina asked. The excitement in her voice was plain, and his pulse quickened. "Yes, of course. This way, if you please, Countess…"

He led her straight through to the back of the house, where the main hallway suddenly opened to a gleaming wall of sunlight and green. Georgina gasped at the sight.

They stepped inside, the air thick and humid and alive with the scent of earth and fragrant blossoms. Rows of trees and potted plants stood in the glass-enclosed conservatory with a small sculpture of the goddess Diana, taking aim with her bow and arrow in the centre of the room. By the front, there were two armchairs and a small round table. Outside, the garden spread open, a dazzling display of dahlias, vibrant lavender, and lush herbaceous borders in rich emerald green.

"Spectacular."

"I'm glad you think so."

"What a delight it must be to take tea or a glass of wine here in the spring and early summer…the autumn."

"I suppose."

"You never have?"

"I cannot say I have ever spent time here, Georgie. I found

all this glass rather insufferable. Cold in winter, unbearably hot in summer, the glare. But the plants and trees seem to like it."

"Well, that's what's important, isn't it?" She let out a laugh, and his gaze shot at her. Her genuine happiness filled his chest with a kind of warmth he had not felt for a very, very long time. Was that hope? Was it delight?

Georgina strolled up and down each and every aisle of trees and blooms and flowering plants. Something told him she would fill this entire house with her hope and delight. A woman had not lived at Ironvine in over a generation, and he could feel the very stones were in wonder at this girl's presence between their walls.

"If there's something, in particular, you'd like to change or to have in here, you have only to inform the gardener."

"My mother and sister talk endlessly of flowers and shrubs, but I never paid much mind. But this, this is inspiring. These flowers and trees seem like rare creatures that should be tended to and cherished, which is why they flourish in this special place, so…yes, perhaps I shall take up an interest now."

A servant appeared. "Tea is served, my Lord."

"Ah, very good. Come, Georgina."

Charles led her to the Blue Silk drawing room, so named for the brilliant sky blue wallpaper in the elegantly appointed room. They sat at the table before a large window, which looked out onto the vast park.

"I shall pour the tea for my husband as is my duty" said Georgina, her lips quirking.

Charles only clenched his jaw. An image of his mother pouring tea for his father flashed before his eyes. Right here, at this very table. Now he had brought a wife into this house of gloom. Would she survive it? Would she survive him?

"Charles? Do you take sugar?"

"No."

She held the cup and saucer out to him.

"Thank you."

She sipped her tea. "Tell me more about Laurent de Mont Clare and his vineyard."

"When Henry VIII ruled, over a hundred vineyards were recorded in England, a number of which produced wine for the royal household. At least that is how the legend goes. My grandfather had told me the tale, and his grandfather had told him, and so on."

"And Ironvine was one of those vineyards?"

"It was."

Her eyes doubled in size. "What an achievement."

"Laurent did well. For a short time, at least. Eventually, it came to naught or to not much wine. The weather turned colder and wetter, epidemics of mildew, and then of course plagues came and went. In the end, it became too difficult an enterprise for the following generations. The vine did not survive."

"That is a shame."

"But even as he tended his vineyard, Laurent continued to offer his expertise to the wine trade, selecting, importing, and the like. Bristol was quite a centre of trade even then. The first Lord Ryvves was considered one of the finest connoisseurs, and if he approved…well…"

"So he remained in royal favour?"

"He did. He had a great many noblemen at his fingertips."

"I like that he persevered in his chosen field. That which interested him the most. I imagine he married and had children."

"The monk had seven children, in fact—and all with his wife."

"A virtuous Earl of Ryvves." She let out a laugh. "Good for Brother Laurent."

"Yes, good for him." He rose from the table and pointed to a small painting on the wall between two large landscapes. "Here they are—the first Earl of Ryvves, his Countess, and their spawn.

She went to the painting and studied it. "It's quite remark-able. The detail. Something about it that is so familiar to me…"

"Holbein painted it."

"Holbein, who painted Henry VIII himself? Oh, Charles, what an honour for your family."

"It is, isn't it?"

Georgina's mouth fell open. "What a rich family history you have."

"History or legend, no one is quite sure any longer. The entire wine-producing business cannot be verified. As succes-sive generations took over, each with its own interests, and as the grape became harder and harder to sustain, farming and livestock became the vital backbone of Ironvine, and wine became a myth from our distant medieval past."

"Why the iron in Ironvine?"

"For the iron mines in the Forest of Dean, which abuts one edge of our lands. Brother Montclare's wife was a daughter of a local Freeminer, who was also a royal favourite."

"Was she? The Freeminers here were the bravest and hardiest warriors for many a medieval campaign against the French. The very best archers in the land," said Georgina.

"I see we are well versed in our local history?"

"My governess was a local lady and very proud of our history. It's beautiful really…"

"What's that?"

"How Laurent honoured both himself and his wife with the name of his estate." She poured more tea for them both. "I like your ancestor very much, Charles."

"I suppose he could have given the estate some florid French name, eh? Thank Providence, he did not."

She let out a laugh. "There's something medieval and very strong about the name he chose. A vine is a terribly unglam-orous thing."

"As are the iron and coal and ochre found in our local mines."

"But they are all precious treasures of our land. And in the Bible, the vine represents the seam of life. Christ likened himself to the hale and stalwart vine."

"Hale and stalwart, eh?"

"They are hardy. They survive. They have many, many branches, and bear much fruit."

"I do not think such vines can be found here any longer. Those are a thing of the past, I'm afraid. All we have left is a story and a name. And that name has become renown for misdeeds and impropriety."

She leaned forward. "You are the Earl of Ryvves now, Charles. You are Ironvine, all that it was, all that it is, and, most importantly, all that it can be."

He swallowed hard at her words, at her earnest tone. How she believed in him. As the second son, he was never supposed to inherit the title, and he'd grown accustomed to that. He'd never imagined himself shouldering it all alone. Taking charge, assuming total control.

Charles took in his new wife as she examined the other paintings in the room. He was no longer alone. Drawing in a deep breath, he allowed the pleasure of that thought—of comfort and ease—to seep through his body for the first time in a very, very long time.

Chapter Thirty

Georgina

HUSBAND AND WIFE each dressed for their first dinner together and met in the drawing room.

"You are quite lovely," said Charles, his voice unusually low and rough, and her face heated. He didn't compliment her with the same glibness that he once had over the years. Now he seemed to take her in as if he were appraising every detail of her with a fervour she'd never before experienced. It was almost disturbing.

And deeply exciting.

"Thank you." Georgina took his arm, and he led her through to the dining room.

The servants pulled out their chairs for them. From the opposite end of the long table gleaming with silver candelabra and elaborate place settings, she asked, "Must I sit so far away, Charles?"

With a grin, he gestured to the servant. "The Countess and I shall dine alongside one another."

Georgina made her way toward Charles's end of the table, where the servants quickly set a new service for her, and she took her seat. "We are terribly modern, after all."

"Aren't we, though?" His eyes flashed at her. "We swindled your family of you."

"Swindled? Such a term, my lord."

"What would you prefer, my lady?"

Her spine tingled every time he referred to her as "my wife," "wife," or "my lady." And, most especially, when he called her "My Countess."

"I suppose you are correct." She tasted the wine as the creamy white soup was served. "I was to be bartered, and I swindled them of their product and opportunity. It all happened so swiftly and on the turn of the direst of circumstances and yet, here we are. I am most grateful to be here at Ironvine with you, Charles."

"You are the mistress of Ironvine, Georgina. Not my kept woman."

Their soup dishes were taken away, and they were served fillets of beef. "Have you ever kept a woman, Charles?"

"Well…" The wine he'd just swallowed burned down his throat. "Yes."

"Here at the house?"

"No. Never here." He cleared his throat. "At a house in London."

"What became of her?"

"She was an actress and had many admirers. I failed in paying her the attentions she required and as often as she required, and she found someone who did and had deeper pockets than I."

"Ah."

"My father kept a mistress here."

"Did he?"

"She was my mother's first cousin and one of her closest friends."

"That must have been shocking for your mother and quite awful."

"It was indeed." He sliced into his beef. "That was when my mother left us."

Georgina did remember overhearing her mother discussing this bit of juicy gossip with her friends over tea once or twice. She didn't remember the particulars as she was young at the time, but she did remember the gasps and shock that had ensued amongst the ladies.

"Your parents did not divorce?" she asked.

"Of course not." Charles continued to eat, his gaze fixated on his dish, his tone suddenly cold. "Mother lived at her brother's house from then on, Penrose Park, which is not far from here. I sometimes was allowed to visit her there, although she traveled frequently before she died."

"Was your father's mistress here for long?"

"Years and years."

"Was she kind to you? Did you get along?"

He laughed darkly as he put his fork and knife down.

"Perhaps not." She drained her glass of wine, and it was immediately refilled for her.

"Kindness and attachments were never an option in this house, dear Georgie. Whatever my father decided on, one had to accept immediately. It was the only way." He sat back and drank. His glass was filled, and he drank.

"Was she like a stepmother to you and Hugh in any way?"

"I suppose. Until she decided she wanted to bed me and my brother."

"Oh." Her stomach tightened, and she put down her forkful of green beans.

Charles leaned back in his chair. "One afternoon, she and Hugh came upon Father rogering a very young girl, the daughter of a tenant. She was but thirteen, I think. They argued, but he would not give the girl up. So she found a way to amuse herself and get his attention."

"By bedding his sons?"

"Yes."

"How old were you?"

"Fourteen, I think. She and Hugh, however, enjoyed themselves a bit too much. Father discovered them and turned them both out, and she was never heard from again."

"But Hugh and your father were able to repair their relationship."

"Of course. Hugh was his heir, after all. He was banished to our house in town for a few months, and had his allowance drastically reduced until he became appropriately humbled. Then he returned to the bosom of his family and was rewarded with a long tour of the continent." Charles gestured for the servant to leave the bottle of wine at his side.

"Your mother did not return after the mistress left?"

"No. My father enjoyed his liberal way of life too much."

The syllabub was served, and she changed the subject of their conversation to the design of the house, the small maze in the front gardens, and Charles's favourite rooms. They retired to the drawing room, where he poured them a sherry.

"Do you play the pianoforte?" he asked, gesturing at the finely carved instrument in the far corner of the room.

"I have taken lessons, of course, but much to my mother's great disappointment, music was never my strength. Did your mother play?"

"She did. She was very good. In fact, she taught me."

"You play? How wonderful. Would you play for me?"

His teeth dragged along his lower lip. "I've never played for anyone before."

"Consider it a wedding night gift for your bride."

His lips parted as if to say something, something saucy, she was sure of it, but he thought better of it and went to the instrument. Music filled the room as he played a vibrant composition. His body relaxed as he brought the vivid melody to life. Her lips parted, a shiver sliding around her neck as she listened, as she watched him play. He enjoyed it, and he was good, and he was doing it for her, offering her this private piece of himself.

She went over and sat next to Charles on the bench. "You, sir, play exceedingly well."

"Don't tell anyone." His long fingers danced over the keys without missing a single note.

"I won't. Our secret."

He finished the piece, his gaze remaining on the keyboard for a moment. Where had he gone? "I haven't played in quite some time actually," he murmured.

"Thank you for my gift." She kissed him on the cheek.

He dipped his head, a small smile curving his lips. A gentle smile, which made her insides melt. "My pleasure, Countess. Now tell me, where do your talents and accomplishments lay? Needlepoint? Languages?" He played another, slower, more dramatic piece.

"Oh no, no." She let out a soft laugh. "I quite enjoy sketching and drawing."

"Wonderful. You must show me your work."

"All my sketchbooks and paintings are at Fairthorn. All my belongings are there—clothes, sentimental objects that my father left me, everything. I'd like to go to my brother's house and fetch my things, only I'm sure I'm not welcome there at present."

"We shall do that on the morrow then. I shall write to Thomas, telling him we would like to come collect your things."

"I would like that very much."

The clock struck a late hour, and he finished playing. "Shall we retire?"

"Yes," she breathed, barely recognising her own voice.

Rising from the pianoforte, he held out his hand to her, and she placed her hand in his. He took one of the many lit candelabra, and they climbed the staircase together, her heart pounding loudly in her chest. Her breath deepened as they finally reached the dark upper landing.

"There are so very many rooms here. I think it would take me days and days to acquaint myself with them all," she said to fill the silence.

"Yes, there are. These here in the centre were meant for the King when he would visit back in the glorious days of yore." He directed her down the East hallway where their chambers were.

"I had the Lord's chamber fully cleaned and redecorated for Hugh, but he never had a chance to use it. Now it's mine." He opened the door to his bedchamber, and they walked through.

"I hope you had decorated according to your tastes and not to Hugh's."

A dark chuckle rumbled in his chest. "I did, in fact."

She entered the Earl's bedchamber. Her husband's bedchamber. The long dark curtains at the windows, and the dark green and gold patterned wall coverings were sumptuous and very masculine. She came to a stop before a great canopied bed of elaborately carved wood bedecked with drapes, a thick coverlet, and large pillows. It seemed to tower over her. Her teeth dragged across her lip as her hands folded together. Her new life as the Countess of Ryvves was now truly beginning.

He placed the candelabra on a table, and the gold and green and polished wood of the furnishings glowed around them. "Georgina, we don't have to do anything you don't want to do. This is new for both of us and—"

"Not new for you."

"But it is. I have never before been married."

Georgina stilled. A piece of her heart melted like the tapers on the candelabra. That he felt that this moment between them was different, beyond all the other relations with women he'd ever had before, stunned her. "Yes, true," she said on a soft laugh.

"I don't want you to feel anxious or obligated to —"

"Charles, I would like to ask you a question concerning our relations."

"Our relations?" He tilted his head, and his features fell into shadow.

"What I mean is how often and where and what time of day will you be requiring congress?"

His eyes narrowed. "Requiring congress?"

"Yes. I would like to be aware of your needs. If you have a particular programme for when you would expect me to attend you in your chamber, or if you prefer to come to mine, and how often per week?"

Chapter Thirty-One

Georgina

"A PROGRAMME?" Charles repeated, his brow furrowing.

"Well…yes. Isn't that how a marriage works? I would like to know in advance what you expect of me so that I may…"

"Fulfill your obligations?"

"Yes, and be prepared to do so properly."

"Properly? There is no proper anything when it comes to you and me in that bed. None at all."

Her brain stuttered. "Oh, I—"

"And how does one prepare?"

"Um…"

"Where did you get this notion of a programme?"

"My sister. Philippa does this with her husband, and they both find it satisfactory. My mother did so with her first husband, and she said it was the best way. They did tell me not to ask directly, but I would like to know so that—"

"I am not a man for programmes in my bed."

"I see. I thought you might find it agreeable—"

His lips curled in aversion. "Furthermore, I do not find the terms "agreeable" or "satisfactory" satisfying in the least."

"Indeed, I shouldn't think a man of your great experience

would. That is why I asked as I only thought as to your needs and appetites, which are most likely quite…"

"Quite what?"

She licked at her bottom lip. "Advanced. Perhaps yours are greater or different from Mr. Holyfloke's."

His eyes blazed as he approached her, and her heartbeat kicked up. She could feel the heat flaring off his body as he grew closer and closer. His warm fingers cupped her chin, tilting it upwards toward him. "I have a very great appetite, my sweet one. Women have appetites as well."

"Yes. Yes, we do."

"I'm finding that I would like to discover yours and fulfill them one by one. Especially as our first time was cut quite short." He spoke slowly, his words an ominous drumbeat on her heart.

"That is quite fair and gallant of you, my lord."

"Fair, eh? You have been told otherwise?" His warm hand slid down her silky throat, cuffing her there, applying the slightest pressure.

Her eyes widened at the possessive nature of the gesture, the all-encompassing claiming of his hand. "Y-Yes."

"You have been told to be obedient to your husband?"

"I have."

"To never say no to him? To spread your thighs for him when he so desires so he may do as he wishes whenever he wishes?"

The breath burned in her throat as he drove one thigh between her legs, inciting a fiery pressure just *there*, a dire need for friction. "Indeed, both my mother and sister said the very same. And an aunt, as well."

"What else did your sister tell you about congress with her husband? Did you ask her or…"

"I asked her, yes."

"Hmm, you're curious." A noise rumbled in his chest as his

thigh moved between her legs, applying pressure to her very centre.

She let out a ragged breath. "I've always been curious."

His fingers tugged at the edges of her dress at her bosom, exposing more flesh, and the cool night air raced over her skin. He brushed his lips across the tops of her breasts. "Tell me what they told you."

"To always express pleasantness even if I am uncomfortable, for I will mostly be uncomfortable. To endure for however long my husband wishes to partake. To always do as I'm told, no matter what he wishes of me."

He licked at her ear and whispered, "And what, pray tell, is your brother-in-law's favourite way to take his wife?" A delicious shiver traveled up and down her neck.

"She on all fours, him taking her from behind," she replied.

He rubbed his thumb against her lower lip. "And how does she find that?"

"She said it was agreeable."

His lips twisted. "Agreeable? That is all she knows, is it?"

"She seemed content."

"Agreeable doesn't interest me, Georgina. Nor does content. And they certainly will not interest you. You are no lifeless instrument for me to use. In and out, done." He licked her throat, and a whimper escaped her. "No, my lady. I require much, much more."

"What is it you require?"

"Your full participation." His tongue lashed over her lips. "Your pleasure mixing with mine."

Her eyes flared. "What you did to me in London….when you kissed my…"

"When I licked your cunny?"

"Hmm," was all she could manage.

"Say it."

"When you licked my cunny," she breathed. Her cheeks

reddened, and his cock hardened against her middle setting off an ache she'd never known before in her cunny.

"You enjoyed it? Say it, Georgie. Tell me."

She pressed herself against his hard body, her hands sliding up his chest. "I enjoyed it. I enjoyed it very much. I did not know that *that* was possible."

"That and so much more. Did you find it illicit?" His tongue trailed up her throat to behind her ear, and she trembled in his hold.

"Yes…"

Their lips were so very close that his warm breath fanned her face. She was mesmerized. A short knock at the door made her stumble back.

"My lady?" came the voice of her lady's maid from the other side of the door.

"Do you wish your maid to undress you this evening?" he whispered hoarsely.

"No. I want my husband to undress me."

A grunt rumbled in his chest. He liked that. Charles shouted out: "Go away." The servant's steps quickly retreated down the hallway. His hands stroked her back and slid down to her waist.

Her breath caught, her insides tumbled and tightened. "I also did not know that women could enjoy congress in general. I hoped, I thought surely they must if men did. How could Nature be so unkind to our sex?"

"Nature is not unkind. She is most fair to the fairer sex. Only men, the bastards, keep it a secret." He pulled her in closer and his hips ground against her as his hands slid down to her rear, keeping her where he wanted her, providing the friction her helpless body so desired.

Her head tipping back, she pressed against him. Intoxicating. "A secret?" she breathed through the haze.

"I believe men are afraid that if all women found this out,

they would become demanding of them and also seek out pleasures of their own."

"A great many women certainly do, do they not?"

He lifted her dress up her body, over her head, and let it fall to the floor. Her breasts strained from her corset. She could feel the heaviness of his gaze on her flesh, feel it in her blood, in her very centre. "Indeed they do. Do you wish to seek out your pleasures, Georgina?"

"I do. I've always wanted to." *And I want to with you, Charles Montclare, roared through her brain.*

He cupped a breast, squeezed a nipple between his fingers, and took it in his mouth, brushing it with his teeth, suckling it, savouring it. Fiery explosions went off in her body, and she gripped his arms. "I have one concern—"

"Which is?"

"I fear that you are perhaps accustomed to a certain level of experience and agility that serves your needs to the fullest… and I do not have that. Yet."

He drew a thumb across her damp lips. "Lady Ryvves, know this—I am thrilled that I am your first in all these things. That your experience begins with me. That you shall discover your agility and your needs with me, and I shall strive to fulfill those needs."

She blinked at his words, his raw, deep voice. The promise of bliss indeed.

"Tonight, you will cry out my name when I bring you to your release, and that shall be devastatingly satisfying to your husband. That is what I require of you, my delicious Countess, your pleasure."

"Release? Ah yes…that is what we call that moment when…"

"That moment, yes. You enjoyed it?"

"I did."

"Tonight, if you wish, I shall lick and tease every inch of

you, Georgie. Kiss every corner, every curve, discover you, as you shall discover me. What say you?"

A shudder shot through her. "Yes, I wish it so. And, may I ask—"

"Ask me anything." Grinning, he pushed off his frock coat. Undid his necktie. Kicked off his shoes.

"Will you seek out congress with other women? If I do not please you, of course, you should…"

He stilled, his shirt hanging open, revealing a smooth sculpted chest, a tense torso that she yearned to touch. He came to her, cupping her chin once more, lifting her gaze to his. "I do not wish to seek pleasures elsewhere. You are my wife, and you please me greatly." His gaze was steady, his tone unrelenting.

Her heart stopped. "How do you know?"

"I know."

"But we only had that once after I brazenly insisted that you…"

"Ruin you." His eyes gleamed at her. "And it was much too swift and brisk, and we did not finish, which was not what I would have wanted for your first time."

She swallowed hard. "What did you want for my first time?"

A grin broke over his lips. "To lavish you with kisses and fill you with hard, deep strokes. To bring you to release not once, but a number of times in a number of ways."

She groaned, and he turned her around and expertly undid her corset, tossing it to the floor, the thud of the heavy fabric making her blink. He pulled on her chemise, and she raised her arms, and up it flew over her head. She was bare. Bare to a man. To her husband. Bare to Charles.

Groans rose up behind her. "So beautiful." His hands cupped her arse cheeks, and she gasped as they slid over her hips down between her legs, where she pulsed with need. His fingers grazed and teased and stroked as her heart beat wildly.

He slid those two fingers into her mouth. Wet fingers. "Taste your desire, Georgina." She suckled them, devoured them. It was her, her taste on him. "I've done that to you. Me." His free hand squeezed a breast possessively, his hard length pressed against her rear. "You deserve a feast, and I shall give that feast to you. Our bodies shall celebrate together." He turned her around to face him, his lips taking hers, his kiss taking her breath away.

Her knees weakened. "Celebrate? What an idea…"

"Yes, woman. Kiss me."

A tremor went off inside her at his command, and she kissed him, her lips parting immediately, her tongue sliding against his. This was what she always wanted, wasn't it? She'd always been eager for sensation, eager to learn, eager to experience all that congress could be.

And now she would with Charles.

Georgina's fingers dug into his flesh as Charles lifted her in his arms and lay her on his bed. He rid himself of the last of his clothes, and her hips twisted at the sight of such male magnificence. Laying down next to her at last, he took her hand and put it to his chest, and slid it down his taut torso. "Touch me. Touch me everywhere."

Chapter Thirty-Two

Georgina

The candlelight glimmering around them, Georgina's fingers swept down his sleek torso, through a thin line of curls, to his manhood.

"I want you to know me," he whispered in the shadows. "All of me."

Her hand enclosed his hard length. Smooth and long and thick. Georgina's heart squeezed in her chest. Her lips brushed over the hard plain of his breast, and a shudder went through him. A shudder that encouraged her, excited her. Meant the world to her.

Sitting up beside him, she pushed him back against the bed, her hands stroking his cock. She let out a soft moan as her fingers found his balls and cupped them. His body seized, and he let out a grunt. He took her hand and spit in it. "Stroke me."

She did so, from the base of his shaft up to the wet tip and down again. "Tell me —"

"Harder. Quicker," he bit out.

She did as he said, and he grew even firmer in her hand. She wanted nothing more than to feel his velvety smoothness between her lips, to kiss the core of him. To give him the kind of intense pleasure he had so freely given her. She would.

"I want to kiss you there. I want to give you the same pleasure you gave me."

"Do it."

She climbed in between his legs. Leaning over, she brushed his cock with her lips.

His hips twisted under her. "Georgie…"

Her tongue stroked his entire length, circling the thick, wet tip of him. His breath shuddered as she coaxed pleasure from him, teased him. "Tell me how, Charles. I want to learn."

"Take me in your mouth. I want to see your mouth swallow me. Want to see my cock between your beautiful lips."

Her hands slid over his hips to his muscled rear and gripped his flesh as she suckled his tip, and with her eyes on him, she took his cock in her mouth.

He dug his hands in her hair. "Fuck, look at you. Yes, yes….Watch your teeth, ah, yes…." Groaning, he angled his hips and slowly eased deeper into her mouth. Her eyes widened, and her lips stretched as she took in his thick length. His entire body clenched and jerked at her intent strokes.

She found a rhythm at last. The very core of her body throbbed as she took in his moans and the tightness of his jaw, his muscles contracting around her, the thickness of him between her lips. Charles let out a growl and with a hand at her chin, pulled her off his cock, and flipped her back on the bed.

She touched his chest, sleek with sweat. "Did I do something that did not please you?"

He let out a dark laugh. "Your mouth is perfection, and I am quite undone, but I must slow us both down."

He took two of her fingers in his mouth, and she cried out as he sucked on them. Releasing them, he brought them to her cunt and guided her hand in gentle circular motions over her nub. "You told me once that you'd touched yourself before."

"But I never found that release that you gave me, only a pleasantness."

"There will be no mere pleasantness any longer for you, madame. Not with me." He spread her legs open wider and raised them, her knees now bent. "Go on. I want to watch you find your release."

"Watch me?"

"Do it." Charles licked up an inner thigh, his gaze locked on hers as she stroked herself. "I could watch you do this all day." His hand fisted his cock, and he rubbed himself, following her rhythm which made a sting flare through her. Their breathing grew louder, heavier.

He leaned down, and his tongue, hot and wet, swiped at her fingers, licking her there where she worked. On a cry, her pelvis arched up, seeking more of him. His tongue lashed down her slit to her backside. As she continued to tease her nub, he slid his fingers inside her wet cunt and stroked. "Don't stop, Georgie. Don't stop."

He increased his tempo, his fingers churning inside her, coaxing a new intense pleasure from her body. Trembling, she cried out. She knew not where she began and where she ended.

Raising himself over her, he removed his fingers, slapped her hand out of his way, and drove inside her, filling her with one deep thrust.

She cried out, her head knocking back. The world stopped.

His lips brushed hers. "You feel my cock inside you, Georgie?"

"I do..." She squirmed underneath him, relishing his weight upon her, the heat of his wet skin on hers. Her body was desperate. It wanted more, she wanted more. More sensation. More of Charles inside her.

"Look at me, love. Look at me."

Her gaze found his as his slow, steady thrusts built that profound pressure in her body.

"Touch yourself again. This way you shall add to your pleasure as I take your cunt, and your release will be even more powerful."

On a small moan, she did as he directed. The lewd sounds of her fingers sliding through her wet flesh made her lust explode.

"My beautiful, beautiful girl." His body pounded into hers. "You're all mine now, all mine."

She melted utterly at his words. "And you are mine," she gritted out as her legs tightened around his hips, keeping him close.

He drove into her hard and fast. "Yours. Yours. Oh damn, Georgie…" he grunted, his cock throbbing inside her.

Helpless in his grip, powerful in his grip, submitting all that she was to him, giving him all that he wanted. There was equality in their claiming. Equal need. A hunger that fed the other's. He was an animal consuming, coming to life. Giving her life.

She couldn't think, only feel, and she gave in, giving herself over to sensation. She could take no more. The pleasure tore through her body, and his name ripped from her lips.

Now she was truly his.

Chapter Thirty-Three

Charles

CHARLES STRETCHED OUT HIS BODY. Opened his eyes to the sun's glare peeking through the openings in the curtains. The pillows next to him bore the indentation of another person's head.

He grinned. *His wife.*

They had enjoyed each other last night. Just as he'd thought, she was not timid but eager to learn. Eager to feel.

And he'd allowed himself to feel it all with her.

He half hoped she'd still be in his bed when he woke, but she'd left. Another thing she assumed wives did, he was sure. Retreat to their own bedchambers to recover after their husbands were done with them.

He'd never actually fallen asleep with a woman before he and Georgina had shared a bed at the inn on the way home from London. Why would he have? That had never been the point of his philandering with ladies. The point was to enjoy her to the fullest and get the hell out because he didn't want to be drawn into conversations afterward nor caught by a husband.

Spitting in his hand, he gripped his hard length and stroked quickly, his hips pulsing. Right now, he wanted to be caught by Georgina.

He wanted to see her response. Feel her eager touch. Feel her fierce determination to please him, to explore, to learn.

Swiving had always been a one-way pursuit for him from the very beginning.

But with Georgie, dear God, Georgie…it was different. It was an experience. Every kiss, suckle, bite, stroke, pinch, nip earned him a delicious moan, sigh, gasp, tighter grip, a cry, a breathy plea for more.

Charles wanted all of her. He was a bloody lucky man.

He'd heard of many a wife turning the other way while her husband got on with servicing himself whenever he wished. She would not refuse, complain, nor say a word. Simply lay there, lay still, endure until he was done.

Not he and Georgina. *Not his wife.* His seed exploded in his hand, and he let out a groan.

He was gloriously fortunate indeed.

Charles got out of his bed, washed, and went to the double doors that separated their rooms. He opened one door gently, just a crack, and there she was. Her hair was being brushed by the young lady's maid he'd just hired for her. His bride was humming to herself, her dressing gown around her, her feet bare.

The girl he always knew, the woman who was now his wife.

All his. A smile curved Charles's lips as heat flared through his veins.

He'd leave her to her preparations. She was settling into a new home as its mistress, and she would have to create a new routine for herself. He would leave her to it. He returned to his bedchamber and wrote a letter to her brother Thomas to kindly expect them later this morning to retrieve his wife's belongings. His manservant attended him and had the note despatched forthwith.

After he dressed, Charles made his way to the dining room, where breakfast had been set on the sideboard. He treated himself to a full dish of eggs and warm rolls, cheese, and a generous slice of ham.

His wife entered the room. "Good morning." Her cheeks flushed the second he met her gaze.

"Good morning. I assumed you would take tea in your rooms."

"I did enjoy a cup, but I found I was hungry for a full breakfast and wanted to enjoy it with my husband, if that is to your liking?"

"Your hunger is very much to my liking, madame."

Letting out a laugh, she served herself. Charles gestured at the servants to leave them, and they darted out of the room. Georgina sat down next to him.

He buttered another roll. "I was surprised to have woken to an empty bed."

She put down the jam. "Oh? I had presumed you would want your chamber to yourself after..."

"Make no presumptions about me, Georgina. I greatly enjoyed our night together, and I fully expect to enjoy our mornings as well."

"Mornings too?"

"This strikes you as unusual?"

Is it not part of the prescribed marital programme you had spoken of?"

"No, it's not." She laughed. "I must say, after giving it some thought, I feel a programme would not work for us, Lord Ryvves." She bit into her crusty roll.

"I am most pleased to hear it, wife, but what has brought about his change?"

"You." She brushed his lips with hers. Gentle, warm. Marvelous.

Sunlight suddenly poured through the room, the clouds having moved. Her skin glowed. Her brown eyes gleamed. The rich blue dress she wore was almost the colour of the sky, not that dark hue he'd noted when she first entered the room. A delicate creature, but no, she wasn't fragile. Georgina was strong and vibrant.

He cleared his throat. "I sent word to Thomas at Fairthorn that we would be coming to collect your belongings."

"Did you? Thank you, Charles."

"The carriage will be out front for us in two hours' time. I'll drive us there."

"I am to see my brother and mother again. They will see that we are married and not living in scandal." She chewed on her lip as she pushed her plate away.

"You're anxious?"

"A bit, yes."

"I'll be with you. We shall all be polite, and we shall not stay long. Don't worry."

"I'll try."

Chapter Thirty-Four

Charles

THE WINDING hilly road that led to Fairthorn seemed to delight Georgina. A smile curled her lips from ear to ear as she took in the lush green grasses and the groves of trees. "Almost there."

His hands guided the reins of the carriage. "Yes, almost there."

She loved the country. She loved *their* country. Who would have thought that the young lady who had so much to recommend her and was the toast of many a party in London since she had come out several years ago, would be so content in the country?

A pinch of bitterness filled his nostrils. Like his pipe when he hadn't bothered to clean it. No. More acrid, thicker.

"Is that smoke?" Georgina pointed to a yellowish-white billow in the sky before them.

Charles urged the horses forward, and they charged ahead, entering Fairthorn. Black smoke curled from the front drive before the manor house. Flames wrestled and flew high.

"Madame, please!" a young maid cried out. "Please, I beg you!"

"Get out of my sight!" Georgina's mother shouted as she

flung objects into the flames. The crying servant girl ran off. Other servants stood and watched, unable to do anything as their mistress held sway over destruction. The flames before her multiplied and grew bolder. The plume of smoke thickened and blackened and billowed as she threw more objects into the fire.

"What the hell is she doing?" Charles brought their carriage to a halt and jumped off.

Thomas ran out the front door, and down the steps. "Mother! Mother!"

"Ah, there they are! Welcome, my lord and lady," said Mrs. Townsend, her face red, shimmering with perspiration. She extended her arm and bowed to them in mock tribute.

"Dear God!" Thomas turned to the servants. "Fetch water. Put this out at once!" They dashed away.

"No, Thomas! All this dross shall burn."

"No, Mother, no!" Georgina's shouts rose from behind him as she rushed to the flames.

"Georgina!" Charles hooked an arm around her waist, pulling her back.

"Papa's paintings, his letters! My sketchbooks!" she cried out, shoving against Charles, but he held her fast.

"You've destroyed Georgina's things?" Charles stood on the other side of the fire from Mrs. Townsend, Georgina struggling, twisting in his iron grip. "Why?" he roared.

"Dear God..." Thomas's lips parted as he took in the destruction.

Rounding the fire, Mrs. Townsend cast Charles a foul look as she tracked toward her daughter. "Trollop. You dare come here with your whore monger to take your belongings?"

"They were all I had left of Father! How could you do this?"

Mrs. Townsend's eyes flared. "Nothing but refuse, all of it, polluting my house for years. Your scrawlings, your father's cheap tokens."

"Do you hate me so much?"

"With your brazen and vulgar behaviour, you made your hate for your family quite plain. You have disgraced us all. Your sister's husband is most displeased with her. I can no longer live here, but your brother must, and what must he endure."

"Mama, please." Thomas darted to his mother's side. "Georgina did not run off to Gretna Green with a soldier or a servant. She is married to a man of great title and wealth. She—"

"That does not blot out her betrayal nor her disgrace. What she did was undignified and shameful." Her cold eyes locked on her daughter once again. "Were you so set on having a Montclare in your bed?"

"Madame," Charles warned her.

Mrs. Townsend's searing gaze landed on him. "Oh, I suppose we should be grateful that the present Earl of Ryvves deigned to marry his dead brother's slut?"

"Mother!" Thomas's eyes widened.

"You are angry that she undermined your scheme to use her for your own benefit," Charles said through gritted teeth. "You are angry that you could not control her."

"Duplicitous schemes are the hallmarks of you Montclares. Every single one of you." Her contempt and spite were as scorching as the flames burning before them and as thick as the black smoke polluting the air.

"Mother, please." Thomas gripped his mother's arm. "I beg you, stop."

She only shook him off and moved closer to Charles. "One night with you and your brother indulging her base instincts and she selfishly turned against her family."

"You have said quite enough, Madame." Charles's voice was loud and firm. Georgina fell lax in his arms, burying her face in his chest, and he wrapped his arm around her tightly. "You will stay away from me and my wife. You are not welcome at our home, either here or in town. If, one day, you come to your senses and wish to make amends to Georgina—"

"Amends? I?" Mrs. Townsend's voice exploded. "Oh, not I."

"Yes, amends for what you have done today, for the vile things you have said."

"Oh, you impudent, unprincipled blackguard. Villain!"

Thomas's back shot up, a hand in the air. "My lord, please forgive her. With recent events, you can understand our mother is in a state of shock."

"Do not apologise to him," Mrs. Townsend muttered.

"I care not what you think of me or my family, Mrs. Townsend. My only care is for the welfare and well-being of my wife. That is all." Turning away from them, he led a listless Georgina back to their carriage.

Securing her in the seat, he climbed on next to her and picked up the reins. Her hiccuping breaths twisted in his heart. He bid the horses forward, and they charged down the drive. "There is nothing here for you any longer, Georgie. Nothing."

Chapter Thirty-Five

Charles

CHARLES'S HORSES sped away from Fairthorn, but the smoke remained in the air.

"I never ever expected this sort of thing from my mother. Such hatred, such cruelty."

"She is a bitter woman. And it seems she's hated my family for quite some time."

"I have no idea why…"

"Now her daughter has married the devil himself."

"I'm sorry, Charles, so sorry for all the awful things she said to you."

"They are nothing to me, and you have nothing to apologise for." He urged the horses on faster, his posture straightening. "I shall buy you all new things, anything you wish…everything you wish…clothes, shoes, hats, ribbons, and books."

"None of those matter to me like my sketches and my father's letters. The small paintings he'd brought me from his trips."

"Of course." His shoulders tightened, and his chest flared with heat. He couldn't bear to see her so distraught. Such violence perpetrated against her by her own mother was an enormous shock. All her life, she had felt safe and secure and rooted in her family at that house. No more.

Now all of that was gone.

"We shall go tomorrow to the tailors' and choose the grandest toilette for you."

"I've already done that with Justine."

"We shall order more and more. I wish to dress my Countess of Ryvves as her spirit dictates."

She only tilted her head, water filling her eyes. "You are so very generous with me," her voice was just above a painful whisper.

He clenched his jaw. "Georgina, you are the most positive and happy of humans I have ever met. To see you thus is killing me." His hand gripped her thigh.

She undid the ties of her bonnet, and it fell to her feet as she wiped at her face. But the tears still fell. A droplet pooled on his hand, wet, warm. She was hurting, and he would not let this go on. He could not bear it.

He pulled the horses to the side of the road, stopping them. "Look at me." She lifted her watery gaze to him immediately. "Oh, Georgie," he murmured softly, stroking the side of her face, and she leaned into his gloved palm. His heart ticked up, his blood racing at seeing her in such pain.

"Your mother showed you her true self. There is no denying it. Feel her betrayal, feel her coldness. It was real. She is angry at both of us. Angry that we've thwarted her plans for you, for herself." He leaned down and kissed the side of her temple. The fragrance in her hair instantly brought him back to her sleeping on his chest last night, their bodies tangled in a decadent harmony.

He swept back a lock of her hair. "But this spectacle she put on for our benefit, whose sole intention was to hurt you, was most childish, and thus, the humiliation lies with her." His thumb wiped through the tears on the skin of her hand, stroking her flesh. "If you choose to forgive her one day, I shall support you in this decision. But for now, trouble yourself no more. You must learn to consider yourself first."

"Perhaps that very thing was my very defect—I only considered my desires, and thus, sacrificed my family's wishes and their happiness."

"Is their happiness greater than yours, of more worth, simply because you are the youngest and a female?"

She had no reply. Her lips pressed together.

"I refuse to allow you to wallow in guilt over her nasty tirade."

"I've never seen my mother like that."

"Everyone hides a deep fury for whatever reason. We become schooled in keeping it bottled up, sealed inside us, and then one day, if the circumstances are all tilted in a certain way—boom—that seal is suddenly broken, and a Pandora's box of rage is released."

"You seem to be familiar with this Pandora's box."

"I am, Georgie. I am." He let out a breath. "Think not of her any longer. The more you do, the more her spite wins and the more it ransacks your spirit."

"Is that a command, husband?"

"It is indeed. We are married, and you are free of any obligation to them."

They rode on in silence.

She let out a sigh. "I shall miss my brother most of all, I think."

"Thomas is a good sort. He may come round after a time."

"Yes. I hope so." She averted her gaze. "I always thought of myself as a good, caring sort of person. Perhaps I am only selfish."

"If you are selfish, then I am truly the devil."

The urge to pull her out of this dark and sticky cobweb of feelings overwhelmed him. An idea came to him, and he changed course at the top of the hill, directing the horses to the left instead of the right.

She sat up straighter. "Where are we going?"

"You'll soon see." He directed the horses off the main road and onto a well-worn path through the woods. He and Brandon and Hugh had ridden through here often in their youth. Charles brought the horses to a stop and tied them to a tree. He held out his hand to her and helped her descend from the carriage. "Trust me?"

Her shoulders eased. "I do trust you."

His chest surged with warmth, and he bowed his head to her, leading her to the nearby footpath.

"This is Wolfsgate land, is it not?"

"It is. Our friends will not mind us enjoying a stroll on their property."

"So a walk in the woods is what you prescribe for my refreshment?"

He only laughed darkly, and the sound made her back straighten. At last, they reached the folly, a temple ruin that Brandon's father had built for his mother when they'd first married.

Georgina let go of his arm and walked in between the faux Greek columns. "Isn't it beautiful?"

You are beautiful, he thought to himself, taking in her delicate smile, her soft dark eyes.

He went inside the folly to the stone bench padded with thick pillows and sat. "The echo is splendid in here. Brandon and I would have contests as to who could make the vilest sounds." A small smile flickered over her features, and he held out his hand to her. "Georgie." She took his hand, and he brought her between his legs. "I want your desires to resound, to fill this space. I want your desire free and clear and loud."

"What are you saying?"

He slid his hands under her dress and stroked the bare skin of her thighs. His thumbs found the nub of her cunny and gently applied pressure and stroked, stroked, stroked.

Her lips parted, a small moan escaping them. She grabbed onto his shoulders.

"That is what I mean, my love, only louder. You have only yourself to please."

Her hand went to his face and caressed it. "And you."

This woman. His heart thumped in his chest. "It would please me for you to take me."

Her jaw slackened. "Me to…"

He undid his trousers, shoving them down, his stiff, swollen cock thrilled to be free at last. "Take it, take what you will of me. Find your desire."

Licking her lips, she tore off her gloves, letting them drop to the stone floor, and reached out and wrapped a hand around his cock.

Charles's jaw tightened as she stroked, stroked, stroked. She licked at his lips, and his breath caught. His head fell back against the damp stone wall, and she bit his lip. His hands cupped her arse cheeks and he brought her closer. Bunching her dress in a fist, he held it up.

"Bring your legs here around me and take my cock."

She blinked.

"Take it, Countess."

She lifted herself up around him, and he slid his cock against her wet cunny. She moaned at the promise of what she would be getting.

"Lift up," he breathed.

She did so, and he positioned himself at her entrance. "Harsh measures are in order to revive you from this dark cloud that has descended upon your spirit. I will not have it. I will not allow anyone to pollute you thus. Take your cock and pleasure yourself. Give voice to your desire. Give voice to your anger."

She lowered herself on his cock, taking him in inch by inch, filling herself in one long thrust. A groan heaved from his chest.

She clung to his shoulders as she moved up and then ground down on him. With one hand, he stroked her bosom, nipping at the delicate flesh. Her fingers dug in his hair. Moaning, she quickened her pace.

"Feel it all, all that I'm giving you. Feel it and show me what that is. Share it with your husband. Share all of it. Your anger, your pleasure." He'd never spoken like this before to anyone, yet the need to help her disentangle herself from her mother's cruelty overwhelmed him.

She quickened her pace, grinding down on him

"You feel so good, Georgina," he groaned against her skin. "My wild girl. You want this, don't you? You want all of it?"

"Yes, all of it." She shuddered as his fingertips dug into the silky flesh of her bottom, urging her on, keeping her close, his hips meeting hers with his own urgency.

Her groans and whimpers intensified. She was angry, she was hungry, she was searching. Sliding his fingers between her legs, he teased her nub. She groaned loudly, her breaths ragged. Charles brought his wet fingers to her lips, and she instantly took them in her mouth and suckled them as she devoured his cock.

What a sight...

"This is what my cock does to my wife."

She only moaned in reply, her gleaming gaze hanging on his.

"Do you want more of me, Countess?"

Her eyes flashed. Another moan. "More." She clung to his neck.

On a grunt, he hammered his hips into hers, the wound in his stiff arm flaring with pain, but he didn't give a damn. Her dress slid from her shoulders, and the sight of her tightly pressed bosom doubled the heat in his balls.

The wall of pleasure built around them both, her jaw set, her eyes pleading with him, urging him on. He kept her close, his wound throbbing. Their gazes locked as they both chased their end together.

"Fuck, fuck…" he grunted.

"Charles…"

Her flesh streaked with red, and her head fell back. Shuddering, she sank on him, her pelvis grounding out its last, her movements slowing, lazy, satisfied. His cock shot its load inside her perfect cunny, and he buried his face in her breasts.

Holding him tightly, they remained locked on one another, their deep breaths filling the ruined temple. She kissed the top of his head. "I believe I am quite rejuvenated, sir." She lifted up from him, and he held her arm as she steadied herself on her feet.

He tucked himself back into his breeches. "Hold up your dress. I want to see you in the light."

A satisfied smile slid over her lips as she did so. He stroked his hand up the silky skin of a thigh, a thigh dripping with his spent seed. He slid it up to her cunt and stroked there, tucking it into her.

"Are you marking me like a beast, my lord?"

"I am a beast with you, Countess." He tugged her close and kissed her deeply.

A dog barked close by, and Georgina let out a slight gasp, her body stiffening in his hold. His arms tightened around her.

"When you're finished, do come up to the house for tea. We'd love to see you," came Brandon's voice from outside the folly.

Georgina burst out laughing.

Chapter Thirty-Six

Charles

THE FRONT DOORS of Wolfsgate flew open, and Justine rushed out onto the steps. "How wonderful to see you both! Come in! Come in!" She hugged Georgina, taking her by the arm and bringing them into the house, Charles and Brandon following them.

Tea was promptly served in the front parlour, the sun streaming through the old leaded paned windows.

"I found our friends at the folly and invited them over." Brandon poured Charles a glass of wine.

"We aren't disturbing you and the children, are we?" asked Georgina.

"No, your timing is perfect. They're both asleep at the same time. Somehow Nanny and I managed it quite nicely today. A true victory." She handed Georgina a cup of tea. The selection of sandwiches and biscuits beckoned.

"I was coming home from one of my tenants whose pasture had flooded," said Brandon.

Charles drank and stretched out his legs. "The river has swollen this week with all the rains, hasn't it?"

"Indeed. There are sure to be more instances."

"I'll check with my steward today."

"What brought the newlyweds out of their home on this fine day?" asked Brandon, winking at Charles.

Georgina told them of their morning at her brother's house.

"How dreadful," said Justine.

"Ambitions and greed get the best of people, twisting things into ugly, ugly messes," murmured Charles, a hand rubbing his wounded arm which ached with the strain of driving the carriage and then happily driving his wife to her release.

"Quite true," said Justine. "My dear, I am quite sorry that you've lost your father's letters and the small paintings he'd left you."

"They are the greatest loss. It's funny to think I used to place so much importance on my lovely things—my dresses, my silver hair brushes, my jewellery. Now I have my liberty."

Justine squeezed her arm. "And a husband."

Georgina laughed softly. "Yes, and a husband."

Justine leaned in closer to Georgina. "You are happy, my friend? I realise it's only been a day or two, but are things going well between you? Is he good to you?"

"They are going well, and yes." Georgina glanced at her husband, his long legs stretched out, his blond hair mussed as he spoke to Brandon, gesturing with a hand. That hand that held her firmly grasped her, kept her safe in his embrace. The hand that knew how to stroke, caress, tease. The deep timbre of his voice blazed hotly inside her. "Yes, my husband is very, very good to me."

The cakes were eaten, tea and brandy were consumed. Hours later, Charles and Georgina rose to leave. As they reached the entrance hall, children's voices rose from upstairs.

"They're awake," said Brandon.

"I do want to see my godson, Graven," said Charles.

"And he'll want to see you." Brandon darted up the stairs. "I'll bring him down."

Georgina's gaze landed on the portrait of Brandon's mother

on the stairwell, on the pearl and diamond and ruby necklace Lady Caroline wore, and that same feeling took hold of her once more. *It must be…*

But how could it be?

"Justine, the necklace your mother-in-law is wearing in her portrait is remarkable."

"Isn't it beautiful?"

"The wolf head and claws for a clasp are quite extraordinary."

"Lord Jeremy had the necklace made for his wife when she gave birth to Brandon."

"Ah. A true Graven family heirloom."

"Yes. I was fortunate enough to have seen it on her once when I'd first come here as a child, but unfortunately, it's been lost to us."

"Lost?"

"After the shipwreck when Brandon was believed to be dead, his uncle and his cousin William pillaged Wolfs-gate. Paintings, sculptures, the finest furniture, and jewellery. At the time, Brandon's father was on his deathbed, and yet he realised what was going on. He gave me his signet ring to hide from them, to keep it safe for Brandon."

"How awful."

"It was. I managed to hide the ring and the earrings Lady Caroline is wearing in the portrait, but sadly, not the necklace. It was one of the first things that William snatched in his hateful fervour for revenge on Brandon."

"Do you know if William kept it for his wife, or did he sell it?"

"I'm not sure. Even though Amanda adores jewellery, I never once saw her wear it. I can only assume he sold it to the highest bidder he could find."

"Must have been worth quite a tidy sum," Georgina mused. *A sum a Duke could easily afford.*

"It is lost to us forever. And neither of us likes to dwell on its loss or those times."

"You are quite right, my dear." Georgina pressed her hand in hers.

She was positive that this was the necklace the Duchess of Oakley wore to the ball in London that night. Positive. It had made an impression on her. Not only because it was a beautiful piece, but perhaps because she'd seen it before here in this very painting.

The nanny came down the stairs with baby Caroline in her arms, and Justine rushed forward to take her daughter.

Georgina reached out to her husband. "Charles, I'd like to show you something—look at Lady Caroline's necklace."

"Ah, it's remarkable."

She whispered, "I am certain I saw the Duchess of Oakley wearing it at the ball in London, but not with the wolf clasp showing."

"Perhaps it is similar. Surely Brandon and Justine have this necklace in their possession?"

"No, they don't. Justine told me that when Brandon was thought to be lost at sea, William and his father stole many items from Wolfsgate, including this necklace."

"I had no idea."

"When I danced with the Duke at the ball, the Duchess and my sister's husband danced alongside us, and afterward we spoke. I admired it from the very first. William must have sold it to the Duke."

"Uncle Charles!" Little feet battered down the hallway. "Uncle Charles!"

He grinned as his godson, Jeremy, lunged at him, his dark mop of hair flying. He lifted the boy up in his embrace. "Well, look at you, young man. You've grown so much since I saw you last. What is your mother feeding you? Magic beans?" He tickled Jeremy's belly, and the boy giggled uncontrollably. "Magic soup?"

Jeremy shook his head and pouted. "I don't like sooooop."

Charles laughed.

Jeremy reached out his hand to Georgina. "Miss Georgina!"

"My darling." Georgina kissed his chubby hand.

"We have a surprise for you," said Charles, and Jeremy's eyes widened. "Miss Georgina and I are married, so you can now call her aunt if you like. Would you like that?"

"Oooo… yes." He nibbled on his thumb, a tiny smile forming on his lips.

Justine rubbed her son's back, taking him from Charle's embrace as Georgina fawned over baby Caroline in the nanny's arms in the hallway.

"Charles, what Georgina's mother did was awful," said Justine.

"It was."

"I am so very pleased that she has you at her side. And I am also greatly pleased that you have her on yours."

He tilted his head at her. "You are confident in me as a husband? The man who once dissembled and played you falsely?"

"Most confident." Justine slid her arm through Charles's, her smile warm. "You have much to recommend you, my lord, and not only your title. I know that you are a caring, generous man, even if you don't let on to the rest of the world that you are, which is probably wise."

"You know I hold your opinion in the highest regard." He let out a heavy breath. "I never thought I'd marry. And suddenly I am and to Georgina."

"Life plays crazy tricks on us, does it not? Crazy, awful tricks of all kinds brought me and Brandon together, and yet, we found great happiness. It was not easy, but every day I knew that at the core was a friendship and fondness that we'd shared from childhood. I think you and Georgina share such a friendship and fondness as well."

"We do, yes."

"Build on that, gently. That is all. The rest will grow, and it may surprise you." She let out a small laugh.

"I must confess, it already has."

Chapter Thirty-Seven

Charles

BEFORE THEY WENT HOME, Charles took Georgina to the village stationer's shop and insisted she buy all the sketchbooks and pencils and supplies she desired. Once they entered the shop, her face lit up. She brushed his cheek with a kiss and went to speak with the owner.

The crisp tone of Georgina's voice diverted his attention from perusing the shop. A prickle of warmth raced through him as she ordered specific pigments and brushes and paper. She knew exactly what she wanted. And now, married to him, she was free to have it. To have it all. To enjoy it to the fullest.

And he would make sure she got it.

A lazy grin curled his lips as he imagined her riding his cock just as she'd done earlier today, informing him, in that very same decisive tone, how she'd like him to move—quicker, harder, gentler, slower, or not at all. Yes, perhaps she would prefer to take charge of their coupling, whilst telling him how to touch her, where to touch her, where to shove his tongue—

"Charles?"

Shifting his weight, he cleared his throat and dragged himself back to reality. *Stationers. Pencils. Paper.* "Yes?"

She touched his arm. "Charles, could we go to the Apothecary?"

"Are you unwell?" His back straightened.

"I am quite well. I would like to purchase ground pigments there. Our village has yet to have a colour shop."

"Of course."

They walked down the high street to the corner. In the window of the bookseller they spied a great many copies of the latest literary sensation.

"Ah, in London I heard talk of this novel, "The Monk." It has caused much outrage and sensation of late," said Georgina.

"The hero is a man of God?"

"The hero is a depraved monk.'Tis a tale of lust, filth, violence, and supernatural horrors."

His lips twisted in a smirk. "Ah, a modern romance?"

"Indeed," Georgina let out a laugh.

"With a monk as your husband's ancestor, it seems you have married fashionably, dear Georgina."

"I have indeed. So gratifying."

"Shall we purchase a copy and entertain ourselves with it?"

She bit her lip. "Yes, why not?"

They entered the booksellers, and Charles purchased a copy.

Next door was the apothecary, where the chemist knew Georgina. Other ladies came there to purchase remedies for their and their families' well being, Georgina would come here to purchase what ground pigments he had available. She placed her order, and the man packaged each one up for her.

"In London, I had managed to go one morning to Rowney's, the famed colour shop," she said to Charles as they waited.

"And missed a stroll in St. James?"

"I did. I had to lie to do it, but I did it."

"Shocking behaviour, madame."

She laughed. "What a delight it was. His specially formulated watercolour cakes are a marvel. I purchased a new water-colour box, chose the colours I wanted, several new brushes, some charcoals and pastels. But I'm sure my mother destroyed them all after I absconded with you."

"You must write to Rowney's today and order everything and more," said Charles.

"Even oils? Oil painting is considered a man's domain, lacking in female delicacy as the oils and solvents are so odorous and messy."

"You shall be able to enjoy that mess in your own atelier in the conservatory, won't you?"

"I simply wanted to make sure that it was agreeable to you."

"There's that odorous word again."

She laughed, and he squeezed her arm tighter. He loved making her laugh. "Enjoy your messes, Georgina."

She beamed at him. "Thank you, Charles."

The apothecary gave Georgina her package, Charles paid, and they left the shop. "I am eager to go home. There is something I'd like to show you that I know you will enjoy."

At Ironvine, Charles led her through the back stone terrace and down the wide staircase to the landscaped lawn with its carefully calculated rows of trees and hedges. Suddenly the tight geometry of the formal gardens ended, and a long rolling hill of bright green grass took over. At the end of the hill, a wood surrounded them, and they walked through where it was darker and quieter, the two of them sheathed in nature.

"This is quite different from the formal gardens around the house," she said.

"Those gardens were my great-grandfather and grandfather's doing. They both loved order and felt if their surroundings reflected that order, it would inspire order in one's life and inner being."

"Were they satisfied with the results of their garden then?"

"Not at all." Charles laughed. "Grandfather had brought some famous designer from Newcastle here to redo it. I believe he even put it in his will that my father, his only child, was to never destroy the garden or change its design, for he considered it one of his great works in life."

"Man's rules imposed over nature. I warrant nature, at some point, will violently rebuff such artifice and strictures put upon her, don't you? I believe she has her own mind and spirit, that try as he might, man cannot control her."

"You may be right. I think my great grandfather put the house and those gardens in motion to rebuff the original Ironvine."

"What do you mean by the original?"

"Remember, the French monk?"

"Brother Laurent, yes."

"He built himself a small castle — ah, careful." He took her hand in his and led her away from a rocky patch.

"Oh yes, of course, I've heard of the Ironvine castle…"

"Does the idea fire your imagination, Georgie?"

"It does."

"I thought it would."

The trees had thinned out, and they emerged on another hill overlooking a thin river at the bottom of the valley. On a small pair of islands stood a lone medieval tower, its fragmented walls connected to a house on land, which was mostly in ruins, half the roof gone. A courtyard overgrown with a riot of colourful flowering vines, thick bushes, and the remains of a stumpy gatehouse. A thin stone bridge stretched over the surrounding pond filled with flowering greens and stones of all sizes. Large ancient trees stretched their aging branches, and clumps of rhododendron gave a wild unfettered feel to the vista.

"I haven't been here in ages," murmured Charles.

The sandstone walls were clothed in climbing wisteria, roses, and clematis. A riot of reds, whites, blues, and purples.

"Beautiful." Georgina stopped in her tracks. "It's like a fairy tale."

"Originally, there were four of those castle towers. Now only that one remains of Brother Laurent's castle, which he used as a home. The house adjoining the castle was built later on, in the early 1600s, but that fell into decay as well. A century later, the family decided to build a new house up the hill where we live today."

She let go of his hand and ran down the hill toward the ruins.

"Careful, Georgie! The water seems high today."

She laughed out loud as she stepped over the great stones to the remains of the walkway, making her way to the castle tower. "It's like a folly, only it's not. It's better."

"How is it better?"

"Because it's a genuine ancient ruin, not a counterfeit meant to inspire feelings. This is real and inspires so much more. And it's your family history." She bent her head to the wisteria and took in their fragrance.

"We never saw it as having much worth or significance. Just an old structure from the past, falling apart, making a mess."

She faced him. "Is that what you've always been told to think, or is that how you see it?" He stilled, his brow furrowing. Had that truth caught Charles by surprise?

"I'm not sure." His gaze roved over the ruins, considering them anew, through Georgina's eyes.

"Wolfsgate's folly was recently built and made to look like a gothic and mysterious ruin on purpose," she said. "But Ironvine's is no theatrical tableau meant to inspire romantic feelings of a lost world, a faraway time. These ruins are authentically gothic and mysterious and have a real history. Ryvves history."

She moved closer to the tower, her hands stroking the smoothed stone as she walked around it. Raising herself up on her tiptoes, she attempted to peer over an opening in the stones to see inside. Georgina climbed up on a rock formation by the wall and lifted up on her toes.

Darting forward, he pulled her arm back. "No, Georgie. This thing is centuries old. It's falling apart. 'Tis unsafe."

"Oh bother…" Her gaze remained fixed on the dark interior, struggling to see.

"For God's sake, woman. Instead of that danger giving you pause, it's excited you all the more."

"I confess, it has." She bit her lip. "I must see inside one day. What secrets may be hiding in there to tell us something of its Montclare past."

"No, Georgie." That familiar cold hardness shuddered through him, and he pulled her back, taking her in his arms and setting her on the ground. "It's not safe."

She stroked the side of his face, easing the sudden tightness of his muscles. "What's wrong, Charles?"

"Nothing."

"You don't like it here. Why?"

"That's not true." He rubbed at his neck as he turned away from her.

"It's made you uneasy." She touched his arm. "Why?"

"From the time when my grandfather was a young boy, it was forbidden for anyone to enter the house and the castle tower. The structure is not stable, and the stones have been known to fall in storms and on their own."

She tilted her head. "You went in, didn't you?"

"In the summer when we were boys, Hugh and I would often come here to climb trees, hide and chase each other, go for a swim. One day we stayed here through sunset. There was a full moon, and it was beautiful. Light shone all over the valley, especially on the castle. Hugh dared me to go inside. I would go first, and he would follow so we could explore the old place together like Vikings looking for loot."

Her stomach tightened. "Did you go in?"

"I did. I climbed up right here." He pointed to the opening high up the wall where she'd attempted to lift herself up. "And that's when he pushed me. I fell into the darkness head first. Cut my face on the rocks, twisted my ankle, broke my arm."

"Oh no!"

"Same arm as the one he shot, in fact. I cried out for him. Shouted. I heard him laughing. And then the laugh faded until all I could hear were owls hooting and bats flapping about me."

"How horrible. What did you do?"

"Crawled about in the mud. Managed to find the hallway that led from the tower through to the house where there was a roof. Exhausted and in wretched pain, I lay there on the stone floor. Thankfully, the moonlight was very bright, streaming through the windows and the gaps in the ruined roof, making all sorts of odd shapes. I was convinced they were ghosts of the past and, as the intruder, they were angry at me for ruining their evening. The walls seemed to move in that eerie light, the very stones coming alive. There were so many odd sounds—the whistling wind, rustling. I feared there were ghosts. I was sure I felt a snake slither over my leg."

"He abandoned you on purpose in such a place at night? You must have been so frightened, felt so alone, in such pain."

He met her gaze, his lips parted. He had never told this story to anyone. He shifted his gaze to his boots. "I did feel frightened. Very alone."

"Did you see anything interesting inside the old house? You probably don't remember."

"Oh, I remember." He shifted his weight, his voice regaining a dash of its usual zest. "There wasn't any furniture, of course, but I was lying down on the ground, looking up, and I was sure the one wall was painted with some sort of decorative—I couldn't quite tell what it was—some sort of ribbon that ran along the walls. On one wall, it went up to the ceiling."

"A ribbon?"

"Might have been a garland…I couldn't make out the details. But I remember trying, to give myself something to focus on, latch onto. The wind had begun to howl through the stones and ruined roof overhead. I was so cold, upset, but being able to see the stars through the gaps in the roof, tracking that glittering garland, calmed me."

"How did you ever get out?"

"Our steward's son found me. Joss is only a few years older than I, a childhood friend of sorts, although my father and brother frowned upon any such associations. Joss found me and helped me to my feet and got me out of there."

"Oh, Charles… And what did Hugh say? Your father?"

"Hugh said that he thought I was playing a game, that I was treasure hunting inside. That I wanted to show him up by not coming out. It hadn't occurred to him that I was hurt or in trouble."

"Rubbish."

"My father only punished me for being wilful and disobedient. They didn't even ask me how I got out." He cleared his throat at the knot that had formed there. "My grandfather was still alive then. He'd said I was the first in a very, very long time to have gone inside the tower. 'Well done, boy,' he'd told me, much to Hugh's annoyance. I tried to feel proud of myself, but I could never quite muster it. I only felt a fool."

"You're no fool, Ryvves." She raised her hand to shield her eyes from the sun as she took in their surroundings, the hills, the woodlands on the other side of the ruins. "How different this aspect is from the manor's park. It's positively wild in comparison."

"It is, isn't it? My great-grandmother had this profusion of trees and these masses of azaleas and wisteria planted so that this 'unattractive mess would be more pleasing', and I quote."

"She did well. It's beautiful. What a blaze of colour, such lush abandon."

He laughed. "I'm glad you like it. This is the perfect time of year for it all. You're quite fortunate that your first seeing it now, like this."

"I like it very much," she breathed.

Seeing the ruins with Georgina now, Charles felt the wild dance of colour and form surrounding them rise up and fill him with a kind of music. Joyful, untroubled.

Charles pointed up the hill. "From the morning room at the house, there is a view across the valley to down here."

"Is there? Oh…"

"I thought you might like that morning room for your personal drawing room?"

"A personal drawing room? For me?" Her eyes widened.

"Ironvine has over five drawing rooms and three parlours. But that one is the most pleasing of all. My study is down that same hall."

Surging on her toes, she hugged him. "I'd like that very much. It's a dream come true."

"It's very true now, Countess." He released her.

"Would you mind if I sketched…"

"Of course not. Go on, do what it is you do."

She took her new sketchbook from her new satchel. "This is a paradise."

He let out a laugh. "Paradise, you say? If only my father were alive to hear this described as a paradise. He wanted to mow the whole thing down and let the moat flood from the river, which is further up, in order to create a lake so he could fish properly."

"Oh no, no. Never do that."

He bowed his head to her, bringing a hand to his chest with a flourish. "So speaks the Countess of Ryvves, so it shall be done."

Chapter Thirty-Eight

Georgina

JERROLD HAD SHOWN her the bed linens, the table linens, the extensive Montclare glass collection. And the entire time, all she could think of was getting back to her sketching. She had an inspiration for a new series of drawings this morning and had begun, but once her maid had arrived, she had to attend to her duties as the lady of the house.

And attend she did.

"And that is the last of the sherry glasses, ma'am."

"That was a great number of sherry glasses, Jerrold. I am in awe." Georgina smoothed back her hair from her face as the two of them walked down the hallway together.

"Yes, ma'am. Tomorrow morning, do you wish us to continue?"

"Certainly. What do you have on the menu for me?" She gave the woman a relaxed smile.

"I thought the silver, my lady."

"Very good. The silver, it is. I look forward to it."

"Give it all away." Charles's sharp voice filled the air. He was in the next bed chamber, standing over two servants who folded clothing, making neat stacks on the large bed. "I don't want anything of my brother's in my house."

She entered the room. "Charles, if you like, I'll take care of everything."

He only glared at her, at all of them, and quit the room, his boots tracking loudly down the staircase.

"These are all his lordship's things?"

"Yes, ma'am," said Jerrold. "When we were told of his death, I immediately had the lord's chambers prepared for the Earl, and the late Earl's belongings brought here to his former bedchamber."

One of the servants folded a pair of breeches, smoothing her hands over it, adding it to a pile of other breeches. There was a pile of white shirts next to it.

"Jerrold, as this is obviously a very difficult time for my husband, I'd like to go through his late brother's belongings to see if there is something that perhaps, one day, the Earl would have wanted to keep. I don't wish him to have any further sorrows. You understand."

"I do, my lady. This is a terrible time for the family. First his lordship's father, then his brother."

"Yes, awful."

"I am right glad that he has you now, my lady. That Ironvine has you."

"Thank you, that is most kind."

"Other than Master Hugh's clothing, there are these two caskets his Lordship kept. I found them in his dresser." Jerrold gestured at two polished wooden boxes on the dresser. "We haven't opened them."

"Very good. I shall go through them then." She prayed they were not locked. She touched the fastening on one. It opened. She let out a tiny breath as she scooped them both up, turning to leave the room when she caught sight of a tall square item cloaked with a fabric covering.

She stilled. "Jerrold, what is that?"

"'Tis an unfinished portrait of the former master, bless his soul. I had it brought here with all the rest of his belongings until we organised everything."

Georgina moved the sheet from the piece. "There he is."

Hugh. The beginnings of a portrait, a study. His features were perfectly captured in washes of pigment and brushstrokes, delicate lines drawn and smoothed over. All so very well proportioned, accurately capturing its subject. Hugh's elegance, along with a subtle hint of patrician condescension. The rest of him, limbs, clothing, were only outlined, sketched, brushed over.

Her heartbeat surged in her chest. A study. The painter was experimenting and deciding what was best to bring out his subject.

Jerrold came up alongside her. "The artist had just begun his work when..."

"Yes, of course," Georgina murmured. "The artist has done quite a remarkable job even if 'twas only a beginning." She moved the sheet back over it. "You were right to have it put here for the time being. Lord Ryvves would find this most upsetting if he saw it."

"Yes, ma'am."

"Please have it brought to my morning room. I would like to study it more closely and I shall put it away there."

"Yes, my lady."

"Thank you, Jerrold." Georgina took the wood caskets and made her way down the staircase to her morning room, and locked the door behind her. Setting the two polished wood boxes on her desk, she opened one. Four thick packets of letters filled the box. So many letters bound with leather ties. She picked up one packet. A woman's hand, to be sure.

"Such beautiful handwriting," she murmured to herself as she turned over the thick paper. The signature was only "Z."

Z?

The Duchess's Christian name was Cassandra.

She looked through a few other letters, handling them

gently. They had all been signed Z. Her teeth dragged along her lip. Was Z the Duchess?

She opened the other casket. A collection of snuffboxes. One had a beautiful horse racing across a green field with an interesting decorative design around the edge. Geometric and very unlike the usual Baroque-inspired artwork.

She opened it. The pungent scent of the snuff hit her nostrils. There was a mirror inside the lid but the top of the box was rounded and deep. Could it be hiding a secret compartment?

Her finger traced the gold rim, and a slight irregularity brushed her flesh. Indeed on the side, there was a tiny button-like piece that scraped her fingertip. She pressed on it, and a small sound erupted. The mirror released, springing forward, revealing an additional interior. "Oh my…"

A miniature painting of a naked couple. The man bore his bare staff like a sword. It was large and upright. He hovered over the naked woman, who was lying on a bed, her legs splayed wide open in anticipation of him, her pink quim plainly visible.

The lady's feet were not bare. She wore the most extraordinary pink shoes with heels. Georgie let out a laugh. The same pink as her quim, in fact. The lady's one hand stroked the man's upright member, her pleased gaze boldly fixed on it. The man gripped one of her shoulders, steadying himself. Readying himself to enter her.

Georgina emptied the snuff from the bowl onto her desk. Engraved there were words. French words: *"A Vous Seule."*

Her heart tripped in her chest. "Yours alone," Georgina whispered. Surely, this had been a gift from a lover. She studied the miniature once more. The male figure had blond hair like Hugh, tall. Was it him? It had to be. The female bore a slight resemblance to the Duchess, but one couldn't be sure.

She had to keep these safe.

Her gaze shot to the elaborately carved Italianate trunk in

the room. *Perfect.* Unlatching it, she carefully stowed Hugh's two caskets at the very bottom, arranging the cloths, odd vases, and bowls that were already stowed in there.

A knock at the door.

She bolted upright and unlocked the door. A servant held Hugh's portrait in his gloved hands. "My lady?"

And right then, a plan formed in her head. A very fine plan.

Chapter Thirty-Nine

Charles

HE'D PICKED her pink roses today.

He liked this, doing something nice for her. He'd always been good at gifts with ladies, tokens of his "appreciation" and "adoration." Jewellery, small pots of perfume, all specially chosen, all expensive, all meaningless. But these flowers from his own gardens that he'd chosen for her and picked himself were different.

They weren't shiny expensive objects meant to elicit gasps and awe and a surge of lustful enthusiasm and gratitude. No, these flowers were a simple thing. No money was involved, and the gesture was not a secret but out in the open, given and accepted freely. Acceptable. Appropriate between a husband and wife.

And yet it was so much more thrilling for him this simple thing in the light of day rather than the sly, shadowy gestures, the planned ploy out to prompt a certain result he desired. This was simply to bring her joy.

He knew she was downstairs in her morning room right now. He went to her dressing area, placing the small bouquet on her vanity. One of her sketchbooks lay there. He had yet to see a full collection of her drawings, and he was very curious.

He opened the book. His lips parted as he turned the pages. Sketch after sketch.

Of him.

Him sleeping. Naked. Studies of his arms, his back, his chest. Even one of his buttocks. Another of his entire naked form, cock at attention, his arm flung over his face. Others where she would sketch the same limb and shoulder over and over until she got it right.

His wife had been sketching him without his knowledge. She had studied him in his sleep, translated what she saw, what she felt onto paper. She kept searching for more. His pulse charged, his balls tightened. Yes, it was bloody exciting, a thrill in a wholly different way than anything he'd ever experienced before.

He went back to the beginning of the book and took in each drawing more carefully. Just as Justine had told him, Georgina was extraordinarily talented. She had a gift.

Taking the sketchbook, he went downstairs to her morning room. The door was closed, so he knocked and entered. But she was not there. Not at her desk taking care of correspondence as she'd told him she did every morning before breakfast.

He quit the room and called out for the housekeeper. "Where is your mistress? Has she gone for a walk in the gardens?"

"No, sir."

"Out riding?"

"No, my lord. Her ladyship is in the conservatory."

"Ah." He tracked to the back of the house and entered the glass-enclosed space, past the rows of orange trees and orchids. He followed the sounds of shuffling and murmuring and some sort of swiping of papers, more muttering and sighing.

He found her on the floor crouched over a large paper, sketching. Her hair had fallen from its tie, fingers blackened with charcoal. Pencils were strewn at her side. She licked at her lip as she drew, her features focused with intent.

"Here you are."

She looked up as if she'd been shocked awake. "Charles? Oh. I thought you'd left already…"

"Not yet."

She sat up straight, biting her lip. Her face reddened.

"How are you finding working here?"

Scrambling to her feet, she grabbed a cloth and wiped at her hands. "It has much good light and I find the airiness quite inspiring."

"I can see that, yes."

"I'm making a mess, aren't I?"

"Georgina. I am most pleased that you are comfortable here and that it suits your needs."

Her shoulders fell. "It's perfect." Her gaze went to the sketchbook in his hand, and her eyes widened, her shoulders stiffening all over again.

He held it up. "I found this."

"I can explain."

"Explain your taking advantage of your husband's naked form without his knowledge?"

"Please forgive me."

He let out a laugh. "There is nothing to forgive."

"One night this week I happened to wake. The moon was quite strong and I'd opened the curtains to enjoy the light, the views of the park, the hills, and see if I could spot the old castle in the valley. I went into your bedchamber and opened the curtains to see the view there, and it was then I spied you on your bed. You are a fitful sleeper and had thrown the covers from yourself. I could not resist."

"Could not resist my naked body?"

Her lips tipped up. "That is correct. The moonlight fell on you in the most intriguing way."

His pulse ticked up at her admission. "Did I resemble a sculpture?"

"No, not lifeless stone. More like a sleeping god. Apollo at rest, vulnerable. I was utterly compelled to record what I saw on paper."

Heat flared in his chest, riveted in his loins. "Did you like it, drawing me?"

"I did. You are a perfect subject. Beautiful long, hard lines, curves, hollows, shadows. I had to work quickly because, at one point, you moved about quite a bit. But I found it to be a good exercise in being swift and nimble."

"You're most welcome, then, madame."

"My apologies, my lord, for I should have asked your permission first."

He stroked the side of her heated cheek with his fingers, and she let out a small sigh which went straight to the pulse beating between his legs. "There's my fine lady, apologising and asking for permission. No, my Countess, if an all-consuming inspiration struck you upon seeing my figure laid bare, who am I to question that? Take what you want of me." His fingers trailed down her silky throat, and she released another soft sigh at his words, his touch. "Indeed, I find myself greatly aroused by your presumption and assertion, my Countess. Am I your *odalisque*?"

Her hand flew to his chest as she laughed. "You are no pleasure slave in a sultan's seraglio, my lord."

He covered her hand with his. "Am I your pleasure slave?" He bent down and took her lips in a long and lingering kiss. Parting her lips, his tongue slid around hers, provoking, demanding.

"I am certainly yours," she whispered as she embraced him. "You are not angry with me then?"

"Why should I be? Do you intend on selling these sketches?"

"Of course not, they're for me."

"I feel sketching is not simply a pastime to you, a ladies' leisurely pursuit as it is for most."

"No, Charles, it is much more than that for me. It always has been. It gives me such pleasure and satisfaction both inwardly and physically. My father always encouraged me."

"He recognised your talent, of course. He was known in artistic circles, was he not?"

"He was." Her face brightened considerably. She loved her father and was proud of him. "He was not only a collector, but a patron, a go-between of sorts for artists and collectors. He enjoyed exhibitions and auctions and helped organize them, which is why he traveled so very much. He received his knighthood from His Majesty for the work he did on behalf of the Royal Collection. But most of all, he loved exploring and discovering new worlds, and the artwork that captured that richness that he saw." She wiped her hands together and brushed her hair back from her face, leaving a smudge on her temple.

"After my father died, my mother stopped my lessons and commanded me to focus on needlepoint and music and dancing, so that I could prepare to attract the best suitors." She met his gaze, licking her lip. "The best husband."

"I should have asked to see samples of your needlepoint before signing that agreement with Holyfloke, eh?"

"If you and Hugh had seen my needlepoint, you would have not signed. Crooked, and sloppy, much, much worse than Brother Laurent's illumination." She laughed, an easy rolling laugh, and he laughed too.

He knew Georgina had attracted the best husband all on her own.

Charles walked about the many sketches on the floor—larger versions of what was in her small sketchbooks. "Is this room to your liking as a place to work?"

"It is beyond anything I have ever experienced before. I love this room."

"That pleases me."

She swallowed hard. He was sure she had become quite used to hiding her work and her enthusiasm for it. Had become accustomed to being told it was wrong and unseemly, and that a husband would certainly not approve and would certainly forbid it. Had she only known encouragement for her talent from her late father?

"Countess, I am quite happy that you have found a use for this conservatory that was built for purely pompous reasons once upon a time. You shall give this hollow symbol of prestige true purpose, and perhaps the little orangerie that has survived all these years will be happier for it and flourish."

"I love the orange trees."

"There's a pomegranate tree too, I think. If you have specific ideas as to what you will require to make this a proper atelier for yourself, I shall hire a few men to fulfil those requirements."

"Charles, are you sure?"

"Quite sure. Adamant, in fact." The need to reassure her came over him. His hand reached out and cupped her face. "You have a talent that you should continue to develop as it makes you so very happy. I find it makes me happy to be able to help you in this endeavour."

She placed her hand over his. Warm and soft. "I am so very grateful."

His thumb stroked her lips, and she let out a small noise. "However, Lady Ryvves, you must make me a promise."

"Anything."

"You shall have no naked male models other than your husband."

"Does this mean you will pose for me one day instead of my stealing your poses in your sleep?"

"Yes, you did steal, didn't you, minx? I will have a price."

"A price?"

"I find your intense scrutiny and study of my naked form very stirring, thus I will require satisfaction."

"Oh?" A knowing grin fluttered over her lips, and he felt compelled by some force to touch her, kiss her, taste her, grip her flesh and he leaned in closer to her for a kiss. Something at his feet caught his eye, and he stilled. A small drawing, a likeness utterly familiar. Those eyes, that mouth curled in that thin way.

"What the devil?" Charles swooped up the paper and studied the drawing and the others at their feet. There wasn't only one. There were tens of them.

"Why the devil are you drawing Hugh?"

Chapter Forty

Georgina

"Why are you sketching my brother?" Charles's features tightened. "Your memory of him is so acute that you are able to produce such an exact likeness?"

"I—"

"Why?" His voice grew louder echoing through the glass room, and her body stiffened. "Do you long for him?"

"No."

"I don't believe you."

"I do not long for Hugh! I never have, you know this."

"Then why? His features are so formidable, so remarkable?"

"No, not to me. This is for the Duchess. I am doing this for her."

"Doing what exactly?"

"I thought to give her a gift, a *memento mori*. I'm painting a miniature of Hugh for her, and these are the studies for it. I found a study for his portrait, and I used it to sketch from."

"You are seeking her out, her friendship, why?"

"I know she has the Graven necklace, and I want to get it back for Brandon and Justine."

His eyes flared, a sharp breath heaving from his lips. "And how do you expect to do that?"

"Firstly, I shall ask Her Grace how she acquired it."

"Impossible."

"But why?"

"I don't want you to have anything to do with them."

"Because of Hugh?" Her eyes widened. "Do you think they had something to do with his death?"

"I am convinced of it, yes. The Duke is a very powerful and extremely wealthy man. He can do as he pleases, and he does. Men like Oakley are very possessive of what belongs to them, and a wife is chief among those possessions."

"Their marriage certainly seems liberal, enlightened?"

"He seemed to allow his wife to keep a lover as he kept a mistress, but who knows what the true boundaries of their liberal way of life are? Hugh may have transgressed in some way, and perhaps that is the reason they broke off. Perhaps the Duke had enough, and he forced them to break? And then the moment they broke off, the Duke took his revenge on Hugh.

"Or perhaps it was her idea to sever ties because she feared her husband's brewing wrath? Or when they came to the ball, something happened between the Duchess and Hugh, and the Duke saw and became angry?" He let out a groan. "All of these ring true to me, and they do not cease to wreak havoc in my brain."

"You are right. There are many possibilities to consider."

"They are all highly likely. Over the years I have come to hear many intriguing things about the Duke's proclivities. Hugh did not share any details with me, so I cannot be sure they are true or simply rumours based on envy." He picked up a sketch of his brother and studied it. "Hugh and I have known Oakley since we were boys, and from the very first he struck me as an unusual character, even then. Wiser than his years, fearless. And in some ways, sinister. A character much like my father, though perhaps not as selfish or small-minded as Father was." A dark scowl shadowed his features. "I cannot explain it, I just know. I have always felt it." He gave Georgina the sketch as he absently twisted the Ryvves ring on his finger. "You must find that very odd."

"I believe you." She gathered all the sketches of Hugh in a pile. "But all the more reason to befriend them. We could find out if they knew about Hugh and Amanda, or if they had anything to do with Hugh's death for whatever reason."

He held her gaze. "She had a spy on Hugh in London. They weren't supposed to be in town that last week, but they suddenly appeared at the ball. She must have learnt of his affair with Amanda, and her jealousy drove her to see for herself."

"Yet she seemed so at ease at the ball, so poised. She must be a very fine actress."

"As a Duchess, his Duchess in particular, she has to be."

"Very true.

"I'm not sure if Hugh and the Duchess spoke at the ball, but that very same night he went to Amanda. Then William caught him and challenged him to a duel."

"So perhaps the Duchess had heard of the duel and sent her spy to watch and afterward, she went to the house to confront Hugh about Amanda. They argued, and …" She swallowed hard.

"Can't bring yourself to utter the words 'she killed him' can you?"

"I am finding it rather difficult to fathom."

"Anything is possible in this world, dear Georgie. Anything."

"I have come to that realisation."

A knock came on the door, and a servant entered. "My lord, a letter and a package have arrived from Fairthorn for Lady Ryvves." In his hands, he held a box.

Charles took it from him and brought it to Georgina.

"What could that possibly be?" Georgina's mouth dried, her heart thudding in her chest as her hand reached out for the letter.

Chapter Forty-One

Charles

"PLEASE, CHARLES. YOU READ IT."

He broke the seal and opened the letter as she opened the box.

Dearest Sister,

Our mother has been deeply affected by your outrageous behaviour, as she phrased it, and your wild course of action, and will not retrench in her feelings toward you or, most especially, toward your marriage to Charles.

Although I am relieved that the Earl of Ryvves did indeed marry you after the unexpected loss of his brother, thus saving you from further disgrace, this union to the Montclare family seems to have only made Mother's feelings regarding your betrayal all the more vicious, resulting in her attempt to destroy your possessions in such a ferocious manner.

Once the fire was put out, I saved what I could, and am sending these items on to you. I know these letters, in particular, have always been a great comfort to you, and I was most pleased to see that they survived along with a few of your sketchbooks, although somewhat charred, and only this one small painting of your beloved father's.

This morning, Mother quit Fairthorn for our sister's home where she will stay. I am sorry to report that she remains angry and unremorseful. I do hope one day our mother and sister shall be able to accept your marriage and all shall be as before.

Although I am gratified that you are now the Countess of Ryvves and live close by, I confess I remain troubled by your wilful behaviour.

Yours,

Thomas

"Your disgrace, indeed," Charles muttered, folding up the letter.

Georgina's fingers spread over the charred leather folder. "My father's letters survived the fire. That is all that matters." She clutched the damaged folder to her chest.

Charles tossed the letter on the table. "This was kind of Thomas, considering he remains troubled."

"Yes, it was." Her eyes gleamed with water as she opened the folder, her fingers running over the missives in neat packets. She'd been very attached to her father, how very unlike his experience with his own.

He drew up next to her as she fingered the letters. "I seem to remember you had just entered society when your father died, is that right?"

"Yes. I was sixteen, a very exciting time, and then the very next day after I was presented at court, we learnt of his death."

"How did he…"

"He was on his way home from Edinburgh for my coming

out. He had promised he would be there. But on that day, he was not there. I was most disappointed, Mother was livid. And the next morning we received word that there had been a carriage accident just outside of London. He'd been trampled by the horses, crushed." She winced. "A horrible way to die."

"And he left you with every ounce of sterling he was worth."

"How do you know?"

"There was gossip at the time about how fine a catch you were, but I know the details because your brother-in-law told me when we discussed the betrothal arrangements."

"And now, as my husband, all is yours."

"Georgina, I made sure you kept a healthy sum for yourself in the settlement so you would never be dependent on Hugh's whims. John Holyfloke was shocked at my insistence on this point."

"Why did you do it?"

"I didn't want you to marry Hugh. I knew you had to, and I wanted to help you escape your fate in Devonshire as you'd asked of me. I knew what sort of husband my brother would most likely be, so I did what I could to protect you. I didn't want you to be vulnerable, at least in your financial security. In that, I could assist you.

"The money your father left you was yours, it was only right. Hugh certainly didn't need the money, nor would I have wanted him to use it at his leisure for other women or gambling or some such. Nor did I want you to be put in a position where you had to continually ask him for money. I wanted you to be able to take care of yourself as you saw fit."

She lunged at him, embracing him. His chest caved in at her emotion, and his arms wrapped around her. "Charles, you were the only one in all this madness who gave a damn about me as a person, not a commodity to be bartered."

His hold on her tightened. No words came, only a flow of warmth from deep inside his chest through his limbs. He had felt so powerless that day, discussing terms with Holyfloke for her engagement to his brother, Hugh smiling effortlessly at his side. He did what he could to gain her the best possible position, which had given him some measure of relief.

But now he was the one married to her, holding onto her in their home.

"I believe it had frustrated both your brother and your brother-in-law to no end that they had no control over your income in order to force your hand in some way."

"I am sure of it."

Releasing her, he gestured at the wrapped canvas. "What is this small painting of your father's?"

She unwrapped it and showed it to him with a smile. A dark-eyed woman practically bare, laying provocatively on a bed strewn with coloured silks in a shadowy and exotic room, her straight-on gaze bold. "I'm so glad to see it again."

"A true odalisque."

"Yes. She's quite..."

"Erotic." He examined the darkly toned painting.

"Hmm, that she is. And utterly without shame or timidity. I always liked that about her." Her gaze fell to his lips. "My father was a patron to a number of artists and often accompanied them on their travels to faraway places. He would bring me souvenirs of his trips abroad, which were small paintings and sketches done by the artists he traveled with.

"He had several larger paintings of the kind from a trip to Constantinople and Asia Minor where he journeyed with several French painters. The pieces were beautiful—ruins, landscapes, musicians and dancers, shepherds, shopkeepers. All of them otherworldly and exotic to me."

"He must have amassed quite a singular collection."

"He mostly sold work to his circle of acquaintances on the artists' behalf. Whatever else he collected, he kept at his house in London, never at Fairthorn. Unfortunately, Mother sold them all along with the house after he died."

"That is a great pity."

"It was most upsetting to me. I wanted to keep it all. I often hoped there had been works he kept somewhere else." She let out a sigh. "He was a true collector with a good eye, as they say."

"Your mother seems not to have shared in your and your father's affection for art?"

"She did not. In fact, I can't think of any interests that bound them together, other than me. Philippa once remarked that theirs was a lovely infatuation that had quickly evaporated under the strains of daily life. What I do know, for Mother told me so herself, was that she did not want to be on her own as a widow. She was still young when her first husband passed away from a sudden illness, and she wanted to remarry to be a part of the course of society as she always had been."

"Indeed."

"My father was dashing and charming, by all accounts. The fourth child of a Viscount, who along with his family name to recommend him to society, had his own house in town and a good income which he used to support his interests and various pursuits. He was not much for the country—hunting parties and the like—nor for the social demands of town. He much preferred to travel and learn and explore. My mother was quite the opposite, so I suppose somehow the arrangement suited them both. Respectability with freedoms."

Charles twisted his lips. *Their freedom, yes. But what of their child?* "Your mother must have enjoyed her life as the lady of Fairthorn without a husband's interference."

"She did, yes." She adjusted the letters in their packets. "On every one of his trips, he wrote to me. Such wonderful descriptions of Rome, Naples, the Levant, Athens—he even sketched Athena's temple at the Acropolis for me—all the wondrous things he saw, the fine food he ate, the colourful friends he made." She touched the leather folder. "I thought them lost to me forever. Now, to have them back…"

"You loved him very much."

"I did. He was a good father. Encouraged my interest in art, would take me to exhibitions, introduce me to artist friends of his, architects. He even arranged for a tutor for me, a painter from London who stayed in the village for a few months while he taught me."

"Wonderful."

"It was. My mother thought it was a ridiculous waste of time and money when I should be practicing the pianoforte, my French, or my dancing just as she and Philippa had done at that age. After he died, she got her way. She stopped my drawing and painting lessons and insisted on only music and needlepoint and the like. An obligation of my sex, which I had to fulfil to please my family, to please society, and most especially, to please men. I resented them greatly after a time."

He stroked the side of her silky face with his fingertips, and she made a small sound that made his pulse leap hotly. "Trust me, my girl, a fine needlepoint does nothing to please my cock."

"I'm quite sure it would not, sir." She burst out into a peal of laughter.

He grinned. Georgina was learning what pleased his cock, but at the sound of her relaxed and easy laughter, he shoved away the image of her naked between his legs boldly pleasing his pego with her luscious mouth. A tight spring unwound in his chest. He liked this, the two of them talking about important things, understanding one another, sharing a story, a brazen jest. Nothing forced.

"I did as was expected of me," she said. "But I continued to draw and paint in secret. I would go to the old nursery in the wing of the house where no one lived. It had a single large window, which would get the best light first thing in the morning, so I would wake very early and go there and work. Everyone thought I had gone on walks or was taking an extraordinary time with my *toilette*, or feeling poorly as one often does, but I only let them think so."

He brushed a stray lock of hair from her cheek. "You don't have to hide anymore, Georgie." His fingertips grazed down the side of her neck to her bosom.

Her lips parted at his light strokes across her delicate skin. "No, I don't."

"I want you to flourish here at Ironvine."

"I am most grateful, Charles." Her voice almost ached with emotion. It meant so much to her, this simple gesture of his. She'd been deprived for much too long.

His heart thumped in his chest. He was accustomed to every gesture having a price, a quid pro quo.

Not with her.

It felt damned good to feed this girl the stuff of her dreams. It was simple and yet satisfying, and it felt good to give to Georgina and not expect nor want anything in return. Charles licked at his lips. He could taste the musk of her quim this very second on his tongue and he craved it now like nothing else.

She picked up the pile of sketches of Hugh she'd collected earlier. "I thought if I could create this token of Hugh for the Duchess, she would have something of him to hold onto as I now have this painting of my father's. If I can give her this small and very private comfort as a gesture of friendship, mightn't I? And thus, mightn't we learn of what she knew of Hugh and Amanda?"

He crossed his arms. "All right then. Paint that thing for her as a gesture of friendship, give it to her, and see how she reacts. It could be telling, I agree. But do not push her."

Georgina lifted up and brushed his lips with her warm ones.

He held her close. "You must proceed carefully with the Duchess. She may not be the friend you hope her to be."

Chapter Forty-Two

Georgina

GEORGINA TROMPED through the grasses back to the house. Wearing trousers and tall boots made life so much simpler. She grinned to herself at the memory of asking Charles's manservant if he had any old clothes of Charles's for her to wear on a walk to the ruins. Luckily, it had rained early in the morning, so she explained how she did not have many dresses just yet, and nothing suitable for a long walk in the muddy wet fields. Two pairs of breeches, shirts, and even a pair of boots were found for her.

Even now under clouded skies, a cool breeze kicking up, the seat of her pants wet from sitting on the stones, knees down in the grass, her heartbeat thrummed. She was so grateful.

Within three hours, Georgina had filled her sketchbook with studies of the castle tower, the ruined wall with its small medieval windows, and the flowers curled around the stones.

She put the finishing strokes on her sketch of a wisteria bloom. Her last tutor had helped her gain momentum with miniatures, and she'd become quite obsessed with mastering that delicate craft. She was a long way away, but it was so gratifying to now have so many new and beautiful subjects at her disposal, and no one to lie to. To be able to give herself over to her tasks uninterrupted was a luxury she appreciated.

Georgina had set up her drawing supplies in the morning room that Charles had said she could have for herself. In such a room, in such a grand house, the lady of said house would most probably take her tea, take care of her correspondence, and invite a friend for a sherry.

She would do that, but this would also be her place to work in addition to the glass-enclosed orangerie where she would work on larger projects.

Her mother had once snapped at her for being untidy in her rooms at Fairthorn. She had just finished a painting, and she'd been so gratified by the entire experience she hadn't realised over five hours had flown by. Everyone else had dressed for dinner, and here she was with paint smudged on her hands and arms, splattered on the old clothes she wore to work in. She hadn't minded, but her mother had been disgusted and scolded her.

"Can't you at the very least sketch like a lady, and not like a tradeswoman or a gypsy?"

After that day Georgina had tried to be good, to only work early in the morning when no one could disturb her, or, most importantly, catch her out. Now here she was in a very large house, with rooms to call her own, so many rooms to explore, and a husband who had no qualms about her working. Would Hugh have allowed it, she wondered.

Charles had been quite busy the past few days with his steward. The man was elderly and wanted to retire, and his son would most probably be taking over for him. Having been away in London for almost two months, Charles had a lot of catching up to do on estate business, but it didn't seem to ruffle him in the least. He enjoyed the work.

"Hello, m'lady. Did you have a good walk?" Jerrold greeted her in the front hall.

"I did indeed, Jerrold."

"Would you like a cup of tea to warm ye up? 'Twas cold out there today."

"It was unusually chilly, and yes, I would very much love tea." She wiped her boots on the small rug in the hall set for that purpose in such weather. "I thought I'd go to the library and find something to read. Could the tea be brought there?"

"Of course, ma'am."

"Wonderful. Also, I was hoping to have a bath before dinner."

"I'll have your lady's maid see to it while you enjoy your tea, and it shall be ready."

"Wonderful. Thank you."

Rain splattered the windows, a lightning bolt flashed in the dark sky. "Thank goodness I came home when I did," she murmured to herself, leaving her satchel with her sketchbooks and pencils and squares of rubber in her morning room, and headed to the library.

So many shelves. So many books. a giddiness filled her like it would when her father would take her to the sweet shop on the high street when she was a little girl. He'd gotten her one of everything she'd wanted.

Now her indulgences and pleasures were her painting and reading. At Fairthorn and at her sister's she did much reading as it was the best way for her to be left alone, to not be criticised for not attending to the other pursuits a young lady should always be immersed in.

Although here at Ironvine, she didn't want Charles to leave her alone, did she?

She'd wanted to start reading that sensational new novel Charles had bought, but hadn't had a chance to start it yet. He'd told her where to find it here in the library. Every time she came in this room the filled shelves took her breath away. A fine library of Ironvine's age and caliber was truly a thing of wonder. Most of the volumes were quite old, each of the highest quality bindings and leather. One shelf at the top left caught her eye. Three volumes were turned around so their spines were not visible.

"Odd."

Georgina used the ladder and climbed up, which was quite easy in her boots. Each of the three books was painted on. The fore-edge of the paper had a miniature painting of a landscape. Green hills, blue sky, a castle in the distance. "How fantastic." Carefully, she slid a volume out to inspect it closely.

The small paintings were detailed and delicate. On another volume, a couple dressed in the style of the previous century walked along a field, a manor house in the background. She looked to the other volume which was painted with two ships at sea. But there on the shelf, she spied something else.

Was that a knob? A handle?

Gripping the sleek wooden handle, she twisted it. A grating shoving sound filled the room, and she turned in its direction. A section of the wall had jerked open. "A jib door."

She placed the books back on the shelf and scrambled down the ladder. Pushing at the false doorway, she entered. Her muscles tightened, her breath cut. Was this a secret inner passage to another part of the house? Or an escape route? Could this be from back when Catholic nobles would hide priests and monks in their homes?

She darted back out to the library and found a candelabra and lit the wicks. She wanted to be able to see everything inside the secret passageway. Bearing the light, she went back through the jib door. But there was no passageway, only a room. A small room with a faint spicy aroma, as if incense had been lit here.

She held the candelabra higher as she took small steps in the room. There was a wider than normal cushioned settee with an assortment of large and small cushions. Was this a private reading room? A glimmer shone on the wall. She blinked. Her breath cut. Her grip on the candelabra tightened as she moved it. The light revealed the richly coloured walls.

"Bloody hell, what is this?"

Chapter Forty-Three

Georgina

THE CANDLELIGHT FLICKERED over a great colourful painting that filled an entire wall. A painting of a man about to roger a woman. His engorged member was quite large between his legs, and he was very ready to mount the naked woman before him whose legs were spread open wide on a messy bed. Angels floated above her, fanning her with their black wings.

Every detail of her nether regions was plainly visible.

Georgina moved the light along the wall. A second man stood over the woman and placed his member by her mouth, a hand stroking one of her perfect breasts. She turned, and her heart stopped as she took in the next painted wall. Images of multiple couples engaged in a wide variety of wanton acts.

Two men taking a woman at once — one laying beneath her, the other over her backside? A man suckling a woman's arse as she took a man's pego in her mouth?

Prickles of heat raced over her flesh, her throat burned. She went about the entire room. Every inch of space was painted with people swiving in a variety of positions. A feverish, fervent apocalypse. And very well painted as well.

She continued her exploration. In the lower right-hand

corner just behind the door, she discovered a depiction of two women licking each other's —

"What are you doing in here?"

Gasping, she swung around toward the deep voice, dropping the candelabra. It banged on the floor between them, and in the shadows, towered Charles.

"How the hell did you get in here?" He plucked at the candelabra and held it aloft, the light suddenly gleaming between them, revealing his sharp features.

Her mouth dried. "I was looking at the books on the shelves., and I...I..."

"Yes?"

"I found three volumes that were turned backward, there was a delightful painting on the fore-edge."

"You saw the handle." His tone was oddly stern.

"I saw the handle, yes." She swallowed hard. She should have ignored the damned handle. She should have asked him first.

Charles placed the candelabra on the low table in the centre of the room. "Luckily I took the tea service from Jerrold and brought it to the library myself."

"Ah yes, tea..." Her stomach knotted over and over. "What is this room exactly?"

"This was my father's private chamber. Here he entertained himself with mistresses, whores, a servant or two."

"The paintings are all quite good."

He let out a sardonic laugh. "Painted by the best." He slapped his hand against the wall at his side. "Here there's a passageway to exit the house for quick getaways if one's spouse were to interrupt while you were rutting a servant or a mutual friend. Or perhaps the spouse of the mutual friend might come calling, looking for his wife, and she could then easily escape and return to her own home undetected."

"Ah, I see."

"Do you?" His eyes narrowed at her, his jaw tense.

"I think you've witnessed a great many things in this house, Charles."

He averted his gaze. "Here is proof for you that all the horrid things people say about us Montclares are true. Profligates, rakes. Debauchery, decadence." His gaze roved over her. "This is my family." He cradled the side of her face with his cool hand, and her breathing deepened. "Your brother was right. By marrying me, you've been polluted."

"Have you used this room?"

"You want to know?"

"Yes, I want to know."

"Never. Had I done, I would have been whipped."

"But you wanted to?"

"I did." Pressing his lips together, he gestured at her. "Why are you dressed like this? Are those my old clothes?"

She shifted her weight under his critical scrutiny. "Yes, yes they are. I asked your man if there were any of your old clothes I might use to walk to the ruins today. With this morning's rains, there was a lot of mud and..."

"This is rather shocking, Countess."

"Is it?"

He tugged sharply on her loosely tied neck cravat, swiping it out of the way to reveal her throat. His thumbs brushed down the delicate skin of her neck, and she let out a cry. "That's better."

"Hmm."

"You like the paintings on the wall? Perhaps you'd like to sketch them?"

"Yes, I would."

His eyes flared. "Would you?"

"They're very good."

"Only the finest for the Earl of Ryvves."

"Obviously the artist was a talented professional."

"He was. When my father did his tour of the Continent as a young man, he'd met an artist in Rome. He invited him here, commissioned him to create a unique atmosphere for this room." He turned her around to face the largest of the wall paintings of the two men swiving the woman at the same time. The woman's wrists were bound by iron shackles held by two monkeys, their expressions lascivious.

Sliding his arm around her waist, Charles pulled her back firmly against his body. His hard chest at her back, his breath hot on her neck, his fingers stroking the sensitive spot behind her ear. Her insides melted as her head melted back against his chest.

"Tell me what you like about the paintings, Georgie."

"I find the artist's use of colour quite rich."

"Colour, yes…the flesh tones in particular…" He chuckled softly. "Have you ever seen such works of art before?" He moved her toward a section of the mural where a great beast of a lion rutted a naked woman from behind, his claws gripping her, drawing blood, his fangs showing, promising torment. The woman shrieked, but was it in horror or ecstasy?

"I cannot say I knew that such a thing existed on such a grand scale."

"Oh, it does. It does." Charles planted a kiss on her shoulder. His scent of rosemary and lemon filled her senses as he planted a kiss on her other shoulder. A small cry escaped her lips despite her attempts to be still, be quiet. "I think you like it, Georgie." His tongue lashed at the rim of her ear.

"I do." She pressed her body back against his., and his hard length pressed against her buttocks. He was hard and that hardness set off a twist of need inside her, for her body now knew what it was to be filled and pleasured by that hardness. "You like it, too." The blood pounded in her veins at the knowledge that he was excited as he held her this way.

They had not lain together recently. He'd kept late hours with his steward and his son, Joss going over accounts and improvements and problems. He'd go directly to his chamber and sleep and then wake early and go riding, then he'd have appointments and much correspondence to take care of.

Was he also avoiding her? Perhaps being with her had been a novelty for him, and now that intriguing shine had worn off? She felt that what they had shared so far had been exciting, and thrilling, yet perhaps it had not been as thrilling for him. He was used to women of experience who, she imagined, knew how to make a man come back for more, more, and even more. She wanted to be that kind of woman for him, not a family obligation.

No, not that.

Nor did she want him seeking out his pleasures elsewhere like his father and brother, and her own father undoubtedly had. Charles's father had even brought the *elsewhere* into his own house, his needs were so great.

Georgina had always been taught that a husband of her class did these things, and a wife could only expect and accept them. She'd understood it. But now that she was actually married and to Charles...

No. No. Impossible.

The way he made her feel in his arms, his kisses, his lust for her...her lust for him.

Yes, it was lust. It was, but it was also something more. And something very real, not a fanciful idea. Something that bolted to the prickly yet affectionate friendship they'd shared for years, something that made their connection more intense, more colourful. Powerful.

Yes. She wanted to be her husband's well-spring of desire.

Georgina covered his hands with hers and brought them to her breasts. Groaning, he cupped them, bound them, stroked them.

"Georgie..."

"I'm not experienced in the ways of carnal pleasures as you are, Charles, you know this. But I would like to be. You've always wanted to have a woman in here. At least, here, I can be your first."

He stilled. "You would like that?"

What she would like was to be his ultimate pleasure. "Yes, I would."

He squeezed her middle, his lips coming to her ear. "This isn't a horror to you?"

"It's shocking."

"It's meant to be."

"But it does not disgust me. It fascinates me."

He tilted his head, an eyebrow arching. "From an art perspective?"

She laughed, her shoulders slackening. "Oh, indeed. But if this is what you spoke of at Vauxhall I think."

"I said a great many things that night."

"You said a kiss was a promise of bliss."

"It is."

"I like our kisses very, very much, and I want to know what that bliss is for you. Is it this?" She gestured at the walls.

"You're trembling, dear Georgie. Are you afraid?"

"What I am afraid of is that you will perhaps think less of me because a wife is not supposed to ask for these things, is she?"

"Not from a husband, in my experience. But from her lover." His eyes narrowed at her. "Georgina Montclare, my Countess of Ryvves, do you wish to experience the bliss of raw carnal pleasures with your husband? Speak."

"I most certainly do, my lord Ryvves."

He yanked at her trousers. A jumble of tugging and pulling.

"The boots—"

"No, leave them." He pulled the trousers down her legs to the boots, constricting her movement. He pulled the shirt over her head and gestured at the other chemise she wore underneath. "Take it off."

She did so, and she was bare to him. An ache burned in her very centre as he placed her hands on the table and set the candelabra on the floor before the painting of the woman being taken by two men. "Stay here no matter what I do to you." His voice was a razor over her flesh.

A shudder quaked inside her. "I shall."

"And look at that painting. Let it fuel your desire and enflame your need. That's what it's there for." His hand stroked a breast.

Behind her, he got on his knees. His hands slid around her thighs sending whispered promises to her centre as they swept over her skin. He blew air between her legs and it tickled her quim. His warm fingers spread her arse cheeks, and she jolted and clenched. Would he enter her there?

A lash of wet warmth found her. His tongue. He was licking her in all her secret places. She melted in his grip, the harsh hardness of the table only added to the sharp unexpected pleasure. His insistent tongue flicked and explored from her cunny up to her ... *oh Lord*. Her pelvis tilted upward to meet his lips and tongue. She was so very wet now. Was it him, was it her?

More friction. More nibbling, more licking. Her cries echoed in the small room.

Fingers easily slid inside her. Two of them churned in her cunny with purpose. His thumb tapped on her sensitive nub, applying steady pressure, and her body seized, a moan burst from her. "Do you feel that, my Countess? Do you feel the pleasure I am giving you?"

"I do, I do, my lord."

He gripped one of her arse cheeks tightly, and it stung painfully along with the intensity of the mounting pleasure he provided. Her gaze was glued to the cock entering the woman's mouth, her tongue long and ready to receive her master. Georgina was at Charles's mercy, exactly where she wanted to be.

Everything she was built swiftly in a towering crescendo, and she could not breathe. "Charles!" She would explode, surely she would. She did, and crashed into a thousand pieces, and was rearranged.

His tongue lashed up her spine. With his hand, he led something wet and smooth to her entrance. His sleek hardness nudged inside her an inch, no more. Her body tingled everywhere. Her flesh knew him, craved him. Demanded him.

She moaned loudly, her hips grinding, hoping in the darkness. A tide of desperate need rose inside her as he pulled on her hair, wrapping it around his hand tightly. "What say you, my Countess?"

"Take me as you wish, my lord."

He thrust his cock all the way inside her with one move, and she let out a long cry. He bent over her, the two of them breathing hard. Was he being kind, waiting to see if she was uncomfortable, in pain?

She was full. Full of Lord Ryvves. Full of Charles Montclare. Full of her husband.

"Am I hurting you?"

"No. You fill me. Give me more."

With a grunt, he rocked back inside her. Her body relaxed more and more with his every hard and fast thrust as she clung to the unforgiving table that offered no comfort, no mercy

"Dammit, Georgie." His pace quickened, his grip tightened, he thrust inside her swiftly, like an animal who knew only need, only *this* one driving need. Their flesh slapped together loudly, the raw sounds echoing in the room, as a musk scent rose around them. Heat. Warmth. Carnal desire. The images surrounding her in the dim half-light came alive. They cavorted and leapt as she and Charles cavorted with them.

She twisted her head on the table slightly to catch a glimpse of him, but he kept his hold on her hair firm and she could not. He grunted and suddenly stiffened as if he'd been knifed in the back. Another low grunt, a sharp howl.

That's what this was, wasn't it? A kind of violence. Sudden, unexpected, brutish, not only the way their bodies met and moved together, but the sensations that overwhelmed her body and her thoughts—erasing all the politeness, dissolving the carefully cultivated niceties. Smashing graceful manners, gentle countenances.

Between lovers, all of them were insignificant. All were obliterated.

Chapter Forty-Four

Georgina

GEORGINA'S EYES FLUTTERED OPEN. Sunlight spewed into her bedchamber through the slight gap left between the great curtains. She liked waking up early. She'd grown accustomed to it at Fairthorn. She would get all sorts of work done in the quiet of her room or her studio room, depending on which project she was consumed with.

A deeply intense rose scent filled her nostrils. Fresh roses lay on the pillow next to her. White like her wedding day roses.

Charles.

Sweet, thoughtful. Romantic. A gesture of esteem.

She lifted the flowers to her face and smelled their intense fragrance. Heady and rich. A smile tugged on her lips. A beautiful gesture that tickled her very heart. As if he were courting her.

After their time in the painted room, exhausted, they drank down the cold tea in the library, the two of them barely uttering two words between them. And then he'd taken her hand in his and brought her to his bed where they continued until they had to dress for dinner. After a wordless dinner, they continued on in her chamber well into the night.

Early this morning she'd awakened him by taking his cock in her mouth, kissing it, lavishing it, one hand at the base of him, stroking as he'd shown her.

Groans and harsh murmurings filled the room. A hand dug in her hair, fisting. His hips rocked with urgency against her face, as Charles cursed like a savage, grunting out her name, which had only made her work him more intently until finally, his cock throbbed his release between her wet swollen lips, his warm seed filling her throat.

He'd taken her in his arms, his breathing ragged, his ringed hand gripping her face. His lips against hers as he repeated, "Georgina, Georgina…" They fell silent in a sweaty embrace, his lips nuzzling her throat, his hand between her legs.

She stretched her arms over her head. Her entire body ached in a most delicious way. He now knew every inch of her flesh, and she his. It had been exciting, startling, beyond anything she'd hoped congress between a man and a woman would be.

Georgina threw off the covers and washed her face in the warm water her lady's maid had brought. She arranged the roses in the pitcher by the basin, her heart thudding in her chest.

Donning her dressing gown, she grabbed her sketchbook and threw open the heavy curtains. Sunlight bathed the room. The view of Ironvine's endless green park filled her vision as she perched herself on the couch by the window.

Her pencil flew over the paper. Drawing quickly from memory, she laid down the lines of Charles's face. The way he'd looked at her when he'd first spied her in his father's secret room. Surprise, apprehension, dread, and a hint of anger that soon grew into fervour and then something darker, richer.

His seduction in that room had been so unique, so commanding. She truly did not know how to describe it properly and very much wanted to. She would with her lines. The lines of his face, his eyes, his lips. *Oh those lips.* Dangerous, powerful, magnificent. The sharp angle of his jaw.

She lost herself in this combination of feeling, memory, sensuality, and technique as her pencil flew over the page, as her fingertips rubbed out lines, smoothed out angles.

For all the information her sister had given her since she'd gotten married about relations between a man and a woman, never once had she mentioned what a man's tongue, teeth, lips, his fingers were capable of doing to a woman's body.

Philippa had always answered Georgina's many eager questions as a proud woman of experience. She enjoyed that prestige in her younger sister's eyes very much. She was sure her sister had never experienced her husband's tongue between her legs, in her…Georgina drove the pencil swifter against the paper as a delicious sting flared between her legs and melted her insides.

The sketch of his face fell from her lap, but she paid it no heed as she quickly outlined his body on another paper. Filled it in. Modified, rubbed.

Yes.

A knock at the door. "Ma'am?" Her lady's maid had come to help her dress. *Already?*

"Come in." Georgina quickly put away her papers and went to the basin to wash her hands.

Today, she and Charles were to go visit the Ironvine tenants. She would meet them all. Charles had mentioned that he liked visiting his tenants and seeing how their crops were going, and their livestock, to hear their concerns. It was important to him.

Dressed and ready, she entered the dining room for breakfast. She looked forward to seeing her husband, but the dining room was empty. He was not there. She ate quickly on her own.

"Are you ready?" Charles stood in the doorway, boots

muddy, face flushed. He took a roll and bit into it. "I went riding early this morning. I've missed it. I love riding here at Ironvine. I didn't want to wake you."

"I did enjoy my lie-in this morning, I must admit."

His lips quirked. "Tired, were you, Countess?"

She choked on her tea.

He let out a laugh. "Should we take the carriage then?"

"No, I'd love to ride."

They finished eating, and after, they mounted their horses and he led her through the edge of the park to a pathway smoothed with the years.

"Do you visit your tenants often?" she asked.

"Quite regularly when I'm here. Of course, I've known them since I was born."

"Thomas and my mother would only pay their tenants visits on Christmas and Easter for the most part. He'd once told me, "That's why I have a steward and pay him quite handsomely.""

"I am of the mind that if I show my tenants that I have their welfare in mind, by inquiry and discussion, by offering assistance where I can, they are more likely to be content. It's a circle, you see. Their satisfaction is mine. Their success is my success. Each adds to the other's measure, each compounds the other's."

She blinked up at him in the glare of the sun. "I very much agree."

They arrived at the first cottage. Introductions were made. They were invited to sit and drink. She asked the woman questions about her day and her duties, and gave the children sweet biscuits she'd had cook prepare. And they went on to the next house. And the next. And the next family.

She'd taken a paper with her in her reticule to jot down particulars of each family so she wouldn't forget them.

"I'm most impressed by your note-taking, Countess."

"It's my duty to know our tenants, not simply to pretend to

take an interest. I don't like to pretend. And if we are to have a good relationship, I feel it should be genuine."

He slanted his head. "Most of the young ladies of our acquaintance would not feel so strongly about this responsibility."

"Certainly my mother never did, except on the holidays when she would give each family a basket of food. She wouldn't even do that much, really. She would stand there at a distance and smile while a servant would do the handing over. She felt that fulfilled her obligation. It was something, of course, but not enough, in my opinion. Not quite right."

They spent the longest time at Charles's steward's home. His son, Joss, a young man about her brother's age, greeted them with a big smile and a hearty handshake for Charles, and a bow of his head for Georgina. "Very pleased to meet you, my lady. Very happy for you both."

"Thank you, Joss," said Georgina.

This was the Joss who had saved Charles from the castle ruins when they were children.

Charles beamed at him. He and Joss spoke easily. It was obvious they were old friends.

On their way home at last, their horses trod slowly along the path back to the house. "At Fairthorn, I had gotten to know a few of our tenants well," said Georgina. "One man especially, Mr. Talley, was like a grandfather to me. He would fix my shoes when the strap would break on my long walks to see him, tell me tales as he worked. Mrs. Talley, his wife, would show me how to knead dough and would give me a bun for the walk home. They had no children of their own. They were always so very kind to me."

"Did your mother know?"

"Oh no. She would not have approved."

"Our tenants have been without a mistress's touch for many, many years, Georgina. Your care shall not go unnoticed and will be greatly appreciated, I warrant."

"I fully intend to visit regularly and help in any way I can."

A small smile warmed his face, lighting up his eyes, and a flare of warmth ran over her flesh. She had made him happy, perhaps unexpectedly so.

And that pleased her most of all.

Chapter Forty-Five

Georgina

"His Grace the Duke of Oakley and Her Grace the Duchess of Oakley request your presence at a dinner party on—"

"You're joking!" Georgina burst out.

"I am not." Charles's somber gaze remained fixed on the invitation.

The servant had brought them their mail as they'd finished breakfast, and the Oakley seal had, of course, been the most prominent in the pile.

"They're here? At their house? At Tidesfar?"

"They are indeed."

"Are we going? We are still in mourning."

He let out a ragged breath. "It's not a ball or a dance, at least. We can't not attend. In recent years, the Duke and Duchess have only taken residency here at their country estate but once a year and then for barely a month's time. The first week they always have a dinner party for the local nobility." His features remained shuttered.

She put down her tea cup. "You do not wish to go?"

"We must go. Our families share a history, other than Hugh. My grandfather hunted with the Duke's grandfather, my father hunted with the Duke's father—both here at Ironvine and at their estate—and later, Father hunted and kept company with His Grace when he first inherited his title."

"Did that continue even when Hugh and the Duchess …"

"It stopped then, much to my father's great displeasure." He let out a short laugh as he handed her the invitation. "Of course, Father was proud of Hugh for taking up with her, only he didn't expect it to go on for as long as it did."

Georgina read the beautifully written invitation. "We shall attend and show them and everyone that there is no ill will between our houses. It shall also be an opportunity to get to know them better now that you are Earl, and judge their behaviour toward us, for if they did have something to do with Hugh's death…"

Charles folded his hands on the table. "I will tell you once more, tread carefully with them. Theirs is no ordinary playground."

There's an intriguing turn of phrase, she thought. "Of course." Georgina knew this would be a perfect opportunity for her to get closer to the Duchess. To offer her the gift she'd made. Another thought occurred to her. Would the Duchess wear the Graven necklace to the dinner where Justine and Brandon would surely be present?

She gave the invitation back to Charles. "As it shall be our first social event as the Earl and Countess of Ryvves, I want to look my very best. I shall certainly need an exceedingly fine dress in black, of course, and shoes and…"

"Do what you will, Georgie. You have access to your own money, you don't need to ask me for it." Charles went through the other letters.

She let out a small breath. *Of course. Charles had done that for her, hadn't he?*

Very much unlike her sister who had to ask her husband for every little thing she wished to shop for. She'd even refined different tones of voice depending on the cost of each article she hoped to purchase. Philippa would then judge the best time to make such requests so her husband would be agreeable.

Her lips tipped up into a smile. Not Georgina. No.

"And I have you to thank for that." She squeezed his arm. "I'd best go to Mrs. Thompson's in the village without delay and put in my order." She dashed off.

In the hall, she stopped herself, dashed back into the room, and planted a kiss on his cheek.

Chapter Forty-Six

Charles

"The Earl of Ryvves, the Countess of Ryvves," the herald announced their arrival at the Duke of Oakley's dinner.

They were greeted by the Duke and Duchess. Georgina was relieved to see that Her Grace was not wearing the Wolfsgate necklace this evening, but another no less impressive piece, this one dripping with diamonds and sapphires which made her even more striking than she already was.

"Ryvves, a pleasure," the Duke greeted Charles. His Grace's gleaming, aqua blue gaze hit Georgina like the summer sun, rendering one helpless in its glare. "My dear, how lovely to see you again. Marriage certainly has made you even more beautiful than you already were in London." He took her hand in his and kissed it. Charles's jaw clenched.

"Thank you, Your Grace."

"My lord," said the Duchess on a smile in a perfectly gracious and pleasant tone. "Congratulations on your marriage."

"I thank you, Your Grace," replied Charles.

Her Grace took Georgina's hand in hers. "Countess, I longed to see you again since we met at the ball in London. I so enjoyed our brief time together there."

"I too, Your Grace. The Earl and I were so pleased to hear the news that you and the Duke have come to stay for a time. We are most excited to be here this evening."

After more tidings of goodwill were exchanged, Charles and Georgina entered the grand hall of Tidesfar, the Oakley mansion. Georgina let out a small gasp. A veritable ballroom.

"Have you never been here before?" he asked.

"No, never. It's spectacular."

The high coffered ceilings lined in gold, the walls adorned with Baroque cherubs and mythological creatures fluttering past, and the polished marble floor all bespoke of a house that belonged to the highest rank of the aristocracy. The number of liveried servants lining the walls and bustling through the guests alone was staggering.

All eyes were upon Charles and Georgina as they moved through the grand hall. Georgina was resplendent in a black silk gown, diamonds glittering in her loosely coiffed hair coiled with a black silk scarf. She was elegance personified. Her fingers curled tighter in his hand as she spotted her brother, Thomas.

Thomas met her gaze, his posture straightening. She nodded at him and he bowed his head in acknowledgment to her and to Charles. Glancing up at him, Georgina gave Charles a smile. She was pleased and relieved that her brother was polite. Thomas went back to his conversation with another gentleman. The man he was speaking to turned and took Georgina in boldly, a grin forming on his lips. Matthew. *Bastard*.

Several couples stared at them, whispering loudly, eyes wide. Was it their sudden marriage? Georgina's mother's disapproval? Was it Hugh's death? The duel? Ignoring them all, Charles guided his wife to where Brandon and Justine stood.

"There you are." Justine embraced Georgina. "You both look marvelous."

"Graven." Charles shook hands with Brandon. "What a to-do, eh?" he muttered.

Brandon clamped a hand on his shoulder as he let out a dark laugh. "Ryvves, welcome to the rest of your life."

"I used to slide in and out of these soirees without much care or notice."

"Those days are over, my friend," said Brandon. "That was a hard lesson for me to learn as well. Both of us inherited our titles in an unexpected and disturbing fashion, did we not?"

"We did. But you, Brandon, were the one destined to inherit, being the only child and son. I was never meant for all this grandeur."

"You were born to it, Charles. Made for this. You see how thinking in extreme terms as 'never' can be a problem?"

"I had lots of nevers, and yet…"

"Fortune is a whimsical creature. We can choose to either flounder or flourish with what she throws in our paths. And yet, both take a wild supply of energy, I can tell you."

"I see the local ton is here."

"But of course. Tonight is an event not to be missed."

"Unquestionably," Charles muttered as his gaze roved over the guests. A woman with dark hair in a coral gown offered him a brazen smile. *Damn. Elinor Whatley.* Charles blew out a huff of air. He'd forgotten about her.

Mrs. Whatley had been one of his lovers here in the country last winter. Her husband, Mr. Whatley, a stout and overdressed young country gentleman, stood next to her, preening himself as he spoke to another lady. He most especially enjoyed pontificating to any willing audience of females.

The year before last, a marriage agreement formed of mutual desperation had been struck between Elinor and Whatley's families, and they had married. The lady had a tiny dowry, two younger sisters, and her titled father—titled but without income—had accrued debts that he could not pay.

Meanwhile, much to Whatley's family's great displeasure,

not one, but four young ladies had turned down Mr. Whatley's marriage proposals in quick succession. What he lacked in personality and handsomeness, and, it must be said, masculin-'ity, Mr. Whatley, an only son and heir, more than made up for this imbalance with his great wealth which Elinor's father greatly appreciated.

Upon their marriage, Elinor's parents and younger siblings lived quite comfortably, their debts paid along with a new, additional income. And much to his parents' relief, Whatley was now a respectable married gentleman above reproach.

Behind closed doors, Elinor squirmed alone in her bed every night. She had told Charles that her husband had only touched her once—on their wedding night. It had lasted no longer than a few moments and he'd seemed, quite surprising to her, disgusted by the act.

After months and months of her husband avoiding her bed, even shoving her away on a howl when she'd attempted to mount him one night as he slept, she finally realised the truth of her marriage and began to take lovers, to which her husband delightfully ignored, and, for which, he was gratefully relieved.

Elinor put her arm through her husband's and whisked him away from his audience and swiftly slid through the guests toward Charles and Georgina. Charles groaned inwardly.

"What is the matter?" Georgina asked.

"Nothing."

Whatley and Elinor bowed before them. "I say, Ryvves, splendid to see you," said Whatley in his loud affected voice which always made Charles wince. "Our condolences for your dear brother, of course. He shall be missed."

"I thank you, Mr. Whatley."

Whatley showered Georgina with a pompous grin. "And congratulations on your nuptials, my dear."

"Thank you, Mr. Whatley," she replied. "Mrs. Whatley." She bowed her head at Elinor.

Elinor barely glanced at her. "Countess." She only had eyes for Charles. Blazing, gleaming, hungry eyes. "So very good to see you again, my lord. What a shame our paths did not cross in town as I'd hoped."

Charles had no reply to her remark other than a cold half smile.

"Ah Lady Graven," Mr. Whatley's voice tittered at Justine. "Don't you look splendid in vermillion this evening?"

"I thank you, Mr. Whatley. How kind of you to say." Justine bowed her head to him. Whatley immediately joined Georgina and Justine's conversation as Elinor inched closer to Charles.

That syrupy rose scent of hers filled his nostrils and dragged him back a thousand years to plowing into her in her drawing room in broad daylight, while her husband was upstairs in his bedchamber plowing into his favourite male servant. How they'd all enjoyed the pretence.

"You are the Earl of Ryvves now, eh?" Elinor's grin deepened. "And married."

"I am."

"Won't that make things more fun?" She let out a soft laugh.

"To what things are you referring, Mrs. Whatley?"

"One great, formidable thing in particular, which lies between your le—"

He pulled away from her, his gaze cold. "Madame, never speak to me in this manner again. Ever. Do you understand me?"

A sour grin flashed over her lips. "Ah. A faithful husband, eh? Very charming." She let out a scoff. "How long will that last, I wonder?"

"My wife and I are none of your concern. Have I made myself clear?"

She pursed her lips, her neck seeming to lengthen. "My lord." She bowed her head.

He stalked off, scrubbing a hand across his mouth as if that would cleanse him of that *tête à tête*. Of Elinor Whatley.

A hand slid through his arm and pressed. Georgina. Her brows pulled together. "You and Elinor Whatley?"

Dammit!

"Pardon?"

"I suppose I must become accustomed to the fact that you have lain with many women of my acquaintance."

His mouth dried, and his breath burned in the back of his throat.

"Was she trying it on with you?"

"Georgina—"

"Was she?"

"I let her know quite clearly and adamantly that all that is no more. Ever."

"Is that what you want?"

He blinked. "Of course I do."

"Don't say it like that. Say what you feel, not what will produce the desired result. Not to simply sweep it all away to make things better faster."

Say what you feel? That was the one thing he could rarely do. He'd trained himself never to do it. But from the very first, ever since he'd known Georgina, she'd always dared him to be honest. Always demanded the truth from him.

"I don't want her. Don't even like her."

"You don't have to say those things."

"I do. They're the truth." His fingers dug into her flesh. "After everything we've been through together, the truth matters to me, and it matters most between us." His heart thrummed in his chest. It did matter, for the first time in his life. The bloody truth mattered.

She held his gaze, her lips easing, curving into a slight grin. "Poor Mrs. Whatley. To have such a husband, and to lose such a lover."

"Georgina—"

"She must have been very keen to reclaim you tonight."

"I was never hers to claim or to lose."

Her chin lifted. "There must be more here tonight?"

"I want only you." He needed her to hear it, and he needed to utter those words. "Tell me you believe me. I need to know you believe me."

She brought her hand to his chest and pressed over his heart, her touch a burning spear. "I believe you," she whispered roughly.

He clutched her hand in his. "I am gratified to hear it."

No one had ever looked him in the eye and believed in him. Believed him yes, for he was a good liar. The falsehoods that he would weave and twist with tiny truths over the years to seduce women, flatter women, flatter men, and get his way, were many. Creating tales that hovered between truth and lies had become his forte.

But with Georgina, that had always been nigh impossible. Now? Absolutely distasteful. Unacceptable. His muscles tightened. He did want to be faithful to her, there was no question of it. An astonishing fact, which was, in truth, empowering.

"Ryvves, how are you?" A group of new guests had arrived, and they greeted Charles and Georgina.

"Ah…" Georgina's hand wrapped around his arm. "Here is another."

He followed her gaze. "For fuck's sake. What the hell is she doing here?"

Chapter Forty-Seven

Charles

AMANDA WAS HERE at the Oakley dinner.

"She must have come with her brother who was invited. There's Andrew—" With a lift of her chin, Georgina pointed out Andrew Blakelock, Amanda's brother, a gentleman, who was a friend.

"Good evening, my Lord Ryvves," came a familiar voice from behind them.

"Aunt Vivian, hello."

Her eyes gleamed. "This is your wife?"

"It is. Georgina, this is my Aunt Vivian, my mother's sister, Mrs. Dunsmore."

"And Alice's stepmother," said Georgina on a bow. "We met in London. How lovely to see you again, Mrs. Dunsmore."

"It is indeed lovely to meet again, and in such happy circumstances. So much has happened since the night of that ball in London. Quite a whirlwind, to be sure." She eyed Charles decidedly.

"A whirlwind, indeed," agreed Georgina.

"We only just arrived from London yesterday. Of course, Alice and I were quite disappointed to have missed your wedding, but no matter, we are thrilled for you both. Congratulations."

"Thank you, Aunt."

"Alice is here with you this evening, is she not?" asked Georgina.

"She is. She went for a turn about the room with a very handsome young gentleman."

"Did she?" Charles smiled at his aunt.

"One would need a companion to take a turn in such a house, for it would be too easy to get lost in this grand *palais*," Aunt Vivian remarked.

Matthew drew up next to Aunt Vivian with Alice on his arm, and Georgina visibly stiffened.

"Georgina, how good it is to see you again." Alice bowed to Georgina in greeting. "Charles. How wonderful that the two of you are married. So very romantic of you."

"Oh indeed. Very romantic," Matthew's voice jeered at them. "Countess." Matthew inclined his head. "Ryvves."

"Mr. Penry took us on a turn around the room. This house is quite extraordinary. More like a royal palace," said Alice, a nervous giggle curling under her words.

"We were just saying the very thing. It is indeed a spectacular house," said Georgina.

"In truth, the Oakleys have, for centuries, been close to the royal family," remarked Charles.

"Really?" said Alice.

Aunt Vivian recounted an occasion from her youth when the Prince of Wales had visited the present Duke's parents.

"How wonderful," murmured Alice.

Matthew turned toward Charles and Georgina, a twist to his lips. "Congratulations are indeed in order. Married hot on the heels of Hugh's untimely death. Last time we saw each other, Ryvves—" his voice jeered emphatically on Charles's title— "your brother and your wife were kissing, eh, Georgina? Stealing your brother's bride is certainly romantic."

"I was never Hugh's bride," said Georgina cooly.

Charles leaned into Matthew, his face stony, lips snarling, voice stinging. "My wife's name shall never again pass from your foul lips. Do you understand, Mr. Penry? My wife is the Countess of Ryvves to you."

"Yes, indeed, she is." Matthew swallowed hard, his face paled.

"Never speak to either of us ever again or speak of us for you shall suffer the cut from me, and what fun that shall be."

Matthew's eyes widened, his lips fell open. "I was only—"

"Leave us."

Matthew's shoulders stiffened and he bowed curtly. Turning to Alice and Aunt Vivian, he bowed and took his leave.

Charles put his hand on his wife's back and her gaze met his. He was relieved to see that she did not seem distressed.

"How wonderful that the possibility of suffering social exile from the Earl of Ryvves is a dire penalty Mr. Penry can ill afford at present."

"How so?"

"That night at Vauxhall Thomas told me that Matthew's family is very much in debt."

"Are they?"

"Last month his family's circumstances drastically changed with a bad investment he and his father had made, but their love of spending did not alter."

"Thus he is in wont of a wealthy wife."

"Which is why my brother was so irritated with me and Matthew at Vauxhall that night. Even though he considers Matthew a friend, he wanted me to stay clear of him."

"Even your brother did not trust his own friend's intentions with his very wealthy sister." Charles's eyes narrowed at Matthew taking Alice on his arm once again.

"He seems to be paying much attention to Alice this evening."

"Yes, he is."

"My brother was quite taken with her in London, but she seems to be easily swayed by Mr. Penry's flirting and flattery."

"Well, Mr. Penry prides himself on his great charm and charisma."

"He certainly does," she replied evenly. "Look at Thomas." She gestured discreetly to where her brother stood, a scowl etched on his face, a glass of wine in his stiff hand as he watched Matthew and Alice converse with a group of guests. "Surely Matthew knows that his good friend has feelings for the girl."

"Of course he does, but he's a selfish nob. And Alice is the easy answer to his problem."

A familiar airy laugh rose up, and he clenched his jaw. Amanda. Matthew was amusing Amanda with a tale, the two of them laughing along with Mr. and Mrs. Whatley. But Alice was not laughing. She did not seem to understand the joke.

CHARLES DRANK a fresh glass of Madeira as he watched the Duke converse with his wife across the room.

"Good evening, my lord," a familiar cool voice said at his side.

His eyes narrowed over Amanda. "What are you doing here?"

"Enjoying a night out." Amanda exchanged her empty glass for a full one from the servant's tray.

"Forgive me, I thought you were in mourning for your dead husband."

"I've had quite enough of mourning. Doesn't suit me."

"Indeed, I mistook you for a typical widow. Are you not humbled in the least by William and Hugh's sudden and violent ends because of you?"

She eyed him, her cool and relaxed gaze a challenge. "It was their choice as gentlemen, was it not?"

Matthew and Alice strolled by them. Alice smiled shyly at Charles, whilst Matthew sent Amanda an appreciative gaze. The idiot was flirting with her as he tried to bedazzle Alice.

Amanda sent Matthew a smug smile in return. Charles let out a dry laugh at that familiar sight. How she enjoyed conquering. He leaned into her, lowering his voice. "I wonder, is Matthew more interested in the widow's fortune or her experienced cunt?"

She met his acidic gaze with her own, just as she would in the old days when they'd have biting conversations in public plotting schemes. "I'm not quite sure if he deserves my cunt."

"Make him work for it. You always enjoyed that, didn't you?"

"Oh, I still do." She sipped her wine.

"Hugh once told me the sculpture gallery here is a spectacular place for assignations."

"Did he?" Her voice rose slightly.

He'd caught her interest with that remark. Charles's lips tipped into a sly grin that he knew she'd recognise. "He did. It's just off the main hall and is lit with torches, which only adds to the illicit atmosphere for such a *rendezvous vous*."

She laughed as she took a delicate swallow of her wine. "I must say, Charles, I find it most satisfying that as I am enjoying my freedom from my husband, you are now saddled with a wife. Poor darling. But that won't stop you, will it?" she said in that slicing yet syrupy tone.

Saddled? No, he wasn't bound against his will, squirming to be free. He actually felt freer, more at ease than he ever had. "I am most satisfied with my marriage, madame."

"With her?" Amanda laughed. Laughed the same way they used to laugh together over gossip, over others' weaknesses. It had once filled him with satisfaction. Was that what his life had been filled with before? Only a series of temporal triumphs and deceits?

"Ah, Charles..." She let out a dramatic sigh. "At this moment, being married is all shiny and new to you both, but that sparkle won't last long. It won't. You—like me, like Hugh—cannot deny yourself. You will be stifled for the lack of—"

"Madame, you are confusing me with my brother."

"You, sir, do not compare to your brother."

"Ah..a compliment from you at last."

"Tell me, Lord Ryvves, were you bothered that I had your brother in my bed?"

"In faith, I was only bothered for Hugh because he had no idea the kind of manipulative beast you are. Now he's dead, and here you are looking for your next victim."

Her eyes blazed, and her jaw tightened. "I was the victim. He was the liar."

"What did he lie to you about?"

"I expected more from him. Much more." She averted her gaze.

"And what in God's name was that?"

She gave her empty glass to a passing servant. "You are boring me, Charles. Go find your new wife and bore her instead."

"I gladly take my leave of you, Mrs. Treharne." He stalked away from her and took in a deep breath to relieve himself of the stench.

Chapter Forty-Eight

Georgina

GEORGINA WAS SEATED at the right hand of the Duchess, a great honour that neither she nor Charles had expected as he left her to sit at the opposite end of the grand table by the Duke. They had just finished their soup course, and the roast meats had arrived at the table.

"How are you finding married life, Lady Ryvves?"

"I am liking it very much, Your Grace."

"He's a good husband to you?"

"He is. I've known Charles all my life, so we are not complete strangers to one another."

"Ah, so you were friends before you married? As were the Duke and I. I believe those sorts of marriages to be the hardiest."

"My good friend Lady Graven and her husband were also friends from childhood before they wed. And their marriage is the strongest and the happiest that I have ever known."

"When two people are betrothed and have not even met yet, those marriages are like games of chance."

"Oh, I quite agree."

"It must have been a great shock to your husband to claim the title after his brother's untimely death?"

"It was indeed. He had just lost his father and now to lose his brother was quite difficult."

"Duelling is a dirty business, but one must stand up for one's honour." The Duchess cut into her fillet.

"Yes, one must."

"Shocking that they both died, don't you think?"

Georgina pushed the small forkful of carrots down the throat quickly, her back straightening even more than it already was. The Duchess was asking her probing questions in a very casual manner about Hugh's death. Charles's warning to be careful with Her Grace flashed in her memory.

"Most unusual, yes. One fell immediately and the other, unfortunately, suffered his wound."

"No one truly triumphs in these situations."

"No, indeed." Georgina's fingers slid around her wine glass.

Several more courses came and went. The precision of the servants in the dining room kept the spectacle and the serving rolling along smoothly.

"Zandra—" the Duke's clear voice rang out from the other end of the long table. "You must hear what Graven just told me."

"Do tell me, darling."

Georgina's grip on her fork tightened. *Zandra?* Zandra, Cassandra. She let out a tight breath, her pulse humming. Z. It was her. The love letters in Hugh's possession were from the Duchess.

At long last, the desserts were brought to the table. An astonishing assortment of ices, colourful cream tarts, fluffy syllabubs, and exotic fruits. Georgina chose a lemon syllabub and it was placed before her.

"Tell me, Lady Ryvves, do you know Mrs. Treharne well?" asked the Duchess.

The Duchess had questions about Amanda, just as Georgina thought she might.

"Mrs. Treharne and her husband were close friends with

my elder brother and my husband from childhood. We all grew up together here in the country."

"Pity, for one so young and attractive to be a widow."

"Yes."

"I'm sure if she wished to marry again she would have no problem finding a suitor."

Georgina dipped her spoon into her syllabub. "Ah, Mrs. Treharne has never had …" Pursing her lips, she put her spoon down. *I mustn't gossip about Amanda with the Duchess.* She must remain steady, neutral.

"Yes?" She tilted her head. She was looking forward to Georgina's remark.

"I quite agree, she would have no problem finding a suitor. She's very beautiful."

The Duchess let out a sardonic laugh. "You, my dear, are quite lovely. And not only your physical beauty, no, your spirit commends you." Her heavily ringed hand reached out and touched Georgina's. Cool, silky, light. A small smile lit the woman's lips. Georgina's face heated and she wasn't sure why. "You and I shall make great friends while we are here, I can feel it." She raised her wine glass to Georgina. A bond of understanding had been made between them.

It's what she'd wanted, wasn't it?

Georgina raised her glass as well and drank, but the wine did not refresh her, it only warmed her further. She caught her husband's tight gaze. She knew he was wary of her getting close to the Duchess. The Duke said something to Charles, who met his gaze and laughed. A false laugh. She could always tell when he did that.

The Duchess rose, signalling for all the ladies to retreat to the drawing room and leave the men to their smoking, drinking, and talk.

Georgina passed her husband on her way out of the dining room. He took up her hand, stopping her. Charles held her gaze as his warm lips brushed her hand, his fingers tightening their grip. Her breath shortened. Was it a warning?

"My Lord," she whispered.

"Do not worry, Ryvves, your wife shall be safe with us." Chuckling, the Duchess led Georgina and Justine out of the dining room, the other ladies before them.

A flash of pink showed underneath the Duchess's dress. Georgina blinked. "What pretty shoes you are wearing, Your Grace."

"Do you like them?"

"Pink is one of my very favourite colours, and I have never seen a shoe in such a bright happy colour."

Except in that snuff box of Hugh's.

She raised her dress an inch and showed them. "They are my favourite. I wear them on special occasions only, as they are rather delicate and the heel is high and not in fashion now, nor is it the most comfortable, but they are quite beautiful and I enjoy them greatly."

"I only have one pair of higher-heeled shoes," said Georgina. "And I agree, they are not the most comfortable, especially if one is dancing."

"I am quite addicted to pretty shoes. I collect them, and I have so many buckles to choose from."

"A delightful addiction if ever there was," said Georgina.

"Luckily my husband enjoys indulging me in my addictions."

He certainly does.

"That is truly a blessing," said Justine, sliding her arm through Georgina's.

"Your Grace, I must ask you—" Mrs. Whatley came up alongside the Duchess, casting a doleful glance at Georgina. She and the Duchess drifted off into the parlour.

"What a grand house, do you not think so, Georgina?" Justine whispered to her as they crossed the centre court, following the other ladies.

"Insanely grand. And they only come here but once a year, and then for only a handful of weeks. Or is it days? Are we to blame? Is our part of England not fashionable enough?"

Justine let out a laugh. "They must have so many interests and responsibilities that keep them elsewhere. Goodness, I don't think I've ever seen such enormous vases before. They dwarf the average person."

"Their porphyry colour is magnificent and rare." Georgina stopped in her tracks, her breath cut. Her gaze hung on a larger-than-life-sized portrait of the Duke in his younger days. Regal, as handsome as he was in real life. The commander of all that he surveyed. A leader who inspired reverence.

"What a fine likeness," murmured Justine. "He is most… impressive. I find that portraits usually give the sitter a false air of majesty and import, but not so with His Grace. In life, he is all that this portrait conveys."

"Indeed." Georgina moved closer to the painting, inspecting the bottom of the massive canvas. "Oh Lord," she murmured to herself. Stepping back, her heart thumping in her chest, a smile lit her face as she took in the entire portrait. "It's a Gainsborough. I never ever thought I'd see one in real life. If he paints your portrait…"

Justine moved to the large painting on the next wall. "This painting is of the two of them — she's remarkable."

The Duke and Duchess stood under a grove of trees, her arm through his, their estate stretched out behind them, Tidesfar towering in the distance. Both of them were younger, at ease with one another, and smiling ever so slightly in the very same way.

Unlike other portraits of husbands and wives she'd seen, this wife was no demure feminine creature. She and her husband were of one spirit, one mind, Her Grace's countenance was just as straightforward and bold in aspect as her husband's.

Georgina glanced at the bottom of the canvas. "Joshua Reynolds…" fell from her lips.

"Very good," came the Duchess's voice next to her.

Georgina swivelled at her voice. "Your Grace, the two most famous English painters of our time have painted your portraits? I mean, of course they have."

"You appreciate fine art, do you?"

"I do. These are extraordinary paintings by extraordinary English artists."

"Georgina is a very talented artist herself, Your Grace," Justine said.

Georgina's face heated. "I would not call myself so as we're standing here before a Reynolds and a Gainsborough."

"And what do you create, Countess?"

Create. There was a word, there was a notion. Justine and the Duchess waited for her reply. "I enjoy drawing and painting portraits very much."

"I would like to see your work."

"I…"

"As you might imagine, we have many social engagements this week, but I could visit you the day after tomorrow?"

Georgina was at a loss for words. Justine smiled at her pointedly.

"You must come to Ironvine, Your Grace. I would be honoured to show you the estate and my sketches."

"Excellent. I look forward to it. Now, come, ladies, before the men arrive and spoil our time together."

Georgina's heartbeat raced wildly. She'd accomplished her task. The Duchess was coming to Ironvine.

Chapter Forty-Nine

Charles

THE MEN finally began to leave the table, yet they lingered in their discussions as they emptied several bottles of port. Matthew quietly excused himself and left the dining room.

"My compliments, Your Grace, your port is magnificent." Charles raised his glass at the Duke as they rose from the table. "I do not think I've ever tasted the like before."

"You have a fine palette then, Ryvves, for I can promise you, you have not ever tasted this wine before nor likely shall again, unless you are, of course, in my company." The Duke chuckled.

"Your Grace brings it over from Portugal yourself?"

"Something like that." He winked at Charles.

"It is very fine, indeed," said Brandon.

In the drawing room, Charles found Georgina with Alice and his aunt. "How are you enjoying yourselves?"

"Very well," said Alice, her gaze darting over the men slowly entering the drawing room.

"Aunt, did you and Alice see the sculpture gallery? The Oakley collection is quite remarkable."

"Not for many, many years."

"Shall we have a look?"

"I'd love to." His aunt's face lit up as she slid her arm in his, and with Georgina and Alice following them, Charles brought them to the long, dark gallery dramatically lit by torches.

"I'd once heard that the Duke's father had gone to Athens and brought back small sculptures he'd come across at some ancient temple," said Aunt Vivian, her voice just above a whisper. "And that the present Duke continues to acquire such pieces."

Glowing firelight cast a warm glow over the lustrous sheen of the many white marble sculptures as they strolled through the rows of sculptures. "They must be here," said Charles. An audible gasp rose up behind them and they stopped.

Alice's eyes had widened considerably as she took in the nude figure of Apollo, the sun god, urgently chasing the maiden, Daphne. Alice was in a state of arrest.

"Wonderful..." Georgina murmured as she walked around the marble figures, her face awash in glee. "What do you think, Alice?"

Charles's pulse jumped at the sight of his wife so enraptured by the sculpture.

"Em...I..." Alice's face flushed, and her lips parted as she took in the spectacle of Apollo pursuing the object of his desire.

"I would say it is a battle between chastity and lust," said Charles.

"Oh...is it?" said Alice.

Aunt Vivian stepped closer to the piece. "The story goes that Eros, the famed god of love, played a trick on Apollo for insulting him. He shot him with a golden arrow of love and he fell hard for Daphne. However, he shot Daphne with a lead arrow so that she would hate Apollo. Thus, whilst the god was inflamed with desire for her, the girl was determined to reject him."

"Quite an impossible situation for a man never before rejected," muttered Charles.

"Can you imagine?" Georgina smirked at Charles.

Aunt Vivian continued, "Daphne had asked her father, also a god, to help her, and just as Apollo caught up with her—this is that very moment—see there, he's just reached her, he's touching her—she instantly transforms into a tree."

Alice only bit her lip.

"I ask you, is that being saved?" said Charles. "Being immobilised into this thing, confined and muted forever, is preferable to being ravished by a god who loves and adores her?"

"Until he no longer loves her," quipped Georgina. "Arrow or no, Apollo was a passionate and unfaithful sort, was he not, Aunt?"

"Quite right, my dear. He was most fickle." Aunt Vivian laughed softly. "Very much a scoundrel."

"Daphne made a choice, and in that, she trumped his hollow conquering," said Georgina. "Maybe she was better off being a tree than succumbing to such a savage, hungry predator."

"I suppose there are women who don't appreciate savage and hungry lovers, eh?" Charles quipped.

Alice's eyes widened.

Aunt Vivian laughed. "A great many prefer a more stable existence, Charles. Perhaps you've never met those ladies, hmm?"

He had no witty reply. He was only transfixed on his wife's molten gaze in the quivering shadows of the torchlight. He knew that Georgina was a woman who wanted a savage and hungry lover for herself as well as stability. Could marriage be that?

A jolt shot through his insides, and he shifted his weight. He wanted to be the one to give that to her. He wanted to experience that with her.

Aunt Vivian's clear voice rang out, "Alice, dear, what do you think of the sculpture?"

Alice remained spellbound by Apollo's hand gripping Daphne's bare hip, holding her in possession, claiming her for himself as she attempted to twist away from the bewitched god. Her attention slid to the god's bare muscular thighs.

Georgina's lips curved into a slight smile, a delicious knowing smile that melted into a softer one, as she moved alongside Alice. "I must say, the movement the artist has created here from stone is sublime. Do you not think so, Alice?'

"Yes, it is remarkable indeed."

"Such a rush of movement fuelled by opposing forces: her fear and his great desire. I can feel it. Can you?"

"Yes, I can," whispered Alice.

Charles's breath deepened, a growl rising in his lungs. He could smell Georgina from here as if he were Apollo himself and she his Daphne. But Georgina did not run away from him. Her body thrilled to his in the shadows of their bedchamber. She'd taken his hand, chose him, became his mate. That growl in his chest became a strange, deep ache spiralling from the very centre of him.

Footsteps and chatter broke the thick spell between them. In the next aisle, wandering in between portrait busts of previous Dukes and Duchesses of Oakley, two couples who Aunt Vivian knew greeted them. They all exchanged pleasantries, and the couples strolled away.

Charles touched his Aunt's arm. "Aunt, I believe one of the sculptures you wanted to see is just over there." He pointed. "His Grace mentioned over dinner that he'd recently acquired The Three Graces."

"Wonderful."

Charles led them to the section of the gallery which the Duke had mentioned to him earlier, and they found the small marble trio of bare goddesses dancing together. "They are lovely."

"Yes they are," murmured Aunt Vivian.

Alice cast a quick glance over her shoulder at Apollo once more, and Charles and Georgina shared a grin.

Low voices and heavy footsteps grew louder and louder. The Duke and three of his friends all headed for the Three Graces.

"Ah, Oakley, a remarkable piece," said one gentleman.

"Indeed. Good for you for plucking it and bringing it home," said another.

"There's so much to be had there, most of it lying about," said the Duke. "The Ottomans don't really care if there's money to be had for it…"

"If you don't take it, I imagine it'll only rot," said one.

"Quite right," remarked another.

His Grace turned toward them. "Ryvves. You found it."

Charles bowed his head. "I did, Your Grace."

The Duke's gaze honed in on Georgina. "Countess." His voice had gone velvety smooth. Charles took in a tight breath as his wife bowed to the Duke, and the Duke's chin lifted, lips curving. Satisfaction. "You are enjoying my recent acquisition?"

"It is a beautiful piece."

He held her gaze. "Once I find something I like, it must be mine."

"Certainly, this is a once-in-a-lifetime find."

His eyes narrowed over her. "I very much agree."

"Did Your Grace travel to Greece to find it?" asked Aunt Vivian.

"No. I have an agent who knows exactly what I like. He found it for me. One day, I hope to go myself."

"Although this piece is beautifully displayed in Your Grace's magnificent gallery," said Georgina. "It is, I find, a shame that it was taken from its native land where it surely has much historical significance."

A gasp, a scoff, a murmur.

Ah fuck. Charles clenched his jaw.

Silence reigned as the Duke turned to Georgina once more as if he were seeing her anew. Her body tightened under his grim scrutiny. "You are a curious creature. I've saved it. The Greeks are not a nation as you and I may know, but a people enslaved by the Ottomans who rule all of the Levant. These conquerors do not appreciate these slivers of ancient Greek history as art, they are but rubble to them and sell them most willingly. But I appreciate them, and I am willing to pay to liberate them, to preserve them, not only for my private pleasure but for future generations."

"Indeed, Your Grace," said Georgina. "Yet perhaps one day the Greeks shall win their freedom and then —"

Muffled voices rose in the distance. "You are spectacular." Desperate voices. Grunts. Groans. A cry. "Here — ah yes. Kiss me."

Charles recognised both voices. Clamping down his jaw even harder in order to not grin as he wished to, he noticed movement in a dark alcove at the end of the hall. His aunt was frozen to the spot. Alice her lips parted, her face pale just as when she'd first laid eyes on Apollo chasing Daphne. Georgina's hand slid around his arm.

"What do we have here?" The Duke let out a dark chuckle as he turned toward the alcove.

At the end of the dark alleyway of sculptures, a man and a woman clutched at each other, his one hand clasped around her bottom, keeping her close as they kissed urgently, their bodies grinding into each other. The woman's blonde hair caught the dim light. The angles of the man's face were made visible. There was no mistaking them.

Amanda clung to Matthew. Matthew gripped Amanda. Hungry kisses, roving hands.

"Oh," Alice gasped, her hand flying to her mouth.

"There's a fine tableau," one of the Duke's friends remarked on a hard laugh.

"Damn me, look at her," murmured another. "Oh, I'd like to…yes, he's got it…"

With much haste, Aunt Vivian steered Alice out of the sculpture gallery. Charles and Georgina remained rooted to the spot. Georgina pressed her body against his.

"My collection always inspires, don't you know?" The Duke laughed and his friends joined him.

Amanda and Matthew stilled, the two of them turning. Freezing. Her eyes were wide as saucers. "No!" she cried out.

"What a magical gallery you have, Your Grace," said Charles. "I do believe Apollo caught his Daphne this evening, eh?"

The Duke roared with laughter, a dark, sharp laugh that had Georgina's fingers tightening around his.

Chapter Fifty

Charles

Matthew and Amanda had vanished.

As the Duke and his friends left the sculpture gallery, Charles led his wife to the next aisle of sculptures, deeper into the dark corridor. He squeezed her hand. "Georgie, you cannot speak to His Grace in that manner."

"I wanted to know why he —"

"There's only one reason. Ever. He's incredibly wealthy and has a very healthy sense of entitlement. And this encompasses all things. Not only sculptures."

"And people?"

"Yes."

"He did tell me 'once I find something I like, it must be mine.'"

"Yes, he did," Charles muttered as their footsteps made clear, clipped noises on the polished marble floor. "Did you enjoy watching Matthew?"

"I do not care about Matthew."

"I asked if you liked watching him."

Her eyes widened. A new idea. "Watching them kiss and…"

"Yes."

"Did you enjoy watching Amanda?" she asked.

Tightening his grip on her hand, he stopped before two marble figures in the throes of a passionate embrace. The male bore wings which were stretched out over himself and his lover. "This is the one."

"Eros and Psyche?"

"Very good."

Her shoulders eased as she pored over the marble statue. "Extraordinary."

"When I was a boy, the Duke's father would have holiday parties to which we as a family would be invited. One was at Christmas and the other was a very grand picnic on the summer solstice. On these occasions, Hugh and I would sneak in here, sneak all over the house really. But we especially liked it in here. We'd chase each other around the statues, ogle at them."

"Were they your first introduction to the female form?"

He let out a chuckle. "They weren't a flat drawing or a painting, and they were over life-size, and...we could touch them," he whispered as if it were an illicit secret, and she laughed. "This one, in particular, would fascinate me. Eros and Psyche are in the throes of their wild passion, so utterly focused on one another. Yet unlike Apollo and Daphne whose plight is tainted with menace, there's a tenderness here between these two, do you not think so?"

"I do, yes." A small smile lifted her lips.

"I always felt as if I were intruding on them, on their intimacy."

Georgina's breathing grew heavier. "They're both enraptured with one another—there's anticipation, excitement, and vulnerability all at once. I can feel it."

"Yes. They've just fallen in passionate love and are about to come together for the first time." Taking her hand in his, he brought their fingers to Psyche's bare breast where Cupid stroked her. The cool smooth as silk stone under his touch along with Georgie's hot fingers in his had his heart thrumming in his chest. He pressed himself against her back, his hard cock nestling perfectly in her rear, and she let out a small gasp as she pressed back. He'd answered her ache. Her body relaxed against his as their fingers continued their trail over the long curve of Psyche's bare hip.

"Tell me what you're thinking?" he whispered.

"The transitions between the different parts of her body are so…"

He let out a laugh. Of course, she was aching for the sculpture.

"I'm sorry, you meant…"

"Go on. Tell me."

She guided his hand. "Here—from hip to waist. So soft, so incredibly smooth…yet it's marble." Their hands trailed along the curve of Eros's arm embracing his love. "How he adores her."

"He does."

She guided their fingers along the edge of one of Eros's stiff and sturdy outstretched wings. "His wings show how aroused he is, but I feel they also show how his desire to protect her and protect their love."

"I agree." His free hand cupped a breast, stroking her, and she let out a small moan that stirred his blood. He felt the same way about Georgina, didn't he? A fierce desire fused with a fierce need to protect her. He nipped at her ear lobe and she shivered in his hold.

Georgina led Charles's fingers over Psyche's arse cheeks, which were pulled tight as she surged up at Cupid, her arms reaching for him and his promised kiss, anticipating his embrace. "What an ecstatic union this shall be…every line tells us that." She brought their fingers around Psyche's thigh, over her belly, along Cupid's arm down to his hand which gripped his lover's chest. "Do you feel it, Charles?" her voice vibrated with yearning, with craving.

He craved.

His arm wrapped around her waist, and Charles held Georgina close, her orange blossom scent filling his senses, the warmth of her skin enflaming him. "I feel it. I feel you, my Georgie," he breathed.

Stroking the edge of his jaw, she tilted her head towards him and her lips found his. Sweet silk.

On a groan he adjusted her in his hold and took her mouth, his tongue plundering, ravaging. Her taste drove him on for more friction, more sensation. Turning in his hold, she drew her arms around his middle, nestling her body into his on a whimper that sent his mind stuttering and his cock hardening.

There in the shadows, the flickering dim light of the torches glinting over the shiny curves and plains of marble at their side, Charles and Georgina became one in their greed for each other's flesh, their need for—

Coughing, the clearing of throats rose about them. "Pardon…"

"Oh my…"

Charles's body tightened, and with an arm around her, he pressed Georgina to his side. Her eyes blinked in the dim light, her fingers digging into his frock coat.

"Ah, 'tis the newlyweds. Our apologies." Mr. Whatley smothered his high-pitched laugh with a lace-trimmed hand-kerchief and made a ridiculous bow while a grinning older woman pulled him away.

"He'll tell everyone now." Georgina sat on a small cushioned settee against the wall, smoothing her hands down her dress.

"Good. As he said, we're the newlyweds." He smoothed a curl of hair against her temple where it belonged. "We've done nothing wrong, my wife, only proven our marital status."

"Isn't that a refreshing turn for your reputation, Lord Ryvves?"

"And for your recent disgrace, Countess."

"Quite right. You'd better kiss me some more."

Cuffing her neck, he brought his mouth to hers and, sliding a hand under her dress, found the wet heat between her legs.

Chapter Fifty-One

Charles

"I THINK Justine might enjoy hearing what we witnessed earlier," Georgina whispered as they entered the grand drawing room.

Charles admired Georgina's flushed face due to the release he'd just given her with his fingers. "I warrant she will." He enjoyed the rear view of his wife gracefully walking toward her friend in the drawing room.

"Ryvves, have you seen Amanda?" Andrew Blakelock came up alongside Charles.

"You've lost your sister, Blakelock?"

"I do not see her with the other ladies." His lips pressed together.

In Andrew's grim eyes, in the set of his mouth, Charles saw not only concern but worry. "I did see her recently. In the sculpture gallery."

"Ah, very good. Thank you." His tight features eased and he moved to leave.

Charles gripped his arm, stopping him. "She was with Matthew."

"Oh." He let out a groan, his shoulders sinking. "I trust you'll keep this between us."

"They were seen."

"Were they…"

"Afraid so."

"Christ. She's going through a rough time of it. She hasn't been sleeping or eating properly."

"Only drinking?"

Andrew's face tightened once more. "Coming here tonight was a terrible idea. Although she is in mourning, I thought that it would be good for her to be in company with people she knows and is fond of. She always so enjoyed a dinner party, and when she learnt of the Oakleys' invitation, she was most determined to attend."

"Was she?"

"Yes," Andrew murmured absently as he looked about the large room. He stiffened, his gaze locking on Matthew, who was attempting to have a conversation with Alice, only Alice looked positively stricken. "Matthew's here, though."

Charles followed his gaze. Justine and Georgina appeared alongside Alice, and Georgina put her arm through the girl's, made a quick remark to Matthew, and led Alice away from him.

Well done, Georgie, he thought.

"I'll go talk to him." On a huff, Andrew stalked toward Matthew. Matthew shook his head. No doubt he professed his innocence. Andrew's posture grew rigid, and he stalked out of the drawing room as Matthew blew out a huff of air. Turning, he caught Charles's cold gaze.

"Port, sir?" A servant with a silver tray of wine glasses blocked his view of Matthew's annoyance.

"Excellent." Charles brought a glass of wine to his lips as he noticed Matthew approaching. The servant left.

"Ryvves, were you in the sculpture gallery earlier with Miss Dunsmore and her stepmother?" Matthew asked him.

"Yes, we were admiring the Duke's collection. One moment

we were enjoying passions set in stone, and then suddenly passions in the flesh flared before us."

Matthew sucked in a breath, his nostrils flaring.

"How is it, Mr. Penry, that you seduced a widow whilst at the same time flirting with an innocent young girl?"

"I—"

"You really have come a long way. Might I remind you that Mrs. Dunsmore is my aunt, and I shall not allow you to ensnare my wealthy step-cousin to your advantage?"

Matthew scoffed. "I am only trying to save my family, my name. You wouldn't know anything about that."

"I suppose you should have considered those lofty principles over the years when you were spending your family's money on all sorts of amusements."

"You and Hugh enjoyed the same amusements."

"We could afford them."

"Yes, yes, with your money and your title, you can do as you please."

"Hate me for it, but it's the truth. Another truth is that now that you and Mrs. Treharne have been seen together in such a memorable manner—by even the Duke and his friends—you might have to marry the widow to save both your families' reputations."

"Oh dear God…"

"I don't think God gives a damn about who you're strumming, but with your little show tonight, you certainly made it everyone's business."

Matthew leaned in closer to Charles, his lips a snarl. "You and your brother always thought you were better than the rest of us, that nothing could touch you. Hugh got his, didn't he? Have you heard the rumours flying about? If you had, you'd be more inclined toward humility at this very moment."

Charles kept his features still, indifferent. He would not betray any emotion to this ass. "Rumours?" He drank his wine.

"That your wife was engaged to Hugh, but you wanted her

and the title for yourself. We all saw how attentive to her you were that night at the ball."

"This coming from Hugh's lackey?" Charles hissed.

Matthew's eyes narrowed. "There's more. That after the duel you turned your pistol on your own brother. It suits. You've always been a cold, slippery, calculating sort, not the amiable, gladsome man your brother was."

"And you've always been a jealous, resentful, petty sort."

Matthew shot him that practiced smirk of his and Charles's hand itched to smash it from his face. "Amanda told me herself that William had caught the two of you in London and challenged you to a duel."

"She's lying."

"Why would she lie when she suffers such agony?"

"Agony, indeed."

"Does your pretty wife know the truth? Everyone here tonight has heard these rumours. You'd best wash that smug look off your face, my lord, don't you think?"

Chapter Fifty-Two

Georgina

THE DUCHESS OF OAKLEY had arrived at Ironvine.

Georgina rushed outside with the servants to greet her as the Oakley coach came to a stop at the foot of the grand staircase. Her footman opened the door, and another held out his gloved hand to assist his mistress.

She emerged from the coach, a lovely small burgundy tricorn hat set at an angle on her head, a black cape over a burgundy and gold dress.

"Welcome to Ironvine, Your Grace." Georgina bowed.

"What a beautiful park you have, Countess."

"I agree. I'm pleased you like it.

"I would have ridden here on my horse, but I've brought you and the Earl a gift."

"A gift? How very kind."

Her liveried footman appeared just behind her holding a large wooden box.

"Lord Ryvves very much enjoyed the Duke's special Port last evening, and so my husband has sent a number of bottles for him to enjoy."

"His Grace is most generous. I thank you. The Port was remarkable."

"Is the Earl here today?"

"He is, yes. At present, he is working with his sword trainer."

"Does he practice with Mr. Swindon? He works with the Duke when we are here."

"Yes, I believe he does."

They entered the house, the Duchess's cloak was taken, and Georgina led her to her morning room. "Tea has been brought for us."

The Duchess took in the large room. "Beautifully appointed. Is it all yours, perhaps?"

"It is."

"Ah. It's always good for a woman to have her own rooms, do you not agree?"

"I do agree. For so long I did not, which is why now I feel most blessed."

"Blessed?"

"I suppose I always thought that when one gets married you have so many responsibilities and obligations that any personal freedoms would be greatly curtailed, especially by one's husband."

"Men are tricky beasts."

"Thus, I feel blessed that my husband does not wish to curtail me."

She let out a low laugh, a laugh that hinted at something other than their direct topic. "You are indeed most fortunate, Countess."

"Do call me Georgina, Your Grace."

"I shall." She smiled.

They drank their tea and ate small iced cakes as they talked about the dinner party. No mention was made of Amanda and Matthew. Had she not heard? Had her husband not told her what he'd witnessed? Georgina managed to curve their discussion to which books they were reading.

The Duchess had read "The Monk" and had very much

enjoyed it. "You must finish it, Georgina and then we can discuss it at length." She placed her empty cup on the table. "Do show me your sketches. I am most eager to see."

Georgina brought her to the large table where she had her work laid out, ready to be seen. Drawings and watercolours of the estate, the castle, and a number of studies of Charles's face.

"You are quite talented, Georgina. You use simple lines yet you've managed to articulate Ryvves's personality, a fleeting emotion. Remarkable."

"Thank you."

"Your parents fostered this talent of yours? Surely you've had a tutor?"

"My father had arranged for a painter friend of his to teach me for some time. But after Father died unexpectedly, the lessons stopped."

"What a shame."

"Much to my mother's distress, that did not make me stop. I could never imagine myself not drawing, not painting."

"It's much more than a pastime to you."

"Much more. I need to do it. It's a part of me." Georgina's face heated. She had only had such a conversation about her work before with Charles. Her Grace had honed right in on her desire. Being able to speak the truth, to not dissemble for fear of censure, was now a thing of the past in her new life.

Her Grace poured over the various drawings of Charles. "I could never sketch the human form properly. I found it so frustrating. Flowers, leaves, fruits, yes, but a face?" Her gaze lifted to Georgina. "Heaven forfend—a figure?" The grin on her face froze suddenly, and Georgina very well knew why.

She'd seen the painting of Hugh which stood behind Georgina, propped up against the wall on the floor.

The Duchess's posture stiffened as her gaze riveted on the oil study of Hugh. "Is this painting yours?" Her voice had cooled.

"No. It is an unfinished portrait of Hugh, recently done. I

found it amongst his things. The likeness is quite good, is it not?"

"Is this why you invited me here?" Her icy tone stopped Georgina's heart. "What is it you want of me?"

Georgina's pulse thudded in her neck. "I too know loss, Your Grace. My beloved father was taken from me much too soon, and I have but one small likeness of him and many of his letters. They are precious to me. Would you like to see the painting?"

The Duchess only nodded and was perfectly still as Georgina placed the canvas against the table on the floor where it caught the sunlight. Hugh's brown eyes and his dark blond hair glowed in the light. The blue coat he wore was a rich hue of cobalt that faded where the painter had smudged the edges, the painting incomplete. Incomplete forever.

The Duchess's face softened immediately, and then just as suddenly, that softness was gone, replaced by stiff lines. A mask.

Georgina cleared her dry throat. "This is a preliminary study the artist made in preparation for painting Hugh's portrait. I recently uncovered it here at the house along with keepsakes amongst Hugh's possessions."

The Duchess said nothing, her gaze pinned on the painting.

Georgina continued, "If I may be so bold, Your Grace, I would like to give you those things that are not even mine to give. They are yours and his."

The Duchess turned to her, her face stony, and a cold knife plunged into Georgina's chest. Had she taken it as an insult that Georgina had taken the liberty to speak to her outright about Hugh? Charles was right, she should have kept her mouth shut. His words of warning flared through her. *Stay away from her.*

Georgina took in a breath. *I must see this through,* she thought to herself as she went to the old trunk and took out the casket. Placing it on the table before the Duchess, she opened it. The Duchess betrayed no emotion as she took in the many bound letters.

"I do not mean to offend," said Georgina. "I wanted to return these to you. You should have them. If you want them, of course."

"You were to marry him, and here you are offering me—"

"Truly, there was no affection between us. I barely knew him. The marriage was one of true convenience and perfect timing benefiting us both. For different reasons, of course."

"I know what his reasons were. May I ask, what were yours?"

"My family had decided to marry me to a friend of theirs, a much older man, to solidify their financial and political bond with him, and he wanted a young wife to bear him more children. In the course of an evening, at that ball where Your Grace and I met in London, I learnt I was to be used for a transaction of status, breeding, and business."

"That is what we women are bred for, Georgina. It is only natural that you felt betrayed and maybe even chained, for your feelings, your entire life were suddenly of no matter to those closest to you, those you'd always trusted had your best interests at heart."

She blinked. "Yes. Exactly. You seem to know of such things."

"I do," she said plainly, not betraying any emotion. But in the sudden purse of her lips, Georgina was sure underneath lay an unsettling story. "So you acted extremely quickly to counter their actions. How did you cross paths with the Earl in London?"

"My family has known the Montclares since before I was born. I came to know Charles through his friendship with my brother. Hugh however, was a stranger to me. That night at the ball, all the ladies were talking of nothing but him, and I realised he was the perfect antidote to my plight. The stellar candidate."

"You took away your family's power over you? Well done. Your family can be cross with you, but they can certainly have no complaint with their house now being united with the house of Ryvves."

"That is fortunate, yes. But they remain cross with me."

"It must have been quite a shock for you when Hugh died. But you regrouped quickly and married his brother. Again, well done."

Georgina averted her gaze to a drawing of her husband on the desk. "Charles has always been exceptionally kind to me."

"More than kind, I think." A grin swept her lips and quickly faded from her face. "Hugh must have suffered in the end. To die at home alone, bleeding, is awful."

Georgina's scalp prickled. She'd expected the Duchess to ask questions about her lover's death. And now she would have to reply to them. But was she inquiring because she didn't know the details like everyone else, or she wanted to know what Georgina and Charles knew?

"Horrible," Georgina agreed.

"Why did Mr. Treharne challenge him to a duel?"

"I am not sure. All that remains an extremely painful subject for Charles, and he has not shared with me the particulars. Although the other man was known to be an unpredictable, volatile sort of character. It could have been any kind of disagreement or offence between gentlemen." Georgina pressed her lips together. Perhaps she had said too much, but she had to give the Duchess something to chew on.

She had to distract her from this line of conversation. "There is something else here that may belong to you and Hugh. Georgina emptied the one casket of its bundles of letters and lifted out the snuffbox. The Duchess's eyes widened at the sight of the curio.

Wonderful.

Her Grace took it in her hands. "I remember when I gave this to Hugh. He loved it so. Did you open it, Countess?"

"I did."

The Duchess tilted her head. She appreciated Georgina's honesty. "Did you like it?"

"The workmanship is exceptional, Your Grace."

The Duchess let out a wicked laugh that had Georgina shifting her weight. "Come, Georgina. Did you see the hidden painting inside?"

"I did."

"What did you think of it?"

"It surprised me."

"How?"

"It has opened my eyes to the kind of painting one can do and its different purposes. My father-in-law seems to have enjoyed the same taste in art."

"Yes, Hugh had remarked upon that once." She opened the snuff box and nimbly touched the hidden spring. The false interior snapped forward, revealing the erotic couple, and a smile creased her lips. "As you rightly remarked, this piece had its purpose. Hugh and I endured many separations, and precious items such as this made it easier to bear. He liked this one very much."

There were more?

"I like the pink shoes very much," said Georgina.

The Duchess laughed, an easy laugh. "They were his favourite. And mine too." She closed the box gently, her fingertips stroking the shiny, glazed exterior. "Tell me, did you find this vulgar or did it excite you?"

The breath burned in her throat. *What to say? How to say?*

"You can tell me anything."

Somehow she knew she could, but at this very moment with the ghost of Hugh lurking about them, Georgina felt it would be like dipping a toe in icy waters with deadly sea creatures ready to latch onto her and pull her in.

"Yes, it did…excite me."

"That is natural. Now that you have a husband and are

familiar with the male figure, with the ways of lovemaking, that excitement shall only multiply."

"Yes," Georgina breathed.

"Of course, if your husband is good to you, all the better."

"He is very good to me."

"I'm very glad to hear it," the Duchess said.

Out of all the young ladies of her acquaintance, Georgina was always the one who was eager to discuss coupling—the hows, the what it would be like, all of it. And she did so often with her sister, and later with Justine. She'd wanted to learn, to understand, to be prepared. She smiled back at the Duchess. Now that she was somewhat experienced, it was satisfying to be able to discuss such things with an experienced, more worldly woman like the Duchess of Oakley yet who was not too much older than herself.

"You realize, this sort of thing isn't only for men?" said the Duchess.

Georgina's shoulders lifted. "I quite agree."

"I am pleased to hear you say so, Georgina." A grin slashed over the Duchess's lips as she drew closer to her. "Did you sketch from the painting in the box?"

"No, no. That painting is extremely personal and I could not transgress…"

"You are most thoughtful. Would you want to paint such subjects, especially now that you are gaining in experience?"

Georgina wasn't quite sure if she was referring to her bedroom skills or her painting skills. "I…perhaps, yes. Yes, I would."

"The artist who painted it for me is a very dear friend to His Grace and myself. He's French. Last year he returned to France, but shortly he will be coming back to England to escape the troubles there."

"How awful, yet how wonderful that he has you as patrons."

"It is one of our great delights. The Duke greatly enjoys

such works of art, and you have a seamless aptitude for the human form. Perhaps I will commission a painting from you as a gift to my husband."

"You would?"

"I would. Such a commission would require your utmost discretion."

"Of course, but what…how would I…"

"You would paint the lady from life."

"The lady?" Georgina bit her lip. The Duchess meant another lady, not herself.

The Duchess eyed her. "Let me be frank—my husband keeps a mistress, sometimes more than one. There's an idea, you could paint all of them together."

All of them? Together?

"Would this painting be a miniature such as the one in your snuffbox?"

"Not necessarily. His Grace does have a collection of many miniatures, but also a variety of large paintings for his private enjoyment. He likes keeping mementos. And each mistress has her own memorable talents."

"I see." Georgina's lungs squeezed in her chest. The Duchess seemed to know an awful lot about her husband's lovers.

"Theirs is no ordinary playground," Charles had told her. This was what he had meant.

She'd wanted the Duchess to trust her, for the two of them to become friends, and the thing of it was, she did like her very much. Right now, she had to risk all that to press on in her quest for the necklace. There was no going back now.

The Duchess's hand stroked Georgina's arm. "We should arrange a visit to our estate in the north for you and the Earl."

"I shall have to ask my husband about his schedule first." *And then he will promptly burst into flames.*

"There shall be, of course, payment for your services and your creation."

"Oh..I...I hadn't thought of that, really..."

"You should. The Duke and I enjoy honouring talent and craft. I would be most pleased at being the one who first inspired you to paint such paintings." She licked her bottom lip. "What a shocking influence I am on you, and we've only just become friends."

Georgina let out a soft laugh. "You are most generous, Your Grace, and I appreciate your candour and our frank conversation."

She smiled at her. "I do as well."

"Instead of money, mightn't I ask you for another form of payment?"

"What kind of payment do you mean?"

"There is something I would ask of you."

"Ask me," said the Duchess. "How could I be of help to you?"

Georgina's throat burned. "The night of that ball in London, you wore the most astonishing necklace."

"Yes?"

"Where did you get that necklace from?"

An eyebrow raised. "You would like the name of my jeweller?'

"That necklace came from no jeweller, but from private hands." Georgina swallowed. "Hands that stole it."

Her eyes blazed. "I beg your pardon?"

"I know that necklace, Your Grace. I know to whom it belongs —"

"It belongs to me." She enunciated each word with a dagger-like sharpness.

Georgina had offended her, and she very well might storm right out of the house at any moment and all would be lost. But this would be Georgina's only chance, and she had to take it. "You had the clasps hidden by your hair that night. Are the clasps not wolves with eyes of diamonds?"

The Duchess's features tightened, and her face paled. "That

necklace belongs to me. It was a gift from Hugh. The most beautiful gift he ever gave me. His final gift."

"Hugh gave it to you? I know who sold it to him. He'd stolen it —"

"Why should I care? What the devil does it matter?"

"Because it was Mr. Treharne, the man who challenged him to a duel."

"No!" Her voice was dragon fire obliterating everything in its path. "That necklace is mine, and it shall remain mine forever. Never speak of it again."

Chapter Fifty-Three

Georgina

ICE SWEPT through Georgina's veins at the cold harshness of the Duchess's voice. Everything had been going so well, and now she'd said too much and made her angry.

"Your Grace, I—"

"I beg your pardon, my lady," came a servant's voice behind her. "Mrs. Treharne is here to see you and says it's quite urgent."

The Duchess's eye narrowed, and Georgina's heart stopped.

Dear God, NO.

She had never lied to a guest before, but she was the mistress of this house and she could, and she most certainly would. "Please inform Mrs. Treharne that I am not available."

"Yes ma'am." The servant dipped her head and left.

"Speak of the devil. Mrs. Treharne is your friend, isn't she?" the Duchess asked in a way that made Georgina's breath cut.

"She is not my friend, in fact—"

"Have you arranged all this?"

"No!"

"Please, you cannot! Ma'am!" the servant's voice rose from the hallway.

"Out of my way!" Amanda's harsh voice exploded, and the door to the drawing room burst open. There she stood, dressed in black, her blond hair softly pinned, her cheeks blooming with pink. The young, vibrant widow.

"Mrs. Treharne—" Georgina's pulse beat like a tight drum.

Amanda took in the Duchess and Georgina and her chin lifted. The silence in the room crackled and boiled forth. "Ah, have I interrupted a little party?"

"You have." The Duchess's eyes gleamed at Amanda as the widow drew herself up under her cold inspection. It only seemed to fill Amanda with new humours. Dark and sour.

""Hugh must be having a laugh right now. What a fine party we are—the mistress, the fiancée, the lover." Amanda's hand fluttered to her chest.

"Amanda, you must leave this instant!" Georgina's heart banged in her chest at Amanda's taunting gaze at the Duchess who remained perfectly calm. A snake readying to strike.

"Look at you, the Countess of Ryvves issuing orders. How did you manage it, Georgina darling? Engaged to Hugh for less than a day, and before he's even cold in the ground, you're in his brother's bed. Did you have to seduce Charles to persuade him to marry you? Poor Hugh didn't realise his fiancée was no innocent but a ... virginal vixen?" She let out a biting laugh. "Did he never get a taste of you? Or perhaps the three of you–"

"Get out of my house." Georgina's hands fisted at her sides.

Amanda's lips curved. "Yes, your house, indeed. Did you and Charles plan on getting Hugh out of the way to claim your fortunes all along? That's the rumour going around, you know. I for one believe it because I know Charles very well. Stratagems arouse him greatly, especially when they involve pretty young ladies."

"That's quite enough," Georgina said.

The Duchess prowled toward Amanda. "How dare you speak to the Countess of Ryvves in such a vile manner in her own home? You come here uninvited, you were asked to leave by the mistress of the house, you refuse, and then you offend her guest, her husband, and the Countess herself."

Amanda remained…amused.

"You are enjoying this, are you not?" said Georgina. "Once long ago I admired you, Amanda, and I also resented you. All the young men around me wanted you—my brother, Matthew, Charles, Brandon, William. Even if you treated them with disdain, somehow you remained a paragon, able to inspire their adoration, their desire to claim you for their own with just a look, a witty remark, a dance."

"I always knew you were envious of me."

"No, I was intrigued. Because what I could never understand, and never more so than at this moment, was that instead of being grateful for your many blessings, you only wished to conquer over and over, indulge in stratagems, all of it to a selfish end. And it never mattered to you who you trampled in the course of your sport. Now, here you stand, alone, with none of these men to love, and none of these men to love you."

Amanda's nostrils flared. "Although I'm finding our little gathering entertaining, I came to see your husband. Where is he?"

"The Earl is unavailable, as am I. You must go." Georgina had never spoken to her so formally, so officiously.

"Your husband must answer for what he did to me last night. He set out to ruin me."

"On the contrary, madame," Georgina said evenly. "You were the one engaged in ruinous behaviour."

"I am so very sorry to have missed the performance," said the Duchess.

Amanda's entire being was fixated on the Duchess as she stalked toward her, her gaze raking her from head to toe. "I declare, I do not know what Hugh saw in you."

Georgina's eyes widened. "Amanda!"

"I know what he saw in you." The Duchess's voice positively slithered around them, cool, relaxed, ready to strike. "And you proved it last evening." A grin slashed the Duchess's lips. "My husband described your behaviour to me in great detail, as did Lord Darnley, Sir Whitten, and Admiral Trainor. They greatly enjoyed themselves, and I was so very pleased. I hadn't realised we'd hired a posture moll for our dinner party."

With a piercing cry, Amanda's arm flew in the air. She didn't like the Duchess calling her a whore.

"No!" Georgina darted forward. Her face stung, her body swung. Her head exploded with pain.

Chapter Fifty-Four

Charles

His sword still in his hand, Charles stormed into his wife's morning room.

The moment he'd seen his servant's face etched with worry, his heart had flown out of his chest, and he'd gone running to find her. "Georgina?" He tossed his sword to his manservant.

Hiccupy breaths filled the air, stabbing at his heart. The Duchess leaned over his wife murmuring.

"Georgie?"

The Duchess turned around and pulled back. And there was Georgina, her one cheek flushed scarlet, eyes wide and filled with water, biting on her lower lip. Fire raced up his spine, swirled in his chest, burst in his brain. "What have you done to her?" He grabbed the Duchess's arm. "Did you strike my wife?" he growled through clenched teeth.

"No, I did not."

Georgina's hand reached out, coming between them. "Her Grace helped me, Charles. I am so thankful she was here."

His hands cradled Georgina's marked face. "Who has done this to you?" His wife flinched at his raised voice. "Tell me now."

"Amanda."

"She is here?"

"She burst in uninvited and would not leave," said the Duchess.

"Mrs. Treharne was just shown out, sir," said a servant.

Charles took in a tight breath. "Your Grace, may I ask you to stay with my wife?"

"Of course."

"Thank you."

"Charles, please," Georgina cried out. "She is not herself."

"No one does this to you. No one. Ever."

He stalked through the foyer to the still open front door, and he spotted a female figure in the front drive stumbling, a dark cape flying out behind her.

He tore down the steps. "Amanda!"

She turned, her face pale and drawn, and stumbled once more.

Charles grabbed her arm and shook her. "How dare you lay a hand on Georgina? How could you do such a thing?" She swayed in his grip, something like a howl bursting from her lips. He knew the signs so very well. "How much have you had to drink today?"

She yanked herself out of his grip. "Just a bit to ease my discomforts of which there are so many."

"Discomforts indeed. Why did you strike my wife?"

"I meant to strike that woman, but your wife got in my way! The impudence!"

"Why would you do such a thing to the Duchess? What is wrong with you?"

"Let me begin with last evening. You've ruined any chances I had to—"

"I did nothing of the kind."

"You encouraged me to go to the sculpture gallery, and then you brought everyone there on purpose."

"The Duke and his friends came on their own."

"Liar! Why would you do this? Is this some sort of revenge?"

"I did no such thing," he lied. In truth, having her so rudely exposed was a delightful by-product of his basic scheme to expose Matthew to his Aunt and Alice. If she felt the stinging pinch of his watch-out-because-I-bite warning, that was an added bonus.

"You wanted to seduce and be seduced last night, did you not?" he said. "If you were careless, that is because of your passions or the wine, or your sudden liberation, certainly not because of me."

"I hate you," her voice simmered.

"You were a great success, it seems. The Duke and his friends all know who you are and are hardly likely to forget you."

"Yes, that is a triumph indeed." The ironic tone in her voice was like water fizzing and hissing on burning iron.

"Now that he knows who you are and what you are capable of, perhaps you could try to gain the Duke's favours. He must have broken with his most recent mistress for she was nowhere to be seen in town this season. Think of the high life you would lead at his side."

Charles would certainly have fun watching her try to seduce the Duke.

Amanda lunged at him, but her fingers only stuck in his chemise, pulling it loose. "How dare you mock me!"

Gripping her shoulders, he took in a breath to steady his temper. "I know you were unhappy in your marriage for a very long time, but now you are free of William. You must only be patient until your mourning period is over, then flirt and seduce and be seduced all you like. Take all the lovers you want, find another husband—"

"I don't want another husband!" She shoved at him. "And I cannot afford to be patient. It seems my husband had altered his will and has left me nothing, nothing except for my small allowance. Whatever William had, he left in trust for our son."

"Did he?"

"I have no home of my own, no income to speak of. All I have to commend myself are my charms and my beauty, which is creasing and fading, but I do not want to crease or fade. I do not want to. I can't." Her lower lip trembled, her troubled gaze darting here and there.

"You have your brother."

"My brother is determined that Matthew marry me to save my reputation."

"Andrew is protecting you. A fine solution."

"Only I've just learnt that Matthew has no money! If I had known that little fact last night I would not have allowed him to flirt with me, let alone touch me." She tilted her head, her mouth firm. "But you knew, didn't you? You knew he was looking for a rich girl, which is why he's had his eye on your Miss Alice. You knew and you encouraged me to—"

Charles raised a hand between them. "You have never needed anyone's approval or encouragement. You get fixated on an idea, and in the end, you always do what you want. You enjoy being praised and admired for your cleverness, which is what you always required of me."

"Damn you!" Her fists bunched in her dress. "I cannot marry Matthew. He's a boy. A disaster. He will demand a king's ransom from my brother for doing us the great favour of marrying me. I will not do that to Andrew. I will not."

"You're stuck then, aren't you?"

Her jaw tightened. "You must help me."

"Why should I? You're the reason my brother is dead, and now you've assaulted my wife in our own home."

She let out a groan like an impatient ten-year-old child. What he'd said was tedious.

Charles put his hands at his waist. "No words of humility or regret, Mrs. Treharne? Look at you, a husband and a lover dead after fighting over fucking you. What a triumph you are for all womankind."

"Shut up," her voice seethed, her hands went to her temple.

"You must apologise to my wife for your offence."

"I will not. And certainly not in front of that woman!"

"That woman is the Duchess of Oakley, and you must tread carefully."

"Oh? She must certainly be jealous to know that I was her lover's final lover." Her eyes were alive with fire.

"Why would she care? Their affair was over well before you and he took up."

"Oh, every woman cares even if she pretends otherwise. Perhaps I should do as you suggested."

"Which was…"

"Would it upset her, you think, if her lover's lover were to seduce her husband? What a delicious thought. Now there is a fine specimen of a man. I imagine he's quite a king in —"

"Shut up, will you," he hissed at her. "Dear God, why do you feel the need to best her?"

"I don't like her. She is pompous and imperious."

"She is the Duchess of Oakley! She could crush you if she wished."

"Oh, let her try. When I get done with her, she will be in tears, begging for my mercy. And I shall not give it. I shall be the one laughing at her."

"Bloody hell, you're already forming a new plan? I'm warning you, Amanda. I highly doubt you or anyone could get between those two. The Oakleys are not to be trifled with."

Her body swayed, her eyes gleaming as she righted herself. "Neither am I, my lord."

"Enough. I demand that you cease spreading these ugly and untruthful rumours about my having killed my brother to usurp his title and take his wife-to-be. All lies and you know it. Why the devil are you hell-bent on being so spiteful? Now, you will go back to the house and apologise to both of them. I demand it. "

Pressing her lips together, she attempted to compose herself. Charles knew very well that apologising to anyone was alien to Amanda, alien and a horror and insufferable in one. *She must be choking on her own bile this very instant,* he thought.

"Apologise." He gestured to the house to where the Duchess and Georgina watched them from the terrace.

Amanda let out a tight breath and stomped toward the house. He followed her up the stone steps. On the terrace, Amanda came to a halt before Georgina.

"Countess, I am very sorry for having lashed out at you in such a way. I apologise. Forgive me for having struck you. I fully intended on striking the Duchess."

Georgina's eyes widened, and she gasped as Amanda flew at the Duchess.

"Amanda!" Charles roared, grabbing her by the waist and jerking her back, away from the women. "Are you mad?"

"I will not bow down to her, not ever!" Amanda seethed.

Charles gestured to his two footmen who stood by the door. "Both of you, take Mrs. Treharne home immediately."

"Sir."

"Never come here again, do you understand?" he said to Amanda. "Never."

She cast them all a cold glance and trotted down the stairs in between the servants.

"Your Grace, please accept our sincere apologies for such abominable behaviour." Georgina tried to save the day. "I never—"

The Duchess took hold of Georgina's arm. "I do not fault you for her behaviour."

"To be assaulted so as a guest in our home. I am utterly mortified."

"I appreciate your mortification, I do. But that woman is

not worthy of it." The Duchess turned to Charles. "What did the two of you speak of?"

"She accused me of setting her up to be seen with Mr. Penry last night. And I insisted she apologise to my wife and my esteemed guest. That outburst was abhorrent. Her demeanor…"

"She was like that when I saw her at her house that morning," said Georgina. "Brazen in a bizarre sort of way, elsewhere at the same time. She was taking laudanum with her wine that morning. She probably still is."

"Laudanum?" Charles's brow furrowed.

"A woman's helper, it's called. My sister sometimes imbibes. She said it would calm her nerves and blur the pains and discomforts a woman must endure. I've never tried it myself."

"Laudanum and wine, ergo…" He gestured in the direction they'd last seen Amanda as he wiped at the perspiration on his face with the side of his hand.

The Duchess stilled, her gaze fixed on his exposed bare chest and left shoulder. His chemise had come completely loose after his sword lesson, his rushing about, Amanda pulling on him. The red scar on his upper arm was plainly visible.

"You bear a fresh wound, Lord Ryvves," said the Duchess.

Charles clenched his jaw as he yanked his damp shirt back into place and buttoned it. "'Tis a scratch," he quoted Shakespeare on a brittle grin to fend off her pointed inquiry, to distract her.

Her eyes narrowed. "Marry, 'tis enough," she quoted *Romeo & Juliet* back to him and Georgina's heartbeat sputtered as the Duchess's features hardened. "The rumours are true, then? You were the one fighting Mr. Treharne in the duel? You were shot and Hugh was safe. Why then is he dead?" Her voice had grown louder.

"That's not the truth," exclaimed Georgina. "I was there, I saw —"

"You were there? Why should I believe either of you? I

shall ask you again, for what purpose did you bring me here to show me that portrait of Hugh, to sweeten and soften me by returning my letters and gifts that were in his possession? Inquiring about my necklace? You deny you are friends with that woman, and yet...what do you want of me, Countess?"

"What is it *you* want of us?" Charles's voice seemed to slice through the air like a sharp axe as he moved between her and Georgina. "You and Oakley haven't resided in your house here for nigh on two years. Suddenly, your long-time lover, the local Earl, is out of the way, and you are in residence, making up for all that lost time, having parties and catching up with your noble duties in the village."

"Charles!" Georgina grabbed hold of his arm as he moved closer to the Duchess, but it did not stop him.

"Now you are befriending my wife, your former lover's fiancée. Asking questions. What is your true purpose here amongst us, Your Grace?"

Her chest heaved, a cry heaving from her lips. "I need to know how Hugh died. Why he died. I need to know. I am in agony. You must tell me the truth."

Chapter Fifty-Five

Charles

"THE LAST LETTER I received from Hugh was just before that final ball," said the Duchess as she sat down in a leather armchair by the window of the main parlour. "He said he was committed to finding a wife."

"You had communicated whilst he was in London?" asked Charles pouring himself a glass of brandy.

"Twice, yes."

"When we saw him and Georgina dancing together at the ball spending much time together, I knew he was pleased, and I'd hoped she would be his choice."

"Is that when the Duke asked me to dance?" asked Georgina. "And you danced alongside us?"

"Yes. His Grace liked you immediately, as did I."

"Why would you do that, seek me out?" asked Georgina. "Did Hugh want your approval for his choice of wife?" Her question hung in the air as the Duchess made no attempt to answer it.

"You never broke." said Charles. "It was all a lie so he could find a bride and claim the rest of his inheritance."

The Duchess lifted her gaze to his. "Yes."

"And after he married, the two of you would reunite?" said Georgina.

"That was our plan," said the Duchess. "But the next day after the ball, instead of hearing word of his engagement, we heard reports of a duel between a Mr. William Treharne and a Montclare, but not which Montclare brother. Many reports noted that you, Charles, were the one most likely fighting the gentleman as it was known that you once had relations with his wife. I was relieved, yet I could not rest until I heard from Hugh."

"You knew he was bedding her, didn't you?" asked Charles.

"No, I did not know."

"Come now. I saw your spy by our house late one night."

"He is the Duke's most trusted man, and he was delivering my letter to Hugh that night. He never spied on Hugh." She let out a sigh. "I did not know of his dalliance with the lady. When we heard that Mr. Treharne had died, and then soon after, got word that Hugh too was dead, I was in shock; it was as if the earth had cracked and broke from under me.

"I could not comprehend it. If you had fought the duel, then why was Hugh dead? I had to know the truth, and so we came to Tidesfar so that I could find out what I could from you." Her glance fell on Georgina.

"I did not fight the duel, Your Grace," said Charles. "Hugh did."

"And yet you bear a wound on your arm? Is that wound not Mr. Treharne's doing? From his pistol?"

"No, it is not. It is my brother's doing. Directly after the duel, Hugh shot me."

"No. It cannot be. Why would your own brother do such a foul thing?"

"It is the truth, Your Grace," said Georgina. "I was there, I saw it. After William was taken away, Hugh shot Charles right there in Hyde Park."

"Hugh had asked me twice to take his place in the duel, but

I'd refused," said Charles. "He was angry with me, desperate to ensure that nothing would endanger his engagement. He feared if it was known he had bedded Mrs. Treharne, had fought the duel, Georgina's family would have grounds to break the engagement we'd just signed the day before."

"Hugh was most angry with me for being at Hyde Park and having seen him shoot Charles," said Georgina. "We argued, and I took Charles from the park to a doctor, a cousin of mine, to be seen to. Charles and I stayed there for a short while, and then we both thought it wise to find Hugh, to confirm that the engagement would go on."

"We went to my house and found him dead on the floor of the drawing room," said Charles.

"A fine story," the Duchess's voice clipped.

"Pray, what is your story, madame?" Charles held her gaze. "For I believe you capable of a great deal, especially if you are betrayed."

"I let Hugh go so he could marry because he had to, because he should. I loved Hugh. I wanted what was best for him.

"And Hugh spent almost every night in London at whorehouses and private clubs with his friends. Surely you'd heard reports. Were you not jealous?"

"No. I fully expected it. I encouraged him to indulge in those entertainments to prove he was a free man. We all enjoy such pastimes, do we not?"

Georgina bit her lip at the Duchess's reply.

Charles rubbed his sore arm. "But if your man was hovering over Hugh to deliver your letters, he might have seen him go off to his secret lover and then report it to the Duke. Perhaps you did not consider Mrs. Treharne such a passing entertainment? It seems Hugh had been with her a number of times—a fact he kept secret from me."

"I never had Hugh followed or spied upon."

"Perhaps the Duke had him followed and killed? If you

and Hugh were broken, your husband finally took a husband's revenge on his wife's lover."

She let out a short laugh. "You don't know my husband. He was glad I'd found Hugh. He was glad that I was happy. He liked him. Furthermore, he knew our plan."

Charles blinked. "Nonetheless, I find it odd that a man such as Oakley wouldn't mind that his wife —"

"You, sir, know nothing of our lives, do not assume you do."

"Quite right." His chest expanded as he dipped his head. "My apologies."

Georgina filled glasses with sherry and brought one to the Duchess.

The Duchess drank. "When I heard of the duel, I did consider that it could be Hugh who had cuckolded Mr. Treharne. I found it most unsettling, for he and his wife were Hugh's childhood friends. Hugh's time was running out to secure a bride, and such an indulgence was a heavy risk for a scandal that would have put a stop to any engagement to a fine young lady from a good family."

"I agree, it was most unwise." He attempted a small smile as he raised his glass at her. "Hugh had once remarked to me that you were a very sensible woman."

"Did he?" she let out a soft laugh, more weary than amused.

"I can only offer that since my brother inherited his title, he thought himself invulnerable, more so than before."

"Yes, he did." Her Grace let out a ragged breath. "Now he is gone, you bear a gunshot wound, and I a chasm inside me that is filled with grief, questions, and doubts." Her grip on her glass tightened.

Georgina drained her wine glass. "Well, now that we are all clear on what we know — who the devil killed Hugh?"

Chapter Fifty-Six

Charles

THE TREES SWAYED in the wind as their carriage brought them into Penrose Park on the other side of the village from Ironvine. Aunt Vivian had invited Charles and Georgina to dine.

Both Charles and Georgina were still emotionally exhausted from their discussion with the Duchess and Amanda's shocking visit the day before last. Charles was relieved the slap had left no bruise on Georgina's cheek, only a red mark that had faded. They rode most of the way in silence.

Charles loosened his grip on the reins. "This morning, I wrote to a friend in London who knows a man trained in matters of investigation. He assures me he is very discreet."

"Now that the Duke and Duchess are no longer the likely suspects, this is a good decision. I must say, I am quite glad that Hugh and I did not marry. I don't mean, of course, that I'm glad your brother is dead, only that as his wife I'm sure I would have been quite alone, unhappy, and grown bitter, much like my mother."

"You would have been, yes." Charles kept his gaze on the road.

Georgina fiddled with her gloves, pulling them off. "Is that why you were in a temper when you came with Hugh to settle the engagement? Because you knew what awaited me as his wife?"

"He would have taken full advantage of you in every way, then abandoned you without explanation whenever he liked to be with her or whomever else had caught his eye, for as often as he liked." He let out a sigh. "Inevitably, he was sure to break the Duchess's heart one day."

"I think he may have already done that."

"I think so." Charles let out a sigh. "Who am I to judge him?"

"Have you ever been true to any woman?"

His lips tipped up. "There she goes, merciless."

"Give me the sordid truth."

"No. Never."

"Never?"

"Only to you, Georgie," he confessed, the weight in his chest shifting. "I find I want to be constant and faithful to you. It's quite a singular sentiment for me. Peculiar, foreign, and very potent. I cannot deny it. It's what I want, just as I want you to be mine alone." He swallowed hard and glanced at her. "Are you mine alone? In your thoughts? Your heart? Do I ask too much of you? Am I being selfish? Bloody hell, I don't know how this works, I—"

"*À vous seule.*" Her posture straightened as her hand gripped his thigh. "I am yours alone, Charles. That is how I feel, that is what I want. You have my complete and utter loyalty." Georgina's dark eyes gleamed in the afternoon sun. "I'm proud and most grateful that I am your Countess." She brushed his cheek with a kiss. A small thing, a gentle touch, and yet it was a balm salving the gashes and scars inside him.

"Ah, there she is," Georgina murmured as the manor rose before them. Smaller and less grand than Ironvine, but a very handsome Tudor-style house.

"It is, indeed." Charles pulled up in the drive, and a footman aided Georgina's descent from their carriage. They entered the hall, and immediately that familiar combination of lemon oil and cedar greeted him, and he took Georgina's hand in his.

The servant announced their arrival as they entered the parlour.

"Ah, here they are, our newlyweds." Aunt Vivian embraced him.

"Aunt." He gave her a kiss on the cheek.

She took Georgina's hands in hers. "Georgina, how good to see you again."

"Aunt Vivian." Georgina hugged Aunt Vivian whilst Charles greeted Alice.

"Georgina, I'm so very pleased to now call you cousin," said Alice.

Georgina embraced the girl. "I too am most pleased, dearest Alice."

Charles's gaze remained on the prospect of the park from the large window where a riot of colourful flowers and shrubs framed the view. As a boy at Ironvine, he would sometimes accompany his mother as she trimmed her blooms, picked her flowers, and tended to the special varieties in the conservatory. He would hold her basket for her as she worked, helping her fill it as he babbled on, asking her questions about anything and everything, and they would talk and laugh.

"What a splendid front garden you have, Aunt," Georgina remarked as she moved toward the window. "The colours are beautiful."

"My sister, Charles's mother, is responsible for that garden. Sophie chose all the flowers herself. She loved to putter about there. Said it eased her."

"Sophie? What a lovely name." She glanced at him with a small smile.

"We shall sit by the great window here and enjoy it with our wine as my sister would have wanted us to." Aunt Vivian gestured at the lovely table prepared for them, and they sat down and enjoyed a glass of sherry.

Averting his gaze from the garden, Charles drained his glass of wine quickly. The wall next to him was lined with small paintings of landscapes, seascapes, ships in ports, small portraits.

"I don't remember all these paintings here before, Aunt. Have you collected them?"

"Not I, nephew. Your mother."

Georgina rose and went to the wall of paintings. "They are very fine. Are these two Sheffields, Aunt?"

Aunt Vivian sat up straighter. "They are indeed. You are familiar with the artist's work?"

"I am, very much so. Anton Sheffield was a close friend of my father's. He often invited him to stay here in the country and would rent a small house for him. I was quite fortunate, for whenever Mr. Sheffield was here, he was kind enough to give me lessons."

"Did he?" Aunt Vivian's eyebrows perched higher on her brow, her head tilting.

"Georgina is a most accomplished artist," said Charles. "She's using the conservatory as her atelier."

"How wonderful," murmured Aunt Vivian.

"Perhaps you could give me lessons, cousin?" said Alice.

"I would love to, Alice. Mr. Sheffield was a very generous teacher, and I'd be pleased to help you in any way I could."

Aunt Vivian stood. "Who is your father, girl?" Her voice was odd, and it had Charles lifting his gaze to her. Her body was rigid as if she awaited an answer to a question she had longed for years.

"My father died some six years ago—Sir Edward Townsend."

Aunt Vivian's face paled, and her hands flew together.

"Aunt?" Charles put his freshly refilled glass down.

"You are Edward Townsend's daughter?" asked Aunt Vivian, her tone almost ominous.

"I am." Georgina shifted her weight under Aunt Vivian's sudden somber scrutiny. "Surely you knew him if you lived here? You knew my mother."

"I knew your mother, yes, but I had married and left for my husband's home in Surrey just before your mother had re-married. Over the years my visits were brief, and I…" She swallowed hard. "Dear Lord," she murmured, a hand to her temple. "I only returned to Penrose Park this past winter, after my husband passed away."

"Aunt, are you unwell? Whatever is the matter?" Charles sat up.

Aunt Vivian's eyes remained transfixed on Georgina. "You…you are Edward Townsend's daughter?" she repeated, her voice low, faraway.

"Mother?" said Alice.

"I must show you both something, something very important. It cannot wait. It cannot wait any longer," said Aunt Vivian. "Charles, as you know, I've withheld your mother's belongings from you since her death. Although I knew you loved her, I feared your father's influence could have swayed you, and I did not want her things destroyed or sold, such as these paintings." She went to the other wall and unhinged a small, rectangular painting in a thick gold frame and brought it to them. "This was Sophie's most precious possession."

Charles and Georgina peered at the painting of a cottage, a blue sea stretching in the background, and a man and a woman standing together in the wild grasses before the small house.

"This a Sheffield as well," Georgina murmured.

"It is, yes." Aunt Vivian brought her hands together.

The artist had captured a casual glimpse of the couple who

held hands. The lady smiled at the painter as she and her partner walked on through grasses buffeted in the wind. The lady's blond hair was loose and long, and one hand was at her temple, keeping her hair from her face. The handsome gentleman held her hand, smiling softly at her. He adored her. They shared an intoxicating secret.

Georgina gasped. "Oh my God."

"Yes, dear girl," Aunt Vivian said. "Yes."

Charles's grip tightened over the braided gold frame, the blood rushed in his veins, rage fomenting in his middle. "Who is this man holding my mother's hand?"

"That is your mother?" Georgina's voice shook, her fingertips grazing the surface of the painting. "This man is my father."

"I shall tell you everything." Aunt Vivian stood before them. "The time has finally come, and in a most unusual way."

Alice gestured to the servant attending them, and he refilled everyone's glasses with wine and left them alone.

Charles's heart clenched tightly in his chest. "What the devil is this?"

"Your mother and Edward Townsend were very much in love," replied Aunt Vivian.

"What? How? When?"

"Always."

Georgina's eyes widened, her lips parting. "I don't understand. What do you mean?"

His brain stuttered. "Are you saying that when she was married to my father she — Is that why —"

"Oh, how fitting. Moral outrage coming from you?" Aunt Vivian's voice hissed.

"Hardly," Charles spit out. "Tell us everything." He took Georgina's cold hand in his.

Sitting down, Aunt Vivian had a long sip of wine. "Sophie knew Edward before she married your father. In fact, the two of them wanted to marry, but our parents would not allow it.

They wanted the Earl of Ryvves for their eldest daughter, and they got him.

"Years later, and after your parents had separated, your father happened to meet Edward at his club in London. He liked him. Edward knew many artists, like Anton Sheffield, and your father wanted to meet Sheffield and a few others. Your father considered himself cultured, a patron of the arts." Her lips twisted. "But it was Townsend who was a true patron to artists. The man had been bestowed a knighthood for all he'd done for artists' causes, sponsoring exhibitions and the like. The Earl of Ryvves was enamoured by that world and invited him and Sheffield and a few others to Ironvine for a weekend."

Charles's eyes narrowed. "I do remember an artist sketching me and Hugh as we had our archery lesson while the adults went shooting. As you say, they were separated then, but Mother was at Ironvine that week, and the artist gave the drawing to her as a thank you gift."

"Do you still have it?" Georgina asked.

"I—I don't know."

"Sophie had it. She framed it. It's over there." Aunt Vivian pointed to the far wall where a simple sketch with a lone wash of green watercolour was framed.

Georgina let go of his hand and went to the piece as Charles gulped in air. He remembered his mother's pleasure at the gift. That she'd had it here in her home, filled his veins with a flood of warmth.

He remembered every inch of that watercolour. Two boys with bows and arrows, one taking aim, the other, the younger boy, faced the artist, head tilted, a slight smile on his face, his stance proud yet rather shy.

"Here is Mr. Sheffield's signature on the bottom," said Georgina, a hand at her mouth.

"That weekend was when your mother and Edward reconnected." Her gaze darted to Georgina. "He'd married the year before. In fact, I believe you had just been born, my dear. Eventually, it all erupted between them, and they became very close and quite attached to one another. He often traveled for his work, and Sophie began to accompany him on these trips. Whenever she and Townsend could, they traveled abroad together."

"I have all her letters from everywhere she traveled. Not once did she mention —"

"Come now, Charles. Would she have told you she was with a lover?"

"No, but —"

"Away from England they could be together freely," murmured Georgina.

"Yes, they could be free. They were on those occasions," said Vivian.

"Did he visit her here?" Charles asked, his throat constricting.

"She wouldn't allow it. Sophie wanted to preserve the agreement she had with your father to see her boys. Can you imagine, if your father had found out? God knows what he would have done —"

"I know what he would have done," fell from his lips, his heart pounding in his chest.

"He certainly would have forbid her from seeing you and Hugh ever again, and that would have been the least of it." She met Charles's hard gaze with her own. "Georgina, this must pain you, and I am sorry for that, but I felt you both deserved to know the truth." She took Georgina's hand in hers. "But the two of you married is truly…"

"I'm glad you've told us, Aunt," said Georgina. "When my mother learnt of my marriage to Charles, she was livid, in a way I'd never seen her before. She said awful things about the Montclares. She said awful things about my father. Even my brother was taken aback."

"She must have known. She must have known of their affair," said Charles.

"Yes, she must have known." Georgina's teeth dragged along her lower lip. "This painting of the two of them, do you know where that cottage was?"

"That was in Portugal. Mr. Sheffield had visited them on his way to Lisbon one summer. They loved it there."

"Portugal…she'd go there almost every summer, didn't she?" said Charles. "When I was young she'd bring me back seashells and starfish she'd find on the beach."

Georgina glanced at him, her eyes full of water, a smile struggling over her trembling lips. His heart twisting at the sight, he took her hand and crushed it in his.

"How did she die exactly?" said Charles. "I want the whole story, Aunt. Did my father ever find out? Did he —"

"No, my darling. No. She'd learnt that Edward had died in a terrible carriage accident outside of London on his way back from a trip to Scotland, I think it was."

"Yes, he'd been in Edinburgh for an exhibition," said Georgina. "He was on his way to meet us in London for my coming out."

"Oh, I see." Aunt Vivian's shoulders sank. "Sophie heard gossip in the village at the sweet shop one afternoon. That is how she learnt of his death. She was in shock. Inconsolable. A few days after she'd gone for a ride on her horse at sunset, her favourite time. But suddenly, there was a terrible storm. One of those odd summer storms, fierce and quick. Even the river had risen as it has now. Her horse came back alone. He appeared on the front lawn, waiting for us to find him.

"By that time the rain had stopped and luckily there was a bright moon. They searched for her, and finally, they found her —unconscious at the edge of the property in the woods. She'd broken a rib and an arm, and had a terrible fever. She never recovered. In the space of a week's time both of them were gone forever." She let out a long, heavy sigh.

"Father would not allow me to come see her."

"No, he wouldn't." Aunt Vivian lifted her chin. "But you came anyway, didn't you, my love? I shall never forget seeing you in the kitchen doorway wet through and through, trembling, so very pale."

"You took my hand and brought me through," he breathed.

"Yes, I did," she said. "You were so brave."

"Aunt, were there any letters between them?" asked Georgina.

"Oh yes, there are letters. Many letters. She'd given them to me for safekeeping at my house. She was afraid the Earl might find them here."

"Wise," muttered Charles.

"Very. I have them with me, along with a few lovely pieces of jewellery Townsend had given her on a trip to Venice." She went to a cupboard and retrieved a leather box. "But mostly he gave her these small paintings which she treasured. Souvenirs of every place they'd gone together."

His vision blurred as Georgina and Aunt Vivian spoke, but their words were unintelligible, their voices far away.

A hand gripped his arm and he shuddered and jerked back. "Charles? Charles? Are you unwell?" A glass was brought to his lips. "Drink, my love. Drink."

Charles drank, coughed, bringing his hand to his mouth. He rose to his feet. "Forgive me, Aunt, but … I…"

"We must go home," said Georgina, sliding an arm around his waist.

"Rest here, my darlings—"

"No," he spit out.

Aunt Vivian rang for the servant. "My nephew and his wife are leaving. Prepare their carriage." She gestured to another servant to take up the jewellery box and the small painting, along with a filled cloth bag. "Secure these items in their carriage."

Georgina touched Vivian's arm. "Aunt, thank you for being

the faithful keeper of my father and mother-in-law's story all these years."

"Ah, you, my dear, are an extraordinary young lady." Vivian embraced her, as did Alice. Aunt Vivian came to Charles and slid a hand against his cheek. The sudden warmth of her palm made his eyes blink. "Take care, my darling. You and Georgina need each other now more than ever."

Chapter Fifty-Seven

Georgina

THE STEADY CLOMPING OF THE HORSES' hooves, the drumming of the wheels of their carriage, lulled her into a kind of numbness as they drove home. The sky had darkened quickly, filling with thick clouds. A storm was coming.

The trees whipped past them on the road, all of it a blur, a blur of memories and emotions washing through her.

Nothing made sense. Nothing added together to make one clear picture, not yet anyway. She strained to remember particulars of her father's behaviour. Had she ever noticed a change in him? She was a child, what did she know of love then? Nothing.

He'd been in love. Truly in love. With Sophie Montclare, Countess of Ryvves.

Oh, Papa. Her heart ached.

Her mother had kept all this anger and resentment pinned inside her for so many years. No wonder she'd taken Georgina's engagement to Hugh and her subsequent marriage to Charles as such a visceral betrayal.

She glanced at Charles. He so much resembled his beautiful mother. *Sophie. Sophie and Edward.* The two of them led a secret life together away from their families, away from society. Defiant and non-conformist and passionate.

She rather liked that.

Thunder boomed over them, and Charles, his eyes pinned to the road, back rigid, knuckles white drove the horses faster. Was he disappointed in his mother? Was he in shock that she had been intimately involved with another man, a married man?

Finally, their carriage rounded the drive and jammed to a halt as raindrops fell fat and thick. Servants rushed outside to assist them. Ignoring everyone, Charles flung open his carriage door and descended. Georgina took the footman's offered hand, but Charles grabbed her, taking her in his arms, and darted up the steps into the house.

Putting her on her feet, he stalked off. Her wet cloak was taken from her, and she waited for the footman to bring in the small trunk with the precious items Aunt Vivian had given them. She found Charles in the drawing room, gulping down brandy.

"Thank you," she said to the servant who'd placed the trunk on the floor as he bowed and quit the room.

"Countess, may I offer you some liquid fire to wash down the knowledge of our parents' illicit love affair?" said Charles, pouring himself another.

"Is that what you are trying to do? Burn the knowledge away?"

"Don't know." He drained his glass and poured another. "Don't know how to feel. Don't know what to think. Don't. Know."

"I don't know either, but I am glad we know the truth." She took the keepsakes out of the trunk and placed them on the round table in the centre of the room.

"Are you not distressed? Not shocked?" He let out a sharp laugh. "Again, you impress me, Countess."

She opened the cloth bag and out spilled packets and

packets of letters. Charles moved to the table, plucked at one stack, yanking off its ribbon. Unfolding one letter, he skimmed the contents of it, his face clouding.

"Am I shocked that my mother-in-law was the woman my father had loved for decades? Most probably his one and only love? I am. However, in this knowledge, I find a great clarity and an even greater relief."

"Clarity?" He glanced up from a letter. "Relief?"

"My parents had a polite marriage, but I never once saw them exhibit any signs of affection or attachment between them. From what you told me, neither did yours."

He tossed the letter to the table and opened another and read, his lips tightening.

Georgina continued, "My father took every opportunity to travel, saying how important his work was, and my mother would wish him well. In fact, she seemed to prefer it. He would tell me that every trip was a rare and splendid opportunity to discover something new. But now I see that each trip was also time he spent with his love. Sophie was his true rare and splendid discovery.

"This is the missing piece of my father that I always struggled to ignore and always struggled to understand. But now I know the truth." She took his glass from his hand and drank. "They had been in love and wished to marry, but were denied their happiness for the sake of what—vanity? Ambition? And years later, after he finally does marry, suddenly their lives cross once more, and those sparks of feeling are still there between them. Amazing. Yet their lives were now different, complicated."

"Yes, both were living a lie and were deliriously *un*happy." He tossed the letter he'd been reading and poured himself another brandy.

"Exactly. After years of simply existing, years of wandering on a desert, they find each other again. Both with severe obligations, and yet, they took a daring leap, risking so much to be together in any way possible. T'was the impossible made real." Her eyes filled with water. "How they must have cherished every moment together."

"Don't cry for them."

"Why not? So many of us natter on about romantic love and affections. We flirt recklessly and make a pretty commotion. But their love was bold and strong and proved to be an enduring bond."

"You are not angry with your father then?" he asked. "That he abandoned you and your mother for another woman. Lived another life with her behind your backs?"

She took the glass from him again and drank. "Did I want him to stay with me longer, more often? Of course I did. I often considered he did not love me enough, that I wasn't good enough for him to stay. But as I grew older, I understood that marriage was simply a bargain struck between a man and a woman. That the husband could do as he pleased whilst the wife had to stay home and uphold the obligation.

"You'd lived that pretence, as did I." He took the glass from her and drank.

"A pretence I grew to abhor. I didn't realize how much I hated it until that night at the ball when I was told I was to marry Sir Reginald. I could feel an iron noose about my neck grow tighter and tighter."

He handed her the fresh glass of brandy, and she took a gulp. "I find it is a great relief to know that my father being away was not about my lacking as a daughter or his inability to love me more or love me better. The time we had together was always well spent. I feel a kind of satisfaction and peace in the knowledge that he and the woman he truly loved lived their love to some measure."

"Yet it did not last, Georgina. One random accident destroyed it all."

"Yes, but look at them together." She held up the painting and took in the man and woman at ease, enjoying a warm breezy summer's day together. A stranger would think Sheffield has captured an ordinary moment in the life of an ordinary married couple, and yet to me this painting speaks of great, great things, significant things. It's like music filling my ears, my very insides to bursting. How is it for you?"

Charles raised his glass at the painting. "I once knew that woman—carefree, at ease. Happy. But then it changed, all of it changed. She changed, she had to. I lost her, that woman." He gulped at his drink. "That was not my father's wife."

"You are angry with her?"

He pounded his fist onto the table, his hair flying in his face, letters fluttered and spun off the table. "I am angry that she bore so many sorrows."

"Tell me of her sorrows, Charles. I want to know her. I want to know you."

"It was always difficult for me to know that my mother had never experienced affection from her husband, from any man. And now that I've learnt she did, I am pleased. I am. Yet my heart aches to know that she had been denied that happiness from the first. Denied the man she loved because her parents had their eye on a brighter star." A sharp laugh escaped his lips. "That bright star was a demon who made her suffer abominably over and over again. And she endured it over and over again for me and Hugh."

Her heart beat loudly in her chest at the tortured ache in his voice, the harsh gleam in his eyes. She wanted to take that horror from him, whatever it was. "I think your mother was incredibly brave to have left your father. She took a stand for what was right for her, a wholly uncommon thing for a woman to do to this very day. She made a bold choice and had the strength to broker a peace with her husband in order to maintain a relationship with her sons, and thankfully, your father agreed."

"Yes, they forged a peace between them." A contemptuous sneer etched his face, a bitter laugh fumed from his lips. "How delicate a word that is, my darling. How dignified. But their peace was none of those things."

Each of his brutally bit out words battered at her chest. She wanted to wipe away the pain that now marred his features, tortured his soul, burdened his heart.

"The Earl of Ryvves might have given an inch in allowing her to live apart from him, and though that suited him greatly, his wife claiming what she wanted remained a burning insult. He was compelled to make her pay for her offence in a way that would please him and disgust her."

Her skin crawled with cold sharp needles, her stomach knotted, but she held it all at bay. She would not betray her disquiet to him. He needed to tell his story at last. He needed her to listen, and she would. She would be his rock. "Tell me."

"He was a cruel man, my father. His cruelty always had purpose. He let her go, but he enforced that she would never forget who owned her, who ruled over her dominion, who had supremacy in all things." He swallowed more brandy and licked at his lips. "After they separated, she was allowed to see us here at Ironvine under supervision, once a month perhaps. And at the conclusion of every one of her visits, she would suffer his savage degradation."

The knot in her stomach stung. "How did you know?"

He grabbed a bottle of port and filled his glass. "When I was very young, when my parents were still living together, I would often visit my mother in her chamber using the secret hallway and the false door. I'd visit her early in the morning or late at night. She would always have sweets and biscuits for us to eat together, and she'd read to me, tell me stories, we would laugh. Sometimes in the mornings, I would wait for when her lady's maid would bring her tea and we would share her break-fast. Those were times of happiness. I had to steal them to have them."

"After they had separated, a month later she came to Iron-vine for her first allowed visit with her children. One weekend.

I'd been both anxious and thrilled. But it went smoothly and I could tell she was relieved, as was I.

"On her last morning, I woke early and went to the secret hallway to wait for the servant to leave. But just as I reached the gib door, I heard his voice, and I froze. I peeked through the crack in the door. My father was in her chamber, speaking to her in that scornful and taunting tone that I knew meant he was building his argument, leading somewhere terrible.

"He'd asked her if she enjoyed her visit, and she'd said yes, that she was grateful to have spent time with her sons. That's when he said, *'your gratitude is nothing to me.'*" Charles's fist went to his chest. "I can still remember my heart pounding so hard in my chest. I even held my breath. I knew, I knew, she'd be punished somehow, that he'd force her to pay a dear price if she wished for these visits to continue.

"They argued, he called her terrible names. She said, "I hate you. I shall always hate you." Charles's eyes closed shut for a moment and then opened. "Father only laughed. Then he ordered her to get on all fours and lift her skirts."

A small cry escaped Georgina's lips.

"I pressed back against the wall, and I heard struggling, muffled grunts, fabric ripping. Then a smack, another, a harder slap. I waited and waited, but I did not hear her. I had to stay to hear her, to make sure she was all right. I had to know."

"Yes. Of course."

"I opened the door an inch more and could see the side of her face smashed into the bedding, her body jerking forward on the bed. I couldn't see him, but I could hear his grunting, his foul language with his every forceful thrust." He let out a ragged breath and drained his glass.

"Not one cry, not one scream. No begging, no pleading. She knew that's what he wanted for his true satisfaction, and she would not grant it to him. She kept all her terror, her fear, her pain locked inside as her hands gripped that bedding. She would not let him break her." He lifted his gaze to Georgina, his eyes heavy. "Yet in that moment, my heart broke forever. And yet… I was proud of her. Dear God, is that not perverse?"

"Because you knew the kind of monster he was. You knew how hard it was to bear."

His head tilted, his chest heaved. "Yes, I knew. And that day my hope that it would stop died. Any hope died." He wiped at his face, cleared his throat. "I finally managed to scramble down the secret passage to the back hallway like a rat chased by flames, down the stairs, and outside where I threw up, much to the footman's horror.

"Out front, the servants were loading her trunks into her carriage. I waited and waited. Finally, she appeared, and I ran to her—to offer her my embrace, comfort…"

"And to be comforted yourself."

"She heard me and turned. Her demeanour was hard as stone. It did not soften as it always would upon seeing me. It was gone. He'd destroyed it. She only said, *'Goodbye, Charles,'* and entered her carriage. No smile, no embrace, no kiss. No endearments. One brief wave goodbye and she was gone."

And his heart with her, Georgina thought.

He let out a deep breath. "When she returned the next month for her visit, instead of being overjoyed at seeing her again, I was only full of dread."

"You were afraid for her." Georgina went to him, her hand wiping his brow, settling against his face.

"I did not visit her in her chamber, I did not use the gib door ever again. I did nothing to stop it, nothing to help her. To comfort her in some way. I only receded. I learnt to never speak of her, pretend I had no use for her, just as Hugh had. I did what was expected of me. Thus, I'd collaborated with him against her. Makes me sick to this day." That muscle alongside his jaw flexed.

"You couldn't have possibly done anything differently. Think of it—he would have punished you or sent you away, never allowed you to see her again. You were just a boy." Her hand went to his chest. "Did Hugh know? Did you ever tell him?"

"Oh, Georgie. I trusted no one in this house, and no one outside of it," his voice was weary, raw. His gleaming eyes lanced her through her like a burning hot poker. One would have thought Charles Montclare, son of the Earl of Ryvves, had enjoyed an idyllic childhood, free of cares and woes, rich with abundance and glorious plenty.

"Truly she suffered, and you understood her suffering. You had compassion for her. So unlike your brother, who simply shed any unpleasantness from himself and carried on." She stroked the sides of his face. "You must know that she did not allow it to destroy her. Her relationship with my father is a clear testament to that, is it not?"

He pulled away from her. "I am glad to learn she had happiness in her life, that happiness which she'd yearned for once upon a time in her youth. But to have it thus taken away from her, by marriage, by death…I only feel a profound sense of grief. I am grieving her all over again, and in a new way." Charles swallowed hard, composing himself. "I only wish I could have shared that new happiness with her, known it, known her like that again…" He rubbed at his eyes. "Dammit…I cannot…" Suddenly, he stalked out of the room, his drink in hand.

"Charles!" She followed him out into the great hall. "Charles!"

Glass exploded and crashed. The large portrait of his father was covered in wine, the amethyst liquid streaming down the great long canvas. Splinters and shards of glass were everywhere, the heady scent of the liquor rising around them.

"You are nothing like him." Georgina's voice rose behind him. "Nothing."

He stormed away. "It is all I know. He made sure of it."

Chapter Fifty-Eight

Georgina

THE DUKE and Duchess were set to quit their estate within a fortnight's time, and Brandon and Justine felt they should invite the Oakleys over to Wolfsgate for dinner before their departure.

Rather, Georgina had instilled the idea in Justine's mind as another plan formed in hers.

She had invited Justine to Ironvine to help her make sense of the massive silver collection as well as offering ideas to redecorate and repurpose the many parlours on the ground floor of the house as well as redecorating the many bedchambers upstairs.

As they poured over tapestries and bedspreads, Georgina mentioned that she had heard the Duke and Duchess would be leaving shortly.

"Are they?"

"I feel I must invite them for dinner, being of the peerage, but as our mourning period for Hugh is not yet over, to host a party would not be…" Georgina watched her friend's features for a response. "Of course, if it were hunting season, Charles at the very least would certainly have the Duke and Brandon and a few others over for shooting and the like, but now in July…"

Justine's gaze shot up from the bedding they had been going through. She was positively stricken. "I hadn't considered they would be leaving so soon. I thought we'd have many more weeks before…" She blew out a huff of air. "Ordinarily, Brandon and I would have considered such a thing immediately, but these past weeks he's been consumed with a business matter and has been going to London and Bristol with regularity. And with the children, I…where is my mind?"

"Where it should be, with your beautiful babies."

"I am so glad you mentioned it."

Georgina took the tapestry from Justine's hands. "All this can wait. Arranging such a dinner party is the most pressing matter. Do not fret, my darling, I can assist you with every detail."

"As Brandon has just returned last night from London, I shall make haste and go home now and tell him that we absolutely must have the Oakleys to Wolfsgate immediately."

"Excellent." Georgina grinned as she gestured to the servant that Lady Graven would be leaving. *Objective accomplished. Desired result achieved.* "If you like, I could pen the invitations?"

"Yes, please, Georgie, would you? That would be an incredible help, I find that such a tedious, time-consuming chore."

"Of course, my love."

Having the Oakleys at Wolfsgate would be the most powerful way to get the necklace back from the Duchess. If that didn't work, nothing would. As the Oakleys were leaving, there would be no more such opportunities, and she would not let it slip away. Especially now that the Duchess and Georgina's friendship had progressed since her visit to Ironvine. This was the time to strike.

～

Five days later, in the parlour of Wolfsgate, Georgina found the Duchess on her own taking in the view from the leaded glass windows.

"Your Grace, how delightful to see you again."

The Duchess held out her hand to her. "Georgina, how good it is to see you."

"I was sorry to hear that you will be leaving us shortly for I very much enjoy our friendship, and I long for it to continue. I think often on your last visit and I—"

"No, no." The Duchess took her hands in hers. "Be assured, I am glad that we cleared the questions between us that day."

"As am I. I have something for you." Georgina handed her a leather pouch. Inside was the gift she'd prepared for her. "Please accept this token of my sincerity and regard for our friendship."

The Duchess opened the pouch and pulled out a large locket. She clicked it open, and a sound escaped her lips.

"I took the liberty of painting a miniature of that portrait study for you as a gift of goodwill. I wanted you to have that most recent image of him as a *memento mori*." Georgina's voice had sunk into a whisper. "I thought perhaps you would take pleasure in it or rather take comfort in this keepsake, for you mourn him alone."

The Duchess did not reply. She only fingered the lock of bright blond hair Georgina had curled into the other side of the locket. Georgina moved closer to her. "It is his, his as a boy. I found it recently in a collection my mother-in-law had kept of her sons."

Her Grace's gaze was glued to the locket. So schooled in controlling all her emotions, reactions, and responses always, she did not speak, did not betray any feeling.

"Have I done wrong? Please, I—"

The Duchess's hand firmly gripped Georgina's arm, her watery gaze meeting hers. "What a blessing you are to me,

Countess," she breathed. "I thank you." Her Grace embraced her.

~

OVER DINNER, the conversation flowed easily, and once the jellies and syllabubs had been enjoyed, the topic drifted to business investments. A sure sign for the ladies that they would quit the dining room shortly.

"The future is investment outside of England," said the Duke.

"Spices, sugar, saltpetre, that sort of thing?" said Charles.

"There's so much more than that, because it's not only about doing trade unique to those regions, it's about owning it out there in India, in China. The possibilities are truly endless and the returns are…significant."

Brandon fingered the edge of his dessert dish. "When I was a boy, my father had invested in a sugar plantation in Jamaica along with a number of other investors."

The Duke raised his glass. "Ah, wise choice. Excellent."

"It's a sound business."

"Have you been to the island?" Her Grace asked.

"I did go, yes. And I must admit, that is when the seeds of doubt were planted in my soul. I saw it with my own eyes, heard it, felt it. We didn't simply own a tract of land and shares in a plantation and its product, a product we then sold and made a grand profit from. That business doesn't only own land and sugar, it owns people."

"You are referring to the slaves?" said the Duke.

"I know it is not a popular opinion, especially as Bristol is at the centre of that industry, yet I do not feel it is right to own a person for my own use, and ultimately, for my own advantage. All the sugar cane planted and harvested, all that sweet profit is made on the backs of these piteous humans who've been ripped from their homelands and brought to the islands

384

as prisoners with nothing offered them but squalor and suffering.

"I shall never forget the sight of a newly arrived slave ship at port unloading its cargo for sale. Cargo…" Brandon let out a ragged breath as he shoved his dish out of his way, his forehead creasing, his eyes narrowing, the memory still fresh. "It is a wretched, sinister business. It is wrong, and I cannot abide it."

"There was a slave uprising on the island of Haiti recently, was there not?" asked the Duke.

"Your Grace is well informed, yes. The sugar trade has been all but wiped out there, and many of those plantation owners have moved on to the neighbouring island of Cuba."

"They haven't abandoned hope, eh?" asked Charles.

"Would be foolish to do so," said the Duke. "Sugar is in extreme demand, a golden asset worldwide. Many islands in the Caribbean now boast a high number of plantations, don't they, Graven?"

"They do indeed, Your Grace."

"And that location is a gateway to the yet untouched Americas."

"Beyond those nasty former colonies, eh?" smirked Charles.

"It's a whole damned continent of yet unexplored natural wonders," said the Duke.

"Unexplored or unexploited?" asked Georgina.

Every guest at the table turned to stare at her, and she stiffened her back. Charles's features remained unreadable except for a slight twitch of his lips and a quirk of an eyebrow.

"Excellent point, Countess," said the Duchess, raising her glass in Georgina's direction. The rest of the guests looked away then, but the Duke's gaze lingered on her, and a cool smile took its time razoring over his lips. From across the long table, she could feel his scrutiny of her as if it were a physical thing. A thing she could not translate. Her shoes pressed into the floor, and her back straightened even more than it already was.

The Duke turned back to Brandon. "Graven, now would be a very, very good time to sell your shares if you are so inclined."

"In fact, I have already." Brandon wiped his hands on a cloth. "It happened quite quickly. I was most fortunate."

"Well done," remarked Charles.

"Indeed," said the Duke. "If you're looking for a new investment, I can assure you that India is the future."

"I agree with you, Your Grace, I believe it is." Brandon folded the cloth into quarters. "But I would prefer this time to not look so far away from home."

"Nothing like surviving a fatal shipwreck to alter one's frame of mind forever, eh?" said Charles.

"Did you, really?" asked the Duchess.

"I did. On the passage home from Jamaica. It was a tragedy that, in the end, gave me back my life in a new and most…unexpected way." Brandon's gaze found his wife's, and she raised her glass to him as he drank the last of his wine, winking at her.

Justine rose. "Gentleman, we shall take our leave of you."

At last.

Out in the great hall, several of the ladies lingered, waiting for their hostess to lead them to the drawing room. Aunt Vivian and Alice detained Georgina for a moment, but as she answered their queries, she spotted the Duchess looking about the house, taking in all the old-style Jacobean accents.

"Forgive me, Alice, I must have a word with Her Grace." Georgina's heart thudded in her chest as the Duchess made her way toward the staircase, her gaze traveling up, landing on the family portraits.

Speak, Lady Caroline, speak, roared through Georgina's brain.

The Duchess stilled, her body stiffened. She'd seen the painting. Georgina bit her lip as the Duchess climbed the steps and stopped on the landing before Lady Caroline's portrait. A hand going to her throat, her lips parting.

Yes. A thousand sparks flooded Georgina's veins as she moved toward Her Grace, but a hand gripped her arm firmly, stopping her.

"There you are, my lovely girl."

That voice. She turned and met those shining, penetrating light coloured eyes. Her flesh chilled.

The Duke.

Chapter Fifty-Nine

Georgina

"Your Grace?" She smiled at him, her eyes darting to where his wife stood before the portrait of Lady Caroline. Justine joined the Duchess before the painting. *Thank you, Lord!*

"Countess. My wife tells me she's invited you and the Earl to visit us at our estate in the north. We eagerly await you."

She shifted her weight under his piercing gaze. This close, he was even more alluring a person. Was it the way he looked at her—as if all his senses were taking her in and calculating? As if he were about to strike or pounce or swallow her whole.

"Yes, Her Grace asked me to paint…whomever Your Grace wished for me to… paint."

"Hmm." A noise rumbled in his chest, the edges of his lips curling. "Yes. To paint."

Her mouth dried. He was positively unsettling.

"Countess, I must tell you. When I first saw you with Hugh at that ball in town, I was quite taken by you. You have a boldness and elegance about you that are not a common pairing. You are passionate about the things you care for and feel no reserve in expressing your opinions."

"I have been told many times it is a fault I have."

The Duke leaned in closer to her. "I find it most refreshing.

Innocent and eager, like your flesh." His fingers brushed over her bare shoulder.

Her chest tightened. "Your Grace, I am a married woman who is dedicated to her husband, and he to her."

His two fingers brushed her lip. "Oh, I do not wish to tear you from your husband, my lady. Only to enhance."

Georgina's breath cut at his delicate, illicit touch, his choice of words. "Enhance?"

"I would wish to exalt you, adore you, unleash the greatest of pleasures in you." His voice rolled with relish over the words he spoke as his warm fingers trailed over her shoulder.

She met his gaze, her feet firmly planted on the floor. There was no other way but to be direct with this man. "I assure you, sir, my husband accomplishes all those things. Unleashes all those pleasures in me."

"I assure you, Countess, I am a good teacher. It would not be time lost nor stolen from your husband, for you will then beguile him with all you've learnt. It is about the experience, that is what I offer."

It would be so easy to be seduced by this man, so easy, she thought. "Ah."

"I am a seeker, my lady. For me, heaven lies somewhere between peril and pleasure—one anticipates the other, they cannot be separated. Only you must be bold enough to seek, and I feel you are. I would invite you on this journey. Be your guide to such an experience."

"Your invitation is most generous, Your Grace."

"It is. I do not propose it lightly."

"Yet I would be unable to accept such generosity."

His eyes glinted over her, lips twisted into an odd grin that made her insides twist. "You were to marry Hugh, were you not?"

"Yes, I was."

"Hugh would have encouraged you in this, if not insisted. Indeed, he would have given you to me, and both he and I would have taken you on a journey beyond anything you've ever imagined."

Her pulse charged. He meant to shock her but she would not give him the satisfaction. She only smiled as serenely as she could. "A remarkable proposal, to be sure. However, I am not married to Hugh, and my husband is a different man. I know of that wild journey beyond of which you speak, for I am on that exquisite journey with the Earl," she replied. "I…I love him."

The breath burned in her lungs. She didn't expect to say such a thing, especially to the Duke, but it was true. And the truth was the mightiest sword. She was falling in love with Charles.

A slight grin grew over the Duke's lips as his gaze darted over her shoulder for a moment. "May I offer one word of advice to you then, Countess?"

"I am all anticipation, sir."

He leaned in closer, his rich, spicy scent that she remembered from dancing with him at the ball in London filled her nostrils, was it clove and cinnamon? His warm breath scoured her neck, his lips brushing the tip of her ear. Every inch of her flesh, every muscle, every limb was on sharp alert. "Never stop seeking together. Never. There is always something new and untamed to discover in seeking a heaven of your own making with your beloved. Always."

Their gazes met, and there she saw no more of that urgent challenge, but calm solicitude. She bowed her head at him. He took her hand and kissed it.

"Darling." An arm coiled about Georgina's waist. *Charles.* Her rigid spine eased.

The Duke released her hand. "Ryvves, your Countess is utterly charming."

"She is, sir, and more."

"You must come to our house in the north and be our guests, for if you do not, my wife would be deeply disappointed, and that is one of the few things on this earth I never forgive." Slanting his head at Charles, he left them.

Charles twisted her around in his arms as her heart thudded in her chest. "Charles, please, don't be angry with me that I was speaking with him alone."

"I'm not angry, Georgie." His lips curved. "I'm proud of you."

"Proud of me?"

"I saw him approach you, and I waited, but you didn't need saving. You handled yourself and him with dignity, and I warrant you spoke your mind and did so clearly yet courteously."

"I did my best. I must tell you, he said the most interesting thing about Hugh," she whispered.

"What did he say?"

"That if Hugh and I had married, Hugh would have given me to him to...play with."

"I had no doubt."

"As you'd remarked, theirs is no ordinary playground, but I told His Grace that I have been conquered by another." She laid her hands on his chest. "You are my husband. You are my bright star, Charles." She quoted him from their discussion of his mother becoming engaged to his father, turning how he'd ironically described his father on its head. "You are my only star, and I love you."

His eyes flared, and he stilled. Was it alarm? Shock? Dread? Suddenly his body slammed into her, his hands around her neck, his mouth devouring hers.

Conquered indeed.

Chapter Sixty

Georgina

"Your Grace?" Georgina stilled. The sight of the Duchess of Oakley standing on her front lawn, her face drawn had Georgina's heart stopping in her chest. Something was wrong. Was she angry with her? Had she heard of her conversation with the Duke?

"I'd like a word if you are free?"

"Of course. It's lovely to see you. Please do come inside."

She handed her a leather case that bore the insignia of a renowned jeweller in London. "This is for you, Georgina."

"For me?"

"Open it."

Her stomach dropping, Georgina unhinged the small lock and opened it. She gasped at the sight of its contents. Lady Caroline's wolf pearls and diamonds and rubies lay in a bed of blue silk. Her grip on the box tightened. "Oh, they are even more beautiful in real life than they are in the painting. Thank you, Your Grace. I imagine this must have been so very difficult for you."

"No. It was simple." She lifted her chin. "At Wolfsgate, the moment I laid eyes on the portrait of Lady Caroline, everything altered. And then Lady Justine came upon me and told me the story of the painting. I asked her about the necklace, and with great discretion, she shared with me that it had been lost in tragic, painful circumstances.

"I felt her sadness acutely, and I also felt that she blames herself. Which is all wrong. It is within my power to put this years-long irregularity to right, to repair wounds, to break the sinister hold of so much arrogance and greed and anger. And so I am." She swallowed hard. "And I would prefer that you returned the jewels to your dear friend, not I. This is your achievement, Georgina. And that will be your greatest reward."

"I thank you," Georgina breathed, closing the box.

"Hugh showered me with a great many gifts over the course of our time together, but this one, this particular one was very special as he gave it to me the day we broke. He said he'd searched for a special piece to mark his promise that he was coming back to me no matter his engagement, his marriage. He would always be mine. That during our separation, this necklace would be a comfort and an inspiration to me."

"Yes, I imagine it was."

"I wore the necklace to the ball in London on purpose. Of course, I knew he'd be there, looking for a wife, and I wanted him to know that all was well on my side. That I believed in him to do the thing he must, that I stood by him. But perhaps I annoyed him with that reminder.

"When you told me the truth about the necklace, I was upset and very angry. I tried to put it out of my mind, but last night at Wolfsgate, when I saw it on its original and rightful owner, it made the storm of my emotions cease. This was stolen from Lady Caroline. It does not belong to me or any other but Lord Brandon and Lady Justine.

"No matter how much Hugh and I loved each other, what was between us could never be permanent, out in the open and I knew that. I had accepted it from the very first. We would never be able to marry, to live a true life together. No…" She let out a heavy sigh. "Ours was but a temporary flicker in the darkness, like a taper that melts and melts until at last the flame dissolves in the spent wax, and its light is no more.

"Hugh would marry and have children, his own family would need him. All things he denied, but I am a married woman, I know."

Her fingers touched Georgina's chin. "Would his wife not accept his attachment to me and our way of life together? Or perhaps would he grow fond of his wife, and love her, even." She removed her hand from Georgina.

"All these realities would eventually wear down our bond, and we both knew it. No matter how hard we denied it, we both knew that when he married, things would change. The necklace was his pledge, his hope against any disappointments, bitterness, doubts, rancour—all things we both abhorred and had never experienced with each other."

She touched the box. "But for Lady Caroline, this necklace was a true token of love and family to be cherished generation after generation. For me, however, it was but a glittering hope and perhaps, a hubristic declaration." She clasped her hands together. "No matter, Hugh's untimely death blasted all that away."

"If only he hadn't–"

She raised her hand. "But he did. And pearls and diamonds and rubies will not bring him back. They can lay beautifully about my neck, but they cannot embrace me the way he did, make me laugh, understand me, share with me, fill me. These precious stones are no substitute for the man, they are but a memento of a moment in time. Yet now they only signify aching loss and broken dreams, foolish hopes, and all that shall never be.

"When you told me that he'd purchased this necklace from the man he'd later duelled with over that woman. I wondered had he not bought the necklace from Mr. Treharne, his acquaintance with the lady may not have been rekindled, and then she and Hugh might not have gotten involved. Might he still be alive?"

"Madness lies there, Your Grace."

"Yes, Georgina, yes, and now that is what courses through me when I behold these jewels. Only that madness, which creates a wave of bitterness inside me." She took in a breath of air and steadied her shoulders. "This necklace was not Hugh's to give, mine to keep, nor was it Treharne's to sell." She took in a deep breath. "This necklace was created by a good and loyal husband for his beloved and should be restored to its rightful heirs and its rightful home. There lies its truth, its true and incandescent promise."

Georgina took the Duchess's hands in hers. "I am deeply moved by your decision and your frankness. I thank you."

"I thank you, Georgina. With your locket, you have given me a finer token of my lost love. It is a true gift of the heart from a true friend. I have not had that, ever from another woman, and I am most grateful that you dared to take the chance to inform me of the truth. You are brave."

"You are brave for accepting it so."

She grinned. "I might have been the type of woman who didn't give a damn. Or worse, would have demanded a high price from you in return and not necessarily money."

"I was sure of the kind of heart you have, and I now know it better still." Georgina slid her arm through the Duchess's and they walked through the gardens.

"I have never had a friend quite like you. I am able to speak with you frankly, and you accept me as I am. You do not dissemble, hoping to say only the right thing, the thing you think I want to hear to impress me, to humour me. And you are sincere in your care. I would ask a favour of you."

"A favour? Of me?"

"Paint my portrait."

"Me?"

"You."

"Your Grace, your family has been painted by Reynolds, by Gainsborough, why would you — "

"My portrait is my choice to make, and I choose you. I have taken overly long in deciding upon a painter for my portrait. Now I know why–my instincts have led me to you. I would like a lady to paint me, and most of all my particular friend, Lady Georgina, Countess of Ryvves. For that, I am grateful to Hugh, for bringing us together."

"Yes, I hadn't thought of that." Georgina met her smile with her own.

"You painting this picture would have great significance for me and insure the finest, truest result that I and my husband will be pleased with. Every time I shall look upon it and am reminded of our time together, see your signature at the edge of the canvas, I shall be filled with true joy, true pleasure. And that is priceless to me."

"This is an honour I dared not dream of."

"Ah no, my love. You must always dream, always dare. You did so in securing the wolf necklace, did you not? For others you do so much, but you must also learn to do for yourself." She stopped and studied her. "Perhaps you feel you are not ready for such an enterprise? I wish to challenge you, not burden you."

"I admit, I do not feel ready for such a great work."

Smiling, she slid her arm through Georgina's and they continued their stroll. "I have a proposition for you then."

Georgina's eyes widened, remembering the Duke's offer. "What kind of proposition?"

"I would like to introduce you to an artist friend who will be visiting us from France. I'd mentioned him to you before, I think. I shall be introducing him at court shortly."

"Ah yes."

"You may have heard of him. Le Verne?"

Georgina let out a gasp. "Le Verne? Le Verne is coming to England under your patronage?"

"How would you like to be tutored by him?"

Her heart leapt up her throat.

"Well?"

Dream. Dare. "It would be a tremendous honour. I would love it."

She let out a soft laugh. "I shall arrange everything, Countess, and then I shall be your first commission. From now on, whenever I am here in the country, I shall send word, and I shall come to you and you shall work. And when you come to town, you shall send me word, and I will sit for you."

"Yes. Yes."

"Good. We are agreed."

"I am astounded at this opportunity, Your Grace. Your faith in me." This woman believed in her, in her talent. The sun shone warm and bright over her flesh. "I am humbled by your trust and grateful for your friendship."

"As am I. From now on, you shall call me Zandra."

"I shall."

"Will your husband agree to this or will he be a problem?"

"My husband loves my work, and he is most supportive of my endeavours."

Bursting through the doorway of the house, Charles strode outside, his chemise wet with perspiration, his face streaked with red, he pulled his mussed hair from his tie. He ripped off his shirt and balled it in his fist as he stormed down the green. His sculpted chest and torso heaved for air. Georgina's mouth dried at the sight of her husband.

"Hmm…" murmured the Duchess. "The Earl continues his sword training with Mr. Swindon?"

"The exercise has strengthened his wounded arm considerably, and he greatly enjoys the sport."

"You must be enjoying it, as well, my darling." The

Duchess let out a soft rolling laugh. "I say that from experience. Where the devil is he off to?"

"Most probably the pond for a swim." Georgina swept the hair from her face. Just the sight of the curved and firm plains of his muscle and sinew enflamed that ember in her chest, setting off that particular ache between her legs.

A grin flashed over the Duchess's lips. "I shall take my leave." She touched Georgina's hand and squeezed. "I must say, there's nothing like a swim on such a hot, hot day, don't you agree?"

Chapter Sixty-One

Charles

The Duke and Duchess revived the Oakley tradition of a summer picnic. They'd decided to open it to all the landed gentry in the area as a charity event to raise money for the poor of the upper village who had their belongings and homes damaged in the recent storms and subsequent floodwaters.

Before they quit the country, the Oakleys would offer a final dash of goodwill to the deserving locals who had fallen on hard times and would remember them fondly for it.

It was a perfect day, not too warm and only a few clouds marred the sky which made for a lessening of the sun's urgent glare just an hour earlier. Couples strolled arm in arm through their formal gardens. Two harpists played their angelic music.

The long tables were laden with a joint of cold roast beef, veal and ham pies, pigeon pies, thin buttered sandwiches, sugar biscuits, fruit tarts, plum cakes, sponge cakes, and cheeses. Ices were most impressively presented in their great platters, as well as colourful fruits. Big silver urns dispensed tea, coffee, along with sherry, and a claret cup punch.

The guests spoke excitedly as they swept up and down the great front lawn, laughed and boasted. The general cheer was quite high. Such an occasion required it.

Charles spotted Georgina where he'd left her, catching up with Justine, and two other ladies had joined them. He had extricated himself from a dull conversation with an elderly neighbour, Mr. Marchmain, about hunting and his recent methods for increasing his stock of wildlife on his estate. He'd excused himself to get more wine which he promptly did at a table at the far end of the lawn, away from the milling crowd of guests.

"I must speak with you," came a familiar voice.

He turned. "Amanda? What in God's name are you doing here? Surely you were not invited after your recent performance at my house?"

"I had to see you."

"Whatever for?"

"I need an introduction to the Duke. I would speak with him on an urgent matter."

"What has that to do with me?"

"You said you'd help me, and you are acquainted with him.

"I did not agree to help you. Why should I introduce you to her husband when I know that you detest her? Surely she's told him of your effrontery in my house. How shall I ever live that down with His Grace? It is a great mark against me."

"I knew his last mistress, Frederica Ashton. We were acquaintances in town and in Bath. And you were correct when you'd remarked that this past season, there was no Frederica. On the occasions that he was in town, Oakley was only seen with the wife."

"How dreadfully dull of him."

"He's always kept a mistress. He must have broken off with Mrs. Ashton. He is free. Surely, he must be in need of a new paramour to indulge his whims."

"I'm sure he takes very good care of his needs and his whims, whatever they may be." He cleared his throat.

"Mrs. Ashton had a very generous allowance, a house of

her own in town, and would live with him at one of his estates in the country where his wife surely did not tread."

"That's what you want, is it?"

"It is. And I'm going to get it."

"I am in awe of your ambitions, Mrs. Treharne."

"It is my perfect solution, and I am not ashamed of it, which is why I need to speak to His Grace directly and right away."

"So you can seduce your lover's lover as you had once remarked so eloquently? Or convince him of your suitability for the position by some other brilliant means before he quits Gloucestershire?"

"I'm not naive to think by simply offering myself he shall accept me. I have something in my possession that he would not want to be made public. I will show it to him and then he and I can come to a mutually satisfying agreement." Was it the slight sneer that wafted over her lips for just a second that chilled his spine? The sudden hardness of her jaw? Scorn and contempt and utter confidence, a heady witches' brew.

"You are going to blackmail the Duke of Oakley?"

"Such harsh language. After he sees what I have to show him, I assure you, in his eyes, his wife shall be disgraced, and I shall be exalted."

"Brazen foolishness. I will not be a part of your schemes."

"Come now, Lord Ryvves, think of it. Next season in town I shall make my debut at his side. What a thrill that shall be."

"Your confidence is most admirable, but I will not be involved. Good day, madame." He stalked away from her.

"Do you not wish to know what it is I have in my possession to show him that will change how he looks at his wife?"

Charles stopped. He did want to know. He would want to protect the Oakleys.

He faced her once again. "What is it?"

A sly grin deepened over her lips. "I have a letter that will provide him with the truth about his whore of a wife. This is my great opportunity to not only sling her down where she belongs but alter my situation in life for the better."

"A letter?"

"I cannot tell you more right now."

"I am not assisting you in this madness."

"If you do not, this could bode ill for your precious wife."

"Are you threatening me?"

"Oh no, no. I'm promising you."

"What the devil could you possibly—"

"Matthew told me that he had every intention of courting Miss Georgina at that last ball in London, proposing to her—"

"Did he now?"

"But then, a surprising turn of events occurred. At the ball, she asked Matthew to position himself in the gardens of the house where she would bring out Hugh for a stroll. Matthew was to watch from a distance. And what did he witness? Georgina kissing Hugh, allowing him many, many liberties with her person. Matthew was to call them out, to force Hugh's hand. But he didn't have the chance, as you arrived and interrupted the brazen seduction, insisting that your brother marry her. Shameless girl to attempt to seduce an Earl into an engagement.

"Naturally when Hugh died unexpectedly, she was in a desperate state and turned to you. Did she beg you to take her? Did you take pity on her with your cock so her reputation would remain untarnished? No, no, there's a better word—intact." She burst into laughter.

"You are vile."

"Georgina is only a younger version of me, only not as clever, I think."

"Oh, she's nothing like you. Never has been."

"She is the me I was before I made the mistake of marrying so rashly out of boredom, impatience, and, it must be said, vanity."

"Pray, what is this? Self-reflection? I am all astonishment."

"I am glad that I must no longer live by William's rules and his petty disappointments in me, nor bear his judgements and punishments. Never again," her voice blazed.

"Still no pity for your dead husband, eh?"

"No. Never."

Georgina's description of Amanda that morning before the duel flashed in his memory. She'd been disheveled, bruised, out of sorts. Extremely bitter.

"I tell you this, Charles. When I saw his dead body brought home, I swore then that I would never suffer such a man again."

Images of William at Hyde Park that morning coursed through his brain. William rubbing at his eyes, stumbling, wavering, bracing himself with effort to raise the pistol. He'd found it odd. So unlike William.

His gut hardened. "You gave William laudanum before the duel, didn't you? Put it in something he drank before he left for Hyde Park so he wouldn't be his sharpest."

She met his gaze evenly. "They both agreed to a duel, did they not? One of them might die, that's the risk taken by gentlemen. That risk is understood and accepted. And it is in that acceptable risk that anything can happen. In that acceptable risk lay my opportunity."

A tight grin cracked over her features. "Hugh was obviously the fitter of the two. William hadn't gone hunting or even held a firearm since we'd quit the country. His pursuits in town had been wholly different—every night at his club, dinner parties, gaming, whores—"

"You poisoned William."

"I only thought to tip the scales even more in Hugh's favour."

"Come now, Mrs. Treharne, in Hugh's favour? Or yours?"

She did not offer a reply. She was pleased with herself. Gloating to him, even now.

"Well, what a great pity you'll never know if Hugh was

grateful for your efforts on his behalf." He turned around to walk away.

"Oh, he wasn't grateful," she spit out. "He was only vile and mean and proved to be a liar of the worst kind."

He stilled. *How the devil did she know what he thought of it?* The blood chilled in his veins. His lips parted to speak.

"I say, Ryvves, are you hiding from us?" Whatley's voice rang out like the crash of cymbals and Charles's spine straightened. Whatley came up close and touched his arm, and Charles jerked away from him.

"I would speak to you, my lord—Oh!" Whatley gasped loudly, his eyes widening at the sight of Amanda. "My darling, Mrs. Treharne, how wonderful to see you!" Whatley lunged at her, giving her a kiss on both sides of her taut face in the French manner. "I had hoped you'd be here. What is a party without your vivacity and wicked wit?"

"Mr. Whatley, you are too kind." Amanda winced at his grip on her hands through a hard smile.

"I leave you both to your enjoyments then."

"Lord Ryvves?" Amanda called out sharply. "Do remember what I promised you, won't you?"

Charles bowed his head stiffly and stalked off, pulling tight on his surging emotions as if they were a school of wild fish he struggled to hold in his net.

She had gone to Hugh after the duel.

She had seen him.

It was Amanda.

He struggled for a breath.

He clenched his jaw. *You and I shall play a final game, Amanda. A grand finale, to be sure, and you shall get everything you deserve.*

Chapter Sixty-Two

Charles

THE HARPISTS' notes filled the air with their delicate music as he rejoined the throng of picnic guests. Rage shuddered through him, a tide of venom, dark and bitter.

Grabbing two cups of punch, he found his wife and the Duchess about to enter one of the mazes together. *Perfect.* "My dear ladies, I took the liberty of bringing you both refreshment."

"Exactly what we needed. I thank you, Ryvves." The Duchess took the cup.

Georgina sipped on the cool drink. "Hmm…perfect." She glanced at him, her unaffected amiable smile filling his vision.

You are perfect, my love, and I will do whatever it takes to protect you. To protect our life together.

"I am here to offer you something else other than punch, Your Grace. Something you have been longing for," said Charles.

"I am all fascination, Ryvves. Do tell." The Duchess sipped her punch.

"How intriguing," said Georgina.

"I shall tell you everything once you bring us to the depths of this intricate maze."

"Is it a secret?" Georgina giggled.

Holding his gaze, the Duchess's features sobered. She understood the need for privacy. "This way."

They followed the Duchess, left then right, straight on, around a half circle. Left again, down a long narrow corridor of green, and, finally, the three of them were enclosed by a high wall of green hedge with no other route before them.

"I know who my brother saw at his final hours," said Charles. In a low voice, he told them what Amanda had let slip.

"Oh no, no." murmured Georgina.

The Duchess's breathing deepened. She lifted her glass to her lips, a slight tremble in her hand. Swallowing, she steadied herself.

"She wants me to obtain an audience with the Duke for her."

"Whatever for?" The Duchess's brow furrowed.

He explained about a letter she claimed to have. "When I found Hugh that morning, his desk was a mess, ink was spilt, papers were strewn about, and there was ink on his fingers when I found him."

"Yet you'd not found a letter?"

"No. She must have taken it. And whatever's in it she wants to use against you, Your Grace. She is of the mind that showing your husband this letter would disgrace you in his eyes. and he would not want it made public."

"And what reward is she hoping for?" asked the Duchess, unruffled by the information.

"To be his mistress."

"Ahh, as a triumph over me, no doubt. This keeps getting better and better," quipped the Duchess.

"I am desperate for a glass of wine now," Georgina said. "I imagine she assumes that achieving the Duke's favour would mean a life of ease and largesse paved with diamonds."

"Oh, they all do." The Duchess's eyes gleamed as she let out a soft laugh.

Was it the sardonic tone in her voice, the cold amusement? *They all expected largesse but that was not the reality of being Oakley's paramour.* Georgina's lips parted at the Duchess's remarks, and Charles placed a hand at her back.

"But would she have the vigour required, I wonder?" A smirk slid over her lips. "His most recent mistress waned quickly under his attentions, and he was most displeased."

His breath stalled. *Poor Frederica Ashton. Had Oakley done away with her?* The Duke's brand of decadence and desire was a darker sort than most could endure or even fathom. Charles was sure Oakley's mistresses were simply not ornaments but workhorses. It was something Hugh had intimated once or twice but never articulated outright. It was whispers he'd heard on occasion at his club in London of the Duke and his inner circle. It was disquieting.

It was perfect.

"Your Grace, the Duke recently remarked to me that one thing in life he does not forgive is someone who disappoints his beloved wife."

"Quite true. In general, my husband does not forgive easily. For my well-being, most especially, Oakley has a very passionate sense of justice. He is most protective of me, and I of him."

"That is the very thing I am counting on in this instance, His Grace's unique brand of justice on your behalf and his authority."

An eyebrow arched stiffly, her lips parted. She said nothing in reply, for she knew what he was implying. The sudden silence between them roared.

"Would His Grace agree to this?" asked Charles.

"Be assured, Ryvves, for me, His Grace will pursue justice most fiercely, until I too am satisfied." A small, tight grin slashed her lips.

The sudden sharpness of her tone, the tension in her upper

lip, and her choice of words, all made her meaning clear to him.

"But would that satisfy you?" she asked him.

"It shall satisfy me greatly. She not only threatens you, Your Grace, but has threatened Georgina's reputation if I do not comply with her wishes. She has already polluted the atmosphere here amongst our friends with her false rumours about Georgina and Hugh and I, and now she has set the stage in motion for more.

Georgina flinched. "What has she done?"

"She and Matthew have woven truths and lies together for their diversion and our downfall. I want her to be swept away from us all and hurled to a most unexpected fate, the opposite of the gilded one which she believes awaits her. If, of course, His Grace were to agree."

"My husband trusts my judgement in helping him make decisions of all kinds. We are partners in all things. After all, we are one in this life. I feel you know this now as a husband."

"I do." His arm slid around Georgina, and he kissed her temple.

"Come." Her Grace led the way out of the maze. "We must speak with the Duke immediately."

Chapter Sixty-Three

Charles

THE DUKE and the Duchess stood together by the enormous marble fireplace in his private study. Georgina was at his side, her hand in his. Charles's grip on Georgina's hand grounded him, centred him when he needed it the most.

"I apologise for taking you away from your party, Your Grace, but this is a matter of great urgency," said Charles.

"I would not be here if I did not believe you, Ryvves. Zandra told me as much, and I can see it on all your faces."

He explained to the Duke that he felt Amanda was the one who'd killed Hugh and had stolen his final letter.

The Duke's eyes narrowed. "This is the same woman who attempted to strike Zandra and struck Lady Ryvves instead?"

Charles and Georgina shared a quick glance. The Duchess had told her husband everything. "Yes, the same," said Georgina.

"It was of no consequence to me," the Duchess said.

Her husband stroked her cheek, his chest expanding. "It is of great consequence to me, my love." His voice was even, but something about the low tone sent a chill racing around Charles's neck.

"Mrs. Treharne wishes to meet with you, Your Grace, to

show you what I believe is this last letter written by Hugh in order to extract some sort of favour from you."

"Money?" he asked.

"Ultimately, but not directly, no. She wants to be rewarded by becoming your mistress."

The Duke's only response was the slow arching of an eyebrow.

"It seems she knew your previous mistress and was aware of the great material rewards she enjoyed."

"And she wishes for such, does she?"

"She does. She's been left without an income by her late husband, who died in the duel, who she'd poisoned prior to the duel to weaken him. died.

"Both men at her hands?" murmured Georgina.

"And after her and Mr. Penry's display at your dinner party--"

"Yes."

"Her brother is adamant that she marry the gentleman, the moment her official mourning time is over. But she does not want him as he is penniless, nor does she wish to marry again."

"She is desperate." The Duke's tongue flicked at his bottom lip for an instant.

"She feels most certain that you would find whatever is in that letter shocking. A betrayal," continued Charles. "But here's the rub in our favour—I believe that whatever Hugh wrote to Her Grace in that letter, you already know. Only Mrs. Treharne does not know the kind of trust that lies between you and the Duchess and Hugh. No one does. Everyone assumes ... quite the opposite."

"Yes, they do," agreed the Duchess.

"The lady is most fervent in her desire to humiliate the Duchess. Furthermore, she is unrelenting in spreading false rumours about me and my brother and my wife, and has threatened to continue to do so if she does not get her way."

"As you know her well, what do you propose, Ryvves?" asked the Duke.

"I would ask you to meet with her, Your Grace, and take the letter from her."

"Make her confess to killing Hugh," said the Duchess.

"And then?" the Duke said. There was a tone of anticipation curling in his words. Two simple words and yet…

Charles met the Duke's hard gaze with his own. "Then do with her what you will."

The Duke tilted his head. "Are you quite sure?"

"I am."

Lifting his chin, Oakley crossed his arms. "What's in this for you, Ryvves, if I do this?"

"The very same thing Her Grace and yourself desire—justice. I shall be satisfied with the justice that you deliver on the Duchess's behalf, my brother's, and my wife's. I would not wish her in gaol, for the sake of her innocent family, but she must be swept away from our lives before she causes further destruction and harm. I forfeit all to Your Grace's capable hands."

The Duke hissed in air at Charles's words. He had hit a vein. The right vein.

Oakley turned to his wife and stroked her cheek. She covered his hand with hers as his gaze burned over her. "Arrange it, Ryvves."

"I shall." Charles bowed his head.

The Duke planted a brief and very sensual kiss on his wife's mouth.

"Your Grace, may I ask—" said Georgina. "Would you truly take her as your mistress?"

A guttural sound vibrated from Oakley's chest, a beast anticipating his favorite meal. He took his wife's hand in his. "I have something infinitely more appealing in mind for the lady."

Chapter Sixty-Four

Charles

CHARLES SENT word to Amanda to meet him at the north edge of Crestdown, her brother's estate, where there was a riding path they'd often use in their youth.

He brought his horse to a stop at the head of the path. How long ago that seemed to him now—he and Brandon and William and Thomas waiting for her to appear brilliantly dressed on her mare along with her brother at her side.

Amanda arrived. She said nothing. Only waited.

"I arranged for a meeting with His Grace as you requested."

Her eyes flared. "He agreed?"

"He agreed. He is most intrigued to see what you have to offer."

Her back straightened. "And her? His wife? Does she know?"

"I only know what the Duke has asked of me to relay to you in the strictest of confidence."

"Very good. When? Where?"

"You must come to my house in two hours' time where he will meet you. You shall do as he asks."

"Of course."

"And if all goes well, tonight you will leave for his estate in the north. You cannot tell anyone where you are going. Not a soul. Not Andrew, not your son, not your maid. No one. This is absolute."

"There, you see..." She closed her eyes and took in a deep breath. She sat higher in her saddle, her cheeks a deep pink in the cool morning winds.

She was pleased with herself. Her dreams were coming true.

~

THROUGH THE WINDOW of the royal parlour on the upper floor of Ironvine, the Duchess, Georgina, and Charles watched as Amanda stood alone on the front steps of his home. The sacrifice awaiting the mysterious all-powerful beast. Only Amanda was no innocent maiden.

A sleek black coach, polished and sturdy, raced down the tree-lined road to the house. Not the Duke's standard coach emblazoned with his coat of arms. It was...discreet. Dark curtains covered the windows. Amanda seemed to stand taller as it came to a stop before her.

The footman darted down and approached her. It was the Duke's man, the same one who Charles had felt was a spy of some sort, who'd delivered the Duchess's letters to Hugh in London. He led her to the coach, and the door swung open. A ringed hand reached out.

Amanda bowed her head, took the hand, and climbed into the coach. The footman entered after her and shut the door behind him."

"Oh my," said Georgina.

The driver called out and with a crack of his whip, the horses charged forward.

"Do you think she will do what he asks of her?" whispered Georgina. "Whatever he asks?"

"She has too much at stake. Furthermore, she feels she's already won since she's caught his interest. She is all zest and zeal now," replied Charles.

"When the coach returns, we shall go outside to meet it," the Duchess murmured. "Now, we wait."

~

POUNDING horses hooves had him putting down his second glass of brandy and shooting up from his chair. An hour exactly had passed. The black coach headed up his drive.

Charles and Georgina and the Duchess descended the front steps of Ironvine, stopping at the coach. His pulse pounded in his throat as the three of them waited for the door to open.

At last, it opened.

The footman exited the coach and holding the door open, stood at the side. The Duke reached out and handed his wife a letter. "This is yours, my darling."

She kissed his gloved hand and took the folded paper.

"What are you doing?" Amanda sputtered from within the coach. Her hair was loose, lips swollen, her face flushed.

The Duke lashed Amanda's leg with a riding crop, and she cried out. "My wife and I have no secrets between us. The contents of this letter were not shocking. All this is well known to me. Do you really think their relationship would have occurred without my knowledge and approval?" His voice was biting.

"But you said…"

"Are you accusing me of lying, madame?" He held the crop under her chin.

Her eyes flared. "No, of course not."

"We agreed, my pet, did we not?" He stroked her throat with the crop. "You tell the truth, and I shall send you to my home in Norfolk to await me."

"Yes, Your Grace."

"Good. Tell them, just as you told me. Go on. It is what I wish of you."

She took in a breath as she lifted her gaze to Charles, and the Duke took away his crop. "I went to see Hugh after the duel. When I got to the house, he was consumed with writing that letter at his desk. He was upset, and when he saw me, he grew angry. He very rudely told me to leave as if I were some street urchin interrupting him.

"I told him how I'd ensured that he was the victor, but he was only irate and annoyed as if I were wasting his time. He informed me he was engaged to be married and never wanted to see me again. I told him his being engaged did not matter to me, but that remark only fed his anger.

"I grabbed the letter from his desk and read it. But the letter was not addressed to his fiancée, explaining the duel, begging for her forgiveness and understanding. No, it was to his great love." Her gaze shifted to the Duchess. "He'd never broken with her. Everything I'd done for him was for naught. Everything I felt all those weeks together. Everything I'd said to him, and he to me—such regard, such affections—all of it lies, puffs of air. False."

"Had you really expected more from him?" said Charles.

"I expected our affair to continue. After playing the penitent wife for so long, Fortune had finally dealt me a stellar hand to play. Indeed, to win. Being with Hugh was thrilling, intoxicating. Did I not deserve this happiness after all the misery I had endured?

"At every ball, dance, and dinner party in London, all the mothers, and their young available daughters quivered around Hugh, and I enjoyed it immensely because I was the one who had him. Me." She glared at the Duchess, at Georgina as she took in a deep, shaky breath. "But all that time he was looking for a bride with an intent to return to his mistress. What was I to him then?"

"Damn you, how the bloody hell did it happen?" Charles's sharp voice made her head jerk.

"He shouted at me to put his penitent missive down as if I were sullying the very paper. We argued. I struck him. He laughed at me. Told me I was acting like a petulant child. I tried to reason with him, but he only pushed me away, and I threw a vase at him. He leapt out of the way, but in doing so he slipped on the marble hearth and fell back against the fireplace. Crumpled to the floor and did not rise up again."

Georgina squeezed his hand tightly, pressing her body against his.

"I rushed to him, and he revived, but in his gaze there still burned that loathing, that anger. His hands flew to my throat. With all my might, I managed to twist out of his hold, and I fell back against a small table. All the figurines fell over on the floor next to me, and I grabbed hold of one."

"The bronze monkey," said Georgina.

"Yes, it was small enough, easy to grip. He cursed violently at me as he struggled to raise himself from the floor. Just like a man who isn't getting what he wants. In my defence I rushed forward and smashed that figurine on his head, and he stopped his cursing. He…stopped."

"Then you scurried home to play the grieving widow?" said Charles.

"I grieved for myself. Hugh was false. Betrayed my heart, played with my trust." She averted her gaze. "He made me dream again, but suddenly in one quick, cold instant, I was hammered back down to the dirt of the earth." She let out a small grunt. "I believed in him." She glared at the Duchess. "But all the while his dream was you. Always you."

"At last the truth," muttered Charles.

Amanda folded her hands in her lap. "What are you going to do now? Make it public? You cannot prove it was me. You can't. You already lied when you told the world William's bullet killed Hugh."

"Come now." The Duke put a hand on her knee and squeezed, and she winced.

"I lied because I didn't want suspicion and questions hanging over Hugh or our house in his death," replied Charles. "I lied because I wanted a clean end to the mess my brother dishonoured us with."

"Dishonour." Her bitter laugh skewered the word. "After all the rumours I've planted, suspicion shall always remain on you and your wife."

"We shall have to bear that as best we can, Mrs. Treharne," said Georgina.

Charles tilted his head at the Duke. "I am satisfied to know the truth, and I am satisfied to have Hugh's letter back in the possession of whom it rightly belongs. And, lastly, Mrs. Treharne, I am satisfied that you shall no longer reside here in Gloucestershire ever again. I bid you goodbye and *bon voyage*."

The Duke stepped out of the carriage and gestured to his manservant, who entered the coach.

Amanda moved forward in her seat, the lines of her face taunt as the Duke shut the coach door. "You are going to my estate in the north under the protection of my most trusted man. I shall meet you there in three days."

A frown marred Amanda's face as she shifted in her seat.

"Behave yourself for there shall be consequences. And our agreement shall be nullified."

She swallowed hard, her gaze troubled. "Until then, Your Grace."

The Duke signaled the driver, and the driver called out to his horses, cracked his whip, and the sleek animals sprang forward, the carriage heaved, and the black coach charged down the road, away from Ironvine.

"How did you find her?" the Duchess asked her husband.

"Stubborn, willful. She'll do nicely."

Charles slid his arm around Georgina's waist and kissed her temple. "It is done," he whispered.

They would never see Amanda again.

Chapter Sixty-Five

Charles

CHARLES AND GEORGINA and the Duke took a brandy in the parlour at Ironvine as they waited for the Duchess, who had gone to Georgina's drawing room to read Hugh's letter.

She returned. "Ryvves, you must read your brother's final words, for I do believe therein lies a truth that you seek."

"Are you sure?"

"Quite sure."

He took the letter, moved to the window and read.

My darling, my dearest Zandra,

I pray this letter borne of tears of regret finds you before the evil whispers of the ton reach you. I have done something utterly stupid, and you must know of it from me. You must hear the whole of it from me.
There we were at the finish line, and I cocked everything up.
With a foolish indulgence, I almost brought ruin to us all.

I beg for your forgiveness, I plead for your understanding. I will not be able to bear living without them, without you. I have failed you, my love, and that knowledge has broken me.

The reckless sins of my flesh are many. You know them all. This was selfish and thoughtless. I abhor my own self for my behaviour, for my choices rooted in weakness, vanity, and hubris. Revulsion overwhelms me as I write these words.

I fought the duel, and I won. The other man is dead. It is over.

Be assured, our privacy remains secure. The world will only know that Charles is the one who fought the duel, for I did the unthinkable. I shot my brother myself, giving him an arm wound as undeniable proof of his participation in the duel. It was the only way to ensure my engagement and that our plans to reunite shall remain unstained and intact.

I can only hope that one day Charles will allow me to explain. That he will understand. That he will be able to forgive me.

But at this very moment, the only thing of worth to me is your forgiveness. All the blood on my hands means nothing before you, my dearest love. No, I have no right to call you by that precious name, yet only you are my beloved now and always.

The thick putrid air of self-loathing gives way to the brisk biting air of contrition. My heart no longer beats the way it once did, once and only with you.

I await word from you to live again. Until then I am haunted, I am ruined.

Ever yours,

Hugh

Charles's heart drummed in his chest as his gaze jumped from word to word. Sorrows to passions to pleading.

This was Hugh?

He'd never known his brother to be so…emotional. Indeed, emotionally vulnerable in any way. So intense in his writing. Positively genuine and genuinely heartbroken.

He read the letter again. *He truly loved her.* He knew of love. Love and affection that he and Father always mocked. That Charles had forced himself to learn to live without because it only led to misfortune, to ugliness.

All this time he thought his brother was simply besotted by lust and his own arrogance of having landed the Duchess of Oakley. But this…he clutched at the paper…was not arrogance. This was humility and repentance and bloody despair. And honesty.

Hugh was deeply and truly in love with her.

And he felt remorse for shooting him.

This was not the Hugh he'd always known—his brother was aloof and confident, sailing through his days on self-satisfaction. Nothing wrinkled his sails, he never allowed it to. Under their father's roof, both boys had learned that sharing one's feelings was not done. It seemed to have come easy to Hugh whilst Charles had struggled, but eventually learned the lesson.

The paper shuddered in his grip as his lungs constricted. Hugh's written lines swam on the page.

A hand pressed into his back. "My darling?"

His chest caved in at the sound of Georgie's voice, an ache twisting the very core of him. No words came to him. He held out the letter to her.

"May I, Your Grace?" she asked.

"Yes, read it," replied the Duchess.

As she read, Georgina's hand slid around Charles's wounded arm, and the aching sting in his arm softened, the burning tension in his limbs released.

Charles was proud of his brother in a way he had never been before and never imagined he ever would be. He bore a scar on his arm to show for it. A scar that would always remind him of weakness, desperation, regret, sacrifice, and love.

Love above all. Love most of all.

"This—this was my Hugh," Her Grace breathed, her eyes gleaming.

Yes, her Hugh. Not his. Not their father's. To him, to the world, his brother had been somewhat selfish, wholly unsentimental. But he'd loved. With all his weaknesses bared, he'd loved.

Georgina gave the Duchess the letter. "I find it a terrible yet beautiful sort of justice that Amanda's downfall was Hugh's love."

Georgina was right, wasn't she? His heart thudded in his chest, a heart he had forced to lay dormant, to become stagnant, cold, and brackish for years, now beat hard and fast and flowed with warmth.

"Georgie," he breathed, digging his hands in her loose hair.

Georgie. His woman, his wife, his Countess of Ryvves.

His love.

A riot of feeling and emotion blustered through him. Feeling and emotion that had been dammed for centuries.

Damn it all.

He buried his face in her neck. "I love you."

Chapter Sixty-Six

Georgina

Georgina knew she shouldn't.

But as she took in the towering wall of the castle ruins before her, every fibre of her being shouted, *yes, I must!*

She'd come here tonight to sketch the castle in the light of the full moon. She'd done a myriad of sketches and watercolours of the ruins in the bright sun and under the clouds, but now, she would finally capture the ruins in the unique silvery light of the great bright August moon.

Darting across the narrow stone bridge over the moat, she'd made her way around the tower to the courtyard of the castle. On purpose, she had worn her boots and Charles's old clothes as all the rains this week had left the valley sodden. Her boots sank into the muddy earth and splashed in the pools of water in the old courtyard as she worked.

Charles was out with Brandon in the village this evening, and she could spend all the time she wanted taking in the various views and perspectives of the castle tower and its house.

She captured the light glittering over the stone walls, and the gleaming surface of the pond. She recorded all that the moon revealed that the sun did not—shadows, contrasts, mystery, allure. The umbrage of the trees and foliage, an atmosphere of gloom, a gothic murkiness.

As she tucked her sketchpad into her satchel, securing it, she glanced up at the moon. She had been here a long while already, and the moon had moved its position since she'd first arrived. Clouds now streaked across the sky like eerie ghostly apparitions.

Perhaps she should have gone inside the ruined castle first and then sketched the exterior, but it all had been so over-whelming when she'd first arrived.

Georgina was desperate to see if she could find that design motif on the walls that Charles had seen when he had been trapped here as a boy on a full moon night. She was sure it was real, not some fantasy, and she dearly wanted to prove it to him, to please him, to shake off all the madness that Amanda and Hugh had left behind.

"I won't take long," she promised herself. She wouldn't go in the castle tower, only the section of the house ruins where Charles had said he'd seen the motif.

She made her way to the courtyard of the house that was overgrown with grasses and flowering trellises. She reached the walls that remained and found the low-hanging window. She stepped up on a pile of stones just under it and heaved herself up. Tumbling forward in the shadows, her arms wrapped around her head.

She landed in muck.

"Ugh." Her boots squelched in the mud and waters as she found her footing. Standing up, she wiped her hands, blinking as her eyes adjusted to the shadowy dark interior. Wings flut-tered, the wind seemed to whistle around her, the musty damp chilling her skin.

Adjusting her bag, making sure it had not come undone in her fall and her belongings were secure, she proceeded to track slowly through the interior, a hand at the damp slime-covered wall to keep her bearings. Finally, she reached the area of the house where the roof remained, where Charles had been stuck as a child.

The upper floor of the house no longer existed. Shafts of light filtered through the ruptures in the stones, the clerestory windows up at the very top allowing in the moonlight. The roof, although intact, was gashed with a number of gaps and the moon and the stars were visible.

"He must have been here," she thought.

A mist filled the air like a diaphanous curtain that grew thicker and thicker, the buzz of insects hovering around her. The walls were covered in moss and vines, and the dingy smell of earth and still water filled her nostrils. Rotted timber lay in a low pile, the ground uneven, muddy, stones upturned everywhere, bird droppings, and so many puddles of muck.

As she sloshed through puddles of black water, she proceeded carefully as the stone floor had collapsed in sections, whilst in other areas, slabs of rock were smashed together, jutting out of the ground as if a great fist had punched at them through the earth. Across the great room, the opposite wall sagged under the pressure of time and weather.

Her hand slid against the wet, cold stone of the ruined wall as she slowly tracked about the room, watching where her feet stepped, desperate not to miss anything. Her fingers slid into deep grooves in the stone, and she stopped. "What have we here?"

Her hands explored the groove which led to another engraving, this one curvy, no—round. What was it?

In the dim light, her hands followed the sculpted lines and another pattern teased her fingertips. Georgina stepped back to take in this carving in the stone better. A long branch with large leaves hanging from it. Was this the garland Charles had seen?

"Where does it start? Where does it end?" she murmured.

Gingerly, she stepped along the wall again, and moved

around the perimeter of the great room, her hands following the long branch. No. Not a branch.

She froze. "Not a branch, it's a vine. A vine!"

She let out a soft laugh as her fingers shoved past the ivy, greedily hunting over the surface of the stone. Yes there… another form was engraved in the wall…a series of round shapes clustered together…a flower? No, a fruit—were they grapes? Was this vine carved along the entire perimeter of the room?

"Oh, Lord…"

Her pulse quickened as she dug her eager hands into her satchel and retrieved the paper and a piece of charcoal. Placing the paper over a section of the engraving in the stones, she quickly rubbed the charcoal over it and the design of the vine appeared under her fingers. She repeated the action over another section. Leaves and a cluster of grapes were visible.

"Oh, Brother de Mont Clare, my first Earl of Ryvves, it's your iron vine, is it not?" She put away the paper and charcoal to keep them dry and safe and proceeded along the wall.

"Now where is that painting Charles saw?"

The moonlight had dimmed considerably with the gathering clouds, and she used her fingertips along the cut stone to guide her, and they led her upwards. Suddenly the vine engraving looped up the wall. Her heart pounded so loudly it seemed to echo against the stones.

Her finger dug into strands of leafy ivy that had latched onto the old stone, and she shoved it out of the way, pulling, tugging to reveal the stone. And as if they'd heeded her inner prayers, the obstinate vines gave way, the hazy clouds dispelled, and the moonlight shone brighter.

Cleared of the ivy, the surface of the stone wall glittered in the light like a thousand tiny diamonds. And there, the grapevine, lush with large leaves and full of grapes, swirled over the wall creating a frame, and at its centre was a shield, rather a coat of arms with a medieval letter R emblazoned on it. Her heart shuddered in her chest.

Laurent de Mont Clare had failed in miniature, yet perhaps, he was better suited to murals. All these years this paint had survived. Her fingers rubbed over it. It was red in tone. "Ochre, of course."

Ochre was a mineral found in the caves by the iron mines nearby the village for centuries. Mr. Sheffield, her painting tutor had shown it to her after he had purchased it from a local miner. He'd been thrilled with the quality of pigment. Deep red, a spicy yellow. It was a mineral that was easily grated or ground by a mortar and pestle and turned into a fine powder that would be mixed with a liquid and turned into deeply pigmented paint.

Of course. Charles had said Laurent's wife was the daughter of a Freeminer. She must have shown him the ochres, and surely he must have been delighted and undertook this mural.

Tears welled in her eyes, and she sniffed in the mildewed air traced with the cool rain. She'd been right, and this discovery was even better than she'd imagined.

The story Charles had told her about his ancestor was true, not some family legend. A colourful tale passed down from generation to generation, yet each succeeding generation believing in it less and less, and the harsh world twisting it into something it was not.

No more.

Georgina was sure that Laurent de Mont Clare was a passionate vintner and wanted to mark that achievement on the very walls of his home. After all, the king had bestowed him a title and estate for that very achievement. Why not herald it for your house, for your family?

If only she had a torch to see any of the colours. But just as Charles remembered, the design seemed to shimmer on the sparkling rock in the light of the moon. This engraving in the stone had been filled with pigment. He must have added something to the ochre to make it sparkly. And the decision to have the design engraved in the stone ensured it would last as long as the castle stood. Smart man.

The moonlight was fading in and out with the gathering of the clouds. She had to be quick. Opening her satchel once more, she found her pencil and quickly sketched what she saw, but the light waned quickly, the shadows around her thickening.

A flash of light blasted through the interior, the paper in her hands suddenly cold stark white. Thunder pealed and rolled in the distance. Her teeth dug into her lip. Rain, again?

A sharp crack and boom drummed over the area. Quickly putting away her paper and pencil, she moved to go. It was now difficult to see. But from what direction had she come?

A torrent of rain battered the stone floor in the roofless section of the house, and she shuddered at the harsh sounds. Rain fell through the cracks and gaps in the old roof over her. Her boots slipped and slid on the wet mossy stones as her hands attempted to grip the cold slithery wall, but she could not gain any traction upon it.

Cold black waters sloshed and rushed around her feet, surging through the room, and her flesh chilled. Which way to go now? *Think, Georgina, think.*

Rain thrashed and battered the stones around her as she plodded in the darkness. The water now swirled around her knees, rushing in from the courtyard. She buckled the satchel higher on her body keeping it safe, at least for now.

She raised up, and her one foot swivelled on the wet ground. Pain flashed through her ankle and she gasped. She'd stepped on a jagged rock. Her hand flew up to the stone wall once again to try and regain her footing, her balance. Ragged wood scraped her palm. Was it a door? The door to the tower.

Although the tower sat in the pond, it was not on the side of the river as the house ruins were. Furthermore, it stood higher than the house. She knew there was a doorway that led out of the tower with stone stairs that led to the bridge over the pond.

She would go there. A plan, she had a plan. Sucking in a deep breath as she swiped at her hair that had fallen in her face, wet, and coiled, she pushed forward in the waters. It was as if she were blind, her hands reaching out for anything in her way. She navigated her feet, her hands step by tiny step.

Was she even going in the right direction?

She arrived at the edge of a wall, the end of it. Her hand reached out into the damp air, her chest heaving, the sound of the water swirling behind her. Her fingers found a different texture of stone. Up and down she felt the surface. They slid upward. Different blocks of stone. Was this an archway? The entrance to the tower?

She moved quickly as the water would allow, still stepping carefully. The water had fully flooded her boots now. Something drove into her side, a hard edge, a flapping. Her body jerked away from whatever creature it was that moved past her, and she slid, the muscle of her back pulling tightly.

"Damn!"

She slid again, and her arms flew out to grab onto something, anything, but there was only black water. Splashing, water blew up her nostrils, and she sputtered, coughing, her throat aching. She tried to right herself, but her left leg wouldn't move. It was stuck. Her foot was wedged between two stones.

She tried shifting, twisting, adjusting. Nothing. A wave of water surged over her. Pushing and pulling her body, filling her nose, her mouth.

There was only water.

Chapter Sixty-Seven

Charles

"Bloody hell, raining again?" muttered Brandon, pulled his cloak over his head as they exited the village pub, The Fang and Feather. "We'll be drenched by the time we get home."

Charles mounted his horse. "It's a good thing I didn't drink very much."

Brandon mounted his own horse. "I have a good feeling about this venture. I'm pleased we are doing this together."

"I am as well, my friend. New beginnings. I think it's very brave what you're doing, pushing for a bill against slavery."

Brandon adjusted himself in his saddle, straightening his back. "It cannot go on. We must do what we can, make our voices heard."

"G'night to 'ee, sirs." A voice came from the darkness, and a hand reached out and stroked his horse's neck. "My lord." Her lips curved into a sharp smile.

"Ella, I told you no."

She'd served him and Brandon their food and drink the three hours they'd been here tonight, and she'd kept trying to flirt with him, but he'd ignored her. He'd had her several times last year before he'd gone off to London to meet his brother for the season's festivities.

Before Georgie turned his world upside down.

"Makin' sure, milord." She licked her lips. "Wouldn't want you to regret nothin' is all."

"Regret what, exactly?" asked Brandon.

She put a hand on her hip. "Not havin' me, o'course," came her reply on a rolling laugh.

Charles's horse stamped impatiently. "I'm a married man now, girl."

"All the more reason, sir."

"Get back inside. Your punters are waiting for you."

She scowled at him, turning her back, shooting Brandon a smile and a bow, making her ample bosom practically fall out of her dress. "G'night to 'ee sir." She waited, hands at her waist, her gaze darting between the two disinterested men. She did not get any response.

"Cor! The two of you, what a waste." She rolled her eyes and sashayed back into the Fang.

"Married, but still in demand, I see," laughed Brandon.

"Aye, but what exactly is in demand here, my coin or my cock?"

"I'd wager on both."

"Imagine, those days are over."

"Disappointed?" said Brandon

"No, and that surprises me. It was a way of life for me, to do what I want when I want. It's how I was raised. And now so much is utterly different. My father is gone, my brother, I have the title and the estate all to myself, and most importantly, but most importantly, Georgina is my wife."

"You've always enjoyed her company."

"Brandon, I cannot do without her. It's rather taken my breath away."

"Charles, you are a wiser man than I was as a new husband. When I came home after the shipwreck, I would spend many nights here at the Fang to avoid truths at home, to avoid Justine, and to find my old self once more, because the old Brandon was such a roaring success. But there was a problem with that thinking."

"Which was?"

"I was not my old self, and I never would be that man again. And I'd come to realise that the old Brandon was a superficial boy. I finally let him go and allowed myself to discover new things. Better things. And I embraced the woman who is both my dearest friend and my lover." Brandon tilted his head. "You're in love with Georgina, aren't you?"

"I am."

"After all you have experienced, you are no longer your old self, Charles."

"Here's the rub, my friend—I never liked my old self much anyway. My carefully crafted polish served to make my life easy. But underneath I always craved something more. A more I considered beyond me."

"Now you have it."

"Now I have it."

"Consider our new business venture," said Brandon. "Sugar was my father's great success, and he meant it for me, for Wolfsgate's future. It was difficult to give it up, but I wanted to, I had to. I am the Baron of Graven now, and it is up to me to decide what my success feels like and looks like. It's not up to my hundred little fears, nor those heavy voices from the past."

"No more voices from the past."

"No more." He cleared his throat. "I'm glad we're doing this together."

A grin lashed Brandon's mouth. "So am I. Brandon extended his hand, and they shook. "Now, I really must get home. I am quite eager to see my wife and tell her the good news."

"I too am most eager to see my wife," said Charles. "Good night, Graven."

"Good night."

With a hand raised in farewell, Charles prompted his horse forward into the rainy night for Ironvine.

No more voices from the past.

Charles urged his stallion into a gallop.

THE MOMENT he rode through the stone walls marking Ironvine, something hot and blazing raced through his veins, curled through his insides.

His desire for his wife.

He urged his horse forward. Faster.

Georgie would be waiting for him in the parlour. Or no, she'd be working in her morning room, organizing, sketching a last-minute inspiration along with a glass of wine. She would smile up at him, and he would take her mouth and….

He slid off his horse, handed the reins to the servant, and charged up the marble steps of his house. The door opened, and his drenched cloak was taken. He wiped at his face. "Where's my wife?"

"The countess retired some time ago, my lord. She did not take supper."

"Ah, then I shall go to her. Have brandy and supper brought to us in my chamber."

"As you wish, my lord."

Unbuttoning his frock coat, Charles took the stairs two at a time. He didn't have a morsel to eat at the pub as the entire tavern disgusted him suddenly. The boisterous crowd, the heat, the heavy smells, the greasy food. Now, he was ravenous.

Learning about their parents' love affair, Hugh's letter—it had all been heavy news, and she had been equally affected but had already found a quiet peace with it. Although it was something they shared, and he liked that, he still struggled to sort through it all.

Rapping his knuckles against her bedchamber door, he swung it open.

"Georgina?"

No reply came, no laughter, no rushing of steps, no sound of his name off her lips. Nothing.

Where was she?

He went through to her dressing room, his dressing room, his chamber. Back to her room. Her dress on the bed. Her chemise crumpled at its side. Her bloomers were tossed on the floor by the bed and the dress. Her shoes.

That only meant one thing. Either she was naked somewhere, or she'd donned her manly clothes to go walking.

Now? In the dark? In the rain?

He rushed down the stairs again and went to her morning room. The door was open. On her desk there lay sketches in a messy pile. He shuffled through them. All of them were drawings and watercolours of the castle and the pond, the colourful lushness of the flowering trees and vines. His gaze lifted to the large leaded glass window with the sweeping view of the valley down below to the castle ruins.

"Ah fuck." He stormed to the front entrance. "A cloak! Someone fetch me a cloak and my gloves! Saddle a horse!"

He flung open the front door, and rain smattered the front steps as he clenched his jaw. "Dammit, Georgie."

His fists curled at his sides. Images of his mother out alone on such a night, lost, in a fever. His heart thundered in his chest. He could not lose Georgie. He could not. He would find her and bring her home. Home. Their home.

"Sir?" Holt held out a cloak, and he snatched it from him. Jerrold came running.

"Your mistress is missing. I fear she is out in this weather, down by the castle."

"Oh no, sir!" cried Jerrold.

"I am going to fetch her. Have a bath ready for her. Holt, find Joss, tell him to meet me there. We'll need tools. Torches.

He'll know what to bring. Find him at once." He charged down the staircase, and stopped, his lungs constricting. Other than his mother, the one person who had been kind to him when he needed kindness the most here at Ironvine was Joss.

"Sir?" Holt rushed to him.

"Tell Joss I need him."

"I shall. Take care, my lord!" Holt shouted after him.

Charles's pulse pounded with his every footstep. He had to find Georgie. He must.

Chapter Sixty-Eight

Charles

CHARLES DROVE his horse at a punishing pace across the fields, through the meadow, and finally down the valley to the ruins. The rains had tempered, and a mist hung in the air. The sweat on his brow was cold, no matter his blood storming through his veins. He signalled his horse, and the animal slowed its pace, its hooves clomping in the mud and water-logged grasses.

The storm had been swift. The pond overflowed. He dismounted quickly and tied his horse to a tree, stroking him as he took in the scene. The clouds now had cleared, and although the moon was not as bright as it previously had been, there was some light once again.

He marched through the water to get closer. "Georgina! Georgina! Where are you? Are you there? Georgie!"

But there was only the sound of rushing waters ebbing in the distance, gurgling water in the grasses, and his boots squelching in the muck. "Georgina!" He approached the court-yard, but to pass through was near impossible—it was deep in water. His only choice was the tower.

The tower where Hugh had abandoned him. The tower where he'd crawled on his hands and knees in the dark to the connecting house, scraped and wounded and so afraid a long time ago.

He'd told Georgie that story, and she had been fascinated by what he thought he'd seen that night when he was stuck here.

Charles moved around the entire stone building and finally reached the embankment by the strip of bridge which led to the tower. His cloak flying behind him, he climbed the stone parapet, his legs tensing, struggling to cling to the wet, worn stones, his wounded arm screaming as he climbed up, and finally, over. Crossing the bridge, he reached the tiny steps of the tower.

The door was his final barricade.

He tried the ancient handle. It would not budge.

Their father would tease them that he had the key to the tower door and would never give it to them, but that had only made their desire to gain entry all the more intense. That was the entire reason he and his brother had become fascinated to enter the tower. But he wasn't that boy any longer. Now he burned with the need to find his wife behind this heavy slab of ancient wood.

"My lord!" Joss rushed toward him, a lit torch in hand.

"Joss!"

"Here we are again."

"Yes, dammit, yes. Thank you for coming."

"D'you know where her ladyship be, sir?"

"No idea yet, but I reckon this will be the best place to enter. The other side has taken on much more water from the river."

"Indeed. I'll go, sir. You—"

"No. I'm going in." Charles gripped Joss's shoulder. "I must. You know I must."

Joss nodded, his eyes heavy. "Let's get this door open then."

The two of them shoved at the door with their sides, splintering and cracking met their efforts. Joss handed Charles the torch, and he pulled out an iron tool from the sack on his back and bashed at the splintered wood. At last, he was able to reach through and grab the interior bolt.

He shoved and shoved. "It be rusted through o'course," muttered Joss.

"Stand back." Charles bashed at the door, creating a bigger opening. Joss took another, a small iron tool from his sack and banged at the bolt. Finally, it swung off the old door.

They shoved, and there was movement. The door gave way.

"Georgina! Georgina?" Charles called out in the dank, dark tower, his throat burning. He held the torch high as they descended the small stone steps inside the old tower. Water met them, rushing around their legs, their hips. The very darkness seemed to blanket him, asphyxiate him. He couldn't breathe.

A hand went to his back.

Charles wiped his arm across his brow. "I have to find her, Joss."

"We will. Let me 'ave the torch, you go on."

He handed Joss the torch, and as the light reached a greater area of the flooded interior, Charles moved around the waters but there was still no sight of her. Although the tower was high, it wasn't extremely wide. Of course, it had seemed huge to him in the dark as a boy, but it wasn't like how he'd remembered it.

Joss descended the steps and searched in the opposite direction. "Nothing," he called out.

Charles made his way toward the narrow arched tunnel that led into the house. He shook off the memories of forcing himself to crawl through it in the dark. His fingers had sunk in the damp earth, his body scraping along rocks and worms and insects.

Now, he pushed through the water filling the tunnel, Joss

behind him with the torch. An object floated and bobbed on the water before them, and he lunged at it, a sharp tingle racing up his spine.

Georgie's satchel. "She's here somewhere."

Joss raised the torch, but there was no sign of her. Nothing. He pulled on the bag, but it was stuck.

Fucking hell.

Charles dove underwater, his hands, instruments of vision in the dark cold abyss. The water was deeper here and growing higher. He followed the strap of the bag.

She must be alive. Do not take her from me. He prayed every prayer he had ever and never uttered his entire life.

He reached the door to the house. It was wedged open. The waters rushed and swirled, louder, rising higher against the half-closed door. The strap of the bag was stuck on the iron trim of the door. He broke the surface of the water. Gasping, sputtering, splashing filled his ears from the other side of the door.

"Georgina! Georgina!"

"Charles! I'm stuck—my foot—I can't..." she yelled out, her breathing heavy.

His heart thudded in his chest at the sound of her voice. *Thank God. Thank God.* "I'm trying to get this door open."

He shoved at the door, again and again. Joss came up next to him and shoved with him. It moved slightly under their pressure.

"I can just fit through," Charles shoved himself through the narrow opening, twisting his body to get through. "I'm coming, Georgie."

In the dim light of the moon coming through the roofless section of the house, he saw her. Arms paddling on the swirling surface of the floodwaters, her face upwards gulping for air.

Joss grunted, straining to move the door. An inch more and he slid through. He swam to her. His hands went around her waist, her jaw. Her skin was cold. "Are you hurt?"

"Only my foot. It's stuck between stones and I—"

Sucking in a breath, he dove immediately, his hands on her legs guiding him to the ground where her one foot was stuck. The boot. He slid his hand against her calf and pulled her foot out of the boot. Her leg slid free and he broke the surface of the water, his arm sliding around her middle and lifting her up. "Let's go."

Her cold lips found his. "Charles."

"Come on! Let's go!" shouted Joss.

They swam toward the door, the waters pushing them that way. Charles pushed Georgie through the opening into Joss's arms. A swell grew behind him, and as he moved it took him with it. "No!" With all his might he dove under the waters, under the wave. But he couldn't escape the power of the waters. He was bashed into the stone wall, water filled his mouth, and everything was dark. The muscle of his wounded arm wouldn't cooperate, and blazed with pain, yet he pushed through. He had to.

Hands grabbed at his arms, his shirt. He slid into an embrace. "Charles!"

He was heaved up. "This way." Joss led them through the waist-high water, to where he'd left the torch on a hook on the wall along with Georgina's satchel. In the torchlight they found the tiny stone steps that led to the open door. All three of them gulped in the fresh air, the moat glistening and swelling before them.

"Thank you both," gasped Georgina in between breaths. "And thank you to my father who insisted I learn how to swim." The three of them carefully crossed the barely visible bridge and got to the horses.

Holding Georgina's hand tightly, Charles embraced Joss. "Thank you, my friend. I never thanked you properly that first time, and I'm very sorry for that. You deserved much better from me."

"My lord—"

"Let me finish. You've always shown me kindness and friendship, and it meant the world to me. Especially tonight. I thank you."

Joss's hand went to Charle's shoulder. "I am glad I could help. Now we must go."

Georgina swept her wet hair from her face. "Thank you, Joss."

"My lady."

Charles helped Georgina up on his horse. "Take that boot off me, Charles."

"With pleasure." He slid off her remaining boot from her leg and threw it in the flooded moat. Mounting his horse, he embraced his wife tightly as he adjusted her in the saddle before him.

His face sank into her neck, and he inhaled her, he inhaled this glorious moment. Her cold skin, the salty taste of it, her body still heaving for air, the moonlight gleaming over his snorting horse, the tower and the ruins gaping at them. The clomping of Joss's horse through the muddy grasses up the hill.

Yes, he would remember this moment forever.

No more voices from the past.

"I love you, Georgie." He bit that spot of flesh where her shoulder began and her throat ended, and she let out a sigh, her body trembling in his hold.

"Charles, I–"

"And don't you dare ever come here again without me. Day or night."

"Yes, my lord."

Gripping the reins, he urged his horse forward, and they galloped home.

Chapter Sixty-Nine

Georgina

With Georgina in his arms, Charles swept into the house and darted up the stairs to the dressing room where the bathtub awaited. Gently, he put her down on her feet. She swayed, and his hands went to her waist, steadying her.

"Thank you all. Leave us now," he said to the servants who attended them.

"It's good to be home," she murmured, clinging to him as he began working on the buttons of her chemise.

"I am glad that you are wearing men's clothes as taking them off you is exceedingly simple, which is good because I am still in something of a frenzy with this evening's events." His voice was piqued but not so very angry.

"Frenzy?" she breathed as he peeled the wet chemise from her cold body.

Shivers raced over her skin as he licked his lips, taking in the thin, wet camisole stuck to her breasts, revealing her curves through the thin cotton. He ripped that off and went straight for the breeches she wore. "I must admit," he said against her lips as he jerked the buttons off one by one. "'Tis odd, but I like it."

"Discovering new things you like in this marriage every

day, are you, my lord?" She let out a soft laugh as he tugged the wet trousers off her. Relief washed through her to be finally rid of the wet clothes, to be here safe at home with Charles, his warm hands on her body.

He led her to the tub, where she carefully climbed in and sank slowly in the hot scented water. "Divine."

Ripping his clothes off, Charles got in the tub with her. Water sloshed and splashed everywhere, neither of them caring.

He took hold of the soap in the nearby dish, made a lather with a cloth, and washed her neck and arms, his jaw tight, his gaze shuttered.

"You don't have to wash me —"

"I do." He brushed her flesh with the cloth, the water clouding with the soap. "Never do that to me again, Georgie. Never leave in the middle of the night without letting me know where exactly…"

"I'm sorry. You are right I should have left you a note and told Jerrold what I was up to. I didn't expect to be out longer than you, nor had I planned on going inside the ruins. It's just that, the moonlight was so bright, and I desperately wanted to find that painted garland that you'd seen as a boy in the old house."

"Georgie —"

"I found it, Charles. I found what you saw as a boy that terrible night."

"The garland?"

"It is a grapevine, and I saw it." She told him all she'd found.

"So it wasn't my overwrought childish imagination?"

"No. It's real and it's magnificent. Although I deeply regret doing such a reckless thing and putting you and Joss in danger —"

"You put yourself in danger."

"But now you know that it was real, that Ironvine's history, your Montclare past, your inheritance is good. Damn everyone who mocks the tale of Brother Laurent." She stroked the sides of his face with her wet, soapy hands. "That darkness you grew up with is not who you are. You are not tainted, my Earl of Ryvves."

Charles took her hand and brought it around his cock, and she let out a satisfied gasp at his firmness. She stroked him, and his jaw slackened, his head fell back on a groan. "Take me, Georgie. Take me."

Positioning herself, she sank down on him, his hand guiding his cock inside her. His thick length filled her slowly and she let out a long moan, rocking over him. Wrapping his arms around her middle, he brought her breasts to his mouth. Greedily he nipped and suckled each one as she drove down on him, water sloshing from the tub as their thrusts became more urgent.

"Never leave me again, Georgie. Never. Promise me."

"I promise. I promise. Now fill me, Charles. Fill me."

He cuffed her neck, his other hand at her hip as he met her thrusts, the water sloshing violently over the tub, splattering on the floor. She didn't care. She wanted all of him. His heart, his soul, his body. Her back arched as the pleasure burst inside her. His fingers dug painfully into her hips as he furiously thrust, finding his release.

Wiping the water from his face, she kissed his cheek, his chin, his lips. "I want to please you and feel that pleasure with you. You gave me that, Charles. With you, I burn. I burn, and yet it is a freedom at the very same time. You've given me that freedom, Charles, that courage."

"I want to give it all to you, Georgie." He rubbed a nipple between his fingers, pinching it tightly.

Wincing, she let out a whimper, her back arching. "Now you're being merciless." She turned in his hold and sank back against him, sliding his hand between her legs.

With his dark chuckle tickling her flesh, he stroked her

quim, and her hips rocked against his hand. "You are also insatiable." He twisted her other nipple as his fingers teased and stroked her nub.

The biting sting coupled with the pressure between her legs had her pleasure mounting again, searing her. "I am insatiable. For you."

"And I for you." His teeth bit into her shoulder as he palmed her breasts roughly. Georgina cried out her release.

They realized the water had cooled considerably, and he helped her from the tub and dried her and dried himself. Donning the dressing gowns that had been laid out for them, they drank brandy on the cushioned divan in Charles's bedchamber. He took her feet in his lap and rubbed them.

"You spoil me, my lord."

"I enjoy it."

She sipped at her drink, enjoying the warmth down her throat. "You realise that if your mother and my father had been allowed to marry when they were young, you and I would not exist."

"A maddening thought." Charles met her gaze. "I am glad that her heart's desire was not lost to her. All this time I thought my mother never knew love, never knew happiness, only —"

She put her fingers on his lips, stopping him from saying the words. Words of darkness, cruelty, the past. "She fought for her happiness and won. Sophie was a triumph."

A slow smile grew over his lips. "She was, indeed. I only wish I had known her in that great happiness. In that freedom she must have experienced during that time with him. That wild, deep joy that I feel now with her lover's daughter." He planted a gentle kiss on her lips.

"We have that happiness, Charles. We enjoy that freedom."

"We do. You and I are here on this earth as a consequence of a collision of circumstances, ambitions, and desires. And years later we came together in another chaotic collision. Had we not experienced that madness in London, we would not have found each other in this way."

Putting her empty glass down, she slid a hand inside his dressing gown and stroked his smooth, hard chest. "We would be lost. Married to others or alone. Unhappy, dissatisfied, and the worst of it—probably none the wiser." Georgina nestled in his embrace, her head against his chest, his heart thumping under her cheek. "I don't even want to imagine it."

His arms wrapped around her firmly. "Our destiny may have been unraveled that night, but we were not helpless, we both made choices. And you were a clear voice in the storm. When you arrived at Hyde Park after the duel, you chose me. When I offered my hand to you to escape your brother's wrath, again, you chose me." He drew a deep breath. "No one has ever—"

She took the words from his lips with a kiss. Sacred words, words of the heart, of the blood. Words that burned in her veins.

"All my life, I learned to close my eyes to the things I didn't want to see around me, but I couldn't close my heart to the things I didn't want to feel. I couldn't close my heart to the things I needed. You, my darling Georgie, have opened my heart. Opened it and filled it. Flooded it." A raw breath heaved from his lips. "I love you."

Her heart surged with heat. "I love you, Charles." A soft laugh escaped her lips. "Oh no, have I ruined the renowned rake, Charles Montclare?"

"Indeed. It would seem that in this affair, not you but I had the sordid downfall."

Chapter Seventy

Charles

The Oakleys were leaving Gloucestershire, and Charles and Georgina had gone to Tidesfar to wish them farewell. The staff had said their goodbyes and listened to their master and mistress's words of thanks and farewell and had retreated.

Before their coach, the Duke smiled at Georgina as he kissed her hand gently. "Countess, I greatly look forward to having you paint my duchess's portrait and work on my own commissions." He tilted his head, the slight narrowing of his eyes unmistakable.

"I shall be ready, Your Grace. I thank you for all you and Her Grace have done for us." Georgina bowed to the Duke.

The Duchess took Charles's arm, and they both moved away a few degrees. She had something private to share with him. "She has arrived and awaits him. We will be there in two days' time."

"Very well."

"You must never ask me more. If there is ever something of import to tell you, I shall do so. That is the way it must be."

"I understand, and I agree. As I told His Grace, I forfeit all to his authority and his pleasure."

"Ah, Ryvves." Her lips tipped up in a slight smile.

"Before you go, I must tell you one thing, Your Grace. The night before my brother died, at that last ball in London, he had remarked two things to me. Firstly, that you were the only woman he could ever love, and also how much he admired your marriage. How he felt it took two very special people to maintain such a unique and rare bond."

Her steady gaze met his. "I would be lost without my husband. He is my rock in all things and I am for him. I know what he and I share is not ordinary, but it is ours. I do hope you find such trust and satisfaction in your marriage, Ryvves. Your wife is a treasure. But, mark me." She turned to face him. "I do not mean a treasure to be placed on a shelf in a curio cabinet and taken down once in a great while when you're not busy to dust it off, admire, and briefly stroke it. Georgina is a woman made of flesh, blood, and bone. A woman of spirit with dreams and desires that deserve respect and, most of all, satisfaction."

He placed a hand over hers. "Georgina is my greatest treasure in this life, and honouring and satisfying her is my greatest purpose."

She slid her arm through his once more and led him to the Oakley coach, where her husband and Georgina awaited them.

Charles shook hands with the Duke. "Your Grace. I wish you safe passage. And again, my thanks."

"Ryvves, you'll be hearing from my attorney in London."

"Your attorney?"

"He'll provide you with names and information for my man in Portugal, who creates that Port you love so much. He won't give you mine for your new venture, but he has other very fine grapes from which he creates magical elixirs. You'll find one you love, I'm sure of it."

"Your Grace, I thank you, truly."

"And I thank you and your Countess for taking great care with my wife when she needed it the most."

"Ryvves, one more thing—" the Duchess said as she took Georgina's hands in hers and kissed both her cheeks.

"Your Grace?"

She eyed Charles, her lips twisted in amusement. "I am enjoying my friendship with the Countess very much. I expect nothing will alter that."

Georgina laughed, that hearty, clear laugh that filled his soul with that unusual lightness. Charles slid his arm around his wife's waist. "I am most pleased and honored to hear it. Know that your and His Grace's friendship will always be special to us both."

Chapter Seventy-One

Georgina

CHARLES WAS true to his word.

Georgina had written down a list of things she would need for the conservatory to be her atelier, and within days, three workmen arrived and re-arranged the space as she needed. They whitewashed one wall so that she could draw on it, paint on it, and clean it at whim, just as she'd had done in the attic at Fairthorn. Only this wall in the conservatory at Ironvine was enormous and washed with bright light from above and all sides. It took her breath away.

Soon after, art supplies and tools and paper and canvas of all kinds arrived from her favourite colour shop in London.

She was thrilled to bursting.

She now had long shelves for her sketchbooks and canvases, and more shelves as storage for her supplies. A stand for canvases, boards, a thick pile of paper, containers for brushes, containers for pencils, and boxes for pigments. Two long sturdy work tables, a variety of chairs, and a large divan, which made her grin to herself—he was planning on having relations with her here. *Perfect.*

No more hiding, no more sneaking about, working in

secret, stealing time to work. Lying to herself and lying to everyone around her. No more.

The Duchess of Oakley was also true to her word. A few days after the Oakleys had left, Monsieur Le Verne, the French artist, sent her a letter saying that he had arrived in England and wished to meet his new pupil. The Oakleys had rented a house for him nearby, and he was ready to begin their lessons.

Georgina, too, was ready.

"Sorry, how long have you been standing there?" Georgina wiped a smudged hand across her forehead, creating more smudge, a flush of red sweeping her cheeks.

"I was admiring my wife as she gave her heart, mind, and soul to her work." Charles uncrossed his arms and went to her. "Quite different from looking at ledger books and doing sums all day long."

"I like it when you look at me that way." She wiped at the smudges of paint and charcoal on her arms, the side of her face.

"What way is that?"

"You're undressing me, piece by piece. Planning on how to make a mess of me. I can feel your touch from here."

"Hmm, how well my wife knows me." He kissed her. "What are you working on today?" He took in the drawings on the floor and her sketch of a vine on the whitewashed wall.

"Trying to get the vine just right along with the dimensions of the entry hall."

"Ah. I'm looking forward to that."

She was planning on painting Brother Laurent's iron vine from the castle in the entryway of their house.

He gestured for the servant, who gave him a small wooden casket. "Thank you." He tapped his fingers on the wood. "I have a gift for you. Is Monsieur Le Verne still here? I wanted him to see this."

"He left about twenty minutes ago." She made a beeline for him and snatched the long wooden casket from his hands.

He laughed softly. "As if you thought jewellery lay inside, but my wife does not get excited by jewellery."

"Sometimes she does." Grinning, Georgina unlatched the lock, opened the cover. Her lips parted, her eyes gleamed. "Oh Charles!" Pots of coloured powders rested inside.

"The very finest pigments from the mines in the Forest of Dean at Clearwell."

"They are the very best."

"The very best, my darling."

"Oh, this red…" She let out a soft moan.

"Joss has a cousin, who is a Freeminer, who specializes in the ochres. I asked him weeks ago for a selection for you. He gathered, milled, washed and dried these for you."

Something caught in her chest and twisted there. "You did this for me?" She touched the side of his jaw. "My darling, thank you."

A smile etched over his lips, almost shy yet deeply satisfied. He loved this, making her dream come true every step of the way. He lifted out one jar. "I was told this one is the finest and rarest pigment of them all, and I wanted you to have it."

Her heart thudded in her chest as she opened the jar. Purple ochre. "The purple is the most unusual natural earth pigment."

"That is what I was told."

She dipped a finger in the fine powder and rubbed two fingers together, mesmerized. "This is exactly what I need for the vine."

"Yes."

Putting the casket on her worktable, where she had drawings and outlines of the grapevine motif from the castle along with sketches of the Duchess she was working on with her tutor, she went to her whitewashed wall and stroked her pigmented fingers across it in a great arc.

Charles let out a sound. "What a bloody outrageous colour."

"It is, isn't it? The colour of royals, so rare, so extraordinary." She worked a bit of oil onto her fingers, creating a paste. Again, she stroked and smudged across the white wall, the tone of the purple different, richer.

He drew alongside her and he dipped his fingers in the purple on the wall, swirling, He brought his hand to her face and smudged purple across her silky skin, down her warm throat to the perfect rise of her breasts.

Georgina swiped her pigmented fingers across his cheek, down his throat, the purple marking his skin. She flew at him and took him in a deep kiss. "I love you, I love you so very much. I thank you, my darling. Thank you."

On a groan, he lifted her up and brought her to the divan, quickly undoing his breeches as she lifted her skirts. Her intense emotions often led to a fierce response from Charles. Actions spoke louder than words, did they not?

"The best thing I've ever done in my life was choosing to leave Hyde Park with you after the duel. The second best thing was when I took you from your cousin's house to mine with your family threatening us." His tone was harsh, intent. "I offered you a choice, and you chose me." He thrust inside her to the hilt, and she cried out, her hands clutching him. "You. Chose. Me." He pounded inside her.

She clung to him, meeting his iron gaze. "You made a promise to me, and you kept it over and over again." The rhythm of her hips met his. "Every day you keep that promise."

The divan jerked and jostled across the sleek stone floor with his every savage thrust. The ochre mixed with their perspiration, and on their wet and heated skin, the purple pigment grew deeper and deeper.

Chapter Seventy-Two

Georgina

GEORGINA HAD DECIDED that she did not want there to be any ill will between her and her family any longer and would take action. The loss of relations with her brother, mother, and sister had been a deep hole. The first step she decided to take was with her brother.

Charles had insisted on going to see Thomas on his own, and told him straight out that although it was unfortunate that their marriage had occurred through subterfuge, he could not be sorry for it because his sister was his greatest happiness, and it was for her that he had come.

"I miss her, Ryvves. I miss my sister desperately," said Thomas.

"Of course you do."

"And although I would never have thought you would be able to make her happy, I am pleased that she and you, my old friend, are well together. As for my mother and sister…"

"All in good time." Charles then invited him to the house for tea.

"I look forward to it." Thomas grinned.

Aunt Vivian and Miss Alice had also been invited to tea a half hour earlier than Thomas was told to arrive. "Oh…I…

hello," Thomas stammered as he stood before their table on the front lawn of Ironvine under a white canopy.

"Brother, what a pleasure to see you." Georgina jumped from her chair and went to her brother.

"Ah, Georgie." He hugged his sister.

She whispered in his ear, "Alice is free. The rest is up to you."

He cleared his throat and squeezed his sister's hands. She led him to their *en plein air* table filled with sandwiches and sweets and fruits.

Charles lit his pipe. "Good to see you, Thomas."

"Thank you, Ryvves." Thomas smoothed down his waistcoat. "Very good to see you."

"You remember my Aunt Vivian, and her stepdaughter, Miss Dunsmore? Ladies, I believe you are familiar with my wife's brother, Mr. Thomas Hackleton."

Thomas beamed at the ladies. "What a pleasure to see you again Mrs. Dunsmore, Miss Dunsmore."

A smile lit Alice's features, her posture straightening. A delicate flower under the summer sun that had gotten a splash of water. "Hello, Mr. Hackleton, how lovely to see you again."

Aunt Vivian glanced at her and smirked. "Mr. Hackleton." She offered him her hand.

"Madame."

Two hours later, Aunt Vivian was asleep with her new fluffy white puppy in her lap, who was also asleep, while Thomas and Alice strolled the long gardens up and down, up and down, walking ever so closely side by side without touching.

Charles and Georgina walked hand in hand on the opposite side of the gardens. Charles kissed her hand. "We did things all backward, you and I."

"How do you mean?"

"These two are courting, are they not? That's what that is."

"Indeed they are." She let out a laugh. "Courting is not something you are familiar with, sir?"

"Personally, no. But as you are a proper young gentle-woman, you deserved to be courted."

"Well, I've had the experience several times over. In fact, once by a gentleman of your acquaintance."

"Who?"

"Mr. Whatley."

Charles stilled, a scowl deepening over his face. "Whatley?"

"Yes."

His eyes narrowed. "Whatley?"

"Mr. Whatley came to see me at least twice, brought many beautiful flowers, and had a torrent of florid words to match."

"Did he?"

"He did."

"And?"

"I refused him." Letting out a laugh, she pulled him along in their stroll. "My mother was very angry with me."

"You are a willful creature, aren't you?"

"I suppose I should have accepted him."

"And why is that, madame?"

"Well, then, I would have surely taken you as a lover, sir." Her eyes flashed at him. "And I would not have let you go."

Charles sucked in a deep breath. "Ah, speaking of Whatley, have you heard the news?"

"Do tell."

"His elder sister is engaged."

Georgina came to a stop. "Is she really? That is news. Is she not almost thirty years of age?"

"She is indeed. Obviously, this is a very special engagement causing a great stir in the family, if not the village."

"I should say so." Georgina seemed to remember that Miss Whatley always had a sullen disposition. Thomas had, on several occasions, danced with her at assemblies and parties, and she had been most waspish and ungracious. He never asked her to dance again. Neither did any young men.

"And who, pray tell, Lord Ryvves, is Miss Whatley's fortunate fiancé?"

"Ah, the happiest of gentlemen, Mr. Matthew Penry."

"Dear Lord, is this true?"

"Why yes. I would not lie about such an important circumstance."

"I am speechless."

"The bride comes with a great, great dowry."

"She must."

"Do you think he courted her?" said Charles.

"I would have loved to have witnessed that to be sure."

"Which brings me back to my point, you should have been courted by your husband-to-be, and you never were."

"Lord Ryvves, you are a traditionalist?"

He chuckled. "My point being, you not only absconded with me in the light of day on a public street in town —"

"May I remind you—you started all of this by stealing a kiss from me on a dark walk at Vauxhall Gardens. My very first kiss was stolen by a Montclare."

"Ah, this is true." His chest puffed out. He was pleased with himself. "And then you insisted I ruin you—your exact words—in my house as an innocent unmarried lady."

"Scandalous."

"Quite. There was no seduction on my part. What kind of Montclare am I? I didn't even have the chance to sweep you off to a bedchamber."

"Must we always do it in a bedchamber?" She shot him a saucy smile.

"What I meant was that for your very first experience instead of having luxuries, we did it in a most heedless and hasty manner. Right there in the drawing room, I ruined your reputation and your innocence."

"It was quite an adventure." Her eyes blazed at him.

"You are shameless, madame."

"I always have been, and you, I must say, always encouraged it. Imagine what a disappointment I would have been to any other man in the ton who would have expected a demure, shy, quiet, undemanding obedient young gentlewoman for a bride."

"A great disappointment." His eyes shifted about the gardens. "Should we try?"

Her fingers dug into his. "More ruination?"

"Filthy girl. I meant courting."

"Ah. Very well." Her eyes flared. "You must let go of me, however. Touching is forbidden."

Releasing her, he clasped his hands behind his back as they walked side by side. He cleared his throat. "What a lovely garden, do you not think so, Miss Georgina?"

"Indeed, it is a lovely garden, sir. The greenery is ever so… green. The breeze flutters just so betwixt the leaves." She sighed dramatically.

"Yes, quite," said Charles.

"But I do know of a better garden, sir."

"Do you?"

"Yes, the one between my legs."

"Georgie!"

"I cannot help it."

"You must."

"I can't. You awakened me this morning with your tongue in my quim and your fingers in my —"

"Shh!" He let out a laugh.

"And then we…well, the rest of the day it is all I can think of, and I find it most trying to concentrate on anything else, my Lord…to work, to read, to stroll even…anything, I tell you. It's a fever you've set off in my very blood."

He stopped in his tracks. "And if your husband is not at home to appease these fevered frustrations, what do you do?"

"I sketch a few erotic drawings, but that only serves to

intensify the fever, and so I find I must take care of myself, as it were."

"Dear God." On a heavy groan, Charles grabbed her hand, and with a glance at his aunt who was still fast asleep, and another glance at the courting couple who were admiring a patch of roses, he led Georgina through the tall hedges and into the small maze.

My lord, where are we going unchaperoned?"

"I need a tour of your perfect garden, Miss Georgina." He charged to the very heart of the maze, a maze he knew from birth. His pace quickened as Georgina raced to keep up with him. "It is the only way I can convey my suffering to you, madame, for, in your presence, I find my heart, my soul, and my body truly ravaged, and only you can offer me solace and rapture."

"Charles." She halted in her tracks, stopping him. "Such lyrical flattery I have never heard before. Truly."

"I should hope not. Come." He walked faster.

Georgina hastened to his side. "I was not joking."

At last, they arrived in the centre of the maze.

She caught her breath. "Ah, this is quite lovely. Will you now recite a poem to me, my lord? A sonnet?"

"Yes, indeed, I shall." He pushed her down onto the ground, and she gasped dramatically. He pulled up the skirts of her dress and dragged his fingers along her damp inner thigh. She let out a moan, her back arching. "Ah, Miss Georgina, you are eager for my poems, I see." His fingers swirled around her nub.

"I am, sir." She twisted her hips in a moan. "Very much so."

"Here's a passionate verse for you—" His face sank between her legs, and he pillaged his wife.

"Oh Lord Ryvves, you are…quite gifted in such … poetry." She grasped his hand and sucked on two of his fingers. Shuddering, she came to her release quickly.

Raising up on a growl, he unbuttoned his breeches.

Planting his hands on the ground on either side of her head, he raised himself and sank his cock inside her in one deep thrust, groaning loudly.

She clasped the taut muscles of his hips. "Your poetry fills me with inspiration, sir. Such bliss…"

He pounded into his wife like a demon devouring, taking his fill. Possessing her utterly. "Would you like me to visit you again, Miss Georgina?"

"I most certainly would, sir." She raised her legs around his back to feel him as deep as possible as he clutched at her hips, lifting her higher to his. "Absolutely. Yes."

Pulling her legs over his shoulders, he nestled even deeper into his wife. He smacked her rump, and a sharp cry escaped her. His eyes darkened over her as he thrust steadily, his lips a snarl. "I look forward to our next visit to your special garden."

Chapter Seventy-Three

Charles

"A PACKAGE HAS ARRIVED for the Countess, my lord."

"Ah, very good," said Charles. "Place it here." The servant put the box before the fireplace in the main parlour where Charles and Georgina were enjoying a glass of sherry together. Bowing, the servant left the room.

Georgina rushed to the box. "Who is it from, my love?"

"It is from Monsieur Le Verne. There is a letter attached." Charles handed her the letter.

She unfolded it and read. "He is in London with Her Grace and has gone to his favourite colour shop and had these new colours mixed for me according to his specifications. He feels I should have them as I'm about to begin Her Grace's portrait." Georgina put the letter down and opened the box. Inside was a great number of small items wrapped carefully in paper. Georgina opened each item carefully yet with great relish.

"What the devil are those?"

"The pre-mixed paint is stored in these small pieces of cleaned and prepared pig bladder —"

"Bloody hell, pig bladder?"

"Yes, to avoid the loss of the paint to drying. Pre-mixed

paint is a new innovation. I shall store them in earthenware containers as he'd instructed me to keep them fresh as long as possible. We had discussed this at length before he left for London. He was very keen to see these colours with his own eyes."

"That was most thoughtful and generous of him to send you a selection."

"Yes, very," she murmured as she picked up her tutor's letter once more and read. "He's gotten me several palettes and a new set of brushes too." Georgina opened another polished casket within the large box and took out a number of long-handled brushes, a grin on her face. "Ah…the textures differ…"

"Very generous indeed."

"What's this? There's something attached to the inside lid…" Georgina worked her fingers inside the lid and produced a folded paper.

"Another letter?"

"A secret one, it would seem." She turned over the folded paper and there was a red wax seal emblazoned with the letter O.

"The Duke and Duchess," said Charles.

She brought it to him. "There must be a very good reason for this secrecy, only I'm not sure if it's good or bad."

Charles broke the seal and opened the letter, and they read it together.

Dearest Charles and Georgina,

I have undertaken the writing of this letter for there is news I must share with you both.

Upon her arrival at the estate, the lady was not at all pleased when she found her bedchamber was neither sizeable nor luxurious as she had thought befitted her new station in life.

But of course, she was wrong about her new station. She would not be the particular favourite of her master, but only one of many who are permanent residents at the house, there to do their master's bidding.

At a party given by the master for his special friends to enjoy the many delights on offer, her being one, she was most obstinate which was enjoyed by the guests. Her quarrelsome attitude led to her punishment, special punishments that for many of us have their own rewards. Thus her instruction in the arts of pleasure began.

However, the lady's fervent attachment to laudanum proved to be overwhelming and her undoing. Once her own supply ran out she grew ever more insistent in her demand for a new supply to which she was denied. Her insistence soon turned into hostility and violence.

She attempted many ways to procure it, even from servants, one of whom she beat ruthlessly, and also from several guests who had none to give but were greatly diverted by her attempts to induce them to do so in order to fulfil her cravings.
One afternoon she happened to recognise the master's mistress, who I believe is known to her and to you as she is from your part of the country.

That day the mistress was leaving her master's service and the estate. The master accompanied her in his coach, escorting her to where she would transfer to another coach to her final destination.

Incensed, the lady stole a horse from a footman whom she injured gravely with a knife to the chest and then attempted to follow the coach.

*But in her desperate state, and in the mud and snow, she was
flung from the horse, dragged and trampled by the animal, and
was found in a ravine.*

I am sorry to report that she is no more.

*If there are inquiries to be made, the mistress is fully prepared
to say that she was traveling with the lady when the accident
occurred. In fact, she is now writing to the lady's brother to
inform him of the unexpected and terrible event.*

I trust you shall destroy this letter as soon as you have read it.

Yours with esteem—

Charles pitched the letter into the fireplace where it was
swallowed by the flames. A heavy sigh dragged from his lips.
"Amanda is dead."

"My brain is spinning. I'm not sure where to begin…"
murmured Georgina, her hand pressed into his back. She sank
into the settee next to him. "So that is what His Grace meant
when he said he had something better in mind for her punishment. She was to be one of his concubines."

"Hugh had never told me outright what went on at that
house, but on many occasions had given me the impression
that such singular revelries took place for a very closed circle
of friends."

"His own private club?"

"Yes."

"What did the Duchess mean by "a special punishment that
has its own rewards'?

Charles's tongue lashed out at his lip. "I believe, it would be
better that I show you rather than attempt to explain." He
settled back on the settee and slid his arm around her.

Her eyes widened then narrowed. "I'm sure it has something to do with the crop the Duke used to correct Amanda's impudence in the coach that day she left, does it not?"

"A shrewd deduction, my love."

"Hmm." She took a long swallow of wine. "The mistress she refers to is most likely Frederica Ashton. Amanda must have been so angry and jealous to see her there with the Duke. To have so violently attacked two people…"

"Her husband had used opium to enslave Brandon in a near paralysed state for almost two years in order to control his fortune, then William used laudanum to humiliate him in public."

"Yes, I remember. At the Assembly rooms." She gave Charles her glass of wine. "Then Amanda used it to weaken her own husband in the duel, killing him."

"Her brother has been abroad with his new wife for months. Whenever he returns home he will find Frederica's letter."

'It's Andrew I feel sorry for, and her son, of course. But she did not consider the boy, did she?"

"Who can ever know another's heart?"

So many lives had ended in a sudden shocking burst. William, Hugh, Amanda. His mother, Sir Edward. He took his wife's hand in his and kissed it. But he and Georgina were here, alive, together. Brandon, Justine, and their children.

And one day, he and Georgina's children.

Their children.

His hand stroked her middle. "I want babies with you, wife. Any signs yet?"

"Not yet."

"Then I suppose we need to try harder." Chuckling, he brushed her lips with his, a hand cupping the curve of a breast.

"We try every day and every night, sir."

"Are you denying me more, wife?"

She took his mouth as she slid into his lap, her fingers plucking at his necktie, undoing it. Undoing him. "I could never deny you." She let out a soft laugh between kisses and nips. "I am not myself without you, my love. No, I could never deny myself you."

Chapter Seventy-Four

Georgina

"WE HAVE A VERY special present for Miss Caroline," said Georgina, glancing at her husband.

Brandon and Justine's baby daughter, Caroline was having her first birthday, and they were all celebrating with a picnic lunch on the front lawn of Wolfsgate.

Georgina presented to Justine the leather box she had wrapped in a sheath of velvet and had tied it with a silk red ribbon herself.

"What is this?" Justine said as she pulled on the ribbon. She pushed the velvet out of the way, and her face slackened. She'd recognized the jewellery box. Glancing up at Georgina, she opened it, and her hand flew to her mouth. "It cannot be."

"It is, my dearest friend."

"What is it?" asked Brandon. Justine handed the box to Brandon. "What the…? Where did you? How did you find it?"

"Georgie found it," said Charles. "It's a long, tawdry, and ultimately love-filled tale which we shall share with you another time." He held his godson in his lap and brushed Jeremy's long dark hair from his eyes.

"But for now," said Georgina, "it has returned to Wolfsgate

and to its rightful family on this precious occasion that we are celebrating today."

Justine leapt from her seat and hugged Georgina. "Oh my love, thank you. Thank you. I can hardly believe it."

"Believe it." Georgina kissed her friend's cheek as she glanced at her husband, his eyes gleaming at her.

"Georgina." Brandon let out a deep sigh. "I am moved beyond words." His voice trembled, and he took in a deep breath. "My love, Lady Graven." He took his wife in his lap, put the necklace around her throat, and kissed her. Jeremy clapped his hands. Justine burst into tears, into laughter, and hugged her husband.

"Georgie, how can we ever thank you for this?" asked Brandon, kissing his wife's cheek.

"I do have a request." Georgina lifted Caroline from her basket and placed her in her lap.

"Anything."

"I would like to paint your family portrait. You, Justine wearing this necklace, the children, and of course, the phantom wolf of Wolfsgate, if I may."

"How splendid!" Justine exclaimed, fingering the wolf clasp on the necklace at her throat.

"It would be our honour, Countess," replied Brandon. "But I fear you must wait."

"Wait? Why?"

Brandon put a hand on Justine's belly. "Because our third child is on its way, and I would have all my family in such a significant work of art."

Chapter Seventy-Five

Georgina

"EACH ONE IS TASTIER than the last. I shall never be able to decide." Georgina put her wine glass down on the table. "But it's not just the flavours, each has its own distinct personality."

"I want you to enjoy the wines, darling, not get frustrated. I know which ones I like best, but the point is, which ones will our punters like and buy incessantly?"

"Excellent point." She brought another glass of wine to her lips and sipped as they took in the vast valley of dark green sloping hills under the hot Portuguese sun.

Today she wore his mother's earrings, the ones Georgina's father had given her. Their long style suited Georgie. Dark antique gold, a small row of blue lapis lazuli adorning the filigreed bottom of each.

After Georgina's course of lessons with Le Verne had been completed, and the artist went on to London to meet with the Duchess, Charles and Georgina took off for Portugal. They had appointments with a winemaker in the Douro River Valley to discuss importing vintage port in newly designed cylindrical wine bottles and not casks to England.

Charles and Brandon's new business venture together was

taking off. Brandon did not wish to travel now as Justine was with child, nor frankly, did he wish to get on a boat ever again. And as Charles and Georgina had not even considered a wedding trip, going to Portugal was perfect timing.

Before they'd left England, Joss had taken over the stewardship of Ironvine from his father. Both he and Charles had begun to discuss their ideas and plans on making a number of modern improvements on the estate.

Georgina had never traveled abroad and was most excited to see new lands and people and record them in her sketchbook just as her father and Charles's mother had done. Traveled and loved.

Tomorrow she and Charles would visit the cottage where her father and his mother had stayed, the one in the painting. The painting that now hung on the wall of their parlour at Ironvine alongside the watercolour of a young Hugh and Charles with their bows and arrows.

In his new wine exporting business, Charles was most eager to use his knowledge of wine, which came with his wealth and his good taste, and now he would put it all to good use. He knew what he liked, he knew what men of his society liked, and he knew what they would like.

"Have you decided, my lord?" asked Fransisco Neves, the owner of the wine company whose acquaintance he had made through the Duke of Oakley.

"I have, Señhor Neves."

As the two men spoke of the advantage of sweeter fortified wines and how they survived the trips over the sea without spoiling, Georgina's thoughts went to Brother Laurent and how proud he would be at this very moment of Charles.

She sipped the full-bodied wine once more. Wine bridged the gap between the sacred and the profane, binding them together. The vine was of the earth, its fruit transformed by man, and the drink then elevated by the holy spirit, consumed by us all to be of one family under God. One communion. One harmonious fellowship of unity, integrity. Wholeness and accord.

Yes, at long last, accord for the House of Ryvves. For Ironvine.

"There is another I think you may like. I shall bring it to you." Señhor Neves left them to bring another bottle.

"Charles, I must say, it's a pity there is no original Ironvine wine to drink. Wouldn't it be fun to look in the castle for a hidden wine cellar?" She wiped a finger at the corner of her mouth. "Although I'm sure if there were any wine left from those days, all your ancestors probably found it and drank it down."

He laughed. "I'm quite sure they did. But that is of the past, and we are looking to the future, my love. A new vintage in a new season for Montclares, for the house of Ryvves. Who knows, perhaps one day, there will be more and more vine-yards in Britain, and Montclares may take up the art. But for now, we can continue in the spirit of Brother Laurent and carry on in the family business. You and I. Together." He raised his glass, his gaze boring into hers.

She raised her glass too. "Yes, you and I. Together."

"We are that vine, Charles," she said. "The branches gnarled and twisted, some broken, others diverged. It is in those contortions and irregularities, those knots and fissures, those offshoots that you and I came into this world and that brought us together."

Señhor Neves returned and offered them fresh glasses and poured from the new bottle. They raised their full glasses. In that deep ruby colour, both saw a world of exciting, wondrous prospects.

And with that sip filling their mouths, Charles and Georgina's eyes met. In that smooth swell of rich flavour and robust sweet warmth were all their possibilities, all their passions. An adventure.

"Hmm, this one," Charles murmured.

She met his grin with her own. "Yes, this one."
A new season, a new flavour. A new vintage, together.

The
End

Books by Cat Porter

- LOCK & KEY SMALL TOWN MC ROMANCE SERIES -

READING ORDER

1 - LOCK & KEY - LOCK & GRACE

2 - RANDOM & RARE - DIG | LOCK & GRACE

3 - IRON & BONE - BONER & JILL

4 - BLOOD & RUST - BUTLER & TANIA

5 - FURY - FINGER & LENORE

6 - LOCK & KEY CHRISTMAS - LOCK & GRACE

7 - THE DUST AND THE ROAR - WRECK & ISI

8 - THE FIRE AND THE ROAR - MORE WRECK & ISI

9 - THE YEAR OF EVERYTHING - EVERYONE IN HIGH SCHOOL

10- THUNDER & FLARE - TRICK & NICOLE

11 - SPARKLE - ALICIA & RONNY

12 - SIN & SURRENDER - WES & LINDY

THE LOCK & KEY MC ROMANCE SERIES BOXED SET: BOOKS 1 - 3

Books 1-3 in one e-book

- THE WIND & THE ROAR DUET -

Beck & Violet - Friends-to-Lovers Rockstar Romance

*(*Same small town as Lock & Key MC Romance series*)*

1- WHIRLWIND

2 - WHISPERWIND

DAGGER IN THE SEA - TURO & ADRI

Mediterranean Romantic Suspense Adventure

About the Author

Cat Porter was born and raised in New York City, but also spent a few years in Europe and Texas along the way, which made her as wanderlusty as her parents. As an introverted, only child, she loved reading and going to the movies, and had very big, but very secret dreams for herself.

She graduated from Vassar College, was a struggling actress, an art gallery girl, special events planner, freelance writer, restaurant hostess, and had all sorts of other crazy jobs all hours of the day and night in New York to help make her dreams come true.

She has two children's books traditionally published under her maiden name. And yes, she loves writing contemporary romances as well as historical romances.

She now lives on a beach outside of Athens, Greece with her husband, three children, and four huge Cane Corsos, freaks out regularly, still daydreams way too much, and now truly doesn't give AF.

She is addicted to reading, classic films, cafe bars on the beach, the Greek islands, Instagram, Pearl Jam and U2, bourbon she brought home from Nashville and whiskey she brought home from Dublin, and realllllllly good coffee.

Writing has always kept her somewhat sane, extremely happy, and a productive member of society.

www.catporter.com

Email - catporter103@gmail.com

amazon.com/author/catporter

bookbub.com/authors/cat-porter

instagram.com/catporter.writer

x.com/catporter103

pinterest.com/catporter103

tiktok.com/@catporter_writer

facebook.com/CatPorterWriter

bsky.app/profile/catporterwriter.bsky.social